SCANDALS

Penny Jordan has been writing for over 25 years. In that time, she has written over 170 books and sold almost 90 million copies worldwide. She also writes under the name Annie Groves and is a mentor for new writers. *Scandals* is set in the rag trade and inspired by the silk manufacturing industry in Macclesfield in Cheshire where Penny lived for 25 years with her late husband. She still lives in Cheshire today. For more information on Penny, please go to www.penny-jordan.co.uk

By the same author
Silk
Sins

PENNY JORDAN

Scandals

AVON

AVON

A division of HarperCollins*Publishers*
77–85 Fulham Palace Road,
London W6 8JB

www.harpercollins.co.uk

This production 2011

1

Copyright © Penny Jordan 2010

Penny Jordan asserts the moral right to
be identified as the author of this work

A catalogue record for this books is
available from the British Library

ISBN 978-0-00-790589-8

Set in Minion by Palimpsest Book Production Limited,
Falkirk, Stirlingshire

Printed and bound in Great Britain by
Clays Ltd, St Ives plc

I would like to thank the following for their
invaluable help:

Teresa Chris, my agent.
Maxine Hitchcock and Kate Bradley, who both
worked as Editors on this book.

Yvonne Holland, Copy Editor, for her sharp eyes and
wealth of knowledge.

Everyone at Avon who contributed to the publication
of this book.

And finally, my business partner Tony, who took on
board much of the research for this book.

To silk – the most magical of fabrics that always casts its spell on me.

Chapter One

Christmas 1991

'It won't be long now. They'll all be here soon,' said Amber.

Jay gave his wife an understanding smile, acknowledging her excitement.

They were in the drawing room at Denham, the elegant Palladian house Amber had inherited from her grandmother. The low-lying December sun was striking beams of pale light through the windows to illuminate the room's soft blue and yellow décor, as Jay and Amber anticipated the arrival of their family.

Amber may have just had her seventy-ninth birthday, but even now she possessed a child's delight in the magic of Christmas.

This youthful enthusiasm she had never lost, combined with her experience of life, had made her the driving force behind the success of Denby Silk, the Macclesfield silk mill, she had also inherited from her grandmother Blanche Pickford, instigating innovative procedures and designs. Amber had opened her own interior design studio in London's Walton Street, and kept the business going during the war, and the even more economically difficult post-war years. Eventually she had handed over the day-to-day running of the business to younger members of the family so that they could continue and expand on her success. Here was a woman who had had the strength to endure the deaths of her first husband, Robert, Duke of Lenchester, and her son, and to go on from that to support and protect her own family here at Denham, as well as Jay's own motherless daughters, before making his life the happiest it had ever been by agreeing to marry him. She had given him two more children, their twin daughters, Polly and Cathy. And now their shared extended family were 'coming home,' to Denham to celebrate Christmas.

Continuing a routine that was almost as traditional for them as Christmas itself, he asked her obligingly, 'So who exactly is coming?'

'Everyone,' Amber assured him, smiling.

Ticking off the names on her fingers, she listed them for him, starting with the eldest: Jay's two daughters from his first marriage.

'Ella and Oliver are flying in from New York. They're bringing Sam with them, but Olivia has a writing commission she has to finish for one of the magazines she freelances for so she'll be coming on a later flight than her parents.

'Janey's going to come over later this morning and stock the freezer, and of course she and John and the boys will be spending Christmas Day with us. Luckily both boys will be able to come home.'

Janey, Jay's younger daughter, and her husband, John, Lord Fitton Legh, lived only a few miles away from them in Cheshire at Fitton Hall. Harry, their heir, was currently working as a land agent for a wealthy landowner in Norfolk, since leaving Royal Agricultural College in Circencester, whilst his younger brother, David, had followed Fitton family tradition and was undergoing army officer training at Sandhurst.

'Emerald telephoned yesterday to say that she and Drogo will be here on Christmas Eve,' Amber continued, 'and that Katie will come to us direct from Oxford.' She paused and then admitted ruefully, 'I know that Emerald is my daughter, Jay, but I do wish sometimes that she wasn't quite so . . . so . . . privileged, and so, well, such a snob. It certainly isn't Drogo's fault, even if he is a duke.'

Drogo, Emerald's husband, had inherited the title of Duke of Lenchester from Amber's first husband, Robert. Emerald's discovery that her father was not Robert, as she had always believed, but Jean-Philippe du Breveonet, a French artist, had led to rift between Amber and her eldest daughter, and even though that rift was now healed, Emerald had insisted that the fact that Robert was not her father was to remain a secret known only to Amber, Jay, Emerald herself, Drogo, and, unfortunately, her ex-mother-in-law, the Dowager Princess of Lauranto.

'Emma and James will be coming with Emerald and Drogo.' Amber proceeded with her list, referring to Emerald's elder daughter and her younger son. 'I'm so glad, James and Sam get on so well with one another. I suppose it helps that they are a similar age.'

'What about Robert?' Jay teased his wife. 'You haven't mentioned him yet.'

Robert was Amber's eldest grandson, Emerald's son from her brief runaway marriage to Alessandro, Crown Prince of Lauranto, a marriage that had been dissolved via the machinations of Alessandro's mother.

Robert, now in his thirties, lived in London where he worked as a very successful architect, running his own practice.

'Robert's driving himself down.'

'And coming alone?'

Jay knew that it was a matter of some concern to Amber that Robert was still single and seemed to prefer to have a constant and rapid succession of women through his life and his bed rather than to settle down.

'Yes, he's coming on his own. I do wish he could find the right person, Jay. Life hasn't been as kind as it might to him. And although I would never say so to Emerald, I don't think that the life he lived with her as a child can have helped, on top of knowing that his father didn't want him. Olivia adores him, I know, but Robert has never shown any interest in her. Oh, don't look at me like that,' she laughed. 'I'm not going to turn into a matchmaking grandmother. As it happens, I don't believe that Olivia and Robert would be right for one another. Robert needs someone who will make him work hard to win her. Much as I love him I have to admit that some things in life have come too easily for him and that has made him rather thoughtless and arrogant. He is a very good-looking young man, independently wealthy and well connected, but that loving sweetness he had as a child has gone, and I do worry that unless he starts to think about others a little more, his life will be less happy than it could be.'

4

'Things haven't been easy for him. He's always admired Drogo, and Drogo has been an excellent stepfather to him, but it is Jamie who will inherit from Drogo, not Robert.'

'Do you think that is the root of the problem, Jay? Do you think that Robert minds that it is Jamie, and not he, who will one day step into Drogo's shoes?'

The anxiety in Amber's voice had Jay immediately seeking to reassure her.

'No. To be truthful I think the problem is the situation with his real father. From the moment he could understand the situation, Robert has known that his father, or, more accurately, his paternal grandmother, has refused to accept or acknowledge him. When Alessandro remarried, Robert must have expected, as we all did, that there would be a child from that marriage to continue the line. But now Alessandro has died without producing an heir, and Robert's paternal grandmother is courting him with a view to him stepping into his late father's shoes. The unwanted unworthy child has become the desired and sought-after future Crown Prince. In view of that it is perhaps no wonder that Robert has become increasingly cynical.'

Amber sighed. 'Emerald is adamant that she does not want Robert to accept either the olive branch that Alessandro's mother has extended to him, or the crown, but the Dowager Princess is a very determined woman who is used to having her own way. She dominated Alessandro and was the power behind the throne during his lifetime. Emerald has always refused to tell Robert about her real father, and although she hasn't said so, some of her antagonism to this recent visit Robert has made to Lauranto to see his grandmother must be because she is afraid that the Dowager Princess might tell Robert the truth. I hope she doesn't, Jay. That information should come from Emerald. I begged her to tell Robert whilst he was still young enough to accept it matter-of-factly and not to make the mistake I made when I concealed the truth from her, but she wouldn't. I know that people who don't know him think that Robert is too proud, that he has too high an opinion of himself, but I think that's just a defence mechanism he's adopted to protect himself. I still remember him asking me if it was true that his father had left his mother because he didn't want him. Poor little boy. Some other boy at school had taunted him about Emerald and Alessandro's marriage being annulled.'

Jay patted his wife's hand. He knew that Robert, her first-born grandchild, had a very special place in her heart.

'What about the others?' he asked her. 'Will Rose be coming?'

At the mention of her late cousin Greg's daughter, from his relationship with his Hong Kong Chinese mistress, Amber's face lit up. She had loved Rose from the minute she had seen her, a tiny, very sick, unloved baby, brought back to Denham by Greg.

Rose had grown up at Denham with Jay's own daughters and Emerald, and she now lived in London with her husband, Josh, a very successful entrepreneur who had built his hairdressing business into a multimillion-pound empire. Rose and Josh did not have any children of their own, but Rose had taken to her heart her husband's illegitimate son from a brief affair he had had before he and Rose had met.

'Rose and Josh are coming. Christmas wouldn't be Christmas without Rose here.'

'So that just leaves Polly and Cathy,' said Jay, referring to his and Amber's own twin daughters.

'Cathy and Sim are driving up from Cornwall with the girls, and Polly and Rocco will be flying in from Venice with their two boys. We are so very lucky, Jay. *I* am lucky,' Amber stressed, reaching out to hold his hand, 'because I have you.'

It was typical of her that she should say that, Jay thought.

'No, Amber, it is I who am the fortunate one,' he told her tenderly.

Theirs had been a wonderfully happy marriage, all the more so, Jay reckoned, because of the despair and heartache they had both endured before they had married one another, Amber through the betrayal of her first love, Jean-Philippe, then through the road accident that had resulted in the death of both her husband and dearly loved son, and Jay himself through an unhappy marriage to his mentally unstable first wife.

She had been so blessed, Amber thought gratefully in turn, and in so many different ways, but the blessing she valued the most had been Jay's survival of the heart attack that she had feared would take him from her. They had waited so long to share their love and be together, that even now she still felt that every minute they shared was a precious gift. It grieved her that not all their children and grandchildren had found such happiness in their lives.

'So that's everyone accounted for then, is it?' Jay teased.

'Not quite. There's still Cassandra,' Amber reminded him.

They looked at one another and their faces fell.

'I know that she's your cousin, Jay, and of course John's stepmother, but no matter how hard I try, I can't forget the past and her cruelty.'

'I know.' Jay gave Amber's hand a gentle pat. Its skin might be soft and loose and mottled with age now, but to him she was still the same beautiful girl she had been when she was seventeen, and his love for her had had to be a secret he could not share with anyone.

Cassandra! Jay had no more liking for his cousin than Amber did.

'What makes a person like that, Jay?' Amber asked sadly. 'It's as though Cassandra enjoys being cruel and mean. I know that Greg was wrong to fall in love with Caroline, but no one need have known they had been lovers. Cassandra was the one who told Caroline's husband about the relationship.'

'Yes. I'm afraid that I too can't bring myself to forgive her for the harm she did,' Jay agreed sombrely.

Amber gave a small shiver. Despite the warmth from the logs burning in the grate of the elegant Carrara marble fireplace, the room suddenly seemed cold, as though the chill of past tragedies had somehow swept in.

'We'll never know if poor Caroline's death was an accident, and she missed her footing and fell into the lake, or if she deliberately took her own life because Cassandra had exposed her infidelity to Lord Fitton Legh. Caroline and Greg paid such a dreadfully heavy price for their affair: Greg disinherited by our grandmother and sent to Hong Kong, and Caroline facing divorce and disgrace. I often wonder if Cassandra would have been more compassionate if it hadn't been for her own feelings for Caroline. She was so passionately in love with her. Do you think Cassandra went on to marry Lord Fitton Legh because he had been Caroline's husband?'

'I don't know,' Jay admitted. His cousin was an enigma to him, a difficult spiteful girl who had turned into an embittered and cruel woman.

'I do wish that she hadn't married Lord Fitton Legh, Jay. She always was a very unkind stepmother for poor John, and she is even now, despite the fact that he and Janey are so very kind to her.'

'John feels he has a moral obligation to carry out the terms of his father's will, not just to the letter but above and beyond it, and his father did stipulate that John must provide well for Cassandra. You know how highly John thought of his father.'

'Yes,' Amber acknowledged, 'but that makes it all the more upsetting that he was such a cold and distant father to John, although of course . . .' She stopped and looked uncertainly at her husband.

'Except that John may not be his child, you mean?' Jay supplied. He saw her face and added quietly, 'Yes, I know that your cousin Greg believed that John was his child—'

'Because Caroline Fitton Legh had told him so,' Amber pointed out, 'but in truth she could have told Greg that he was John's father because it was what she wanted to believe herself.'

'None the less, Lord Fitton Legh brought John up as his son.'

'And John worshipped him. Him and Fitton. Fitton is his life. Janey complains that sometimes she thinks the house and the land mean more to him than either she does or their sons. John isn't very good at articulating his feelings and I do sometimes wonder if their marriage is as happy as we thought it would be when they first married. It would destroy John, I think, if he were ever to suspect that Greg, and not the late Lord Fitton Legh, was his father, and that he himself had no right to the title or to Fitton.'

'So have we now finally accounted for everyone?' Jay asked ruefully.

'Yes,' Amber confirmed, looking up as they both heard the familiar sound of the tea trolley outside the drawing-room door. 'Here's Mrs Leggit with the tea,' she announced unnecessarily, smiling at their housekeeper as she came in. 'We've just been discussing Christmas, Mrs Leggit. It would be lovely if we have snow.'

'They've had some already up in Buxton, or so I've heard,' the housekeeper answered, adding as she headed for the door, 'Mind you, they are much higher up there, than we are down here.'

'Christmas, the family and snow. Wouldn't that be perfect?' Amber smiled at Jay as she handed him his tea.

'Perfect,' he agreed.

Chapter Two

It was snowing and Olivia hated snow in New York. It wasn't like proper snow at all – not like snow in Aspen, or Switzerland. New York's snow made yellow cab drivers even more bad-tempered than they were ordinarily, and turned to slush on the sidewalks. She just hoped that it didn't snow heavily enough to ground the planes at JFK so that her flight to Manchester was cancelled. To Manchester and to Robert.

Her rich chestnut shoulder-length hair gleamed with health as she stepped out of *Vanity Fair* magazine's reception and waited for the lift to take her back down to the lobby. Tall and slender, her classically elegant features and blue eyes, enhanced by discreet makeup, Olivia carried with her an air of calm confidence that right now belied the excitement she felt inside. Soon she would be seeing Robert. She sighed ruefully at herself. When was she going to grow up and behave like a proper twenty-five-year-old and not a wide-eyed teenager in the grip of her first crush? Never, probably, where Robert was concerned, she admitted. She had loved him for so long that she couldn't imagine not loving him, she admitted as she stepped out of the lift into the lobby of the building that housed Si Newhouse's publishing empire of glossy magazines. She was wearing the new butter-soft leather boots she'd seen in Barneys and not been able to resist, and they were about as suitable for slushy pavements as a pair of high-heeled summer sandals. The hem of her long dark cream cashmere coat would also, no doubt, be marked, but she'd felt she had to wear it since that Mecca of fashion, *Vogue* magazine, also had its offices in the building. She was sure she'd seen Christy Turlington, one of the so-called supermodels, in the lobby when she'd come through.

At least now she'd delivered the article she'd been working on for *Vanity Fair*, a real coup for her, and she was keeping everything crossed that they liked it, even if the deadline had meant that she'd had to stay home instead of accompany her parents and younger brother on their flight this morning.

Still, it wouldn't be long before she was following them, and then there'd be Denham, her grandparents, Christmas, the whole family and Robert.

Engrossed in the pleasure of thinking about her cousin, she almost walked straight into the man heading for the lift, her stomach clenching in dismay and dislike when she looked up and recognised who he was.

Tait Cabot Forbes, political investigative reporter *sans* equal, *sans* pity for his victims, *sans* everything, really, that made a human being human. Tait was a walking, talking, writing law book, looking for someone to break one of those laws so that he could pillory them without mercy. He could have built a skyscraper out of the reputations he had shredded so mercilessly in his freelance newspaper articles and on his TV programmes, and she hated him.

There had been a time when Olivia had actually admired him, and even seen him as something of a hero for his brilliant exposés of those whose moral failings were damaging humanity, but that had been before he had decided to wage war on her parents.

Family meant a great deal to Olivia – all her family, but most especially her parents and her teenage brother. Olivia didn't just love her parents, she respected and admired them, and to have their reputation besmirched all over the pages of the New York press by a man who was notorious for bringing down those he targeted had been an assault on them she could never forgive.

'Well, well, if it isn't the doggedly devoted daughter,' Tait greeted her. 'Still public enemy number one, am I? I don't suppose that exchanging Christmas kisses is in order then?' he teased when Olivia tried to step past him.

She hadn't intended to lower herself to speak to him but his comment proved too much for her self-control.

'I'd rather kiss a rat,' she told him angrily.

'Flattery. It does it for me every time,' Tait retorted, giving her what she thought of as a shark smile, all polished white teeth in a face tanned by a lifetime of summers spent sailing off Cape Cod.

He was good-looking, Olivia acknowledged grudgingly, if one liked that big healthy Eastern Seaboard all-American male look. In fact his hair and eyes were dark enough for him to have Italian blood. Now wouldn't that be a thing, a Boston Brahmin – top-of-the-heap WASP – with Italian immigrant blood in his veins?

Olivia knew that her antagonism towards him wasn't shared by her female media colleagues. The word on the New York street was that Tait wasn't just the best-looking reporter, he was also the best in bed.

'Your folks spending Christmas here in New York, are they?'

'No. Not that it's any of your business.'

The melting snow had slicked down his thick dark hair so that it hung over his forehead in damp spikes, the bright lights in the lobby highlighting the small lines fanning out from his eyes and the thickness of his eyelashes. He might have women falling over themselves for his attention, but Tait Cabot Forbes was exactly the kind of man who turned her off, Olivia thought. Unlike Robert.

Robert. It was comforting to be able to blot out Tait's face by focusing instead on her own personal mental image of her cousin. Robert was her perfect man. The courtly behaviour he must have learned as a young boy living with his grandmother and stepgrandfather made him unique in Olivia's eyes: a true gentleman of the old school, who set high moral standards for himself and who believed in such old-fashioned virtues as honour and loyalty.

And love? Olivia gave a small sigh. She knew perfectly well that all Robert felt for her was mere stepcousinly affection, even if he had been kind when she'd been in the throes of her painfully obvious teenage crush on him. The fact that the teenage crush had now become a carefully hidden woman's love was her business and her problem, and definitely not something she would allow out into the open to humiliate her and embarrass Robert.

'Tait.' The sound of a woman's voice, filled with delight as she spotted the reporter and came hurrying over, gave Olivia a chance to escape. A very welcome chance, she thought thankfully as she slipped past Tait and out into the street. Once there, without having intended to do so, she looked back, only to see Tait exchanging the 'Christmas kisses' she had refused with the pretty blonde who had hailed him.

Christmas kisses. She was in her mid-twenties and the last time she had had anything that came close to being labelled a 'relationship' had been during her first year at college. But she had her work, she reminded herself, and her ambitions, and of course her wonderful parents.

In London, at Lenchester House, the London home of the Dukes of Lenchester, the object of Olivia's love was sitting in the library with his stepfather.

Drogo and Robert sat opposite one another at either side of the marble fireplace in the armchairs that had been commissioned from Hepplewhite by the third duke. Heavy silk velvet curtains in a rich shade of amber, woven especially at Denby Mill, home of Drogo's wife's family silk business, hung at the windows. The depth of their colour meant that the room was always filled with a warm golden glow, as though sunshine was pouring through the windows, no matter what the time of year.

The chairs were upholstered in a complementary pineapple-patterned cut velvet in amber and cream, the colour scheme originally chosen for the room by the previous duke, Lord Robert, in honour of his new bride,

Amber. The Savonnerie carpet covering the parquet floor had been woven during the time of Napoleon Bonaparte, its colouring of deep gold and blue on a beige background a perfect foil for the curtain and chair fabrics. Drogo could well understand why Lord Robert had chosen such a colour scheme over the more traditional dark red so often used in such masculine rooms.

'So now that you've been to Lauranto and had a chance to discuss things with your grandmother and her advisers, how do you feel about stepping into your late father's shoes officially?' Drogo asked his stepson.

How did he feel about it? Robert suspected that if he answered his stepfather's question honestly, Drogo would not only not understand him but would also be concerned for him. To outsiders their situations might seem similar: Drogo too had stepped into an inheritance and title he had never expected to be his, and in a culture and a country that was alien to him. That, though, was where the similarities between their situations ended. Drogo hadn't grown up knowing that he had been rejected as not good enough to inherit. He had not had to endure the childhood taunts and mockery that Robert had known because of that public rejection. He had not grown up having to accept that his father did not want him. So how could Drogo be expected to understand the savagely visceral feeling of satisfaction it gave him to have his grandmother courting him, with a view to him stepping into his late father's shoes, even if only because she had no choice as there was no one else? How could he expect Drogo to understand how much he now wanted what he was being

16

offered, when he had not known himself until the first letter had been sent and the first approach to him made? It was his birthright, and he felt that a wrong had been righted by a higher authority than that of his father or his paternal grandmother, but above all, he was determined to prove that as Crown Prince of Lauranto he could be better than any Crown Prince before him, and certainly better than the father who had rejected him. That was what was driving him now – not altruism, which would probably have motivated both his stepfather and his grandfather, not Lauranto itself and its people, but ambition. He wanted this for the child who had been dismissed as unworthy even before his birth, and who had gone unwanted and unrecognised until desperation had forced his grandmother to recognise him.

He would make Lauranto his. He would stamp his personality on it, so that in future Lauranto would *be* him, and so that future generations would say that he had taken Lauranto to its greatest heights. He would leave his mark on it in everything he did, from its architecture, to its finances and its laws, and ultimately via the sons he would give it. No, his stepfather would not understand how he was now relishing the driving thoughts of retribution and triumph.

Drogo studied his stepson as he waited for his response. Tall, with thick dark hair, brilliantly blue eyes, and an almost classically perfect profile, with a strong jaw, neat ears and a well-shaped nose, Robert combined the good looks of both his parents, although his temperament was very different from that of his mother. Robert had a tendency to withdraw into himself and shut others out, and sometimes it seemed to Drogo that his stepson was at war with himself.

'It will be a challenge,' Robert answered him, having weighed up how much to say to his stepfather. Alessandro –' Robert gave a dismissive shrug – 'I just can't think of him as my father. You've always been that, Dad, and there's no way I'd ever want to change that – I suspect that Alessandro was something of a lightweight and dominated by his mother. He was a figurehead who allowed others to run the country for him. The country needs modernising and that will be a huge challenge. My grandmother and her advisers are absolutely dead set against any kind of change. The country is run on almost feudal lines, with the poorest treated almost like serfs, especially those working on the estates belonging to the clique of barons favoured by my grandmother. The children of these workers leave school at fourteen to work on the land, whilst the children of the "nobility", and the very small professional and middle class, are in the main educated abroad. There is no crossing of social lines. The court lives by a formal routine more suited to the Victorian age than ours; the exchequer is almost empty. All that will have to change.'

'Have you told the Dowager Princess how you feel?'

'Not yet. We have agreed to have further meetings in February. By then I should have formulated my terms for accepting the Crown.'

'So you do intend to accept it?'

'I don't see that I have any option.' That much was true, although Robert knew that Drogo would interpret his statement as meaning that he felt he had a duty to step into his father's shoes for the sake of the people, rather than because he had a driving need to take up the challenge for himself.

'Oh, Robert, no. I can't believe you are giving in to that old harridan and letting her persuade you into accepting the Crown, after the way she's behaved,' Emerald announced coming into the library in time to hear Robert's comment.

She went over to kiss the top of Drogo's head. 'And I can't believe how difficult it is to get this family organised. I've had to take Jamie out this morning and buy him new Wellingtons, he's grown so much whilst he's been at Eton. Emma is still fussing about what she's going to take to Italy with her when she goes back there with Polly after the Christmas holiday, Katie isn't even home from Oxford yet, and we're supposed to be leaving for Macclesfield tomorrow morning.'

Whilst Drogo smiled indulgently at his wife, Emerald warned her elder son, 'It's your decision – I know that, darling – but once she's got her claws into you Alessandro's mother won't rest until she's taken over every aspect of your life, including finding you a wife. All she wants you for is to produce future heirs.'

Robert smiled, looking unfazed by his mother's comment. Emerald sighed inwardly: why was it that her eldest child, conceived in the wild passion of her youth, should be so lacking in that wild passion himself? Like any mother she wanted to protect her children from emotional pain, but sometimes she found herself almost wishing that Robert would fall passionately and even hopelessly in love, if only so that he would know what passion was. Emerald couldn't imagine how anyone's life could be fulfilling without having tasted that emotion,

19

even though as a mother that wasn't something she would ever say to her children, especially not to Robert, who sometimes looked at her as though he was the older and wiser of the two.

'The country has a population of three million, most of whom are scratching a living under the burden of a feudal system,' Robert told his parents. 'It's practically bankrupt financially and the governing élite are certainly bankrupt morally.'

'But that doesn't mean you have to become Saint Robert and go riding to its rescue,' Emerald pointed out.

Robert laughed. He knew his mother, and he knew all about the old enmity that existed between her and his paternal grandmother. They were both very strong-minded and determined women who liked getting their own way.

'I've agreed to go back and talk with my grandmother again in the New Year, once I've had a chance to think things through. The country does have potential, its people could be so much better off if things were handled differently. All the royal and government build-ings in the old city are early eighteenth century and desperately in need of renovation. As an architect I'd love to get my teeth into that challenge.'

That was true, but Robert was deliberately promoting that project as a means of concealing from his mother how he really felt.

'Think of it,' he teased her. 'All that scope for using Denby Mill silks. Surely that would be a form of revenge worth having? The mill could do with the business, after all, from what you've been saying.'

Emerald sighed, distracted, as Robert had intended that she would be.

'That's true. This current fashion for glazed chintz swagged everywhere has affected our sales, although we have had some success with the new Sweetpea design. I envy Angelli Silk, and their historical connections with Italy's opera houses, which mean that they get the commissions when they need refurbishment.'

'Denby Silk has its contracts with the National Trust,' Robert pointed out.

'We do have some contracts with them, yes, but they don't use us exclusively. The American market is where the future lies and where we need to succeed. I'm going to have a word with Ella whilst she's over about seeing if we can get some of the top-rank New York interior designers to start using our silks . . . and it's all very well you sidetracking me, Robert,' she continued, returning to their earlier topic of conversation, 'but if you go ahead and become Crown Prince you will have to marry, because it will be your duty to produce an heir.'

Robert had dated any number of young women over the years but hadn't as yet shown any inclination to settle down, and for a very good reason, but it was not one he could communicate to his mother. The early years of Robert's life, before his mother had married Drogo, had been very turbulent. Emerald had partied hard and lived life to the full, as the saying went. One of her lovers had been a notorious East End gangster, Max Preston. Robert had been seven then.

Memories he preferred to keep safely locked away would surface abruptly against his will: his mother's frightening changes of mood; the sound of slammed doors and screaming arguments; the sounds from her bedroom one night when he had woken up in the dark feeling afraid and alone, and had gone there seeking comfort. He had been afraid for her when he had heard the noise, the man's voice thick and harsh, his mother's begging over and over again, 'Please . . . please . . . please . . .'

He had opened the door and seen . . .

Perhaps every child inadvertently witnessing a parent having sex retained the same feeling of revulsion that he felt. Perhaps, like him, they put those memories in a box and buried that box very deeply with a stone slab on top of it. Perhaps they also grew to adulthood too sharply aware of the danger of out-of-control passion, fearful of it and determined, like him, never to let it take control of them. Perhaps. But Robert didn't know, because it wasn't the kind of thing that anyone discussed.

Now, whilst sexually his taste ran to intelligent, feisty, exciting, passionate and even challenging women, his experiences as a child meant that he had decided that he would never want to commit permanently to such a woman. They were too intense, too adversarial, too demanding and high maintenance emotionally and mentally for the men who loved them, and to their families. Life with them was a roller coaster that mowed down everything and everyone in its path. Robert had no intention of allowing himself to ride such a roller coaster. Better to enjoy the passion and the excitement, but to keep the woman who provided it at a safe distance, to make sure she was dispensable. For that reason he had decided that he would not marry. There had been, after all, no need. But the death of his father and his grandmother's approach to him had changed all of that.

If he was to satisfy his now driving ambition to become Crown Prince of Lauranto then he would have to marry, as his mother had just pointed out.

His mother and his paternal grandmother would fight – virtually to the death, he suspected – to be the one to select his bride for him, so it was far better that he selected his own bride. He had, in fact, already done so. The right wife for him, as Crown Prince of Lauranto, would be a wife whose whole loyalty was to him, who supported him unquestioningly, and whose temperament was such that she would accept that her role must be a supportive rather than a leading one. She must love him and only him, but at the same time she must not be passionately possessive or openly sexual in her attitude or behaviour. She must have the intelligence, the education, the confidence and the right kind of nature to be his consort, and she must, of course, look good. It was a long list of requirements but Robert knew someone who filled them all.

Olivia, the cousin he knew already loved him. Olivia, who was elegant, well groomed, well educated, calm, and whose loyalty to him would be absolute.

However, he had no intention of telling his mother what was in his mind – yet.

It was only later, when Robert had returned to his own home – the penthouse apartment in a stylish new block for which he had been the lead architect – that Emerald showed Drogo how anxious she really was about her son's future.

'Is it selfish of me to hope that Robert will turn down Alessandro's mother, and refuse the Crown?'

'I don't know,' Drogo replied carefully, 'but I do know

that it won't help if you keep running her down to him, because ultimately if he does decide to accept that could put him in an awkward position.'

Strong-willed Emerald might be, but she hated feeling that her husband disapproved of something she'd said or done.

'But she is such a horrendous monster,' she insisted, turning on the slender heel of her damson-coloured Charles Jourdan court shoes and walking towards the window, the cut of her Chanel tweed suit, flecked with lilac, damson and white against a black background, discreetly outlining her curves.

Even with the sharp winter light falling on her, to Drogo she still looked as stunning as she had done when he had first seen her.

When she finally turned and saw the look of love and concern on her husband's face, she walked back to him and put her head on his shoulder.

'I only want Robert to be happy, Drogo – is that so very wrong?' She paused and then added in a voice shorn of her normal confidence, 'Sometimes I wonder if it's true what they say about being careful what you wish for.'

'Meaning?' Drogo invited.

'When Robert was born I felt triumphant because no matter what Alessandro's mother might choose to think, Robert would always be Alessandro's first-born son – and his rightful heir. Since then I've wished so often that you had been his father. That way he'd always be here, with us, part of us and our way of life.'

It was so unlike Emerald to show any hint of vulnerability or regret, that Drogo took her in his arms, wanting to comfort her.

'If he accepts what Alessandro's mother offers him,' Emerald went on, 'then he won't be part of us any longer. I worry for him, Drogo. We've brought him up to be comfortable in the life he has here in England; Alessandro's mother will want him to be Alessandro's son, charming but weak, royal but malleable, a handsome puppet prince.'

'You're underestimating Robert,' Drogo tried to comfort her. 'He is his own man, Emerald.'

'It would all have been so much better if he had been your son – not that I'd want James disinherited, of course – but, Drogo, how on earth am I going to face owning up to a son who is the Crown Prince of somewhere as ridiculous as Lauranto? Everyone who's anyone knows that a European title is merely a joke compared with a British title.' Emerald gave a small shudder, reassuming her normal mantle of assured superiority. 'We can't let him make even more of a Ruritanian comedy of himself by marrying some girl with the trumped-up title of "Princess" just because it suits Alessandro's mother.'

'No, better by far that he marries someone we have chosen for him,' Drogo agreed straight-faced.

Emerald leaned back within the circle of his arms and looked up at him. 'It's all very well you laughing, but these things are important, Drogo.'

'I'm prepared to agree that if Robert does step into Alessandro's shoes then it will be important that he marries someone he loves, someone who understands the demands of his role and her own, and who can deal with the problems those demands may cause them both, but as for us choosing that someone – just think how you would have felt if your mother had chosen your husband for you.'

Still looking up at him, Emerald told him derisively, 'She did – she chose you, even if she has never said so.'

'Mmm. Well, there are exceptions to every rule,' Drogo allowed, with a grin, before bending his head to kiss her.

Chapter Three

'It's definite then, Nick? This separation, I mean. There's no chance of the two of you . . . ?' Rose Simons asked her stepson sadly.

'No, none. Sarah has made that more than clear. She's even had the locks changed. Her father's idea, no doubt.'

Nick's voice might be as crisp as the shirt he was wearing – laundered, no doubt, professionally rather than by his wife – Rose thought wryly, but she knew her stepson, and she knew the vulnerabilities and in-securities Nick was so adept at hiding. Too adept? Was that part of the reason why he and his wife had separated? Because the experiences of the first twelve years of Nick's life had made him wary of trusting others?

To the outside world Nick might be an aggressive and very successful corporate raider, whose photograph appeared regularly in the financial press, accompanied by articles praising his economic acumen, but to her he was still, in part, the troubled orphaned child she had taken to her heart.

Nick pulled out one of the matt chrome bar stools from the kitchen island unit where his stepmother had been chopping vegetables for the curry she planned to make for supper. The kitchen of the Chelsea town house Josh and Rose had bought together after their marriage, with its streamlined and highly individual chrome and glass décor, might not look as cosy and domesticated as the hand-painted, extortionately expensive Smallbone kitchen Sarah had insisted on having fitted in the over-priced house in The Boltons she had fallen in love with, but Nick knew which kitchen he felt most at home in and where he felt most valued.

His stepmother had her own unique style, which owed much to the fact that she was a very successful designer of both commercial and private house interiors, working from the family-run Walton Street shop, first opened by her aunt Amber, and something to the oriental genes inherited from her Chinese mother. To those who didn't know her, from the top of her polished still-black pixie-cut hair, to the hem of her strikingly simple black dress, Rose Simons breathed a style that appeared intimidating, but Nick knew the loving heart Rose concealed beneath her couture clothes and her businesslike manner.

He couldn't think of any other woman he knew – and he knew plenty – who, on opening her front door to a scruffy, dirty, snotty-nosed unknown boy of twelve, who was announcing that her husband was his father, would have reached out, as Rose had done to him, to say calmly, 'Well, I am pleased to hear that because if there's one thing this house lacks, it's a boy living here.'

'Nick . . .'

'It's all right,' he told her now. 'I'm not going to do anything stupid, like going round there and kicking up a fuss. I've already tried that, after all.' He rubbed his hand against his jaw, the contact making a faint rasping sound. He was the image of his father, Rose thought, as she put the sliced vegetables into a bowl, and covered it, her movements practised, calm and minimal, in harmony with the pared-down elegance of the kitchen. Rose liked things to be easy to understand and assess instead of complicated; she liked things to be out in the open instead of hidden away, and all that was reflected in her designs. Just as a cluttered, overfilled mind could conceal forgotten secrets and thoughts that ultimately could grow and fester, so, she felt, could cluttered 'space' lead to the same potential hazards.

Nick wasn't like that, though. Nick was a child damaged by the misery of the early years of his life, and Rose's heart ached for him.

Although he was trying to conceal them, she could see his bitterness and his anger over the draining, long-drawn-out misery that had been the ending of his marriage, even if those emotions were now banked down under a thin seal of acceptance.

'What . . . what's going to happen about the children?' Rose had dreaded asking. She and Josh adored their grandchildren, and Rose considered herself fortunate to see as much of them as she did, thanks to the fact that she and Josh lived virtually within walking distance of Nick and Sarah's house.

'Sarah's agreed that I'll be able to have reasonable access. *Reasonable access.* Hell, they are my kids, I made them, I—' He broke off and pushed his hand into his hair. 'Sorry . . . but when I think of what this is doing to them, and all because of Sarah's ruddy father. The poor little sods were crying their eyes out when I left.

Bloody Sarah – you think she'd have spared them that, at least until after Christmas.'

Christmas.

Rose bent her head over the bowl, not wanting Nick to guess what she was thinking. For her Christmas meant going 'home' to Denham Place, near Macclesfield, and to Amber, her aunt. It meant being part of the large gathering of siblings, cousins and parents that now spanned three generations. But Nick had never truly been comfortable within that group, always holding himself deliberately outside it, and since the boys had been born he had opted out of going altogether, 'because Sarah wants to go up to Scotland to be with her parents.'

'Will you be seeing the boys over Christmas?' Rose asked.

'Not a hope in hell. Sarah's taking them to her parents. They've never liked me, especially her father. No doubt they'll have some kilt-wearing chinless wonder waiting in the wings to offer her the comfort of a male shoulder and the right kind of background. Jesus,' Nick exploded, 'when I think of the way I've bloody half-killed myself to give her the kind of lifestyle she kept on whining that she wanted, only to have her turn round and say that she wants us to separate because I'm always working.'

Rose didn't say anything. How could she? She knew as well as Nick did himself that there was some justification in Sarah's accusation, and that the reality was that he loved his work. It enabled him to express the aggression within him that came from his struggle to withstand the cruelty of his childhood, living with a stepfather who had beaten both him and his mother,

30

until the man had fallen into the road after a heavy bout of drinking and had been hit by a bus, dying of his injuries in hospital. Nick's work gave him not just financial independence, but also something he needed very badly, and that was the triumph that came from out-doing others who, for one reason or another, considered themselves to be his betters.

Rose loved her stepson but she wasn't blind to his faults or the inner demons that drove him.

There was one thing, though, about Nick that filled her heart with pride and gratitude and that was his abhorrence of physical violence. He could so easily have developed the same behaviour patterns as the man he had once believed to be his father. Even at twelve, with the deprivation he had suffered, he had been a tall, muscular boy. Rose knew she would never forget the evening the headmaster of the excellent local school they had got Nick into had come round to tell them about the taunting Nick had suffered from a group of boys in his class, and the way that Nick had endured that taunting and walked away from it without resorting to the violence they were obviously trying to goad him into.

When Rose had talked to him about it later, he had confided to her that his mother had made him promise before she died that he would never use his fists on anyone, 'because him that beat us both up isn't your proper dad, and I want to be proud of you when I think of you with your proper dad when I'm gone.'

Later that night, Rose had cried in Josh's arms. 'I can't bear to think what Nick's had to go through,' she had told him. 'He's only twelve and he's had to watch his mum dying, and then come and find you, not knowing how he'd be treated.'

'Well, I could hardly deny him, could I?' Josh had said bluntly. 'Not when he's the spitting image of me. But I'd still not have taken him in if you hadn't been willing to have him, Rose.'

The thin, dark-haired boy had indeed been unmistakably Josh's son when he'd knocked on their door and announced that Josh was his father from, as they'd discovered later, a brief fling he'd had with a young married woman, way back before Rose had even met Josh.

And, of course, Rose, childless by choice because of all that she'd suffered herself because of her mixed race, had taken Nick straight to her heart. Josh had taken a bit more convincing that the boy should stay, but within a month Nick was walking like his dad and talking like him, and Josh, when he thought Rose wasn't looking, had been bursting with pride in his son.

'Well,' Rose said now, 'you're welcome to come to Macclesfield for Christmas with us, you know that, Nick.'

'What, and have Saint Robert sympathising with me, whilst secretly they're all thinking that they don't blame Sarah. Because, let's face it, Ma, I don't fit in with them and I never have. Posh people with posh kids, that's what they are. No offence meant. As it happens I've got a mate who's going to be spending Christmas in the Bahamas and he's invited me to join him. Sun, sea and pretty girls – what else could a man want, eh, Ma?'

Rose wished she could do more to help him but she knew how independent he was. Nick had inherited Josh's sharp instinct for a good business deal. After university he'd studied for an MA and then gone to work on the trading floor of the London arm of an American bank. The Gordon Gekko world of money and Nick had almost been made to go together, Rosie recognised, and neither she nor Josh was surprised that he'd become so successful.

She also understood perfectly well why he had fallen for Sarah, then a newly qualified young accountant, whom he'd met through work, and why Sarah had fallen for him, but she had worried that they were rushing into marriage with expectations that couldn't be met.

Rose knew there had been differences between them for a while – arguments that had caused problems between them, which neither of them had seemed willing to resolve. Sarah's father was a wealthy titled Scottish landowner, who, Rose privately thought, was inclined to bully his wife and daughter and who didn't like Nick. But Rose suspected that Nick sometimes went out of his way to provoke his father-in-law into hostility towards him. Rose actually felt sorry for Sarah, guessing that there were times when the young woman felt torn between her father and her husband.

'Of course, Sarah's father is going to be crowing, but if either of them think that I'm going to allow my sons to be packed off to his old public school then they can have another think.'

Rose sighed. She knew that the subject of the education of Nick and Sarah's two young sons, Alex and Neil, had led to the most bitter of their quarrels. Sarah's father felt the two boys should be educated at his old public school, as boarders 'to make men of them', whereas Nick wanted the boys to attend his own old school.

Nick might like to come across as a bit of a cockney wide boy when it suited him, and in order to infuriate his father-in-law, but the reality was far more complex than that.

'Cup of tea?' Rose went to fill the kettle when he nodded. 'Remember when you first arrived here, Nick?' she asked him as they waited for it to boil.

'Do I?' he laughed. 'I was nearly crapping meself as I stood on the step, not knowing what to expect. Christ, I hadn't even known Bert wasn't my father until my mother told me when she was dying. When you opened the door and saw me there I bet you felt like sending me packing, a snotty-nosed scruffy kid, claiming that your husband was his dad.'

'What I saw, Nick, was a young boy with more courage than a man three times his age. Not that it wasn't a shock.'

'You're the one with courage,' Nick told her, going to the fridge to get the milk. 'We both know that Dad would have had me out on my ear and handed over to Social Services, if he'd had his way. But you wouldn't let him do that. You told us both that my place was here.'

'Josh was just shocked. He'd never really have turned his back on you. He simply had no idea that you existed.'

'It was you, though, who swung things in my favour, Ma. You who loved me before Dad did.'

Rose put her hand on his arm. 'I was so grateful to your mother, Nick. I still am. When she sent you to us she gave me the best gift I could ever have had, aside from your father's love.'

'But . . .' Nick challenged ruefully. He knew his step-mother. He knew how much she loved him, how protective she had always been of him, knowing from her own experience how hard it could be to find acceptance when you were 'different'. He had gone from living on welfare, to having a father who could afford to give him the very best of everything. It had been Rose, though, who had understood that he needed to find his own level, and who had supported him.

'No buts,' Rose assured him. 'Just don't let your pride lead you into doing something you might regret, Nick. You've got two sons—'

'You mean I've provided Sarah's father with two grandsons,' he interrupted her bitterly, 'because that's what she thinks is more important. It's no use. I've tried . . . Sarah would probably say that she's tried as well, if she were sitting here, but all the trying in the world can't put right what's gone wrong between us and, to tell the truth, I don't even think that I want it put right any more.'

'Oh, Nick . . .' Rose hugged her stepson tightly.

In so many ways he was the image of his father, and she would have loved him for that alone. But there were other ways in which he was uniquely himself and she loved him for that as well. Josh had grown up as an only child of loving Jewish parents, who had themselves grown up in the East End of London. His childhood had given him self-confidence and an optimistic self-assurance. Nick had been brought up in an atmosphere of male violence and female fear. He had Josh's self-confidence, but in Nick that confidence had a much harder edge to it, twinned with cynicism and sometimes even suspicion about the rest of the human race. Where Josh was exuberant and physically affectionate, Nick found it difficult to show his feelings. Whilst Josh had always been ambitious, Nick was far more driven. The so-called 'big bang' in 1986, when the financial system in London had become deregulated, had made Nick a very wealthy man, taking him from the trading floor to heading up his own department within one of the world's most successful merchant banks, but it was rare to see Nick smiling and even more rare to hear him laughing.

'When's Dad due back?' Nick asked, changing the subject.

'He said he'd be home in time for dinner, but you know how these sessions with the advertising people run on.'

Out of the success of his original hairdressing salon Josh had built up his business, mainly by lending his name to hair-care products and merchandising, and these days he was more of an entrepreneur and businessman than a hands-on hairdresser, although he still insisted on cutting Rose's hair himself.

'Black gold, that hair of yours was,' he often told her. 'That style I cut for you and the photographs Ollie took of it were where it all began for me, Rosie. You're my good luck.'

'Why don't you stay and have dinner with your dad and me?' Rose suggested.

Nick shook his head. 'I've got a client to see this evening, and I need to sort myself out with a decent flat before Christmas.'

'I can't give you your Christmas present yet because it hasn't arrived,' Rose told him.

Nick had come to them with no possessions, and

when Rose and Josh had gone round to the house where he and his mother had been living, they'd found a handful of photographs of Nick as a baby with his mother. Recently Rose had sent the best of these photographs to Oliver in New York, and he had promised to produce some new photographs from them, to be framed and given to Nick as his Christmas present. They were Rose's way of saying to him that neither she nor anyone else had the right to exclude his mother from his life, nor to ignore all that she had done for him, and Rose knew that when Nick saw them he would understand that, just as she knew that beneath his sharp-edged exterior he could be both vulnerable and sentimental.

Christmas presents . . . Nick looked away from his stepmother. He hadn't had time to go with Sarah when she'd taken the boys to Hamleys and Harrods at the beginning of December. He'd stopped going Christmas shopping for the boys with her after he'd bought them both battery-driven child-size cars. He'd been thrilled with the cars. As a child he hadn't even been able to dream of things like that. He'd raced home from work the day they were due to be delivered, only to find that Sarah had sent them back.

'But, Nick, that kind of thing is so dreadfully vulgar,' she had told him.

'Like me, you mean?' he had fired back, and she hadn't denied it, simply turning away from him, saying quietly, 'Daddy says that we really ought to be thinking about getting the boys used to riding. He's sorting out a couple of ponies he thinks will suit them.'

'Ponies? They are my sons, not some ruddy little

Lord Fauntleroys,' he'd told her before he'd stormed out of the house.

'Hurry up, you two, otherwise Katie is going to miss her train.'

The sound of her best friend's brother's voice from the bottom of the stairs had Katie making a grab for her case whilst Zoë put her finger to her lips and mouthed, 'Let's pretend we aren't here. He'll have a heart attack. You know what he's like about being on time for things.'

Katie could have said that since, on this occasion, what he wanted to be on time for was the train she needed to catch for London, teasing him didn't seem very fair. But long experience of Zoë had her shaking her head instead, whilst downstairs Tom swore audibly.

Zoë burst out laughing and called out, 'Ooooh, Tom, fancy you using such naughty words.'

Well pleased with her joke, Zoë turned back to Katie, tossing a parcel towards her. 'Catch! Happy Christmas, and don't you dare open it until Christmas morning.'

'Yours is in your suitcase,' Katie responded. 'I sneaked it in last night.'

'What is it? Tell me. Is it a naked poster of that gorgeous boy who serves in the uni bar? The one who looks like he could be a modern-day Earl of Rochester?' Zoë was mad about the seventeenth-century notorious rake and poet, and Katie wasn't surprised when she struck a pose, grasping two handfuls of her top as though it were a lecturer's gown, and quoted, '". . . *with an avowed contempt of all decency and order, a total disregard to every moral, and a resolute denial of every*

38

religious observation, he lived worthless and useless, and blazed out his youth and health in lavish voluptuousness". He must have been the most deliciously wickedly dangerous man, far more so than Lord Byron,' she sighed. 'I would love to meet a man like that, a reincarnation of him, wouldn't you, Katie?'

'Who, Dr Johnson?' Katie teased, referring to the author Zoë had just quoted.

'No, silly, John Wilmot, of course. Just imagine how exciting it must have been to be with him.'

'He was a womaniser and a rake,' Katie reminded her.

Zoë gave a small ecstatic sigh. 'Exactly,' and then demanded, 'Tell me what my present is.'

Katie shook her head.

'Please . . .'

'No.'

'Katie, do you want to catch this train or not?' Tom bellowed.

Zoë ran to lean over the banister. 'Katie does, but I don't want her to. Why do you have to go home for Christmas when you could have come with us to Klosters? I thought you were my best friend.' Zoë adopted a tragic pose. 'You don't love me any more, do you?'

'Zoë, stop fooling around for once, will you? Of course Katie wants to spend Christmas with her family.'

Katie blew Zoë a kiss and dragged her case down the stairs, giving Tom a look that was both grateful and apologetic.

It was funny how things could jog along in the same way for so long and then suddenly change overnight – or in her case, over a lager in an Oxford pub when she and Zoë had met up with Tom, newly returned to the UK, having completed his Master's in America. She'd known him virtually all her life, but sitting there in the pub, listening to him talk about America, watching the way he smiled and pushed his dark hair out of his eyes, Katie had realised that the excitement she suddenly felt had nothing to do with the fact that he was Zoë's brother. And then he'd smiled at her as though he guessed what she was thinking and she'd smiled back. Now it wasn't just because of Zoë that she was looking forward to going skiing after Christmas.

Katie and Zoë had been best friends from the first term at the small exclusive junior school they'd attended in Kensington, and then all through their time at St Paul's Girls' School, before coming to Oxford. Katie, used to the bossiness of an older sister with an over-developed sense of responsibility about such things as properly tied shoelaces, neatly brushed hair, and not dragging one's feet in puddles, had been fascinated and bewitched by Zoë, with her mop of red curls, and her delight in challenging authority, from the moment they had met. It had been Katie who had giggled when, that first break-time, Zoë had held a wriggling worm up to her mouth, pretending that she was eating it, whilst the other girls had fallen back in shocked horror, one of them actually bursting into tears, and that had sealed their friendship.

'See you in Klosters,' Zoë called now from the upstairs window of the pretty house her parents had bought for her whilst she was at Oxford, and which the two girls shared.

'Honestly! Girls! Why do you have to cut things so

fine?' Tom mock-grumbled as he pulled away from the kerb.

Katie had never known a brother and sister who were such opposites as Tom and Zoë. Where Zoë thrived on taking risks, Tom preferred caution; where Zoë was tiny, and had a mass of dark red curls, Tom was tall, with the physique of a keen sportsman, and his hair was straight and black.

Zoë claimed that it was the wild Irish blood she had inherited from her mother's family that was responsible for her sometimes reckless nature, while Tom took after their father's family, conservative bankers whose small private bank, in which Tom worked, was still family owned.

'Tom is quite happy just to exist,' she was fond of saying, 'but I want to live.'

'I hope I'm not going to miss the train,' Katie said anxiously as Tom drove steadily towards the station. 'My mother will kill me if I do.'

'You won't,' he assured her. 'Knowing my dear sister as I do, I made sure I came to pick you up with time in hand.'

Katie gave him a relieved smile.

As Tom had predicted, they arrived at the station in good time, and Katie was secretly thrilled when he insisted on accompanying her onto the platform, carrying her case for her, and waiting with her until the train pulled in.

'Thank you for the lift.'

As he placed her case on the train for her and Katie stepped into the carriage, she automatically aimed a brief 'thank you' kiss at his cheek, her eyes widening

41

when Tom cupped her face and kissed her back, not on her cheek, and not as the irritating friend of his equally irritating sister, but properly. Really, truly properly. Not with tongues – they were in public, after all – but almost. And it was a long kiss, a meaningful kiss, a lovely, wonderful, wonderful kiss, Katie decided, pink-cheeked as Tom released her and stepped back, saying softly, 'See you in Klosters.'

'Oh, yes. Yes!' Katie agreed fervently. The train was pulling out but she couldn't bear to go off to find her seat until the platform and Tom had finally disappeared from sight.

She had already had the best Christmas present ever, she decided blissfully, as her train rumbled south towards London, cold air, not warm, predictably coming out of the heating vents, making her glad of the thick tights she was wearing under her miniskirt, as she huddled into the warmth of her black peacoat.

Beyond the carriage window rolled the disappointing green of the Oxfordshire countryside. Christmas should be white, not green and wet. But there would be snow in Klosters, of course. Katie's tummy fluttered with excitement and anticipation.

She was looking forward to being with the family – of course she was – especially Granny and Gramps, who were such darlings. She hoped everyone would like the presents she'd got them – books this year; she liked to have a theme. The book she'd bought for Zoë was a beautifully bound copy of the Earl of Rochester's poems that she had found in an antiquarian bookshop in Falmouth during the summer.

Normally after Christmas Katie's parents took Katie,

her elder sister, Emma, and her younger brother, Jamie, skiing, but this year her parents and Jamie were flying out to Australia instead, where her father had business interests, whilst Emma went to Italy to spend a term studying fabric design at Angelli's.

Silk was the lifeblood of their family, although that might not be immediately obvious to outsiders. Her own ambition, once she had finished university, was to set up an archive library-cum-museum documenting all the patterns Denby Mill had produced, along with their provenance. Her grandmother, Amber, would be an invaluable help. And how much Katie was now looking forward to seeing her. Christmas at Denham Place, even without snow, would be utter bliss.

Through the plate-glass window wall of his penthouse apartment, sitting in the Eames lounge chair with his feet on its footstool, Robert stared out across the London rooftops. The chair was positioned exactly so that its occupant could see both out of the room and into it. Robert knew that he had a perfect panoramic view of the city, but the images inside his head weren't of St Paul's, the Thames and the distant horizon, but of the classically elegant buildings of cream stone and the cobbled square they dominated and surrounded: the royal palace and the offices of state of the Principality of Lauranto. What a project it would be to bring those Palladian buildings back to their original glory, to restore the dingy, shabby harbour below the ancient walled capital city back to the charmingly picturesque place it had once been. It would take money, of course – investment, investors. Olivia's parents were the principal trustees of a very large charitable trust, and responsible for finding suitable causes for it to invest in and support. Oh, yes, Olivia would definitely be the ideal wife for him.

She had grown into an elegant, intelligent, socially adroit and confident young woman, with that aura of polished gloss that New York women possessed; a woman that it wouldn't be hard for him to marry. In fact, it would be extremely easy for him to marry Olivia, Robert recognised. Extremely easy and very suitable.

Chapter Four

'Darlings, how lovely!'

'I'm sorry we're later than I said we'd be, Mummy,' Emerald told Amber, 'but the traffic was simply awful. Is Robert here, only he's got all the presents? We simply didn't have room, what with everything that Emma is insisting on taking to Italy with her.'

'Yes, he's here.'

'And the others? Have they arrived yet?'

'Yes, everyone's here apart from Olivia, and Robert has gone to the airport to collect her.'

Detaching herself from her mother's embrace, Emerald asked, 'I take it that we're all in our usual rooms?'

'Yes, of course, darling.'

'Drogo, can you take everything up? There's something I want to have a word with Cathy about before I forget. Where is she, Mummy?'

'In the kitchen with Janey, I think.'

As their mother headed in the direction of the kitchen, Jamie told Katie, 'Granny and Gramps have got the tree ready for decorating.'

'Yes, and it's my turn to put the fairy on top this year,' Katie answered

It was a family tradition, started when they had all been small, that the children took it in turns to place the fairy on top of the tree.

The front door opened, as she spoke, to admit a surge of cold air, and Harry and David, Janey and John's sons.

'Made it after all, have you?' Harry joked. 'We were going to give you another half an hour and then start the tree without you.'

'It's lovely to be here, Granny.' Katie hugged Amber, firmly ignoring her stepcousin's teasing.

Amber hugged her granddaughter back, their contact making her aware of the physical differences between youth and age. Whereas her own thinness represented a withering away, Katie's slenderness was due to an abundance of youthful energy. Katie's flesh felt firm against strong young bones, whereas Amber's now hung slack and soft against bones that were thin and fragile. Katie even smelled of youth and freshness, Amber thought fondly.

'It's lovely to have you here,' she responded. It didn't do to have favourites amongst one's grandchildren but Katie had an extra special place in her heart, perhaps because she shared Amber's own passionate love for the history of the family silk business.

Katie was dressed in what Amber assumed was the current uniform of youth: black tights encasing her long slender legs, a short skirt, a skinny-looking jacket, which looked like something a seaman might wear, and thick, heavy-looking boots. Gold hoop earrings swung from her ears – Amber well remembered the fuss there had been when Katie had gone behind her mother's back to have her ears pierced after being told she must

46

not – her long thick nut-brown hair swinging on her shoulders.

Katie released her grandmother to turn and eye the bare branches of the Christmas tree.

'It's no use you looking at it like that,' Emma reproved her sister, coming over to join them. 'We can't start decorating it until Robert comes back with Olivia. It wouldn't be fair.'

It was typical of her sister to claim the moral high ground, Katie thought. 'I wasn't going to, Emma. I was just telling Harry that it's my turn to put the fairy on the top.'

'We can't start but we can get organised for when Robert and Olivia get here,' Harry pointed out. 'We'll need a couple of pairs of tall stepladders. Where did you put them after you'd put those curtains back up for Granny?' he asked his younger brother.

'Outside in the garage.'

'Right, we'd better go and fetch them.'

'Let's go and sit down in the drawing room and you can both bring me up to date with all your news,' Amber suggested to her granddaughters.

The kitchen at Denham was a big comfortable room with a table in the middle large enough to seat a dozen people, but with the six female members of the second generation of Jay and Amber's family gathered round, all talking at once, it wasn't just the soup simmering on the Aga that was giving off heat and filling the space.

'Janey, you've done enough. Do let me help. I know you, you'll have been working flat out for weeks getting ready for this,' Rose pressed.

Although there was no blood relationship between them, Rose had grown up with Ella and Janey, gone to St Martins with them, lived and worked in London with them, and the two of them were the closest she had to siblings.

'No, honestly, Rose, I'm fine. It's only soup, after all. I would appreciate a hand, though, when we take the tea into the drawing room, and if you wouldn't mind buttering the scones . . . ?' The two of them fell easily into the kind of efficient domestic routine that came from years of living together. '. . . It makes it easier for Amber and Dad. They're in those boxes, and the butter's our own. John and Dad have been experimenting. John wants to open a farm shop at Fitton. I've brought a trolley from Fitton Hall so that we'll have two. We won't take it in, though, until Robert and Olivia get here.'

Rose made her way to the worktop and opened the first of the Tupperware boxes, whilst Janey looked at her a little enviously. Rose always looked so . . . so contained and calm. Even the way she dressed reflected that. In fact, everyone looked better than she did, Janey thought glumly: Emerald in her Chanel; Polly in what Janey suspected must be Armani; Ella, her own sister, in something that was chic and obviously Fifth Avenue, and even Cathy, who wasn't in the least bit interested in fashion, was wearing a pretty dress. No one looking at them now would ever guess that *she* had been the one who had been passionate about clothes and design when she'd been young. Unlike the others, Janey recognised, she'd put on weight, but there was no point feeling sorry for herself or hard done by because her life meant that she simply never had either the time or the money to spend on herself. Maintaining Fitton Hall was like having an ever-open extra mouth to feed, which gobbled up money and always needed more. Fitton, it could be said, was the cuckoo in the nest of her marriage.

Janey knew that it hurt her husband, John's, pride that her father paid him to manage their estate along with Fitton's land, but without that money they could never have managed, despite all they tried to do to bring in extra income.

Her father and stepmother were both generous and tactful, discreetly paying both boys' school fees, helping them through college and Sandhurst, and providing them each with a small allowance. They should be grateful to them, and she was, which was why she tried her hardest to repay their generosity by making sure that she was always on hand to help and keep an eye on them. John, though, sometimes chaffed resentfully against their need for what he called 'charity'.

Things wouldn't be so bad if John's father hadn't provided quite so generously in his will for his second wife. It irked John that, despite the fact that she was drawing such a generous annual income from Fitton, his stepmother still expected John to pay for the upkeep of the Dower House.

Janey tried not to feel too sharply aware of the difference between them as she looked from her own work-reddened hands and short unpolished nails to Rose's discreet manicure. Rose was so fastidiously controlled in everything she did that she probably wouldn't get so much as a smear of butter on the black dress she was wearing, whilst if *she* had been wearing it, no doubt it would already be covered in greasy smears . . .

Janey made a big effort to gather herself, to raise her game. She was just feeling down because Cassandra was being so very difficult at the moment, she told herself. It was hard to remember sometimes that Cassandra had been such close friends, not just with her own mother, but also with John's mother, when Cassandra was constantly complaining and making life so unpleasant for poor John.

Goodness, but Janey was letting herself go, Emerald thought critically, glancing at her stepsister, before looking round the kitchen for her younger twin sisters and then heading determinedly in their direction.

'Whilst you're both here,' she began without preamble, 'there's something I wanted to discuss with you about Walton Street.'

'Emerald, it's Christmas,' Polly protested, 'and I haven't seen Cathy for over six months.'

'This is important. London's booming, thanks to the banking industry. There's been a big influx of Americans buying up property. Robert's inundated with commissions from them, but Walton Street hasn't seen a corresponding increase in sales—'

'That's because everyone wants polished cotton for their curtains, preferably from Tricia Guild,' Cathy interrupted her.

'I know that, Cathy. What I've been thinking is that we should try and get into the American interior design market, with Ella's help, make a move away from the private homes market over here and think instead about targeting the corporate market. We should expand into commercial soft furnishing, specifically hotels. There's a huge demand for top-quality hotel accommodation at the moment, and that's going to increase. If we can get in on the ground floor of that kind of development it would give us a huge advantage. I was at a cocktail party the other week and one of the other guests was complaining that he simply can't find anyone of the right calibre to oversee the soft furnishings side of a new hotel he's building.'

'Well, it's certainly worth thinking about,' Cathy agreed. 'But we'd need larger premises, and more staff. And you'll have to sweet-talk Rose into agreeing. She's the one who co-ordinates the interior designs, after all.'

They all looked across the kitchen to where Rose was buttering scones.

'What are you three up to?' Ella's amused voice broke into their conversation.

Of all of them, Ella was the one who had changed the most, Emerald reflected, turning from a plump, anxious and defensive young woman, who never bothered much with her appearance, into the elegant *soignée* New Yorker she was now. In fact, it was almost as though, with regard to their appearance, Ella and Janey had changed places so that now it was Ella who dressed fashionably and Janey who didn't. But then, Emerald acknowledged, it would be next to impossible to live in New York and be married to a man like Oliver, who had once made his living photographing beautiful women and clothes, and not be affected.

She eyed Ella's effortlessly elegant draped cream jersey top and skirt with a definite twinge of lust.

'It's Donna Karan,' Ella answered her unspoken question, looking amused, her English accented with a faint American drawl that was as sensual as her clothes.

'Perfect for travelling as it doesn't crease. Olivia bought the darlingest pieces from her leisurewear collection when we went out shopping together.'

Although she was speaking to Emerald, Ella's real attention was on her sister. Janey worked so hard, Fitton Hall was a demanding mistress, and she certainly wouldn't have wanted to share her husband with it. They'd flown over first class and she'd taken advantage of the extra luggage allowance to fill a large case with clothes for her sister. In New York, heading up a charity meant attending a constant succession of society events and maintaining a high profile, and that meant a constantly renewed wardrobe. She'd have to wait until she could catch Janey on her own, so that she could do things discreetly. Janey had her pride, after all, and no one was more prickly about this than John.

'We were just talking about the business,' Emerald told her. 'We really need to get a foothold in the American interior design market.'

Emerald had always had a good head for business, Ella acknowledged.

'If we go ahead, with profits being so low at the moment it will mean us not taking anything out of the business this year, especially if we do expand,' Polly pointed out.

'Well, that's all right, isn't it?' Emerald shrugged impatiently.

'For us, yes,' Cathy agreed, 'but it might not suit Janey.'

Amber had made the business over to all of them in equal shares shortly after Jay's heart attack, and although neither Ella nor Janey worked in the business, their share was the same as everyone else's – a mutual decision from everyone concerned.

'I can sort something out about that,' Ella said quietly.

'And I'll speak to Rose,' Emerald told them.

'Right that's the scones done,' Rose told Janey. 'What's next?'

'There's some cream for those who want it, and some homemade jam. I don't want to overface everyone now, otherwise no one will want any supper, which I thought we'd make help yourself this evening.'

'Good idea.'

'Heavens, who on earth is going to eat all these scones?' Emerald demanded.

'The children,' Janey and Rose said together, both laughing.

'Speaking of children, I take it, Rose, that Nick and Sarah have gone up to Scotland?'

Rose's heart sank a little. She didn't really want to discuss the failure of Nick's marriage but she didn't have much option.

'Sarah has, but Nick's gone to the Bahamas. Things haven't been very good between them for a while and they've decided to separate for a while to give one another some breathing space. Sarah's father never approved of her marrying Nick and I suspect that she feels torn between the two of them.'

'Oh, well, he wouldn't. Sarah's mother came out the same season as me, and I remember him from then. Aunt Beth was touting him as one of the debs' delights but there was nothing remotely delightful about him. He was frightfully dour, as they say in Scotland, with red hair and dreadful skin. And he was a terrible snob, always going on about his title.' Emerald pulled a face.

'I was astonished that Sarah actually defied him to marry Nick in the first place . . . Rose, there's something I want to discuss with you about the Walton Street business.'

Rose nodded. 'And there's something else we should all discuss whilst we're here, perhaps.'

'What's that? Ella queried.

'Well, it will be Amber's eightieth birthday next November. I know that's nearly a full year away, but since we're all together it seems a pity not to take the opportunity to discuss how we might celebrate the event.'

'Well, of course we shall have a family party,' Emerald agreed. 'Drogo and I could host it.'

'A party, yes, but I was thinking of something else, a special gift,' Rose said firmly.

'That means that you've already thought of something,' Emerald guessed shrewdly.

'Yes,' Rose agreed, 'but what I've got in mind is rather a large project and it would need us all to agree and to contribute to it.'

'So what is it?' Polly demanded.

'Well, this does in a way tie in with what Emerald has been saying about the need for us to look in new directions to promote the business. As you all know, through my own private practice I deal with clients who want new interior designs for their shops, hairdressing salons, et cetera, and I'm beginning to see a move away from the pretty-pretty to something more dramatic.'

'And . . . ?' Emerald urged impatiently.

'I'm wondering if we could introduce a new design to Denby Mill's existing portfolio, based on the length of silk featured in *The Silk Merchant's Daughter*. I know that Amber has that piece of silk, and I've always thought how wonderful the colours in it are, all those rich dark ambers, plums and charcoals, shot through with lighter colours.'

Emerald had heard enough. She could never and would never feel comfortable about the famous painting of her mother, the work of the French artist Jean-Philippe du Breveonet, and which she herself had once tried to destroy.

'That piece of silk is priceless and antique. It could never be replicated.'

Rose nodded in agreement. She had expected resistance to her idea from Emerald, who for some reason was always antagonistic to anything to do with the French artist and the paintings he had done of Amber.

'You're right,' she agreed, 'but what I was thinking was more along the lines of us creating an entire new range of designs, using the colours from the silk and incorporating them into modern styles – stripes, block prints, architectural designs – the kind of patterns that would appeal to interior designers and really stand out from what's on offer at the moment.'

'That's a terrific concept, and I love it already,' Cathy announced, joining the conversation. 'Rose is right about the colours in the silk. Every time Sim and I go to the National Gallery we look at the painting and marvel at it all over again.'

'It sounds a good idea,' Janey concurred.

'I thought that if we could work on it in secret so that Amber doesn't know, we could with luck have it ready for launching by her birthday. I thought we'd name it and launch it in her honour.'

'Name it? What?' Emerald challenged, unable to conceal her dislike of the idea. She couldn't help it. Anything to do with the artist who had secretly been her mother's lover and her own father made her feel angry and vulnerable. The last thing she wanted was attention being drawn to the series of paintings, which were currently on loan to the National Gallery and which the artist had given into her mother's care during the war, just prior to his own death. For years those paintings had remained shut away, but Sim, Cathy's husband, had persuaded Amber to let him show them in his own small gallery in Cornwall, where they had attracted such a lot of interest that the National Gallery had asked to borrow them.

'We could call the range "Amber", I suppose,' Ella suggested.

Rose shook her head. 'You don't have to agree with me – this is only a suggestion – but what about calling the entire range simply 1912 as in "The 1912 Range"? That is the year Amber was born, and I think using that date will set the range apart from the current crop of floral patterns and names, if you'll all forgive the pun.'

'Rose, that's a brilliant idea,' Janey approved, clapping her hands together.

'It is very stylish,' Ella agreed. 'I can see that appealing to the high-end American market.'

'It does sound rather elegant,' Emerald agreed reluctantly, 'but you're forgetting something important, Rose. To come anywhere near replicating the colours in the original silk, we're going to need that piece of fabric, and Mummy keeps it under lock and key. She'll be bound to ask what we want it for if we wish to borrow it.'

'We can ask Jay to get it for us,' Rose told her promptly. 'If we tell him what we're planning he'll help us, I'm sure. And, Polly, how would you feel about taking it back to Italy with you and asking Rocco to look into matching it? Denby Mill has its own strengths but Angelli Silk has the best reputation in the world for its dyes.'

Angelli Silk was the centuries-old Venetian silk manufacturing house still owned by the family of Polly's husband, Rocco. It was now in partnership with Denby Silk.

'I can see it now,' Janey enthused, 'gorgeous stripes in all those rich colours: chocolate brown, dark amber, plum, and crimson.'

'With just a thin line of off-white and black,' Cathy put in, equally excited. 'We could add some fun designs in, perhaps spots.'

'Or etched cartoons,' Ella added, her own imagination taking fire. 'Perhaps the outline of an elegant 1912 female profile?'

'Or a hat?' said Polly. 'Or maybe just the figures 1912? Oh, Rose, you really are a genius. This is just such an innovative and wonderful idea, and yet it follows the tradition of great-grandfather so well.'

The great-grandfather to whom Polly was referring was Amber's own father, whose designs Amber herself had used to produce some of Denby Mill's most popular ranges.

Listening to them, Rose exhaled in relief. She had been worried that there might be objections to her suggestion, and was delighted that it had been received so well.

Rose's idea was a good one, Emerald acknowledged,

and she could already see the huge potential the range could have, and she loved Rose's suggestion for its name. She would just have to put to one side her feelings about the painter and the painting, and focus instead on the benefits.

Her plane had just landed at Manchester airport. It was silly to have excitement fluttering inside her just because she was going to see Robert. Silly, pointless but inevitable, Olivia acknowledged wryly.

As she was travelling light, with only hand luggage, Olivia was one of the first passengers to reach the arrivals hall. She looked for her father's familiar face, and then came to an abrupt halt when she saw an equally familiar but unexpected face and heard Robert saying her name.

'Robert, you've come to meet me.'

Of all the inane things to say, and did her voice have to sound so thready and, well, silly?

They were walking side by side, the rail separating those waiting from new arrivals between them.

Robert looked so English in his dark overcoat, worn over a dark suit, his shirt white with a soft red stripe, his tie a slightly darker shade of red. His shirt would have been made to measure for him in Jermyn Street, his suit would be from Savile Row and his shoes from Lobb. He looked exactly what he was: a well-brought-up upper-class Englishman, and he had come to the airport just to meet her. A wave of giddy delight and joy washed over her.

'Is that all the luggage you've got?'

They had almost reached the end of the barrier.

'Yes. Mom promised to bring everything else.'

'Yes, she said to tell you not to worry, they've brought all your presents for everyone with them.'

'I wasn't expecting to get a commission so close to Christmas.'

They were standing face to face, Robert reaching for her case. And that was when Olivia realised that something extraordinary and previously unimaginable except in her daydreams was happening. Robert was looking at her mouth in *that* way – that way that said that he was thinking about kissing it . . . kissing her. Her heart was jumping and racing. She could hardly breathe. She felt . . . oh my, how she did just *feel*. This was crazy. She wasn't a teenager any more and—

Another passenger bumped into her, jolting her forward. Robert's free hand fastened protectively on her arm.

Olivia was attracting a good deal of surreptitious interest from other members of his sex, Robert noticed, and he could understand why. Watching her come towards him before she'd seen him, he had felt his heart lift – with triumph in his own judgement and the acknowledgement that he had made the right decision.

From the top of her shiny thick mane of tawny brown hair to the toes of her pale beige boots, she exuded the confident discreet allure of a beautiful well-groomed woman. The confidence was only a veneer, though, he suspected. He had seen the way she'd reacted when he'd looked at her mouth. And that had pleased him.

'I suppose it's raining?' For goodness' sake relax, Olivia begged herself as, still holding her arm, Robert guided her towards the exit. Her cashmere slacks were warm but thin, and she could feel the muscular hardness of

Robert's thigh against her own. This was ridiculous. She was nearly twenty-six, and adult.

'Of course. This is Manchester. The car's not very far away, though.'

They were outside in the cold damp early evening air.

'It's really good of you to come for me.'

'I had my reasons.'

'What reasons?' she asked, whilst her heart bounced.

Robert mustn't have heard her because he didn't answer.

They reached the car and he unlocked the passenger door for her and held it open while she got in. The interior smelled of leather, the plush cream seat enfolding her.

Robert's Aston Martin was his pride and joy, she knew. The radio was playing – traditional carols being sung beautifully by a choir – the sound just that little bit too loud for them to talk. Olivia wanted to suggest that Robert turn down the volume but felt reluctant to do so in case he didn't want to be bothered chatting with her. There was eight years between them and, of course, when they had been growing up that gap had seemed huge. But an eight-year gap was supposed to be ideal between a couple, wasn't it? A couple? She was crazy thinking in those terms just because Robert had looked at her mouth. So she was crazy, Olivia thought defiantly. It was Christmas and she could be crazy if she wanted. Crazy for Robert, crazy for the feel of his mouth on hers. Crazy full stop, she warned herself.

Robert glanced at Olivia when they stopped at traffic lights. She suited the car perfectly, both of them classically stylish and beautifully put together. The lights changed and he put his foot down on the accelerator.

It might be dark but the road was familiar enough for Olivia to recognise its landmark: the branches of the trees behind gated properties bare of leaves; the bends in the road, swept by the Aston's headlights; Christmas trees sparkling in windows and fairy lights shining in trees.

This was northern Cheshire, moneyed, successful and very proud of itself. They came to another junction, turning right to dip down into Wilmslow and then out again, through Alderley Edge, the road then climbing but skirting the Edge itself, with its mysterious silence and stories of Merlin.

Olivia smiled to herself, thinking that it was predictable that Robert, with his keen eye for style and his love of perfection, should choose to drive to Denham through this smart stockbroker belt part of Cheshire instead of taking the route that was their shared grandparents' favourite, through Macclesfield and then past the family silk mill.

They were in the countryside now, fields stretching to either side of them in the darkness, Olivia knew, even though she couldn't see them. To the left of the road lay Fitton Hall, and to the right Denham Place, the magnificent Vanbrugh building that was their grandparents' home, inherited by Robert's grandmother Amber from her own grandmother Blanche Pickford, and which, so the family story went, Blanche had bought to spite Barrant du Vries, the aristocrat she had loved but who had not thought her good enough for him.

Now the du Vries land was part of Denham, and Felton Priory, formerly the de Vries home, was the headquarters of a multinational company.

'I wonder what Blanche thought when Granny and Gramps married.' Olivia voiced her thoughts. 'After all, Barrant du Vries was Gramps' grandfather.'

'What on earth made you ask that?' Robert turned his attention from the road to look at her.

'I don't know. I was just thinking about Denham and how Blanche bought it to get one up on Barrant.' She gave a small shiver. 'I don't think I'd want to have such an intense relationship.'

Robert's smile was amused and indulgent. Olivia's comment confirmed his judgement of her.

As they turned off the main road and onto the drive that led to Denham, Olivia could see the lights blazing in the large gatehouse, which was currently occupied by the Leggits in their roles as housekeeper and general handyman-cum-gardener.

Whoever had planted the beech trees lining the drive had known what they were doing, because not one of them had fallen during the appalling storms of October 1987, which had done so much damage throughout the country. But the drive and the house itself would benefit from some well-designed and targeted outdoor lighting, Robert decided as he brought the car to a halt halfway down the drive, at the exact spot where it could not be seen either from the gatehouse or Denham itself. He should mention it to his grandfather, but not right now. Right now he had something else he needed – and wanted – to do.

Robert had stopped the car. Why? Olivia shifted in her seat so that she could turn to look at him.

'Remember when I said earlier that I had my reasons for coming to pick you up?'

'Yes . . .' Olivia's heart was thudding so fast and hard that she wanted to put her hand over it to quieten it.

'Well, this is one of those reasons.' He leaned towards her purposefully, as though he was going to kiss her.

No, not as though he was *going to* kiss her – he was kissing her.

Olivia closed her eyes. Robert's lips brushed her own tantalisingly lightly, once, twice and then a third time, before settling on them gently, their caress deliberately careful, that deliberation extraordinarily sensual. He wasn't touching her in any other way, and yet his kiss felt far more intimate than if he had been doing.

It was such a pleasure to be kissed in such a way: an old-fashioned kind of kissing, with an intimate pleasure all of its own way, instead of as a prelude to being groped. The mere touch of lips on lips was so heart-warmingly wonderful that she didn't want it to end.

When it did she opened her eyes, slowly luxuriating in the pleasure that still clung to her senses, to find Robert watching her, his breath warm against her skin.

'I've been wanting you to kiss me since I was sixteen,' she told him.

'I hope it was worth the wait? I've been thinking about you a lot recently,' he continued, without waiting for Olivia to answer him. 'Thinking about you and looking forward to seeing you, and to telling you – showing you – how much I've looked forward to us being together.'

Was this really happening? Should she pinch herself just to see? Was Robert really saying what she thought he was saying? Had he really kissed her, or was she just dreaming that he had? The unexpected shift in their relationship had happened so quickly, and so unexpect-edly that it was having the same heady effect on her as though she had drunk several glasses of champagne, Olivia thought dizzily, suddenly realising that Robert was still waiting for her to say something, but all she could manage was a mundane, 'That's nice.'

Robert laughed. 'And this is even nicer.' He kissed her again. She really was perfect. So grateful and delighted, just as he had expected. He reached for Olivia's hand, sliding his fingers between hers and then lifting her clasped hand to his lips.

'I know this must seem sudden, but I've been waiting a long, long time for you to grow up enough for me to tell you how much you mean to me. That time is now, Olivia, and if I'm speaking out of turn or saying some-thing you don't want to hear—'

Robert was telling her that he loved her? Robert, whom she'd adored and thought the most perfect man there was, for as long as she could remember?

'No. I mean, yes, I do want to hear it. Oh, Robert, you should have told me before. I've been old enough for years.'

'Dearest darling Olivia, you have just made me the happiest I have ever been.'

In the time it took her to catch her breath, Robert had released her hand, kissed her forehead gently and restarted the car. If Olivia was disappointed that he hadn't kissed her again – perhaps even taken things a little further than mere kisses – then she was also touched that he was being so respectful of her. It proved that he was every bit as wonderful as she had always believed.

The house was just the same, the hall smelled as it

always did at Christmas – of pine from the tree and wood smoke from the fire – those smells mingling with the scent of cinnamon and women's perfume.

She could see her grandfather standing talking to her father. Her father's skin brown from Hamptons summers, his thick hair greying now. Her parents had such a good, strong marriage, the kind of marriage she wanted for herself.

'Darling.' Her mother hugged her. 'I've brought your clothes and your presents. Did you get your article in on time?'

'Yes, thank goodness.' As she returned her mother's warm hug and listened to her questions, Olivia was trying desperately hard not to look across to where Robert was talking to his grandmother. Her face felt as though it was burning, and her heart was racing. She felt as though everything was a little unreal, as though she and Robert were enclosed in their own private bubble of happiness that distanced them from everyone and everything else.

Robert was looking at her, smiling. It was almost impossible for her to focus on Amber's face when Robert was standing next to his grandmother, and her gaze just wanted to fill itself with him.

Olivia turned back to her mother. 'I need to run upstairs and get cleaned up.'

'Don't be too long, Olivia,' Katie begged her. 'I'm dying to start decorating the tree, but Granny made us wait until you and Robert got here. You seemed to be ages.'

Chapter Five

'Oh, look at these baubles. I remember Granny buying them at Flora's in Macclesfield,' Katie, sitting on the floor, going through one of the large cardboard boxes of decorations, enthused, holding up the glittering ornament.

Flora's was a garden centre famous for its Christmas decorations.

'Oh, and these!' she exclaimed, holding up a fabric bauble made from velvet and glittering beaded silk. 'Aunt Janey made them, didn't she, from pieces of our own silk?'

'I thought we were supposed to be decorating the tree, not reminiscing,' Harry teased her, but Katie didn't pay any attention. She loved this part of Christmas.

On the other side of the tree Emma was working far more industriously through the contents of her box, insisting, 'You can't put that there; it doesn't go. We agreed we'd stick to a colour theme this year, remember?'

'But these are so pretty,' Katie protested.

'Here's the fairy,' Harry told her. 'I'll hold the ladder for you whilst you put it on.'

Scrambling to her feet, Katie took the fairy from him and started to climb the ladder.

The tree was tall and very wide at the base – so wide, in fact, that even though she was leaning forward she couldn't quite reach the top.

'Come back down, Katie, and I'll move the ladders,' Harry suggested.

'It's OK. I can reach if I just lean over a bit more.'

'Katie, no!' Harry protested, but Katie laughed down at him before stretching up on tiptoe to try to reach the top. But her foot slipped, the sound of her own gasp of shock mingling with Harry's anxious, 'Katie!' as she lost her balance and crashed down, her fall broken by Harry, who rushed to try to save her.

'Are you all right?'

'What's happened?'

'What on earth was that noise?'

'Katie fell off the ladder.'

'Katie, are you all right?' Her father was crouching on the floor beside her, saying calmly, 'Let's have a look at you. Don't try and move.'

Move? That was the last thing she felt like doing. She felt sick and dizzy, and there was the most dreadful pain in her arm.

'How is she?' That was her mother, sounding impatient and anxious at the same time.

'Is she hurt?' That was Aunt Rose.

'She's broken her arm, by the look of it. We'd better get her down to A & E.'

Broken her arm? But she was going skiing next week, and she had to go because Tom would be there, and she desperately wanted to see him.

However, when Katie tried to tell everyone that, the pain in her arm became so intense that she fainted instead.

'Here you are, Janey. This is the last of them.'

Janey took the empty Tupperware containers from Ella and put them into the back of the Range Rover.

'Dad and Amber both look well,' Ella continued, watching as Janey closed the back of the car.

'Yes, they're marvellous,' Janey smiled.

Ella had taken the opportunity of the distraction provided by Katie's fall to have a few minutes on her own with her sister.

'A lot of that is down to you,' she pointed out. 'I really don't know how you cope with all that you've got to do.'

'Oh, I don't mind. Dad and Amber aren't any trouble at all.' She paused and then acknowledged, 'I wish I could say the same about Cassandra. She's become so very difficult, and John finds it very hard to deal with her. To be honest, she wears me down. I felt so envious of all of you when we were in the kitchen earlier; you all looked so groomed and glamorous.'

'Oh, Janey.' Ella gave her sister a fierce hug.

'You are the best of all of us.'

As she released Janey, Ella, feeling awkward, said, 'I've brought some clothes with me that I thought you might be able to use. I know you don't get much chance to shop these days.'

'And if I did I wouldn't have the money to buy designer clothes. Oh, it's all right,' she assured Ella, 'I don't mind eating humble pie – which is just as well as we'd probably all starve if we didn't.' Anything of Ella's with a waist in it would have to be let out, of course, Janey thought, since she was nowhere near as svelte as her sister, but luckily that was something she could do herself.

'I don't know how we'd manage without all the help we get from the family, and I'm especially grateful to you, Ella, for giving up your share of the Walton Street business profits to me. They've installed the new central heating in the Dower House, which Cassandra insisted she was entitled to, and bought me this very handsome vehicle.'

'You deserve it, Janey, and more. I'm sorry that Cassandra is giving you such a hard time.'

'I can't understand why she is being so mean,' Janey responded. 'Especially when she and our mother were such great friends.'

Ella wondered if this was the time to tell Janey about the real relationship that had existed between their late mother and their father's cousin. Even now, after all these years, she hated thinking about the time as a child she had opened her parents' bedroom door to see her mother and Cassandra naked on the bed together, Cassandra caressing her mother intimately, but before she could bring herself to speak, Janey's elder son came out of the kitchen to join them.

'Uncle Drogo has just rung from the hospital. Katie has broken her arm but it's a nice clean break and the hospital says it will mend well.'

'Well, thank goodness for that.' Janey greeted Harry's announcement with relief. 'Go and find your father and David, will you please, darling, and tell them that I'm ready to leave? I've got to get back,' she explained to

Ella, after Harry had gone, 'otherwise I won't be able to get organised for the morning. I've left everything you'll all need for breakfast in the fridge.'

'Modern life is a far cry from the days when houses like these were run by an army of servants,' Ella remarked as they closed the door on the cold night air, and then took off their coats, a sturdy well-worn Barbour in Janey's case, and a luxurious camel-coloured wool and cashmere coat in Ella's. 'I wonder what Blanche would make of things if she was alive today?'

'She wouldn't approve at all,' Janey laughed.

'If you've got time we could go to our room and I could give you those things I mentioned?'

'You're so tactful, Ella,' Janey told her, 'trying to be discreet and make sure that the others don't see me accepting my big sister's charity, but truthfully, I don't mind. Pride is a luxury I simply can't afford, and I am truly grateful to you.'

When she got back to New York, she'd buy her sister something lovely and special and brand new, Ella promised herself, fiercely blinking away the tears she knew Janey would hate to see.

'What makes it all so much more difficult with Aunt Cassandra and John is that she will keep reminding him of what close friends she and John's mother were. She says it in that sort of way that implies that John owes her something above and beyond the very generous provisions for her made by his father in his will. I know it's mean of me but I can't help wishing that she hadn't decided not to go and stay with her friends in Brighton this Christmas.

'Oh, I know what I meant to say,' Janey continued,

changing the subject. 'Your Olivia and Robert looked very happy in one another's company when they arrived this evening. Is something going on there?'

The amused and questioning note in Janey's voice distracted Ella from thinking about the brief sharp prick of warning she had felt when Janey had been talking about John's mother and Cassandra.

'They've always got on well together.' Ella sidestepped Janey's teasing question. Naturally she'd noticed Olivia's glow of happiness, and she'd seen the looks that Olivia and Robert had been exchanging, but if something was going on between them it was a very new 'something', and one she wasn't sure she liked.

'I'm sorry for causing so much trouble, Dad,' Katie said as Drogo stopped the car in front of Denham.

'And so you should be, Katherine,' Emerald scolded. 'You're old enough to know better than to take such silly risks.'

'Yes,' Emma chipped in with big-sister superiority. 'Harry told you to come down.'

Drogo shot his younger daughter a sympathetic smile. 'Not in too much pain now, are you?' he asked her.

Stupidly it was her father's kindness that brought her close to tears, rather than her mother and her sister's criticism, Katie acknowledged, as she sniffed and shook her head. 'My arm aches a bit but that's all.'

'You're lucky you didn't end up with concussion after a fall like that,' Emerald told her, her crossness a cover for the shock and anxiety she had felt when she'd hurried into the hall to see her daughter lying crumpled there.

'It was Harry who saved her from that by breaking her fall,' Emma announced. 'I bet he'll be bruised black and blue with you falling on top of him like a sack of potatoes,' she added. 'Of course, you won't be able to go skiing now. Not with a broken arm.'

'I'll be able to manage,' Katie protested. 'You see loads of people out there with arms and legs in plaster.'

'Yes, but they've normally had that plaster put on whilst they've been out there. They don't fly out to ski with it on, do they?' Emma retorted.

'Dad, I can still go, can't I?' Katie pleaded. 'Zoë's expecting me to, and I could sit out whilst the others ski.' Of course she wasn't going to say anything about Tom, but it was the thought of not seeing him that was making her feel sick and miserable.'

'Well . . .' Drogo began, but Emerald shook her head.

'Don't be silly, Katie. Of course you can't go. What would be the point? And apart from anything else, your father and I would never have a moment's peace, worrying about you, if you did.'

Somehow, after that, David's, 'I've put the fairy on the top of the tree for you,' wasn't as comforting as it might have been. She wasn't going to be able to go to Klosters. Zoë would be furious with her – she was furious with herself; furious and miserable.

'At least it's not your right arm, darling,' Amber tried to cheer up her granddaughter, 'and you're welcome to stay on with us, you know, until your parents get back from Australia. I know it won't be as much fun as Switzerland.'

Katie forced a wan smile, whilst over her head Emerald gave her mother a grateful look.

73

'If you're sure it won't be too much for you and Jay, Mummy, that would be wonderful.'

'Emerald, I am seventy-nine not ninety-nine,' Amber pointed out with a touch of asperity in her voice. 'It will be a good opportunity for me to do something about sorting out some of the old records of our fabrics. I've been meaning to do it for ages. It will be a step towards organising that archive you've been talking about, Katie. Jay and I salvaged snippets of fabric and wallpaper from Felton Priory before it was sold, and they are really interesting.'

Staying on here at Denham would be much better than being at home in London on her own, Katie knew, but it wouldn't be Klosters. Even so, she forced herself to look appreciative, knowing that under almost any other circumstances she'd have been thrilled by such an opportunity.

Family tradition meant that everyone had an early night after their arrival, and with Katie back from hospital, those mothers with young children started to gather them up ready for baths and bed.

'I'll come up with you and Sam, Mum,' Olivia told Ella. 'I need to collect my case from your room, and hand over some parcels to Santa,' she added with a smile in her younger brother's direction, laughing when he gave her a scathing look and told her, 'I'm fourteen years old. I stopped believing in Father Christmas when I was six.'

Laughing back, Olivia ruffled his hair and teased, 'So does that mean you don't want any presents then?'

Ella hadn't intended to start asking questions – after all, Olivia would tell her if there was anything she wanted her to know – but it was impossible for her to stop herself from commenting lightly, once Sam was in bed in the room he was sharing with Jamie, and Ella and Olivia were back in Ella and Oliver's room, 'You and Robert seem to be getting on well.'

'Well, I suppose it's natural that we should gravitate towards one another. After all, we are the eldest members of our generation.'

Olivia's airy response did more to increase Ella's concern for her daughter than to reduce it. That kind of evasion just wasn't like Olivia.

'Has he said anything to you about his visit to Lauranto? Sooner or later he's going to have to decide whether or not he wants to succeed Alessandro and become Crown Prince, and if he does—'

'He picked me up from the airport, Mom, that's all. I hope everyone's going to like their Christmas presents. Oh, and you'll never guess who I saw just after I'd dropped off my piece to *Vanity Fair*.'

Olivia plainly wanted to change the subject.

'Who?' Ella asked her.

'Tait Cabot Forbes,' Olivia grimaced, explaining when Ella didn't respond, 'You know, that dreadful journo who wrote about Maisie changing her will, and you and Dad.'

'Yes, I know who you mean, darling, but once your father had spoken with him privately and explained the situation he didn't pursue the matter.'

'No, but he didn't apologise in print for what he'd said either, did he?'

'Well, he couldn't really, could he? Not when your father had said that what he told him was in the strictest confidence.'

Ella gave her daughter a loving smile. Olivia was extremely loyal to those she loved – it was one of her strongest characteristics and a lovely one – but sometimes it made it hard for her to accept that life was not always black or white but came in various shades of grey.

'Tait is a journalist,' Ella reminded Olivia, 'and a very good one, and he was only doing his job, after all.'

Olivia nodded. But no matter what her mother said she was not prepared to forgive Tait Cabot Forbes for the way he had publicly tried to accuse her parents of doing something wrong, and she would certainly never forget it.

His whole article had been based on supposition, suspicion and spite. In it he had tried to claim that her parents must have put undue pressure on their elderly friend Maisie Fischerbaum to change her will, cutting out the trustees to whom she had originally entrusted her estate, and instead appointing Ella and Oliver as the sole trustees of her billion-dollar foundation, and responsible for deciding which charitable causes would benefit from it. The fact that she had made this change in her ninetieth year, using a new solicitor and without saying a word to the original trustees, had led to a good deal of gossip behind the scenes about her decision and her parents' involvement with her, Olivia knew. However, she also knew that the reason Maisie had changed her will was because she had been devastated to discover that shortly after the death of an old friend of hers, his trustees had ignored his wishes and used his money in ways of which he would not have approved. After that Maisie felt that the only people she could trust were

Olivia's parents. They had tried to reassure her, but Maisie had refused to change her mind, and the new will was drawn up in secrecy at her insistence. The original trustees hadn't done anything illegal and Maisie had been worried that if it got out that she no longer trusted them to carry out her wishes to the letter, they might either sue her for defamation, or have her legally declared to be unfit to continue to conduct her own financial affairs.

After her death, when the gossip had started, Olivia had urged her parents to go public with Maisie's reasons for changing her will, but they had felt honour-bound not to say anything in case Maisie's distrust ended up reflecting badly on her original trustees, who, after all, had done nothing wrong. It was typical of her parents to protect others at their own expense, Olivia knew.

Her parents might have forgiven Tait for his article now he had backed off, but Olivia didn't intend to do so. He hadn't actually taken back what he'd said or apologised, had he? And besides, there was something about Tait as a person, as a man, that made her feel on edge, and . . . and judged. He was so . . . so pleased with himself, and arrogantly and, yes, sexually male. Not like Robert, who was so very much more *gentlemanly*.

Robert . . . Olivia hugged to herself the thought of the kiss they had shared.

'Here's your case,' Ella told Olivia. 'Amber said to tell you that you're in the lilac room.'

'She knows that's my favourite,' Olivia smiled, reaching for the strap of her roller case.

Each of Denham's many bedrooms was decorated in

a different colour to coordinate with the Denby Mill silk used for its soft furnishings.

The panelling in the room Ella and Oliver were occupying was painted a soft grey blue, to contrast with the butter-yellow silk curtains, their Greek key design border a deeper richer gold. The Greek key design provided a border for the blue-grey and off-white trellis-patterned carpet, whilst the bedcover, the seats of the two bedroom chairs and the lamps on the mantelpiece were covered in the yellow silk.

Within seconds of Olivia going, the bedroom door opened again and Oliver walked in.

'You look thoughtful,' he commented.

'Mmm . . . I think there could be something going on between Olivia and Robert.'

'Robert? How can there be something going on between them? She hasn't seen him since last Christmas, has she?'

'No, but when they came in together tonight, there was definitely something there, and she did have that crush on him at one stage.'

'Robert,' Oliver repeated in the tone of voice a man uses when he suddenly realises that his little girl has transferred her affections to another male.

'She hasn't said anything to me,' Ella admitted. 'In fact, if anything she was rather evasive when I brought up the subject, so I could be wrong, but somehow I don't think so.'

In their room – the room that had been hers when she had been growing up, but which her mother had had redecorated five years ago, along with the rest of the house – Emerald dropped into one of the pretty Louis Quatorze-style chairs, the elegant arch of her feet in the high heels she insisted on wearing no matter what the fashion, revealed as she crossed her legs.

'Why must our children be so exhausting, Drogo?' she demanded.

'Probably because they're your children,' Drogo answered with a smile.

'I would never have tried to do anything as pointlessly silly as Katie,' Emerald claimed, quickly changing the subject to continue, 'Poor Janey, she's beginning to look quite old. She really should take a bit more care of herself.'

'I doubt she has the time – or the money,' Drogo said mildly.

'They'd be a lot better off if they let Fitton and moved in here with Mummy and Jay. After all, John could run both estates just as easily from here as he can from Fitton. Denham's a far more comfortable house, and Janey would be on hand to help Mummy and Jay when they need it.'

'Fitton means far too much to John for him to ever want to do that, and even if it didn't, John would still have the problem of Cassandra living in the Dower House.'

Emerald gave a small exasperated sigh.

'I do hope that Rose isn't going to get too involved with Nick and those children of his now that he and Sarah are separating. Not now, when we're hoping to expand into the commercial market. If we do get contracts to provide the soft furnishings and the interior designs for hotel bedrooms, then we're going to need

Rose. She fusses far too much over Nick – I've always said so. He isn't even her child, and there's no real proof that Josh fathered him.'

'Apart from the fact that Nick looks exactly like Josh, you mean,' Drogo pointed out. He was used to his wife criticising her relatives, and he knew that in reality Emerald's critical manner was just a cover for the concern that her nature would not allow her to express openly.

'It's all very well us coming here to Denham, Drogo, but the family would be every bit as comfortable at Osterby as they are here. More so, in fact, since Osterby is properly staffed.'

Since Osterby, the Lenchester family seat, was of a similar size to Blenheim, whereas Denham was of far more modest proportions, at Emerald's comment Drogo gave her a wry look.

'Osterby might have the grandeur and stature of a would-be palace, but Denham is a proper home.'

'It isn't as though Mummy and Jay couldn't afford to employ more staff. Mummy inherited all Great-grandmother's money, after all, and that was millions. Heavens, when Mummy grew up here, there were dozens of servants. Now, apart from the Leggits and the estate workers, there's no one. Janey's actually cooked virtually all the food for Christmas herself. I really do think we're going to have to say something to Mummy. I mean, Janey was actually talking about drawing up a rota for kitchen duties!' Emerald wrinkled her nose, making Drogo laugh. 'It's all right for you,' she objected. 'My manicure will never last until we get back to London.'

'You do realise that you are the world's worst snob,

don't you?' Drogo teased her. 'And that we're going to be in the Australian outback for nearly three weeks when we leave here?'

'You might be in the Australian outback, counting your sheep or whatever it is people do on sheep stations; I shall be staying in a decent hotel in Sydney or the Whitsunday Islands.' A sudden smile illuminated her face, the other side of her nature breaking through like a patch of brilliantly blue in an otherwise grey sky.

'I am so lucky to have married you, Drogo.' She reached up to cup his face, leaning forward to kiss him, and then stopped to add in her normal manner, 'but not, of course, as lucky as you were to marry me.'

Chapter Six

'Happy?'

Olivia nodded, turning her face towards Robert, the wind tangling the normal sleekness of her hair, her hand held warmly within Robert's clasp as they walked together through Denham's frost-rimed formal gardens, their Wellington boot-clad feet crunching on the gravel pathways. They startled a couple of male pheasants that had been foraging for food and that now walked slowly away in that manner peculiar to pheasants, meant to convey the impression that they actually weren't there at all.

'Yes, I am happy,' Olivia reaffirmed. 'And you?'

'Not as happy as I would be if I was kissing you, but I think we're already the subject of enough family curiosity, without stoking up any more for the time being, don't you?'

His answer couldn't have shown better how similar their thinking was. Olivia loved that there was no game-playing between them, no having to contrive artificial tests and tricks so that each could lure the other into being the first to admit to their feelings. It had charmed and delighted her that instead of holding back from her, in the style favoured by New York men – who promised to ring and then didn't, only to do so just when you'd given up, requiring a girl to pretend then that she wasn't interested, or risk losing face – Robert had been prompt and plain about seeking her out this morning, after picking her up at the airport yesterday, discreetly creating an opportunity for them to be alone together via the simple expedient of announcing after breakfast, 'Come on, Olivia. It's Christmas Eve, and you and I are on holly-finding duties. Christmas wouldn't be Christmas at Denham without holly.'

'Mom's already been quizzing me, saying that we seemed to be "getting on very well",' she informed Robert ruefully, loving the way his eyes crinkled at the corners when he laughed.

'That's probably because my mother will have been warning her not to let you seduce me,' he teased her, mock solemnly.

Olivia aimed a playful punch at his shoulder with her free hand, retaliating, 'My mother has been warning me to remember that you've got a decision to make about Lauranto.'

'Is that an issue?'

Oh, she did like his directness. It made everything feel so easy and natural.

'Not for me,' she answered him truthfully. 'It must be a difficult decision for you to make, though?'

'I do feel I have a duty to the people of Lauranto. My grandmother is set in her ways; the whole country is in need of modernisation.' He turned to her. 'And I, Olivia, have a very great need of you in my life.'

So this was happiness, this giddy, dizzy, disbelief, this

delight that made everything – every sensation, every sense, every thought – feel as though it was imbued with a special wonder.

Hand in hand they continued through the garden. The crisp winter air smelled of frost and wood smoke from Denham's chimneys, the sky swept clean of clouds by the sharp easterly wind blowing down from the Derbyshire hills, the Cheshire plain cradled snugly between those hills and the Welsh mountains to the west. The Romans had marched and fought and settled here, mining the area's rich deposits of salt, building the fortress city of Chester, but it was a county that belied the bloodiness of its history, blanketing it with its rich farmland, which spoke more easily of orderly contentment and peace.

They'd reached the end of the walled garden now, the land beyond it parkland scattered with the handsome specimens of trees originally planted by Denham's first owner.

With unspoken mutual consent, Robert opened the age-silvered oak door in the wall to let Olivia pass through ahead of him. To the west of the formal garden lay the vegetable garden and the Victorian succession houses, whilst in front of them, beyond a pretty wooded area in which winter crocuses were still showing their lavender petals, lay the ha-ha that separated the formal gardens from the park, with its muntjac deer.

'I do love Denham,' Olivia sighed happily, before adding consideringly, 'I like Osterby as well, of course, especially its peacocks.'

'Noisy brutes,' Robert complained before relenting and telling her, 'There are some in the palace garden in Lauranto.'

As he spoke he pulled the wooden door shut behind him, and reached for her.

Olivia went willingly into his arms, raising her face for his kiss. She could feel the silky warmth of the scarf he was wearing against her hand. She could smell the clean soap scent of his skin, mingling with the tweedy wool smells of his jacket and scarf. His lips were cold at first and then deliciously warm, the sensation reminding her of the childhood pleasure of hot chocolate sauce poured over ice cream.

As he had done before, Robert simply kissed her, taking his time, making the sensation of his mouth moving against her own a subtly sublime pleasure that had her toes curling in her Wellingtons.

When he finally released her it was to take her hand again, telling her as they headed for a holly tree on the edge of the thicket, 'I've got to revisit Lauranto in February. When I do, I'd like you to come with me.'

Olivia stood still. She could feel the unsteady beat of her heart, and the colour coming up under her skin.

'You . . . you would?'

'Yes. Very much. As I was saying earlier, there's a lot that needs to be done, for the people, for Lauranto's heritage, and I'd like you to see everything as it is, before—'

'I'd love to go with you.'

This time when Robert kissed her, Olivia knew that, without the words being said, a commitment had been made between them, an awareness shared of what could be, along with an acknowledgement that they would travel to that destination at their own pace.

Robert observed the glow of happiness illuminating

Olivia's. Everything was going to work out. In fact, it was all going to be perfect. Olivia was perfect and he could love her for that alone, he told himself.

'Come on,' he said. 'We'd better go and get that holly, otherwise it won't just be our mothers who are asking questions.'

Emma, Katie, Harry and David had taken possession of the billiard room from which the younger members of the family were currently barred. Despite the cold outside, the windows were open, the better to dispel the telltale scent of the roll-ups they had been passing round, the smoking of which had produced a shared mood of beneficent relaxation, spoiled only by David, who had started giggling and been unable to stop until Harry had dragged his younger brother to the window and held his head out of it, to bring him down.

It was the day after Boxing Day, and after two days of charades, sardines, and similar hearty party games shared with the littlies, the four of them were all agreed that they deserved some chill-out time that was a bit more relaxing.

'The thing is,' David remarked earnestly, 'it's not as though smoking a joint does anyone any harm. I mean, it's not like doing heroin or coke, is it, so the parents making a fuss about it is just a joke really.'

'You're the joke, fathead, if you think that Dad wouldn't make a fuss if he caught us,' Harry responded.

'Oh, Dad. He'd probably think a chap should be cashiered from his regiment, he's so old-fashioned.'

'In the twenties heroin and coke were all the rage, and accepted. It wasn't even against the law,' Katie offered. She was still feeling very down about not being able to go to Klosters. She'd had a miserable telephone conversation this morning with Zoë, who had sounded even more wildly off the wall than normal, whispering into the phone that she couldn't talk properly now but that she'd met 'my fate and my soulmate in the shape of my own personal Earl of Rochester'.

The sudden warning rattle of the door handle had the four of them leaping to their feet, Harry calling out in an impressively firm baritone, 'If that's any of you kids, you're barred, remember.'

The door opened and Olivia stepped in, smiling as she told them, 'I'm not really sure if I come into the barred category or not, but I can warn you that Polly's boys have asked her why they can't play billiards, so if I were you . . .'

She could smell the telltale sweet scent of the dope and she turned to exchange a knowing smile with Robert, who was standing behind her. She'd finally crossed the bridge now that had previously divided them, leaving her on the side of the 'young ones', whilst Robert had been firmly on the side of the adults, and it felt good, Olivia acknowledged, it felt very good indeed. She watched in amusement as Emma and Katie started frantically flapping their arms in an attempt to move the sweet-scented air out of the window.

'Here . . .' she delved into her handbag and removed a small atomiser of scent to spray into the air around the door, '. . . this might help to provide a distraction.'

'Softie,' Robert teased her later as they walked out into the garden together, the only place they could really be sure of any proper privacy. 'I dare say that the parents will do the same for them as they did for us, and pretend not to notice, knowing that in a very short space of time they'll have grown out of it.'

'Our parents maybe, but I am not so sure about Uncle John.'

'Mmm . . . I see what you mean. He's a good sort but more suited to the Victorian age in some ways, stiff upper lip, doing the right thing and behaving in the right way, and *very* conscious of being Lord Fitton Legh.'

'That's a bit unkind,' Olivia objected.

'But true?'

A little reluctantly, Olivia nodded.

Although as yet they'd done no more than exchange kisses, Olivia knew that Robert was serious about her, and about them.

'I don't know if I'm going to be able to wait until February to see you again,' he told her now.

'I think you've been reading my mind,' she admitted.

'Delaying your return to New York and coming back to London with me would probably be a bit more obvious than either of us wants right now, but if I were to be able to snatch a couple of days in New York in, say, a couple of weeks' time . . . ?'

'You'd be very welcome.'

'I normally stay at the Pierre.'

'My apartment has a spare room.'

They looked at one another, Olivia both smiling and blushing a little at what she could see in Robert's eyes.

'You're quiet.'

Rose smiled at Josh. 'I was thinking about Nick,' she

admitted. They were in the car on their way home from Denham. 'I do wish there was something we could do to help him with Sarah.'

'He's a grown man and not a boy. He knows enough about the world to have sussed out why her parents wouldn't exactly welcome him as their son-in-law.'

When Rose looked at him, he reached out and covered her folded hands with one of his own. She was so neat and compact and precise somehow, his Rose. And so vulnerable still, even after these years, still so sensitive to her own mixed-race heritage and the revulsion her great-grandmother had felt at the fact that Rose had a Chinese mother.

'Rose, he's working class, and Sarah's father's a titled, upper-class snob.'

'Sarah chose to marry him.'

'Did she? Or did Nick choose for her? Look, I'm not knocking him – he's my son – but he had a hard upbringing before he came to us. It's bound to have affected him. He isn't like me, we both know that. Nick's got an edge to him, a need to win, simply for the sake of winning. To someone like Nick, brought up the way he was, marrying an upper-class girl like Sarah would seem like winning, and would be a goal he would set himself simply for the sake of that win.'

Rose shot Josh an unhappy look. 'That's not fair,' she protested. 'Look how hard Nick worked to buy Sarah that house. She and the boys have the best of everything.'

'Of course they do. That's part of the buzz for him, being able to give her more than the upper-class husbands of her friends can give them. It's all about proving himself, Rose, about proving that he's the best, but now he can't, can he, because Sarah's father is standing in his way, determined to prove that *he's* the best.'

Rose gave him a troubled look.

'Nick's my son and I love him, Rose, of course I do, but that doesn't mean that I'm blind to his flaws and faults any more than I am to my own. The trouble is that Sarah's father is obviously intent on using those faults against him.'

'Sometimes I think I shall never understand our children. Katie's going round with a face like a wet weekend, insisting that she should still go skiing, with that broken arm.'

Folding clothes and putting them in the open case in their bedroom at Lenchester House, Emerald continued, 'And then of course there's Robert. Not a single word has he said to me about Olivia, and yet it's obvious that something is going on between them. It's only because Ella told me that Robert's invited Olivia to go to Lauranto with him in February that I even knew he was going back, never mind taking Olivia with him. I really don't like the idea of him getting involved over there, Drogo. I don't trust Alessandro's mother one little bit.'

Emerald paused and looked at her husband. 'Do you think Alessandro's mother will tell Robert about you know what?'

Drogo walked over to take her in his arms. He knew the real Emerald, the vulnerable Emerald she hid from the rest of the world. 'About your father, you mean?'

Emerald nodded. 'The Princess hates me and she always has done.'

Drogo knew how much it would hurt his wife's fierce pride if the truth were ever to come out, although typically, rather than admit this, Emerald told him, 'It would be dreadful for the children if they were suddenly to learn that their grandfather was a painter and not a duke, as they have always thought.'

'I doubt very much that Alessandro's mother will say anything. It's in her own interests not to, apart from anything else. She wants Robert to take Alessandro's place. Alienating him by revealing the truth to him isn't something she would want to risk.'

'You're right.'

Drogo squeezed her arm gently. He knew how much, even now, she still hated the thought that her father had not been his predecessor, the late duke, but instead Jean-Philippe du Breveonet, painter of the picture of Amber, *The Silk Merchant's Daughter,* now hanging in the National Gallery.

Chapter Seven

Outside, January snow might be falling on the New York avenues, children might be begging to be allowed to skate on Central Park's frozen ponds, but here inside the Limelight disco on Sixth Avenue, in the Chelsea district of Manhattan, the air was heated to almost tropical warmth, as the élite of the fashion and publishing world gathered to 'Celebrate the month of January' at an 'afternoon' party hosted by *Vogue* magazine. Olivia had been invited, she rather suspected, in lieu of her mother, who was visiting friends with her father in Palm Beach.

Loud music, a mix of rock and industrial, pounded her eardrums. Waiters and waitresses, dressed in very little other than what looked like tinfoil and sequins, to reveal their perfectly honed bodies, danced and pouted their way through the guests in time to the music, carrying trays of champagne and tiny morsels of food, which Macey Greenberg, Olivia's friend, had suggested cynically might contain some extra energy-giving or hallucination-inducing ingredients in view of the number of guests, including models, who were well known to have a drug habit.

'That wouldn't be any good for the models,' Olivia had pointed out, before Macey had left on a mission to snag an interview with a not-as-yet-out gay singer for the music magazine for whom she freelanced.

Glamorous parties were supposed to be exciting, and Olivia was prepared to admit that she might have enjoyed this one if she hadn't just realised that Tait Cabot Forbes was also one of the guests.

She'd seen him ten minutes or so ago, deep in conversation with the editor of the *New York Times*, no doubt planning to savage and potentially destroy yet another innocent victim so that he could claim some ego-boosting headlines for himself, Olivia thought bitterly.

Above the music she could just about hear the affected squeals of the group of very thin and very pretty young models, clustered together several yards away, the air around them blue with cigarette fumes as they smoked to keep their hunger pangs at bay. Poor things, Olivia thought sadly. She didn't envy them at all. Watching them, she found it odd to think that once her own father had made his living photographing girls like them for fashion magazines.

Their extreme thinness emphasised Cindy Crawford's far more sensual curves, the supermodel very much the centre of attention as the press photographers gathered round her.

One of the current crop of top fashion photographers was talking with an editor from British *Vogue*, who had flown in for the party. The Fashion Pack, including New York *Vogue*'s Grace Coddington, were all dressed in black, just as Olivia was herself. Pictures of the party would fill the new copy of *Women's Wear Daily*, of course, and be pored over by its dedicated readers.

Her own Ralph Lauren dress was on loan from her mother, who had insisted that she borrow the sophisticated heavy black jersey tube of fabric that somehow magically became a ravishingly elegant dress once it was on, with a slashed neckline and just the hint of a small sleeve. With it Olivia was wearing a pair of diamond cuff bracelets, also her mother's, and she had put her hair up, the whole effect, so her friend Macey claimed, very *Breakfast at Tiffany's*.

Olivia was just looking round for Macey when she felt a firm tap on her shoulder. Turning round, she was surprised and annoyed to see Tait Cabot Forbes standing behind her.

'I've got a proposition to put to you,' he told her without preamble, adding, when she stiffened, 'No, not that kind of proposition. What I'm proposing is that we bury that hatchet you're carrying around with you. It must be getting heavy and burying it will save you having to look for an opportunity to bury it in me.'

'You mean like you tried to stick a knife into my father's back?' Olivia challenged him.

Tait spread open his hands. He had big hands with long fingers, Olivia noticed, his skin tanned and his nails clean without looking overmanicured in the way favoured by some New York men. His traditional Brooks Brothers shirt allied to law-school-graduate smartness made him stand out in a room in which most of the other men were attached to the fashion world and dressed flamboyantly.

'There was nothing personal about my investigation

into your parents' relationship with Maisie Fischerbaum. That's what I am – an investigative journalist.'

'Earning your money and making your reputation by trying to destroy my parents.'

'I got it wrong. I admit that. I've apologised to your folks.'

'In private, but you never apologised publicly.'

His expression said that he was beginning to get annoyed with her. Good, Olivia thought. What had he expected? That she'd roll over and be thrilled because he'd attempted to talk her round? It took more than a too-good-looking face and way too much male confidence to do that.

'Because your father asked me not to publish the reasons why he and your mother were appointed as trustees. I respected that, just as I respect your loyalty to your folks, but I'm beginning to get a bit tired of feeling that glower of yours burning through my skin every time you set eyes on me. So, how about we call a truce?'

'You can call whatever you like,' Olivia told him fiercely. 'As far as I'm concerned you are still the man who tried to hurt my parents by writing things about them that weren't true.'

Olivia turned on her heel and walked away from him. She would have walked past Macey as well, she suspected, she was so wound up and angry, if her friend hadn't stepped in front of her waving a glass of champagne under her nose.

Olivia wasn't going to turn round and see if Tait Cabot Forbes was even still there, never mind looking in her direction. In fact, what she'd like to do more than anything was leave the party early and go home in case Robert telephoned, which he sometimes did just before he went to bed. He hadn't been able to come over to New York yet, as he'd hoped, but he'd promised he'd be over as soon as he could, and he'd told her that he'd informed his grandmother that Olivia would be accompanying him on his February visit to Lauranto.

Robert. Thinking of him, hugging the thought of him to herself was so much better than thinking about Tait Cabot Forbes. So very much better.

'Katie.'

'Tom.'

As she saw Tom coming towards her, Katie stopped dead, blocking the way of a group of determined middle-aged county Sloanes up in London to make the most of the final days of Peter Jones' January sale. With a great deal of tutting, the group reformed with the skill and expertise of campaign-hardened bargain hunters, leaving Katie and Tom to exchange smiles and then swift hugs.

'I missed you in Klosters.'

'I wanted to be there.'

'I told Zoë to tell you how sorry I was about your arm.'

'I expect she forgot. You know what she's like.'

It was what they were not saying, rather than what they were, that mattered, Katie knew.

'I was going to get in touch but Zoë said that you were staying with your grandparents.'

'I was. I only got back yesterday.'

'You'll be going back to Oxford soon,' Tom guessed.

'Zoë planned to go straight there from visiting her godmother in Cheltenham.'

'I'm going back this weekend,' Katie confirmed.

'Have you got something else on right now, or would you like to have lunch with me?'

'Yes. I mean, no, I haven't got anything else to do and I'd love to have lunch with you,' Katie told him immediately.

'Good.' Tom looked so handsome and grown up in his dark suit, crisp striped shirt and, of course, his essential banker's red tie, Katie thought admiringly.

'Will San Lorenzo be OK?' he asked her, mentioning the very upmarket restaurant in Beauchamp Place, which was one of Princess Diana's favourites.

Glad that for once she had given in to her mother's chivvying and worn 'something decent' – the 'something decent' being a neat-fitting dark plum Armani dress with a dropped waist, under a toning dark plum and grey tweed jacket, worn with plum leather boots, the outfit a Christmas gift from her mother, who had said that she was tired of seeing her daughter looking scruffy – Katie nodded her head and tried not to look too impressed.

Half an hour later they were being shown to a table in San Lorenzo's airy cream-painted restaurant, thanks, Katie suspected, to the fifty-pound note she had seen Tom discreetly slip the head waiter.

'Just as well it's January and the jet set are still either in the Caribbean or on the ski slopes,' Tom told Katie ruefully, 'otherwise we'd never have got a table.'

Katie felt a bit like Cinderella, she decided, plucked from the mundane and everyday into a magical world, with Tom, of course, playing Prince Charming.

Over Bellinis Tom studied the menu whilst Katie studied their fellow diners, unable to stop herself from leaning over to whisper excitedly, 'Don't look now but over there, just being shown to the window table, I'm sure that's Jerry Hall and Marie Helvin.'

'And Michael and Shakira Caine are sitting just behind you,' Tom informed her back.

'Tell me about Klosters,' Katie begged him, once they had ordered and been served. She loved Italian food and had decided to go for the special house cannelloni, whilst Tom had ordered the liver.

'Well, there was, you know, lots of snow, and mountains,' Tom teased her.

'I was so disappointed that I couldn't go.'

'I was disappointed that you weren't there,' Tom answered.

They exchanged looks, pleased but slightly self-conscious on Katie's part, and meaningful and very male on Tom's.

'This is such a treat for me,' Katie told him. She felt flushed and happy, and just a little bit out of her depth.

'And for me,' Tom told her, in such a deliciously sexy dark voice that Katie curled her toes into the soles of her boots and thought that she'd never ever be able to so much as walk through Beauchamp Place again without thinking about Tom and remembering today.

'Zoë's told me about meeting her Earl of Rochester,' Katie laughed. 'I'm dying to hear more about him.'

Immediately the smile died from Tom's eyes.

'What is it?' Katie asked him.

'There was a bit of an upset over that. Axel Von

Thruber – I'm assuming that's who you mean – isn't someone my parents would ever approve of Zoë befriending. You know Zoë – of course she kicked up a fuss when the parents initially said that she wasn't to have anything to do with him.'

Katie nodded, well able to imagine the 'fuss' her friend would have made. Zoë hated any kind of restrictions being put on her, and in fact they were something like a red rag to a bull to her.

'I have to say, though, that I agree with them, which, as you can imagine, hasn't made me very popular with Zoë. The fact is that Von Thruber has the very worst kind of reputation.'

'You mean he's very sex, drugs and rock 'n' roll?'

'If only that were all he is,' Tom answered grimly. 'The drugs he favours aren't just the odd reefer, and as for the sex, well, let's just say louche doesn't even begin to describe his lifestyle. He's well known on the Eurotrash young jet set scene, or maybe I should say that he's notorious. The trouble is, I suppose, he's had too much of everything far too young. He inherited millions on his twenty-first birthday and he's due to inherit millions more on his twenty-fifth. It doesn't help, of course, that he is very good-looking,' Tom admitted wryly. 'And I suppose that Zoë, being Zoë, was inevitably drawn to him like the proverbial moth to a flame. Fortunately, though, now she's come to her senses and seen him for what he is. Zoë can be very naïve. Initially I suspect she saw his decadence as glamorous, and of course the fact that everyone was warning her against him, and our parents so obviously disapproved of him, only added to his allure.'

'Zoë's always liked boys with a bad-boy image,' Katie admitted.

'Axel Von Thruber isn't a bad boy, he's bad full stop, degenerate, destructive, the kind of person who enjoys damaging and corrupting others simply for the pleasure it gives him. But thankfully Zoë came to her senses, possibly as a result of seeing him with someone else, from what she said to me.'

'Oh, poor Zoë. She must have been hurt.'

'Yes, she was, but better that she has her heart broken than her whole life, which is what would have happened if she'd got seriously involved with him. Anyway, why are we talking about my sister, when we could be talking about ourselves? Are you still planning to go into your family's business once you've graduated?'

'Yes. I'm going to be helping my grandmother set up a proper archive of Denby Silk's history. I'll be working here in London at the Walton Street shop, but of course I'll be travelling up and down to Macclesfield and Denham to collect papers and things from there. Ultimately Mummy wants to get more press interest in Denby Silk's fabrics and she wants me to get involved in the PR side of the business from an archive point of view.'

'I'm glad you're going to be working in London.'

'Yes . . .' Katie felt slightly breathless.

'Not that Oxford is very far away from London,' Tom continued.

'No.'

'I could easily drive down and take you out for dinner, if you don't mind being dragged away from your books?'

'No. I mean, I'd like that.'

Katie only realised as she scraped away the last delicious morsel of her ice cream dessert that virtually everyone else had gone. She had been enjoying being with Tom so much that she hadn't realised how long they had been in the restaurant.

Having Tom help her into her jacket before they left San Lorenzo reminded her of how excited and elated she had felt that very first time with her first proper boyfriend the year before she had gone to Oxford. They had parted amicably after six months apart at different universities and she hadn't been seriously involved with anyone since. What she felt for Tom, though, was far more than a young girl's desire to explore her sexuality, Katie recognised. Tom was special; what they could have together if they both wanted it would be something special. Her instincts told her that and she sensed that Tom's were telling him the same thing when he took her hand as they walked down Beauchamp Place, and gave her another of those smiles that promised so much.

'What now?' Tom asked her. 'Have you got some shopping to do, or . . . ?'

'Not really. I was going to call in at our Walton Street shop. Mummy's cousin Rose works from there, on interior designs for the shop's clients and for her own private commercial clients. She's borrowed some of Great-grandfather's original drawings from Grandmother and I'd wanted to have a look at them. It's a bit late now, though, so I'll go tomorrow instead, and go straight home now. Mummy and Daddy are taking Jamie back to Eton tomorrow so we're having a special family dinner tonight.'

'Shall I walk back with you to Lenchester House?'

'If it isn't taking you out of your way. Lunch lasted an awfully long time. I hope it hasn't interfered with other things you should have been doing.'

'No, only a board meeting.'

He burst out laughing when he saw Katie's expression.

'A very dull board meeting, chaired by my father, who is proposing to the other directors that I am made up to director level later on this year. It's a formality really, nothing more, and I didn't need to be there.'

'It must be a big responsibility being on the board of the bank,' Katie opined, impressed and rather possessively proud on Tom's behalf.

'It's what I've been educated and trained for. The bank has been in our family since the seventeen hundreds, after all, although we've never been as well known or as big as some of the other private banks.'

They'd reached Sloane Street, crossing it to mingle with shoppers coming out of Harvey Nichols, before turning to cut down behind the store as they headed for Lenchester House.

'It's been lovely being with you, Katie,' Tom told her as they stood together on the pavement in the shadow of a bare-branched tree in the private garden in the square onto which Lenchester House fronted. 'It's made me realise just what I missed out on with you not coming to Klosters. We'll have to make up that time we lost.'

'Yes,' Katie agreed, her breath a white vapour cloud in the growing dusk of the cold late afternoon.

Tom pulled her towards him, drawing her in to the warmth of his body. It was quite private where they were standing, sheltered from view by the gardens in front of them and the tall buildings behind them.

Tom cupped her face, his hands still warm from the gloves he had been wearing, but his lips cold as they touched her own in an exploratory kiss that possessed just the right amount of male confidence. Katie kissed him back happily, deepening the pressure and intimacy of the kiss, and then snuggling up to him as Tom drew her closer.

It would be so easy and feel so right to invite him to come in with her, and she would have done if they had been in Oxford and not here in London.

As though he shared her feelings and her thoughts, Tom released her, telling her softly, 'Come on, it's cold and I'd better get you home.'

Outside Lenchester House, they stood and looked at one another.

'This isn't how I would choose to have today end,' Tom was just saying, when a taxi drew up alongside them and her mother got out.

'There you are, Katie! Oh, hello, Tom. Katie I thought you were planning to go to the shop?'

'It's my fault I'm afraid.' Tom stepped in to placate her mother. 'I bumped into Katie and persuaded her to take pity on me and have lunch with me.'

'Oh, well. Would you like to come in, Tom?'

'No. I'd better not. Katie's already told me that you've got a busy evening ahead with Jamie going back to Eton tomorrow.'

As her mother headed for the door, Tom smiled at Katie and told her quietly, 'I'll ring you in Oxford.'

'Thanks for . . . for lunch,' Katie managed breathlessly, the words for her mother's benefit, but the look she gave him uniquely and privately for his.

Chapter Eight

Valentine's Day. Could there have been any better way to spend it than with Robert, starting with coffee and bagels at her favourite café, followed by a stroll round Central Park, and then a whole lazy afternoon in bed together? Olivia didn't think so. It was their first time, and it had been everything she'd been hoping for, a tender, long, loving journey of mutual exploration, during which Robert had brought her to orgasm orally before entering her, then delaying his own satisfaction until she was ready to come again, this time with him.

Now they were having dinner at one of New York's most exclusive restaurants, Le Cirque on East 65th Street, where all the most famous New Yorkers dined, and tomorrow they were flying back to London together, and then travelling on from London to Lauranto.

'Happy?' Robert asked her.

'Mmm, very.' She was still in a post-coital state of relaxed satiation that was making her feel languorous and boneless.

For their evening out she'd chosen to wear Halston, a slither of perfectly draped red jersey that left one shoulder bare.

'You look lovely,' Robert told her. 'Very regal.' He paused and then added, 'It might not be a good idea to take the dress to Lauranto, though. My grandmother likes to be the centre of attention and she'd probably interpret you wearing such a dress as a challenge to her. That was part of the reason she and my mother never got on, I'm sure. If my mother had been a bit more willing to take a back seat, and if she'd tried to win Grandmother over to her side, things might have worked out differently.'

Robert was holding Olivia's hand and caressing her fingers as he spoke, and, she thought, it must just be her wretched journalistic mind that was raising the question of whether Robert had said what he had merely because he regretted that his mother hadn't perhaps done more to create harmony between herself and her mother-in-law, or because he was warning her that he expected her to play the role he had just outlined.

The last thing she wanted was for their first proper romantic evening together to be spoiled by an earnest discussion about his grandmother and the politics of dealing with her. So it was up to her to ensure that the evening *wasn't* spoiled, by not dwelling on what Robert had said or reading too much into it, Olivia told herself firmly. She was not headstrong and self-willed, as she suspected Emerald had been as a young woman, plus she had the freedom of being American and female, at a time when American women were claiming the rights and respect due to them and allying those rights and that respect to the female skills of diplomacy and tact.

'I hadn't really thought of packing an evening dress

for our visit to Lauranto,' she told Robert, truthfully, 'but if you think I should . . .'

'Although she hasn't said so, I wouldn't be surprised if my grandmother has some plan up her sleeve for a formal event to introduce me to Lauranto society.'

To introduce him, but not to introduce *them*, Olivia noted, promptly berating herself for needing them to share everything, as a newly in love couple. Robert was involved in the most delicate kind of negotiations, which had been ongoing before they had got together as a couple. She should support him through those negotiations, not make them even more difficult for him.

'I'll make sure I pack something suitable, just in case,' she told him.

'I knew I'd be able to rely on you, Olivia,' he smiled approvingly. 'That's what I love about you – your calmness and your ability to rise above the need to indulge in female emotional drama.'

'That isn't a very kind thing to say about my sex,' Olivia pointed out. 'It makes it sound as though you don't like us very much.'

'I don't like emotional histrionics,' Robert admitted. 'And much as I love my mother, I marvel sometimes at my stepfather's patience with her. My mother sees any obstacle put in the way of her being right as a personal challenge. It's very wearing. She's a woman who demands an awful lot emotionally from those who love her. It's all very dramatic and high octane. Personally, my taste runs to a woman – a very special woman who I already know – who is calmer and more considerate of the feelings of those close to her.'

He meant her, of course, Olivia recognised, a faint

107

flush of colour staining her skin when he released her hand to reach into his pocket to produce a small turquoise-blue gift-wrapped box, the colour betraying that its contents had to be from Tiffany.

A little unsteadily Olivia unwrapped it, her eyes lighting up with pleasure and love when she saw the beautifully plain two carat solitaire diamond pendant inside.

'It's beautiful. Thank you.'

'No,' he corrected her as he removed the pendant from the box and leaned across the table to fasten it on for her, 'you are beautiful, and I am the one who should thank you for allowing me to think I might be able to claim the most valuable of all gifts – your love and loyalty.'

Olivia's eyes stung with happy tears but, mindful of what Robert had said about female emotion, she blinked them back.

You could always tell a woman who was happy, Robert congratulated himself. Olivia wore her happiness in the way she moved and held herself, and tonight she looked like a queen, never mind a princess, tall and proud and positively glowing with sexual satisfaction and happiness, the red gown she was wearing almost caressing her body rather than clothing it, for all that it was simply draped over her curves rather than clinging to them.

'You do realise, don't you, that at some stage I am going to have to talk with your father, and I want it to be sooner rather than later?' Robert pointed out to her, his open declaration of the shared future he envisaged for them both delighting and surprising her. She had known, of course, that he was thinking of marriage.

Given their family relationship it had never been on the cards that they would merely have a brief affair – it simply wouldn't have been possible – but even so, she hadn't expected to hear him talking about marriage quite so soon.

Not that she minded. Robert had an awful lot on his plate and probably simply didn't have time for a long-drawn-out, deliciously sensual courtship.

Olivia's father was someone he definitely wanted to have on board, when it came to the plans he was mentally formulating for the financial future of Lauranto, Robert acknowledged.

What he wanted to achieve, both in terms of restoring Lauranto's magnificent buildings to their former glory and modernising the country itself, would take a great deal of money, and Robert intended to find different ways to make being part of a project appealing to those who would provide that money. Olivia's parents were in charge of a charity with billions of dollars at its disposal; they knew other people in similar circumstances, they had rich friends, and surely they would be willing to work towards the future of their daughter and their grandchildren by discreetly encouraging such people to invest in Lauranto?

He was glad he'd thought to warn Olivia about the best way to deal with his grandmother. Olivia wasn't his mother, of course, and would be unlikely to challenge his grandmother outright, but there was a certain American directness about Olivia that perhaps needed to be toned down for his grandmother, and even replaced by something a little more subservient, at least until she had won his grandmother's approval of her.

Olivia was an intelligent young woman. Another couple of hints to the effect that his grandmother had had her own ideas about who he should marry should be enough to ensure that Olivia understood the situation.

The thought that he might have openly raised his concerns with Olivia and discussed them with her as an equal in a shared enterprise was not one that occurred to Robert. He was too used from childhood to having to get on the good side, to 'bargain', with those with power over him – the bullies at school, sometimes his own mother – to feel that he could ever speak openly and honestly to others about his own desires and wishes.

The grey morning light filtered in through the blind they'd forgotten to close last night, striping bars of New York light on Robert's throat and shoulder, revealing the dark stubble shadowing his jaw. He was still asleep, his dark lashes fanning across his cheeks.

Their babies would have those lashes. Olivia's insides compressed and ached. Their flight wasn't until midday, hours away yet, plenty of time for her to give in to the indulgence of simply watching him.

Simply watching him, she had said, she reminded herself a few seconds later, not kissing him, but the temptation of his light-barred skin was too much for her to resist. He tasted of salt and cologne and his own skin. A wave of love for him rolled slowly through her. She was so very lucky and so very, very happy. She kissed the curve of his throat and then gasped in mock shock when his arms suddenly tightened round her.

'I thought you were asleep,' she protested.

'So you decided to wake me? Well, now you've got to pay the price.'

The words, silly, foolish words exchanged by lovers the world over in one form or another, meant nothing and yet spoke of so much: intimacy, desire, commitment, trust, love.

Robert rolled her underneath him, kissing her slowly and erotically, his hand cupping her breast, his thumb rubbing the already erect nipple, the slow dance of their intimacy already becoming a familiar pattern that had her arousal increasing in anticipation of each step. Soon he would kiss her breasts, first one and then the other, and then he would look at her and smile, and she would smile back at him before he kissed them again, this time a little more roughly, taking the eager flesh into his mouth whilst his hand shaped the curve of her hip and then covered the mound of her sex.

Years from now, when they were a long-married couple, she would remember her own delight as she welcomed him into her body and she would give thanks then, as she was doing now, for the happiness their mutual love had brought her.

Katie didn't know what on earth to do. She'd arrived back in Oxford yesterday, two days after Zoë, and since then Zoë had talked nonstop about Axel Von Thruber, whom she quite plainly adored almost to the point of worshipping him. And now Zoë had just dropped the bombshell that Axel had moved to Oxford, supposedly to do some research into his family's genealogy and British connections, but, in Zoë's eyes, purely so that the two of them could pursue their relationship.

'Axel is renting a huge house on Southmoor Road. He's got loads of friends, and they'll be coming to visit him, of course. I'd thought of moving in with him myself, but I didn't think that would be fair to you, unless of course we both moved in – there's plenty of room. Oh, Katie, I can't wait for you to meet him, although I warn you, I saw him first, so no falling for him, because if you do—'

'Zoë,' Katie protested, 'you're not supposed to be seeing him, never mind thinking of moving in with him. Your parents don't approve of him, and—'

'Who told you that?' Zoë demanded.

They were in the kitchen of the pretty two-bedroomed terraced cottage they shared on Hayfield Road, the leek and potato soup the Lenchester House cook had added to the hamper of goodies she had packed for Katie to bring back with her, simmering on the cooker and filling the room with its rich smell. Katie had been hungry when she had started to reheat it, but now her stomach was churning with anxiety.

'Tom told me,' she answered. 'I bumped into him in Sloane Square and we had lunch together.'

'You had lunch with Tom? You're supposed to be my friend, not his,' Zoë told her sharply, tossing her head. 'I bet he only took you out to lunch because he wants you to spy on me.'

Katie tried not to let Zoë see how much her accusation had surprised her, not because she thought for one minute that there was any truth in it, but because Zoë could say such a thing about the brother Katie had always believed she looked up to and admired.

'Why should Tom want me to spy on you when he

doesn't even know that Axel is here in Oxford or that you're still seeing him?' Katie pointed out.

'And it'd better stay that way, because if he does get to know, I'll know that it's you who has told him. I love Axel and he loves me. I know he does. Oh, Katie, wait until you meet him. Then you'll understand. The parents are just so stuffy and Tom is just as bad.'

'Tom said that Axel has a really bad reputation.'

Zoë pulled a face. 'Like I said, Tom is stuffy. Axel is exciting. Being with him makes me feel properly alive. Being with him is just so . . . so mind-blowing, in every sense of the word.'

'I expect it will be, seeing as he's got a reputation for taking and selling drugs.'

Katie knew that she sounded prim and prudish, but she felt she had a duty to Tom to try to make Zoë see reason, as well as a duty to protect her friend from a man whom Tom had been adamant would hurt and even, potentially, destroy her.

'Oh for fuck's sake. So he likes to shoot up occasionally – so what? I've seen you smoking dope, and don't pretend that you haven't.'

'Zoë, smoking the odd reefer isn't the same as using heroin,' Katie pointed out. 'You know that as well as I do. We made a pact that we'd never, ever touch the hard stuff, remember?'

'When we were fourteen, and we thought that giving a boy a blow job was disgusting,' Zoë reminded her. 'Anyway, I'm not using, silly. As if I would!' She pulled a face and then gave a dismissive shrug. 'And I don't know about you, Katie, but I've grown up since then and I found out a long time ago that I actually like doing disgusting.' Zoë was making fun of her, Katie knew, trying to taunt her into an argument that she, Zoë could win, but Katie wasn't going to be taunted. This was too important.

'You told your parents that you agreed with them and that you didn't want anything more to do with Axel,' Katie reminded her.

'You mean Tom told you that I'd agreed with them. I had to, Katie. They were threatening to send me home. My father even said that I needed my head testing if I couldn't see that Axel is dissolute and corrupt. They locked me in my bedroom after that row. When I told him, Axel and I really laughed about what my dad had said. My parents think I ought to fall for someone like Tom, but it's Axel I want. He's so exciting, so dark, and . . . and dangerous. Wait until you meet him, then you can see for yourself.'

The soup was ready but Katie had lost her appetite for it. Every word Zoë had said had increased her alarm.

'I don't—' she began uncertainly.

But Zoë interrupted her, almost flying at her as she rushed up to grab hold of her arms, shaking her as she demanded, 'You don't what? You don't care about what I think and feel any more, only about what Tom says? Katie, you are my best friend.'

'Yes, I know that, but—'

'But what? What Tom has to say is more important?' Zoë guessed.

'No, of course not,' Katie denied. She felt so torn between what she had promised Tom, and Zoë's rightful claim to her loyalty, and a part of her even felt resentful because Zoë was putting her in this position.

114

'I love Axel, Katie. I need him, and I need you to understand that and to remember that you are my best friend. Wait until you meet him.'

'I don't think I want to meet him, Zoë.'

'But you must. I want you to. I'm seeing him tonight at the Jericho.' The Jericho Tavern was a live music venue on Walton Street, and very much a part of the student scene. 'Forget what Tom thinks. Come with me, Katie, and see for yourself what Axel is.'

Katie wanted to refuse but how could she? And besides, didn't she owe it to both Zoë and Tom to make her own judgement of Zoë's Rochester? Reluctantly she nodded, and then went to remove the pan of soup from the hotplate.

Zoë had changed in the short time they had been separated; the nervous energy and exuberance that were so much a part of her had intensified and taken on an edginess that made it impossible for her to keep still. She was smoking far more, and eating less, and she had lost weight, but there was no denying the radiance that lit up her whole face every time she mentioned Axel. Perhaps Tom was wrong about him. Perhaps he and their parents were overreacting. Either way, she owed it to Zoë and their friendship to find out more about Axel Von Thruber, Katie admitted. After all, she and Zoë had always been best friends.

Nick lit a cigarette and leaned back in his chair. The new girl with the good legs and the great tits, who'd been giving him the eye all week, looked up from her desk and smiled at him. She was wearing a black skirt and a white shirt with just enough buttons open to show a hint of cleavage. She'd go far, he thought cynically. She'd been here less than a month and already she'd worked out that she was in a man's world and that the best way to get what she wanted was to appeal to the male ego. Wasn't that what all women did, one way or another: find a man, let him think they wanted him and then get what they wanted from him?

He'd had a row over the telephone with Sarah during the weekend when she'd announced that she was taking the boys to Scotland when their half term began at the end of the week. They were still pretending to be civilised with one another about things, still pretending that their separation was something designed to help their marriage instead of end it, so when he'd blown his top, pointing out that he'd hoped to have some time with his sons himself, she'd accused him of being verbally abusive and threatening. Abusive and threatening? She hadn't got a clue about what it was really like to be on the receiving end of abusive threats. He had, though. Nick dragged the nicotine deep into his lungs, his narrow gaze focused unseeingly on the busy department in front of him.

He'd grown up hearing the sound of a raised male voice from his parents' bedroom, followed by the soft whump of hard fists on soft flesh, mingling with the mewling cries his mother had struggled to suppress so as not to wake him. Too young then to understand the cause of what he could hear, he had known none the less that the sounds were something to be feared, to be kept hidden and secret.

He'd been older, at school, when the man he'd thought of as his father until his mother had put him right on her deathbed, had started using his fists on both of them after Nick had tried to protect his mother.

Nick could feel the bile gathering at the back of his throat. They said that a boy brought up with violence became a violent parent himself, only able to express his own emotions in the way he had seen them expressed himself as a child. It was a circle as vicious as the violence itself, but he had been lucky. His mother had seen to that. After his father had used his fists on them both, she had told Nick not to mind because he was 'better' than his father, that he'd got something that made him 'better' because it was born in him and no one could take it away from him. It was only after she had died, having told him that Josh was his father, that he had realised that she had meant that his genetic inheritance from his real father elevated him from the lowlifes, the petty thugs and criminals amongst whom they'd lived. His mother might not have thought enough of herself to find herself a decent husband, but she had thought enough of him, her child, to ensure that, in the end, she gave him a better class of father. Having Josh as his father had allowed him to escape from the life he might have had, to enter a completely different world. It was a world of affluence, social acceptance, and a certain degree of status, and Nick had known then that when the time came he would ensure that his mother's gift to him was passed on to his own children, his own sons.

Part of the reason he had worked so hard for his financial success had been that he had seen that success as a means of buying his children a better genetic inheritance.

When he had met Sarah he had been blown away,

117

knowing immediately that she was the woman he wanted as the mother of his children. Sarah, with her Sloane Ranger accent, her similarity in looks and behaviour to Princess Di when she had simply been Lady Diana Spencer.

Nick had laid siege to Sarah with all the relentless determination of a man who would have victory, whatever the cost. The physical manifestation of his emotional desire for what she represented had filled him with a passion that had overwhelmed them both.

Sarah had been three months pregnant when they got married, and Nick knew that her parents, but especially her father, would never forgive him for that.

A movement to one side of him caught Nick's attention. The new girl was smiling at him. He couldn't remember the last time Sarah had smiled at him like that, giving him a 'why don't you take me to bed' smile.

The row that had been the original cause of their separation had been over another woman, poison dripped into Sarah's ear by her father, because 'it has come to my notice that Nick has been seen having dinner with a very pretty young lady' – and then kissing her as they left the restaurant arm in arm.

He had tried to tell Sarah that the woman in question was a client – which she had been – but Sarah had refused to believe him, and in the end he had lost his temper and had told her that it would have served her right if he had been sleeping with someone else since there was no sex on offer at home. Accusations had flown and, although they had made up, other arguments soon followed. The truces between could only ever be temporary when what had been said in anger could never be unsaid.

Chapter Nine

'Well, what do you think of it so far?'

It was just over an hour since they'd arrived in Lauranto, flying in from Milan in a private jet because Lauranto as yet had only a small private airfield.

'I think it's beautiful,' Olivia replied truthfully, as she sat close to Robert in the back of the highly polished elderly Mercedes, with its equally elderly uniformed driver, a pennant bearing the flag of the Royal House of Lauranto flying from the car's bonnet.

The drive to the main city of Lauranto and the palace had taken them from the airfield on the small plateau high in the mountains that were Lauranto's natural border, where pristine snow covered the steep mountain sides and the fir trees that cloaked them, reflecting the bright sunlight pouring from the clear blue sky. Every now and again a rabbit or a deer would stop to stare at the car, brought up short by the intrusion into its territory.

The road wound down along the mountain sides, the mountains themselves towering up on one side of them, and falling away on the other far below them to the endless blue of the sea.

Olivia didn't think she had ever seen such an idyllic and unspoiled landscape.

'If you think this is beautiful, wait until you see the city itself,' Robert told her.

He looked the closest she had ever seen him to excited, and knowing why he was so filled Olivia with tenderness for him. As an architect it was only natural that he should be thrilled by the discovery that one of his ancestors had had the good taste to have the entire centre of the original walled city rebuilt in the seventeenth century in what, Robert had told her, was now practically a world heritage site all of its own.

'The buildings have never been touched. They are perfect examples of the architecture of the period: the palace the administrative offices, the square, the military quarters and stables – everything. Even the furniture is original, commissioned when the palace was first built,' he had told her.

'I hope the kitchens and the bathrooms have been modernised,' had been Ella's practical comment when Olivia had passed on to her Robert's descriptions.

'That is such a very American thing to say,' Olivia had laughed, 'and you are not American, you're English.'

'I might have been born English, but I think American,' Ella had insisted.

'What's that smile for?' Robert asked Olivia now.

'I was thinking about my mother, and how much she and Dad love America. Sam and I both have dual nationality, of course, but I guess I do think of myself as being more American than I am English.'

Robert reached for her hand. 'I hope that you're going

to love Lauranto and want to adopt it,' he told her with a smile.

The city was up ahead of them, a mass of buildings huddled within the city wall, here and there green roof tiles and the odd gilded cupola emerging from the snow to gleam in the sunlight.

'It looks so . . . so neat and pretty,' Olivia couldn't resist saying as she turned to Robert, 'like something out of a fairy tale or a Disney movie.'

That sense of having strayed into a Disney movie stayed with her once the car had pulled up in front of the imposing façade to the royal palace and she had seen the uniformed guards, all blue, gold and white, in their sentry boxes, and heard the sound they made as they presented arms and then saluted when she and Robert stepped out of the car and onto the steps.

They might have climbed the stone steps together, but she was immediately, if discreetly, made aware of her subservient role when a man whom Olivia assumed must be a court official stepped forward to take her place at Robert's side, giving her a small neat half-bow, leaving her with no other option than to walk behind Robert as they entered the palace.

The man was elderly, his bearing not just upright but formally stiff, Olivia noted, as their small procession came to a halt in the icy-cold marble-floored hallway, and its elegant Louis XIV-style wooden panelling ornamented with heavily gilded swags, cherubs and, over the doorways, what Olivia assumed must be the honours and arms of the House of Lauranto. It wasn't exactly the most welcoming place she had ever stepped into.

Stiff formality was obviously the order of the day here, she realised ruefully.

Another official, white-gloved and tail-coated, wearing a blue sash over his coat studded with decorations, was bowing to Robert, turning his back to her as he whispered something in Robert's ear.

Then Robert turned to Olivia, giving a small smile as he told her, 'Apparently my grandmother wants to see me immediately on an important matter of state.'

Olivia didn't say anything. The plan had been that they would arrive, rest and then change, ready for her to be presented formally to the Dowager Princess before dinner.

'Someone will escort you to your room. If you wait for me there, I'll be with you as soon as I can.'

This was ridiculous, Olivia thought as she found herself inclining her head almost as though she was about to curtsy to Robert, instead of kissing his cheek in a far more natural manner, but she could sense Robert's own tension, so instead of making a show of their intimacy, she allowed her 'escort' to draw her to one side so that they waited until Robert and his escort had disappeared through the double doors, guarded by two more uniformed soldiers, before she was escorted up the truly beautiful wrought-iron return staircase, and then up another flight and along a corridor carpeted in a tired-looking red carpet, past heavy gilt-framed portraits of unsmiling men and women, until finally they reached a room, outside which a stern-looking, thin, middle-aged woman, wearing a black dress, her hands folded in what Olivia suspected was a warning to her not to attempt to shake one of them, was waiting.

With another small bow her escort turned on his heel and departed without uttering a single word, leaving Olivia to be shown into the room by the equally silent woman.

The room – a bedroom, with an elegant tester bed, hung with blue silk – was icy cold with no fire burning in the grate, the chill not improved by the pale blue décor, Olivia thought as she looked round.

'You will wait here. The maid has unpacked for you. Tea will be sent up for you.'

At last someone had spoken to her, and in English, even if it was only in a way that made her feel like a nuisance – and very much an unwanted nuisance.

Two hours later, when she had drunk her tea, even though she would have preferred coffee, and there was still no sign of Robert or anyone else to explain what was going on and when Robert would appear, Olivia began to wonder if her treatment was an accident or deliberately intended to unsettle and even upset her.

Her mother had warned her that she might find Robert's grandmother antagonistic towards her, and she had certainly expected to be received with a certain degree of wariness, but this, if it was deliberate, was something else. *If it was.* She mustn't jump to conclusions, Olivia warned herself. After all, Robert's grandmother might be able to control her circumstances but she could not control her response to them or her inner mind. Those lay under her own control. It was up to her whether she chose to regard this as a deliberate act of antagonism and hostility towards her or whether she saw it as an opportunity to accustom herself to the fact that in future there could and would be times when she would be isolated from Robert in unfamiliar surroundings as he was called to some duty.

She had brought with her, more out of habit than anything else, both her electronic portable typewriter and the battery-run Dictaphone device she used, both when doing interviews and making notes.

Her typewriter, as she had suspected, was not compatible with Lauranto's electrical sockets, which looked so outdated that Olivia doubted it would be possible to find any adaptor for her modern American electric devices, but she was soon able to record her initial thoughts and impressions of Lauranto, diary style on the Dictaphone, though, of course, edited so that her real thoughts with regard to the lack of warmth shown to her by Robert's grandmother remained locked inside her head.

It was early evening before she finally saw Robert, apologetic, his kiss almost perfunctory, although Olivia sensed he was just a little bit wary of her reaction to his lengthy absence and her consequent solitude.

'Your grandmother must have had a great deal to discuss with you?' she suggested, giving what she hoped would be the right kind of opportunity for him to open up to her.

'Yes, she did.' He grimaced and shook his head. 'I'm rather in the doghouse, it seems. Apparently I didn't make the nature of our relationship as clear to her as I should have done. She thought I was bringing you with me as a friend.'

'As a mistress, you mean?' Olivia corrected him gently.

Robert looked relieved. 'Yes, exactly. When I told her that the role I hope you will play in my life is that of my wife, she was not best pleased.'

'Because you want to marry me?'

'No. Because I hadn't made things clear. Now, according to my grandmother, there hasn't been time for the officials to prepare the necessary court circular to inform people that I was bringing my bride to be with me, which means that the necessary formal events have not been organised, which in turn means that you cannot be presented to the Court and the people of Lauranto in the way that the future wife of the Crown Prince should be presented.'

'We haven't made any formal plans ourselves yet, or spoken to our families, so it wouldn't really have been possible to make any kind of formal announcement here. I'm sure your grandmother understands that. She can't, after all, expect you to be *au fait* with every nuance of Lauranto court procedure when you haven't been brought up here, so to blame you –'

'No, she isn't blaming me,' Robert hurried to assure her. 'She isn't blaming anyone other than herself. No, it's more that she feels that you might be hurt and offended at being kept in the background because your role can't be made public as yet.'

'Divide and conquer', was the phrase that immediately slid into Olivia's mind. That was what the Dowager Princess was doing, she felt sure. She could well imagine how Emerald would react to such tactics even now, never mind when she had been headstrong and young. But Olivia was not Emerald, and she had no intention of being dragged into a confrontation with his grandmother.

'I'd much rather stay in the background and see how things are done than risk putting my foot in it,' Olivia responded calmly, slipping her arm through his as she lifted her head for his kiss. 'Besides, we'll have plenty of time for us, at night, in bed,' she added softly.

Immediately Robert tensed and stepped back from her.

'I'm afraid that isn't going to be possible either. It seems that I'm going to be sleeping in the Royal Bedchamber – alone – at the other end of the palace.'

'Ah . . .' Inwardly Olivia was both angry and upset, but she was determined not to show it.

'So am I actually going to get to meet your grandmother, or is that against court protocol as well?'

'Of course you're going to meet her. In fact, she's suggested that the two of you have a private chat before dinner tonight.'

'A private chat. You mean that you won't be there?'

'She wants to get to know you. And besides, she's arranged for me to have a pre-dinner meeting with Lauranto's Council of Elders.'

Imposingly regal, with her straight back and silver-grey hair piled up on top of her head, her gaze impassive and steely as she stared down at Olivia from the top of the short flight of steps that separated the main chilly vastness of the drawing room from the smaller area between the marble fireplace and the central windows opposite it, Olivia had to struggle against the temptation to drop Robert's grandmother an attempt at a curtsy. With a commanding wave of her hand the Dowager Princess indicated that Olivia was to join her.

Olivia wasn't sure if the Princess was wearing the

full-length dark plum gown because it perfectly suited her colouring or because it was a regal form of half-mourning. She certainly didn't feel she could ask. The Princess's 'May I call you Olivia?' was pleasant enough, but Olivia wasn't deceived. This was a woman who liked to be in control.

Olivia knew that her own plain full-length black gown was easily a match in both elegance, suitability and cost to the Princess's, and mentally she thanked both her own mother and Robert's for their warnings that she would need what Emerald referred to as 'proper clothes', meaning top designer. The Chanel gown she was wearing might be ready-to-wear, but it had cost a small fortune, and was on loan from her mother, as were the brilliant two-carat diamond ear studs. The Cartier diamond bangles, though, were an unexpected 'loan' from Amber, who had sent them up to London via Emerald. Just thinking now of her step-grandmother gave her courage. Amber was the sweetest and the kindest person she knew. Olivia's inner smile deepened when she saw the way the Princess's glance found and then rested on the Cartier bangles.

But Olivia didn't feel like smiling when Robert's grandmother said coolly, 'I never think it's a good idea to wear copies of something as recognisable as Cartier, no matter how good they are. One always knows they must be fake, unless of course, my dear, you have had a very generous gentleman friend in the past who has given them to you.'

'Actually, they aren't fake,' Olivia told her calmly. 'But you are right: I could certainly never afford to buy myself anything so expensive, nor would I want to do so.

They are on loan to me from Robert's other grand-mother. They were a wedding gift to her from her first husband and she's very generous about lending them within the family for special occasions.'

There, let the Dowager Princess chew on that information. She wouldn't want her to choke on it, but she wouldn't object if it caused her indigestion, Olivia acknowledged angrily.

'Ah, yes. Of course, Amber. I had forgotten that she must have quite a collection of good jewellery from her interesting life. It obviously can't be that she has passed down through her genes to the female members of her family the ability to marry well, since you are not related to her by blood, but then they do say that nurture can have just as much of an effect on a child as nature. Tell me, Olivia, when did you decide that you wanted to marry the Crown Prince of Lauranto? It's obviously a recent decision.'

Now the gloves were off, Olivia knew. Perhaps she ought not to have been surprised by the Princess's hostility towards her, but she was.

'I don't want to marry the Crown Prince of Lauranto,' Olivia answered quite truthfully. 'The man I want to marry is Robert, the wonderful stepcousin I have loved for as long as I have known what committed adult love is. I would be happy to marry Robert if all he had to offer me was himself, because that is all I want. It is the person he is I love, not the trappings of what he will have to be to the outer world, should he decide to accept the responsibility of stepping into your late son's shoes.' Olivia gave her adversary a calm level look. 'What you obviously see as the benefits and advantages of royal privilege and position I see as potential burdens that will have to be shouldered not only by the man I love but also by the sons we may have. I love Robert more than enough to want him to make his own choice about the future we will share. Should he decide to accept the Crown, then I will work alongside him to help him to do the very best he can for Lauranto and its people.'

There was a long silence, during which Olivia had to fight the urge to shiver as she bore the almost reptilian unblinking stare of the Dowager Princess.

'Your mother and her sister have both produced sons, as has Robert's mother – that at least is in your favour, in that you should be capable of producing a male heir.'

'Male or female, I shall love the children Robert gives me equally and wholly.'

The Princess actually laughed – a sharp mocking sound that was almost a physical blow.

'No mother loves all her children equally, or indeed wholly. Ask your step-grandmother, or indeed Robert's mother.'

There was a small pause and then she announced, 'It is time to join Robert for dinner.' She rang a small hand-bell. The double doors to the room were flung open by two flunkeys in their gold and blue livery, who had been standing outside when Olivia had entered. They made low bows to the Princess as she swept past them, forcing Olivia to follow on behind her.

Normally Katie loved a night out at the Jericho. It had the best live bands in town, from Goth, through to heavy rock and industrial music, with new bands clamouring for a chance to showcase themselves. Clotheswise, anything went, from urban to Victorian Goth, out-of-touch Sloane Ranger, rock-chick leathers and denim, to plain, simple jeans and T-shirts. Tonight, though, Katie's enjoyment of the evening was being spoiled by her apprehension about meeting Axel – or not so much meeting him as having to make a judgement about him.

Zoë always spent ages getting ready for their nights out. She was an extrovert, after all – an exhibitionist, Katie's forthright and disapproving elder sister, Emma, preferred to say – and this evening was no exception. Katie wasn't sure she altogether really liked Zoë's newly invented Goth slut meets rock chick, meets dominatrix style, and she certainly suspected that Tom would not have approved of his sister's appearance in the black tightly laced corset trimmed with red lace, which matched Zoë's red lace mittens, and the short net tutu-style skirt she had told Katie she had found in a children's shop, and which clashed horribly, in Katie's view, with Zoë's hair. Beneath the red tutu Zoë was wearing black fishnet tights, her favourite Doc Marten boots relegated to the bottom of the wardrobe in favour of shiny black PVC high-heeled thigh-length boots.

'What do you think?' Zoë had asked Katie eagerly before they had set out.

Comparing their reflections in the mirror and contrasting her own black T-shirt, favourite jeans and Doc Martens with Zoë's outfit, Katie had told her bravely and truthfully, 'It would look fine if we were going to an S & M fancy-dress party.'

Instead of being annoyed, as Katie had half expected, Zoë had laughed triumphantly. 'Good. That means that

Axel will love it. He's heavily into bondage and all that kind of stuff, especially if it's really, you know, *dark*.'

Remembering that comment now, Katie felt her stomach muscles tighten. Zoë had always enjoyed saying things for their shock value, but in reality Zoë's lifestyle had always been far more circumspect than she made out to the wider world. Was it still? Was she just saying these things because she wanted to shock her? Katie hoped so. It wasn't that she was naïve or even prim about sex, it was just that . . . It was just what . . . ? Katie asked herself. But she knew the answer, and it was that she didn't want Zoë to be hurt. Zoë, despite the care-for-nothing, confident, extrovert face she showed the world, was vulnerable, so vulnerable that Katie suspected she would do anything to get and keep the love of the man she set her heart on. And Katie was afraid that that meant that if that man chose to do so he could abuse and manipulate her in any way he wished.

The club was heaving with people enjoying themselves, the noise from the band currently playing making it impossible to hold a conversation, the effect of its beat like mainlining adrenalin straight into the body, Katie thought as her foot started tapping and the desire to join the dancing crowd gripped her. Over in a dark corner, close to the wall, a small line had formed, the man at its centre keeping an eye on everyone coming in as he took money and doled out drugs.

'Dance?' Katie shouted in Zoë's ear.

Zoë shook her head, pointing in the direction of the bar, yelling back, 'I want a drink first, or something a bit stronger, if you fancy it?'

Katie shook her head, but plunged through the crowd in Zoë's wake, heading for the bar.

'What's that?' Katie asked ten minutes later, indicating Zoë's glass.

'Black Russian. Vodka, Coke and Tia Maria. This is just a double. It's best if you have a triple vodka in it, though. It's Axel's favourite drink. You should try it.'

Katie shook her head. 'Too expensive. Want to dance?'

'Not yet.' Zoë was looking all around the bar as she spoke, suddenly stiffening and grabbing Katie by the arm as she yelled, 'Axel's over there on the other side of the dance floor, come on.'

There was no point in protesting or objecting, or suggesting that they wait until Axel found them. Zoë steamed through the dancers like a torpedo on a mission before coming to a halt in front of a man who was standing so much in the shadows that Katie had to wait for him to move slightly to receive Zoë's eager kiss before she could see him properly.

He was, as Tom had said, good-looking, or rather, Katie thought, extraordinarily malely beautiful. There were no other words to describe him. His features were perfect: his skin a perfect golden tan, his mouth sensually shaped, his nose straight, his eyes long-lashed and elegantly shaped above sculpted cheekbones. His long dark shiny curls, which fell to his shoulders, could have made him look feminine if it hadn't been for the stubble on his jaw and the open air of dangerous cruelty that came from some alchemic combination of the curve of his mouth and the look in his dark eyes. Katie felt herself shiver. This man was dangerous and, more than that, he was bad – evil somehow, in a way that sent a chill

132

through her like cold water pouring down her spine. There was no reason, no logic, for the way she felt. It had nothing to do with anything Tom had said to her, or anything Zoë felt about him. It was simply immediate, atavistic, ancient in the sense that he himself called it up from the deepest and most instinctive part of her. She wanted, Katie realised, to grab Zoë's hand and drag her friend away from him.

Zoë was still fussing over him, kissing him, her free hand, Katie realised, on his groin, whilst he was looking over Zoë's shoulder at *her*, assessing her, mentally stripping her, not just of her clothes so coldly and carelessly, as though it was his right to do so, that Katie knew he was someone she would loathe.

A feeling of something close to relief filled her. She had worried about this meeting, dreading either not being able to decide what she felt and thought about Axel, or that she would secretly disagree with Tom, but now that the moment, the judgement, was here there was no questioning necessary. She knew – had known immediately – that there was about Axel some evil that made her want to step back from him, a darkness, an emptiness that repelled her and made her afraid and concerned on Zoë's behalf. The closest she could get to explaining it was to repeat inside her head the lines from *Macbeth*: 'By the pricking of my thumbs, Something wicked this way comes.' What she felt was as instinctive, as immediate, as personal as that.

Hard on the heels of her dislike came an equally strong surge of pity and dismay for her friend.

'Axel, this is Katie. Remember I told you about her when we were in Klosters? Katie and I thought we'd come round and help you settle into your new place,' Zoë continued without waiting for him to answer her.

'I'm already settled in.'

'What do you think of my outfit?'

Zoë's comment sounded more desperate than sexy, but Katie was still hurt for her friend when Axel looked her up and down and told her cruelly, 'It makes you look like a drag queen, an ugly drag queen.'

'You said you liked me in bondage,' Zoë protested.

'Did I? It must have been the coke.'

'Why are you being like this with me? In Klosters—'

'In Klosters you were amusing, a diversion; now, I'm afraid, you are an irritation and a bore.'

Zoë's gasp of pain felt like a knife in Katie's own heart. She turned towards her friend but Zoë wasn't interested in her. Instead she was clinging to Axel, crying openly as she pleaded with him, begging him to tell her that he was just joking.

'I'll do anything to please you, Axel, you know that. In Klosters you said I was the hottest girl you'd ever had, you said—'

'In Klosters you were available and I was hungry enough to take what was on offer. Now I'm not. Take a look around you, and tell me what you see. No, don't bother, I'll tell you what I see instead. I see girls, desirable girls, pretty girls,' he emphasised. 'You are not pretty, Zoë, you aren't even plain, you are downright ugly, Ugly, eager and available, yes, but pretty and desirable, no.'

Zoë gasped again as he pushed her off him and she collided into someone. In the strobe lighting Zoë's face was milk white, her freckles standing out against her pale skin, her despair and disbelief almost agonising to watch, whilst inwardly Katie felt shocked that her friend could humiliate herself in such a way.

Axel had turned his back on them and was walking away. Zoë tried to run after him, crying out his name, but he had been swallowed up by the crowd.

'Zoë, he isn't worth it,' Katie told her.

'No, I know,' she agreed emotionlessly. 'It's over, Katie. I don't want anything more to do with him. I was a fool, and Tom and my parents were right. Let's go, shall we?'

Thankful and relieved, Katie nodded. Watching and listening to Zoë, Katie had begun to feel horribly concerned that her friend would insist on continuing to see Axel, despite what her family had said. And concerned for herself, she could admit now. Zoë would have demanded that she said nothing to Tom about the fact that she was still seeing Axel, but Tom would have wanted and expected Katie to inform him what was going on. That would have been a horrible position to be in. But now, thank goodness, she did not need to worry about it any more.

'I was a fool, a complete and total fool ever to have listened to a word Axel said. I hate him, *hate* him now, Katie,' Zoë announced as they walked home, Zoë marching so fast that Katie felt as though her friend were spitting out her fury against Axel in a hail of words as stinging as any bullets.

'I'm not surprised after the way he's treated you. I didn't like him, Zoë,' Katie added forthrightly. 'There's something about him that . . . well, I'm just glad that you're not going to have anything more to do with him.'

'But you can see why I liked him, can't you?' Zoë demanded, standing still in the middle of the road, the streetlight revealing the black mascara tear stains on her face.

'I mean, he is—'

'He's horrible, Zoë, creepy, and . . . and cruel . . . and dangerous.' Too late Katie realised that using the word 'dangerous' might not have been a good idea when Zoë started to cry.

'Yes,' she agreed, 'he is dangerous – beautifully, deadly dangerous – like a drug that spreads through your veins and possesses you, like a spell that holds you. He is everything I always imagined Rochester must have been, Katie: wild and reckless, dark and dangerous, sexy and sadistic, capable of seducing both our sex and his own.'

Katie shuddered, revolted. 'Rochester died in the most horrible way,' she reminded her friend.

'Yes, of syphilis,' Zoë agreed, before adding fiercely, 'Axel did love me in Klosters. He warned me then that sometimes when he's on a high he says and does things that he doesn't really mean.'

A trickle of anxiety dropped slowly down Katie's spine. Zoë had turned round to face the way they had just come.

'Men like him will say anything to get what they want from a girl,' Katie told her.

'*Men like him?*' Zoë mocked her. 'And what would a Miss Prim like you know about men like Axel, Katie?' Her smile turned to a frown. 'Or are you just saying that to put me off him because you fancy him yourself?'

'Fancy him? I think he's loathsome. Come on, Zoë, it's cold standing here.'

Determinedly she linked arms with her friend, urging her to start walking again.

'Ah ha, there is one of the peacocks you promised me,' Olivia smiled as they turned a corner to see one of the fowl standing on the gravel path in front of them.

Robert reached for her hand, congratulating himself on the wisdom of selecting Olivia to be his wife – and his consort. Whilst it might not be true to say that she had completely won over his grandmother, Robert sensed that the Dowager Princess recognised that, in Olivia, both he and Lauranto would have someone wholly committed to them in every single way.

'You deserve a reward for all you've had to cope with these last few days,' he smiled. 'I know my grandmother hasn't exactly made things easy for you.'

Olivia gave him a rueful look. 'That's a definite under-statement. She'd much rather you married someone with royal blood who she has chosen herself.'

'I know, but I would much rather I married you, if you haven't been put off . . . ?'

Robert knew that she would not have been. Olivia wasn't like that. She was calm and sensible, and not given to making emotional scenes or using emotional blackmail, which of course was a large part of the reason he had decided to marry her in the first place. There was no need to fear with Olivia that she, like his mother, would deliberately create hostility between herself and his grandmother.

'No. I haven't been put off,' Olivia assured him. She loved it that Robert could be like this: not hesitant – he was too confident for that – but actually taking the trouble to ask her for her confirmation. It showed good manners and consideration for her feelings. It wasn't exactly passionate, though, was it? It wasn't a declaration that she mattered more to him than anything or anyone else? Quickly Olivia brushed the unwanted thought aside.

'Good.' Robert stopped and turned to face her. Since they were in the palace's formal knot garden, which was overlooked by many of the palace's windows, Olivia wasn't surprised when he didn't kiss her.

'There's so much I want to achieve for Lauranto, Olivia, and to do so I need you by my side.'

'I suspect your grandmother and the Court would prefer me to stand several paces behind you,' Olivia pointed out ruefully, before adding, 'I know what you mean, though. The people here . . .'

'The people, yes,' Robert agreed, 'but actually I was talking about the buildings. Such a heritage must be preserved. It is unique, invaluable, and ultimately it will prove to be a huge tourist draw for Lauranto. It's a crime to have allowed it to fall into such disrepair.'

'I dare say there was no choice. Your grandmother has made it plain that the country is very poor.'

'Yes, and I have been thinking about how that can be remedied. One of the things I plan to do is speak to Nick to find out how best we can establish Lauranto as an offshore tax haven.'

'A sunny place for shady people?' Olivia quoted lightly, but Robert could see that she didn't like the idea.

'A perfectly legitimate way of raising the revenue that Lauranto needs if it is to preserve its heritage and improve the lot of its people,' he corrected her. 'That and tourism are, in my opinion, the best way to raise the money we will need. Tourism, though, means building new hotels, a new marina, and investing money that we simply don't have at the moment. That money will come in more readily if Lauranto is seen as a good place to invest.

'It's my destiny to preserve this heritage, Olivia – I feel that very strongly – and there's no one I would rather have to share that destiny with more than you. You handled my grandmother superbly, far better than my mother ever managed to do.'

'So you have decided to accept the Crown then?' Olivia asked him, though she suspected she already knew the answer.

Robert turned to look at the building behind them, and gestured towards it. 'I could walk away from the Crown, but I don't think I can walk away from this.'

And she certainly couldn't walk away from him, Olivia admitted. Not that there was any need for her to do so. She was half in love with Lauranto already, her philanthropic instincts aroused by the plight of its people.

'I think we should be married sooner rather than later,' Robert told her. 'Do you agree?'

'Is this my proposal?'

'Your official one, yes. Your private one will come later, when I can be sure of having you to myself.'

'I could stay over in London when we fly back tomorrow?'

Robert shook his head. 'It's a lovely thought but my diary is full of work commitments I feel I have to see through, even though I've decided to step into my father's shoes.'

'When do you plan to tell your grandmother?'

'I already have,' Robert told her carelessly. 'I told her last night at the same time as I told her that I intended to marry you.'

Olivia nodded. It was unreasonable and silly of her to wish that she had been the first one to learn officially of Robert's plans. After all, he had discussed their possibility at length with her, and she had guessed that he would accept the Crown. Perhaps it was because she and her values were so American that a small part of her resented the fact that she felt she had been side-lined and almost relegated to second place whilst Robert discussed their shared future with his grandmother.

'My grandmother has given me this to give you,' Robert announced, reaching into his pocket to produce a worn leather-covered jewellery box, flipping it open to reveal an old-fashioned, almost ugly-looking but obviously very valuable diamond ring, its large central diamond flanked by two smaller diamonds, all three of them throwing off brilliant prisms of light in the sharp winter sun.

Robert removed the ring from its velvet pad, and slipped the box back into his pocket. Then he took her hand, obviously intending to slide the ring onto her finger. To her dismay, Olivia found that she wanted to pull her hand away, to curl her fingers away from the ring. Inside her head she had an image of Robert's grandmother.

'It isn't . . . wasn't your grandmother's, was it? I mean, if she wears, it, then I wouldn't want . . . that is, perhaps just a simple Tiffany ring . . .'

Robert was amused. 'Don't be silly. This is the Lauranto betrothal ring. My grandmother gave it to my father to give to . . . to my stepmother, but apparently she rarely wore it, and now she has given it to me to give to you.' A ring given to her in reality by Robert's grandmother and not Robert himself. Was she foolish to want a ring he had chosen for her himself?

A ring taken from the finger of a dead woman, a woman with whom she had no connection.

'When we make our next visit my accession to the throne and our betrothal will both be announced in a court circular. You will be presented to the Court as my wife-to-be.'

Robert's wife. That was what this was about for her, nothing else.

Robert slipped the ring onto her finger. It felt cold and heavy. If she'd have preferred a single elegant Tiffany diamond, Olivia told herself that she had enough common sense to understand that Robert's grandmother's gift was an important form of acceptance of her as Robert's future wife. But still there was that small sense of disappointment, that feeling that her taste and preferences had not been Robert's first consideration. Was she having doubts about Robert and their future together? Of course not.

'Engaged? You and Robert are engaged?'

Olivia smiled ruefully at her mother. 'Robert wanted to come back to New York with me so that we could break the news to you together, but his diary is just so full that he couldn't. And I wanted you to know before the official news gets out that Robert is going to step into his father's shoes. There's going to be a formal announcement in tomorrow's *Times*, which will include a mention of our engagement. Robert wants to get the business moguls of the City onside so that he can start arranging finance for the work that needs to be done in Lauranto. The country is so beautiful, Mom, but so poor.'

Ella tried not to show how uneasy she felt about Olivia's news. She'd known of course, how her daughter felt about Robert, but the truth was that this marriage wasn't what she wanted for her daughter, not deep down. For one thing it would mean that Olivia's future life would lie on the other side of the Atlantic, and for another, the whole idea of Olivia having to toe the line, playing second fiddle to Robert and possibly his grand-mother because of their royal precedence, just went totally against everything Ella had come to feel so strongly about since moving to America. But she didn't want to spoil Olivia's obvious joy, so she hugged her fiercely and made as light of her feelings as she could by saying that she suspected that Oliver was going to have something to say about the fact that Robert had not come to New York himself to talk formally to him before making any announcements.

'Dad worry about something as old-fashioned as Robert asking him for permission to propose to me?' Olivia laughed. 'Did he ask Gramps before he proposed to you?'

Ella was forced to shake her head. 'Our circumstances were slightly different, or at least I hope they were,' she said, reminding Olivia, 'You were born less than nine months after we married, remember.'

Olivia laughed.

'Very different,' she agreed. 'I doubt that either Robert

or his grandmother would want the next heir of Lauranto arriving in the world anything under a suitably respectable full nine months.' As she spoke Olivia was aware of a faint nagging something at the back of her mind, at her acknowledgement of how much his grandmother's opinion mattered to Robert, but she brushed it away. It had no place in her happiness or her love.

'When do you plan to marry?' Ella asked.

'Late summer, Robert says.'

Robert says. What about you? What do you say? What do you want? Ella wanted to ask her daughter, but at the same time she could see how happy Olivia was. She positively glowed with joy and delight. That was the lot of loving parents, Ella reflected: out of the love they had for their children they had to accept, and then somehow learn to love as well, the partner chosen by their child, for that child's sake, no matter what their own real feelings. Not that she disliked Robert in any way. Far from it. It was just that she wanted the man her precious daughter married to put her first, second and third, and she wasn't convinced Robert would do that, not given his commitment to Lauranto.

Chapter Ten

'It's no use you pouting like that at me, Char, sweetie pie. You promised when you moved in next door, after I'd tipped you the wink that the house would be going in a fire sale, that you'd repay me by standing in for me when I had to be away.'

What Nat was saying was true, Charlotte acknowledged.

Charlotte wasn't the name she had been given at birth. That name had been Charmaine, a name so 'common' that she was glad that she'd had the sense to deny it, and her past, and rename herself Charlotte when she'd been orphaned and sent to the children's home. Charmaine Carter, had then become Charlotte Cardrew, and she'd stuck fiercely to the name she had claimed so that by the time she left, it was as if she'd never been called anything else. But now, thanks to her brief marriage to the late Sir Peter Meredith, who had died without an heir, in a whorehouse in Thailand, after a drug-fuelled bout of his favourite sexual activity, she was Lady Meredith.

'What do I know about basement swimming pools?' she demanded, arching one beautifully shaped beige eyebrow, and making a small *moue* with her equally beautifully shaped and discreetly painted red lips. 'I can't understand why you want one in the first place. They are so *nouveau riche*.'

'That's why.' When she pulled a face he added with a grin, 'Look, I'm a famous pop star – a gay famous pop star – people expect excess of me, in all things.'

'Excess but not bad taste. Gay men are well known for their excellent taste.'

'Yeah? Well, my good taste will have to be limited to choosing you as a friend. Besides, you're going to like meeting this guy.'

'He's rich?'

'Yes.'

'And hetero?'

'Definitely, but it isn't what he is you're going to enjoy so much as who he is.'

'He's an architect. So what?'

'An architect whose mother just happens to be the Duchess of Lenchester.'

Immediately Charlotte's gaze hardened, her face becoming expressionless and her body still.

Nat, though, knew perfectly well that her motionless silence was simply camouflage. They'd grown up together, he and Char. They'd known one another before they'd ended up in the same children's home for the same kind of reason: both orphaned by mothers too worn out by the squalor and misery of their lives to make the effort to go on living, both deserted by fathers who didn't give a shit about them.

Nat knew all about the past Char had left behind her, her alcoholic mother, her gangland father who'd ended

146

up hacked to pieces by the 'friends' he betrayed. They'd lived in the same street, sat on the same grimy kerbstones with their feet in the gutter, knowing that the street was safer than what lay behind their front doors: a father who knocked both his daughter and his wife around, in Char's case, and a mother whose pimp regularly beat both her and Nat, in his.

Char had told him all about the posh rich woman her dad was shagging. She'd shown him the blood-smeared pages of the magazine she'd pinched from her mother, showing 'Lady Emerald and her son.'

They'd thought then that the violence they faced at home was as bad as life got. The children's home had taught them different.

There, they'd experienced the same deprivations and humiliations, and witnessed the same abuse – emotional, physical and sexual. Even if Charlotte had used her wits to evade being subjected to it herself, that life had still left its scars. The perpetrators might have differed, but the lessons learned had been the same. Sex was a commodity; human flesh was a commodity; there was nothing about any human being that could not be used and then rendered down for profit. The clever thing was to make sure that that profit ended up in your pocket, not the pocket of someone else. Nat and Char had both learned that lesson well before they had reached the legal age of consent.

Not that you'd know it to look at them now. He with his success as a chart-topping pop star, who'd come out about being gay; Char, who looked like a modern and better-looking version of Grace Kelly, all icy elegance, and hauteur, the kind of woman that made a certain kind of man foam at the mouth with lust to get her into bed.

'So what's this about then?' Charlotte finally broke her silence to demand, adding wryly, 'It isn't my birthday.'

Nat laughed. 'Nope, but I reckon I owe you. I haven't forgotten the way you got everything sorted out for me over Cary.'

'That's what friends are for. I wasn't going to stand around and let him blackmail you, was I, especially when I knew damn well that he'd set you up with those photographs he had of the two of you.'

'Set me up and buggered me up. The arsehole.' Char's lifted eyebrow made him grin. 'OK, so I enjoyed that bit of it – at the time, but it wouldn't have gone down well in certain parts of America, and I had that tour coming up.'

'Which, as I remember, earned you thirty million dollars.'

'That's what the taxman thinks,' Nat boasted. 'The other thirty million is stashed away in an offshore tax haven.'

'So tell me a bit more about this . . . architect.'

'There isn't much to tell. I've seen some of his work and liked it, so I got his number from someone who'd had work done by him. I didn't know then just who he was. Not until I saw his photograph in yesterday's *Times* and read about him becoming the new Crown Prince of Lauranto.'

'And getting engaged,' Charlotte added.

'That too. So, will you see him for me and let him take a gander round the house, or do you want me to cancel him?'

'I'll think about it and let you know.'

'I'm leaving tomorrow morning.'

'Tough. Besides, you know you enjoy being kept in suspense, or should that be in suspension?'

'Miaawww,' Nat retaliated, unabashed by her reference to his enjoyment of the act of sexual asphyxiation, a pleasure introduced to him by the perv who'd buggered him less than a week after he'd been taken into the children's home.

He'd had his revenge, though. But then he'd made sure he'd cried his eyes out at the funeral, with all the rest, over the 'untimely' death of 'the wonderful man' who'd given up so much of his time to do voluntary work with homeless children. And certainly hadn't been the only one there who'd secretly enjoyed the fact that Frank's love of the orgasmic thrill of a near-death experience had turned into his actual death.

Back in her own smart Belgravia town house, with its cream stuccoed frontage, its gloss-painted iron railings and its ground-floor window boxes planted by The Chelsea Gardener, Charlotte paced her second-floor drawing room, her stilettos sinking into the thick pile of its carpet, just off-white enough to be elegant rather than vulgarly Hollywood.

She wasn't Charmaine Carter any more, the illegitimate child of an East End enforcer who had thought her cockney mother not good enough to live with, never mind marry, but who had carried on coming round knocking her half senseless and then filling her with drink until she let him have the kind of sex he most enjoyed with her – the kind of sex he'd never have been able to get off the posh society types he liked mixing with and boasting about. Pain and fear, those were what had turned her dad on, especially if there was a bit of blood, and some screams, mixed up in it. He'd despised her mother, and yet he'd been as jealous as hell if he thought anyone else had been sniffing round her, using the slightest violation of the 'rules' she was forced to live by to inflict more violence on her. Charlotte herself he'd simply ignored as though she just didn't exist. He hated kids, he'd once told her, and if he'd had his way she'd never have been born in the first place. Her mother had told her that the only reason she hadn't miscarried was because he had beaten her up so badly that she'd ended up in hospital for virtually the last three months of her pregnancy, so saving her from any further violence.

Even as a child, before her mother's death, Charlotte had sworn that she wasn't going to end up like her mother and she hadn't.

Now she was Lady Meredith, a baronet's widow, titled but not accepted by the upper-class society into which her late husband had been born. Not that she gave a fuck about them. She was every bit as good as them. In fact she was better.

She stopped pacing. The mirror over the Georgian fireplace had been removed from its original setting by an enterprising designer eager to assist the new up-and-coming 'rich' class of Londoners, who wanted to 'restore' their smart London properties to their original elegance.

Charlotte had taken things a step further, sourcing the fireplace herself, having researched the history of her house. The fortunate occurrence of a neighbour putting his family home up for sale had enabled Charlotte to point her supplier in the right direction to find her the fireplace she wanted.

The mirror gave her back a reflection of herself, her blonde hair drawn back into the smooth soft chignon she favoured (it showed off the perfection of her bone structure as well as the antique pearl earrings that had been a gift from one of her lovers).

Her eyes were the one feature about herself she disliked. They were the same colour as her father's. Fortunately dark blue contact lenses hid that fact. She was, Charlotte knew, a breathtakingly beautiful woman. It wasn't vanity to think that, it was simply reality. As ungenerous as fate had been in choosing her parents for her, when it came to selecting her looks, fate had been very generous indeed. Tall, slender, but with high, taut perfectly teardrop-shaped breasts, Charlotte did not follow the fashion for having a deep tan. Her childhood had given her the confidence to make her own rules. Before Coco Chanel made a tan fashionable, tanned skin on a woman immediately labelled her as poor. Only the labouring classes worked outside, their skin exposed to the sun. Indeed, in previous centuries women of the aristocracy had painted their faces with poisonous white lead to keep their skin pale.

Charlotte had, as the Americans say, 'done the math': pale skin equalled privilege, privilege equalled wealth and status, and, most important of all, 'class'. Like her naturally blonde hair and elegant bone structure, her pale skin was something to be carefully maintained.

The double-aspect drawing room overlooked the street at the front and her small private garden at the back. The room was furnished with antiques and decorated in shades of cream with touches of taupe, grey and black, a colour palette that echoed the soft creams and beiges of Charlotte's clothes.

No one, not even Nat, her closest friend, knew about the books on etiquette and elegance she'd pored over when she'd been creating her signature 'image' as Lady Meredith, after Peter's death. Peter's mother and the rest of his family might refuse to acknowledge her and have anything to do with her, but she certainly didn't care about that. She loved the fact that Peter had inherited the title from a bachelor uncle, and his mother and father had no titles which meant that now Charlotte was Lady Meredith, she would take precedence at any formal functions they might attend together. Not that that was likely. Peter's parents moved in very different circles from her own: dull county circles filled with equally dull bucolic men. Charlotte liked rich intelligent good-looking men, preferably married. She couldn't marry again. If she did she'd lose her title, and potentially her independence, and she wasn't prepared to sacrifice either of them.

'But you could have a rich husband,' one of her less bright female friends was wont to say. Charlotte's experience of rich husbands was that spending money on their wives wasn't something they were very keen to do. When it came to their mistresses, though, things were very different. Not that Charlotte had ever thought of herself as a 'mistress' so much as a 'lover'. The word 'mistress' had such unpleasant vulgar connotations, implying something akin to ownership – almost as bad as marriage. No, Charlotte was not a mistress. She was a publicly charming, elegant, sophisticated woman, who in private could be gratifyingly skilled at understanding a man's need for sexual satisfaction and secrecy.

Out of all the men she'd slept with Charlotte definitely preferred Americans. Especially American WASP men. They were so Protestant and moralistic, so guilty about breaking their marriage vows, and so generous about 'compensating' her when the affair ended. But then she played her part too, always buying into their claims that they were unhappy at home, that they'd leave their wives, etc, etc, whilst knowing perfectly well that all they wanted was someone to shag. Their need for discretion suited her as well. Outwardly she had a reputation to preserve. No one expected a woman of thirty-two to live like a nun, but there were certain conventions that had to be adhered to. The wilder excesses of her youth were something she had brushed under the carpet – the years she'd spent modelling, and being groped and shagged by the fat, bald, bloated-faced men who controlled the fashion business. Her marriage to Peter, a drug addict with a death wish, who could only get it up with the worst dregs of the street girls, after they'd beaten him half senseless, and who'd only married her because she'd agreed to dress up and play the part of one for him as part of their marriage deal, had enabled her to cross the deep chasm that separated her past from her present.

Not that she needed to sleep with a man these days in order to benefit her bank account. The 'pillow talk' of some good Protestant American bankers had included tips on which shares she should buy, which had led to her making a very nice amount of money indeed. She had also discovered that she had rather a good head for money and wise investment, so that now, whilst she might not have Nat's thirty million pounds stashed away, she wasn't very far short of it.

Now she was titled, comfortably off, beautiful and living the life she'd imagined for herself all those years ago, sitting with her feet in the gutter alongside Nat, both of them studying the photographs in the copy of *Vogue* her mother had bought because her father had boasted about the 'posh bint' he was shagging.

Emerald and her son. Charlotte could still see those photographs now. But it hadn't been Emerald who had drawn her angry resentful gaze so much as her son, Robbie, a boy, according to the article, who was only a year older than she was herself, and who had everything that she did not have. Robert Lenchester. Son of a prince. The child of a rich spoiled society mother who protected him from everything. She had hated him for that, for being isolated and protected from her kind of life. She'd held imaginary conversations with him in which she'd force him to agree to change places with her, just for a while, because it wasn't fair that he had such a good life and she had such a bad one.

They were two children growing up worlds apart, but whose worlds had come together because their parents were fucking one another. Her mother had obsessed about 'Lady Emerald', far more than any of her father's other women.

'She's nothing,' she could remember her father saying to her mother during one of their fights. 'She's another stupid slag just like you. You're all the same in the sack, except that the posh sort open their legs wider for it.'

Robert. Charlotte hadn't thought about him in years, and there was no real reason for her to think about him now. And no reason to want to see him either. She'd tell Nat to fix a new appointment for when he'd be around himself.

Katie was worried, worried and miserable, and not just because of the way Zoë had suddenly started behaving. Tom hadn't telephoned her as he had promised he would. At first she'd thought that she must have missed his call but then, humiliatingly, when she'd asked Zoë if Tom had telephoned to speak to her, Zoë had clapped her hand over her mouth guiltily.

'Oh shit, I forgot to give you Tom's message for you after I went home last week. He said to tell you that he hoped you hadn't taken anything seriously he'd said to you when he took you out for lunch, and that he was sorry if you had. He said something about enjoying teasing you.' Zoë gave a dismissive shrug. 'That's typical of him, wanting to make fun of you to get at me because you're my best friend. Oh!' she had exclaimed when she'd seen Katie's stricken expression. 'Now you're upset. Don't be, Katie. That's Tom all over.'

Katie had been devastated – she still was – but there was nothing she could do except learn to live with her disappointment and hurt, and pretend not to feel as upset as she actually did. Somehow the fact that she had fallen in love with her brother and felt that he might feel the same way about her was not something she could discuss with Zoë, close friends though they were. The fact was that whilst Zoë loved talking to her about her own heartache and misery, she did not really want to listen to anyone else talking about theirs, Katie acknowledged ruefully. That wasn't Zoë's way. Reluctantly she remembered Emma saying at Christmas that Zoë was selfish and thoughtless.

Zoë had had a lot to deal with herself, though. She had been dreadfully upset by Axel, and it was only natural that she should be preoccupied with her own heartache, Katie thought. Katie had admired the way Zoë had been so resolute about not wanting anything more to do with him, and she had done her best to support Zoë by going out with her and keeping her occupied.

But these last few days something had changed. Zoë had become increasingly secretive and withdrawn, and even downright nasty at times. Katie had put that down to her natural heartache. After all, she knew how that felt herself. But then three nights ago Zoë had flown into a temper. They'd been in one of Oxford's pubs together, having a quiet drink, when Katie had been approached by a boy she knew from Macclesfield, Miles Saunders, whose family socialised with her grandparents. He had been with a group of friends, male and female, and he'd suggested that Katie and Zoë join them. Thinking nothing of it, Katie had agreed. She'd enjoyed their company and had had a good time, and she'd thought that Zoë had felt the same. But on the way home Zoë had started making fun of and imitating one of the girls, Fran, whom Katie had particularly liked. When Katie had objected, Zoë had lost her temper and accused Katie of wanting to be friends with Fran, preferring her company to Zoë's own. Of course, Katie had denied any such thing but Zoë had refused to be placated.

Since then things had gone from bad to worse, very much worse. The following night Zoë had simply not come back to the house, after they'd left for their morning tutorials, until the following morning. She'd refused to tell Katie where she'd been, but there had been dark shadows under her eyes, her face was deathly pale, and the look in her eyes made Katie feel really afraid for her.

Then this morning she'd seen the most frightening thing of all, when she'd taken a cup of tea up to Zoë, who was still in bed, wanting to put things right between them.

She'd been surprised to find Zoë awake, lying on her back in bed, still fully dressed, staring up at her bedroom ceiling, and smoking a roll-up.

'Zoë!' Katie had begun, but Zoë had put out her cigarette and rolled over, her back to Katie. And that was when Katie had seen the weals on Zoe's arms, thin blood-encrusted cuts that looked as though someone had raked Zoe's arm with finger nails like knives. There had been no doubt in Katie's mind that the wounds had been deliberately inflicted. Inside her head she'd immediately had an image of Axel, smiling that cruel taunting smile of his.

'Zoë, your arms,' Katie had protested, shocked and anxious for her friend.

'It's nothing,' Zoë had told her angrily. 'I fell over and scratched them, that's all.'

Katie suspected that it wasn't the truth. And that left her with a very difficult dilemma. She knew that Tom wouldn't approve of what Zoë was doing and, more importantly, that he would be concerned for her as Katie was herself. But Tom hadn't telephoned her, as he had promised he would. Because of that Katie was reluctant to telephone him, at Zoë's parents' house in London, where he was still living. If she rang him he might think that she was using Zoë as an excuse to get in touch with him, and Katie didn't want that.

Katie had put the tea on Zoë's bedside table and sat down on the edge of the three-quarter bed, the only space not heaped with piles of clothes, books and other possessions.

'I know you're cross with me, Zoë,' she'd begun, 'and . . . you're seeing Axel again, aren't you?'

The effect of her words on Zoë had been electric. Her friend had whirled round, her hands bunched into fists, her eyes blazing with fury.

'What if I am? It's none of your business what I do, Katie. Now leave me alone, will you? I wish I'd never suggested that we live together. Sometimes, Katie, I think I hate you more than anyone else I know,' she had spat.

Chapter Eleven

Robert glanced at his watch as he paid off the taxi driver. It was a Patek Philippe that had originally belonged to his namesake and grandfather, Robert, Duke of Lenchester, and it made it doubly precious to Robert that his stepfather, the current duke, had given it to him. He hadn't wanted to keep this appointment, but the wealthy pop singer who wanted to consult him about installing an underground swimming pool beneath his house had refused to be put off, insisting that having seen some of Robert's work there was no one else he wanted as his architect. In the end it had simply been easier to give in, Robert acknowledged.

From the second-floor drawing-room window of Nat's house, Charlotte watched discreetly as Robert strode towards the house. In the short space of time she'd had available, she was rather proud of the information she'd gathered about the newly engaged, soon-to-be Crown Prince of Lauranto. What a very fortunate man he was. As fortunate a man as he had been a child. One of those people for whom life always seems to turn out well, without that person having to do anything to earn or merit the good luck that came their way. Charlotte could feel her stomach muscles tightening. She was halfway to disliking him all over again already.

Robert climbed the stone steps and lifted the knocker on the door painted to such a high-gloss finish that he could almost see his face in it. The dark red paint was matched exactly by the colour of the geraniums tumbling from the window boxes either side of the door, their colour contrasted by their green leaves.

Everything about the outside appearance of the house – and its neighbour to its left – was immaculate and elegant, although Robert didn't know whether that was due to an unexpected private flair for elegance from its publicly flamboyant owner, or pressure from his neighbours.

Charlotte took her time opening the door, and was pleased when she caught Robert out glancing at his watch when she did open it.

Shaking down the cuff of his shirt along with the sleeve of his Savile Row suit, Robert turned and then froze.

That the woman standing in front of him was possibly the most beautiful woman he had ever seen was an immediate given, as was his surprise, since Nat Richards was totally open about his homosexuality. But these were not what held him motionless whilst his heart pounded in a surge of male awareness and recognition.

The woman watching him, waiting for him, might look ice cool and haughty but, Robert sensed, she possessed a sensuality so powerful, it was like a current of power directly connecting to his own body. He wanted her. Normally he would have set up a discreet flirtation with her, and then, if that succeeded, moved things forward until they became lovers. Normally. But that normality now lay in the past. It had to. His normality from now on meant marriage to Olivia and fidelity. Robert was determined that he would be faithful. Being faithful mattered. The child he had been knew that.

He stepped back from the door, angered by his inconvenient desire and the woman who had caused it.

All this was taken in by Charlotte's unwavering dark blue gaze. She was every bit as aware of him as she knew he was of her. It gave her a savage sense of satisfaction to see in his eyes what she had seen in the eyes of so many men. He wanted her. Knowing that made her feel powerful and in control. It gave her the edge, made her 'better' than he. Now she could admit that she had hoped for this; that he would look at her and want her, just as she had once looked at the magazine and wanted so desperately what he had and was. Oh, yes, he wanted her and he could have her, but he would have to pay, and the payment he would have to make would be in her humbling of him and all that he represented.

So life choices are made in the space between two seconds, between two heartbeats, one path rejected and another chosen, a foot set upon that path and a fate sealed. A sense of power and excitement tingled through her, an awareness of the challenge she had just accepted fizzing through her veins. She could step back from it, and from him. All she had to do was close the door and exclude him. She could choose a different destiny and leave him to his – the Crown, the oh-so-suitable wife-to-be, the life to which he had been born. She *could*, but Charlotte knew that she wasn't going to.

She stepped forward. 'Charlotte Meredith,' she introduced herself. She could never say those words without mentally wanting to insist, 'Lady' Meredith, but of course that was not the done thing. Instead she continued calmly, 'You've come to see Nat, I know.'

Charlotte's voice was low and musical – she'd had elocution lessons to rid herself of her original East End accent when she'd been modelling. Her smile, designed to melt any resistance, was warm, sensual and slightly self-deprecating, 'I'm afraid he's been called away on business. I hope you won't mind having to make do with me instead.'

Her smile said that of course she knew that no red-blooded man in his senses could possibly mind.

Robert could almost feel the force field of her confidence as she stepped back, inviting him into the hall.

She wore that confidence like a challenge that mocked others less favoured by fortune, and Robert could feel himself reacting to it, and to her, with defensive rejection. In fact, everything about her made his skin prickle with wariness; wariness or awareness?

'I really think it would be best if I came back another time,' he announced curtly. 'It is, after all, Nat with whom I need to discuss the feasibility of a basement swimming pool.'

One dark beige eyebrow arched. 'Why? After all, you've drawn plans for and supervised the construction of other similar projects – surely it's only a matter of taking a few measurements?'

'It isn't quite as simple as that. By their very nature such projects present their own problems.'

Charlotte made a small *moue*.

Her lips were full and painted a soft matt red, as though she'd been kissed and the bright shine of her original lipstick removed.

'In that case perhaps you'd prefer to measure my basement since I live next door, and Nat's enthusiasm for your basement swimming pools has tempted me to think about installing one myself.'

Her allure was played to be irresistible, but not to him. He had other plans.

'My diary is rather full at the moment. However, I would be pleased to give Nat the names of several other architects you could both consult.'

The gloves were off and they were confronting one another as antagonists.

Anger stiffened Charlotte's spine. She knew when she was being rejected. She ought to. She had experienced enough rejection as a child to know rejection inside out.

'Thank you, but I'm sure I'll be able to find someone suitable myself.'

Robert inclined his head, saying calmly, 'As you wish,' before he turned to leave.

He heard the sound of the door closing with a soft click before he reached the bottom step.

He could feel his chest expanding as he breathed deeply to steady the pounding of his heart. The palms of his hands felt damp with sweat, his heart racing as though he had had a narrow escape from danger. He had a sudden longing for Olivia's equable calming presence.

In the hallway of Nat's house Charlotte gave way to her fury, her hands balled into tight fists, her face burning, the years ripped away to reduce her once again to that child sitting with her feet in the gutter, who she had promised herself she had left behind for ever.

Robert stood alone in the empty street, letting the cool air chill his overheated body.

Olivia. He needed Olivia. His thirst for her was the thirst of a reformed alcoholic for water, knowing that water was better for him whilst inside him a thirst raged for alcohol.

He would go to New York tonight, on the first flight he could find. Once he was there he would be safe. Once he was there, with Olivia, he would be able to forget Charlotte Meredith.

'Got anything planned for tonight, Katie, only if you haven't I wondered if you'd like to come with me to this party? Unless, of course, you're seeing your new friends.'

'Don't be silly. I keep asking you to come out with me when I see them, but you won't.'

'Because they're boring. Not like this party I've been invited to.'

'It isn't Axel who's giving this party, is it, Zoë, because if it is I'm not going.'

'No, it's someone else. A friend. I have friends too, you know.'

'Zoë, I wish you wouldn't be like this.'

'For goodness' sake stop going on at me, will you, Katie? You're as bad as Tom. All he did over Easter was lecture me. I don't know how his new girlfriend puts up with him. I certainly wouldn't.'

Katie's heart gave a treacherous and sickening thump. This was the first time Zoë had mentioned Tom having a girlfriend, and it was horrible how Katie was feeling almost sick with jealousy and misery, after everything she'd said to herself about not thinking about Tom and getting on with her life as well. She had deliberately not asked Zoë about Tom, and now she couldn't help wishing that her friend hadn't said anything about him. It was silly to keep on feeling so hurt because she knew she meant nothing to him.

'What's wrong? You've gone really pale,' Zoë told her.

'Nothing's wrong, and yes, I will come to the party with you.'

Zoë might have spoken the truth when she had said that the party wasn't being held by Axel, Katie acknowledged, as she surveyed the crowded living room of the first-floor flat, but what she hadn't said was that Axel would be a guest. And not *a* guest, but very much the most important guest, Katie recognised, as she watched the almost worshipful group surrounding the Austrian aristocrat, who was holding court in the centre of the room.

Katie's heart fell. To see Axel surrounded by such an adoring sycophantic crowd of girls wouldn't please Zoë at all.

Katie looked towards the kitchen, where Zoë had taken the booze they had brought with them, promising to return with their drinks, wishing now that she hadn't agreed to come.

The requisite hard rock music played at eardrum-blistering level pounded from giant speakers, the smell of pot mingling with the scent of the incense sticks lit by a quartet of girls, dressed and made up like refugees from the seventies, with their long hair and spaced-out gazes. Other partygoers, like Katie herself, were casually dressed in jeans and T-shirts, but most of the guests were wearing Goth-type outfits and sporting a variety of facial piercings, from single studs right up to multiple piercings in eyebrows, ears, noses and lips.

A muscular-looking boy, dressed in tight leather jeans, wearing a leather waistcoat over his naked tanned and oiled chest, grinned at Katie as he walked past her, offering, 'If you're up for a shag, I'm willing.'

Katie smiled back, shaking her head, pleased when he took her refusal good-naturedly, giving her another smile before he was swallowed up by the crowd.

Zoë had been gone for what felt like ages, but whatever was delaying her return, it wasn't Axel, because he was still standing less than a couple of yards away from her, being fawned over by his female admirers.

Zoë was coming towards her at last, but she wasn't alone, she was clutching the arm of a stoned-looking rocker, leaning into him when he offered her his joint and then giggling when he started to grope her breast.

'What happened to my drink?' Katie asked when Zoë and her companion finally staggered over to her.

'I've brought you Kieron instead,' Zoë told her. 'He's Irish and wild, just how I like my men. Come on, Kieron,' she ordered, 'let's dance.'

The room was so packed that there wasn't really room to dance, but somehow Zoë managed to make some, or maybe it was the way she was dancing that had a space clearing around her and Kieron as she began to circle him, her movements deliberately sexual.

A group of men gathered round, the men slow hand-clapping as Zoë gyrated in front of Kieron until he grabbed hold of her and started to kiss and fondle her.

With every movement Zoë made, Katie's concern grew. It was obvious that Zoë wasn't putting on her floor show for Kieron, but for Axel. It was to Axel that she looked, for Axel that she wriggled and pouted and thrust her pelvis in time to the hand-clapping.

'I want to dance too,' one of the girls with Axel announced, pushing her way towards Zoë. Tall and thin, with blonde hair, the girl began to gyrate next to Zoë, mimicking and matching Zoë's movements, moving closer and closer to her.

When she put her arms round Zoë, the onlookers cheered, one of the men yelling, 'Hey, Axel, come and look at this, a bit of girl on girl.'

The atmosphere in the room had changed, male sexual anticipation and excitement charging the air, making Katie recoil and wish she could leave.

The blonde girl was caressing Zoë's breast now. To Katie's disbelief, Zoë did the same to her, the pair of them grinding their pelvises together, and pawing at one another's breasts, whilst the men started to cheer and encourage them.

Katie felt sickened and dismayed. Zoë didn't know what she was doing; she couldn't do.

Some of the men were chanting, 'Get 'em off, get it on.' Katie turned away and then froze as she realised that Axel was standing right next to her. How had that happened? She hadn't seen him move. But then she'd been too busy watching Zoë.

His, 'Want to have a closer look, or would you prefer

to join in?' accompanied by a taunting smile made Katie's stomach heave.

'No,' she told him shortly. She wanted him to go away. She wanted Zoë to come away. She wanted them not to be here. She turned her back on Axel and then gasped in horror as she felt his hand close round her wrist, his thumb stroking its inner surface, his voice a murmur against her ear as he stood behind her.

'I can do something to you that would turn us both on much more than those two slags.' His teeth tugged on her earlobe.

'Let go of me,' Katie hissed, her whole body recoiling in revulsion from his touch.

'Come on, you know you're loving it,' he mocked her.

On the dance floor the blonde had released Zoë and was now removing her top and her jeans, leaving her naked except for her thong and her shoes. Not to be outdone Zoë started removing her own clothes.

Horrified, Katie tried again to pull away from Axel, desperate to stop Zoë from showing herself up even more than she had done already.

'You want to join your friend?' Axel was propelling her through the crowd towards the small floor space that held Zoë and the blonde.

Zoë looked up, saw them and immediately froze, her expression one of disbelief and then fury. Her intention of undressing forgotten, she hurled herself at Katie screaming, 'Let go of him, you bitch, he's mine.'

'Oooh, a girl fight. Clear the floor everyone,' Katie could hear Axel demanding. 'Let's get them stripped off and oiled up. I love it when girls fight.'

Trying to hold Zoë off, as well as explain to her that

she was completely wrong and that she had no interest whatsoever in Axel, the meaning of Axel's words only really hit Katie when she saw everyone turning towards them.

'We're not staying here. We're leaving,' she told Zoë. 'We can talk later.'

Somehow she managed to drag Zoë through the crowd with her as she headed for the door, the cold night air making her breath catch rawly in her lungs once they were outside.

'Let go of me,' Zoë demanded pulling free of her, her expression and her voice filled with bitterness.

'You're trying to steal Axel from me. But I won't let you, Katie. He's mine.'

'I don't want Axel, Zoë. I think he's loathsome,' Katie responded.

'Liar!' Zoë hissed with venom.

'Oh, Zoë,' Katie protested, 'can't you see what he is, and how he manipulates people?'

'You're the one who's doing the manipulating, trying to persuade me that you don't want him when I can see that you do. You were all over him.'

'No I wasn't. He was the one who came on to me.' Too late Katie realised that she had said the wrong thing.

Her face contorted, Zoë screamed, 'Liar, liar . . .' before turning back towards the flat they had just left.

'Zoë,' Katie protested, 'don't go back in there. Come home with me.'

When Zoë stopped and then walked back to her, Katie thought that she had won, but then Zoë stopped in front of her and spat in her face.

'That's what I think of you, Katie. I hate you. You're

not my friend any more. You aren't anything to me. I'd like to be a witch and make a little doll of you that I could stick pins into so that you could suffer what you've made me suffer. But you won't take Axel from me. No one will. We're bound together for ever. Nothing can change that.' And then she turned away and ran towards the flat disappearing into the building whilst Katie wiped the spit and her tears with fingers that shook.

'Robert!'

Olivia could hardly contain her surprise and delight when she answered her intercom to discover that her late-night visitor was her new fiancé. As she opened the door to him she started to ask him why he hadn't phoned to warn her of his visit.

But Robert didn't let her say more than a couple of words, taking her in his arms with far more insistence and passion than usual, and then kissing her until she was breathless.

'I take it that you've missed me,' she teased him, when he had finally stopped kissing her.

'I've been thinking about you, and us, all the way across the Atlantic,' Robert told her truthfully, cupping her breast with his hand and rubbing the pad of his thumb over her already erect nipple as he breathed in the scent of her. Now that he was with her it would be all right – he would be all right – and that damned unwanted ache *she* had made him feel would stop tormenting him.

'I've missed you, Livvy. Feel.' Olivia didn't know which surprised her the most, the raw admission in Robert's voice or the way in which she took her hand and placed it against his erection, unmistakably rigid and swollen beneath her touch.

He was kissing her again, his tongue plunging into her mouth, seeking hers, thrusting against it, his hands hard and impatient as he yanked off the T-shirt she was wearing and then her bra, dropping them onto the floor of her narrow hallway and then groaning against her mouth in obvious pleasure as his fingers plucked and tugged, her eager-to-be-caressed nipples sending fountains of pleasure and arousal shooting through her body. In the mirrors either side of her narrow hall walls she could see their reflections, Robert's visible urgency enhancing her own delight and arousal. She had never seen him like this before, so hungry for her that he was almost out of control.

When he reached for the zipper of her jeans, she helped him, shucking them off her body, feeling proud to stand in front of him wearing only her brief white cotton string, the dimmed gold lighting of the hallway casting a golden glow over her skin so that it seemed to shimmer as she looked at her reflection.

Looking into the mirror, Robert watched her arousal softening Olivia's expression. She was beautiful, sensual, responsible, everything he could want in a woman, and it was Olivia he had committed himself to. Olivia he must want and not—

Olivia gasped, torn between surprise and delight, when Robert dropped to his knees in front of her, his hands gripping her body as lowered his head to the dark triangle of hair that covered the mound of her sex, his tongue moving below it to part the lips, his movements impatient, replacing his normal finesse with something darker and far more erotic.

Robert was losing control, giving in to his desire for her, to his passion, Olivia recognised on a shaky thrill of delight as she looked down at his dark bowed head and felt the warm wetness of her own arousal rushing to meet the fiercely demanding stroke of his tongue, and yet, at the same time, she felt oddly awkward and unable to relax.

She leaned forward and touched Robert's shoulder. 'The bedroom will be more comfortable,' she smiled as she held out her hand to him. More comfortable or less primitive? Because it was the primitive nature of their mirror images that had checked the rising tide of her desire, Olivia knew.

Taking her hand, Robert nodded. For a moment there he had almost lost control, almost forgotten he was with Olivia. He was glad that Olivia had stopped him. And glad too that he had come to New York and to her. He was safe here with Olivia. Her calm good sense made him safe. It was all right, everything was all right, there was nothing for him to fear, especially not a momentary unimportant reaction he had had to a woman who meant nothing to him at all.

It was later, after they had made love, that Robert told her that before coming to her he'd gone to see her parents, to apologise to her father for not asking his permission before he had proposed to her.

'You've gone very quiet. Not wishing you'd said no already, are you?' Robert teased in the darkness as Olivia lay next to him, her head pillowed on his shoulder.

'No,' she laughed. 'Certainly not. I was actually thinking about what Mom keeps saying to me about the wedding being very complicated.'

'Not really. We get married in London in September. A month later I am crowned in Lauranto's cathedral, the Archbishop having been given a dispensation by the Pope that allows him to do so, since my grandmother has had a law passed removing the bar to a member of the royal family marrying outside the Catholic Church, and then once I am Crown Prince my grandmother will give a ball to introduce you to Lauranto society as my wife.'

'When I said it was going to be complicated I meant that getting married in London makes things complicated.'

'How?'

Even the best of men could be dense when it came to the nuances of female behaviour and pecking order, Olivia reflected.

'Your mother seems to have taken control of the arrangements for our wedding. Traditionally it is the bride's mother who does that.'

'Yes, of course, but since my mother is based in London it makes sense for her to arrange everything.'

'Well, yes, but the point Mom was trying to make last night is that she and Dad would prefer us to get married here.'

'Here? In New York?' Robert shook his head. 'That wouldn't do at all. I had a hard enough time of it persuading my grandmother not to insist on us marrying in Lauranto and converting to Catholicism.'

Olivia was astonished. 'She wanted us to do that? You never said anything about that before.' It surprised her that he should have kept something so important from her.

'No, I didn't,' Robert agreed, laughing, 'because I didn't want to frighten you off.' Reaching for her hand he said softly, 'Look, how would it be if I suggested to my mother that she invites yours over to London so that they can plan the wedding together.' It does make sense to have it there really, you know. Think how difficult it could be for Granny and Gramps to make the journey to New York, and then there's the rest of the family. They'll all want to be there.'

He had a point, of course.

'Stop worrying,' Robert told her, reaching out to smooth what she hoped was an imaginary line on her forehead with the sweetest of tender touches. 'Our mothers grew up together, don't forget. They'll find a way of compromising over the wedding. It isn't where it takes place or how grand it is that matters to us – we both know that. What's important is the private commitment we'll be making to one another, and that is just an extension of the commitment we've already made. Seeing you getting upset makes me feel guilty because I know perfectly well that all the brouhaha of a big wedding is the result of my decision to succeed my father as Crown Prince of Lauranto. It's all about my mother wanting to put on the right kind of show for my grandmother. It's about my grandmother's belief that the marriage of Lauranto's Crown Prince must be accompanied by pomp and circumstance. It's about impressing others, when the reality is that all your parents want is for you to be happy, and all we want is one another. I'm sorry if the wretched trappings of being Crown Prince are going to spoil our special day, Livvy.'

Oh, he knew how to touch her heart with his honesty

and his love for her. Olivia knew that, right then, he could have asked her to get married anywhere and she would have agreed.

'I've told my grandmother that after our marriage I shall be taking you away and that nothing and no one will be allowed to interrupt our honeymoon.'

'Oh, Robert, I suppose I am being silly, getting all het up about the wedding.' When he smiled at her, she lifted her shoulders in a small shrug. 'I suppose I just feel guilty myself because your mother has taken over arranging the wedding. She has two daughters of her own, after all. Mom only has one – me.'

'Ah,' Robert told her wickedly, 'but your mother's one daughter is marrying a crown prince.'

'Mmm. And, like you said, Mom will be able to go over to London and organise the wedding with your mother.'

'All of which means that I'll get to see you more often.'

'Have you managed to sort out our having our own private apartment in the palace yet?' she asked him, changing the subject.

'I think so.'

'And?'

Robert gave her a teasing smile. 'I'm not going to say any more – I want it to be a surprise for you.'

Olivia leaned close to him to accept the kiss he was offering her, closing her eyes automatically as she did so. Not just to accept his kiss but also to blot out her mental image of Robert's London apartment, with its air of sleek austerity and the feeling it always gave her that she was somehow an alien in its almost sterile mini-malism. It wasn't that she wanted to, as Robert put it so succinctly when he talked about the kind of décor he most disliked, 'behave like a psychotic Victorian and shroud everything in yards of fabric, so that furniture ends up looking like badly wrapped parcels of laundry.' Far from it. Denham's gentle faded elegance came closest to her own style and taste, perhaps with a touch of New York smarts and Hamptons simplicity added in to underline her American upbringing. Like any woman she wanted to put her own stamp on her home, but that could wait until after they were married, she comforted herself. Right now, enjoying Robert's kiss was far, far more important and pleasurable than worrying about the décor of their future home. And besides, she genuinely didn't want to spoil Robert's surprise.

'When do you have to go back to London?' she asked him.

'Tomorrow. I shouldn't be here now, but I needed to see you. I needed to be with you and hold you, Livvy.'

He felt her smile as she turned towards him, lifting her face again for his kiss.

Chapter Twelve

The Lamb and Flag pub, next to St John's College, was a favourite with students, and tonight, even though it was early in the week, it was busy, the air thick with cigarette smoke that drove out the freshness of the March evening air.

Katie was with Fran, Fran's new boyfriend, Rick, and Miles and some other students, but her mind wasn't really on their conversation, which was all about the upcoming Commem Ball. Instead she was thinking about Zoë and the party and the terrible quarrel they had had. How could Zoë accuse her of trying to steal Axel from her? The evening and its events were something Katie could hardly bear to think about, especially that final dreadful scene with Zoë, who had not spoken to her since. It was all so awful that she didn't even want to remember it, never mind discuss it with anyone. All she could do was push it to the back of her mind and hope that Zoë, who was avoiding her, would calm down and come to her senses. She was grateful for Miles' tap on her arm to distract her unhappy thoughts.

'If you haven't already accepted an invite to the

Commem Ball, I was wondering if you'd like to go with me?' he asked her quietly.

Katie liked Miles. He might be on the quiet side and seriously brainy, but he was easy to be with – a friend rather than a boyfriend, and someone whose friendship she really appreciated.

'No, I haven't, and yes, thank you, I would.' She'd been so caught up in her heartache over Tom, and Zoë's difficult moods, that she hadn't given much thought to the ball, which was being held in late June. But now that Miles had invited her to go with him, she was glad.

'We could make up a foursome with Fran and Rick,' he suggested.

'What's that? Did I hear my name?' Fran demanded.

'I was just suggesting to Katie that the four of us should go to the Commem Ball together,' Miles answered her, 'you and Rick and me and Katie.'

'Oh yes. Great,' Fran enthused.

'If you like we could meet up one Saturday morning and go shopping for our ball gowns. Everyone seems to go to either Annabelinda or Droopy & Browns,' Fran suggested to Katie as they walked home from the pub later that evening. Fran was sharing a house with three other girls only a couple of streets away from Zoë and Kate. She pulled a small face. 'I know the ball isn't until the end of June, but we won't get anything decent if we leave it. Mind you, the dresses in both shops are fearfully expensive, so thank goodness my parents have offered to pay.'

Katie knew that her own parents would do the same for her. They had reached the corner where their shared

178

route home ended. 'I'd thought about hiring a dress but my mother would throw a blue fit,' Katie admitted ruefully to Fran. 'She's the world's worst snob.'

Fran giggled. 'Mine's the same.'

It saddened her that she would be attending her first Commemoration Ball without Zoë, but Zoë had made her feelings clear last night when she had said that she hated her and no longer considered her to be her friend. Axel had driven a wedge between them, and Zoë's emotions were like the furthermost ends of a seesaw – either right up or right down. And, Katie thought, it was Axel who currently controlled whether the seesaw was up or down.

It was only just gone eleven o'clock, so Katie knew that she shouldn't really be surprised to find the house in darkness; after all, it had still been light when she'd gone out, and presumably Zoë had gone running after Axel – again.

Katie unlocked the front door. As she stepped into the small hallway, she reached for the light switch, freezing with shock as she heard a sound coming from the sitting room that lifted the hair at the nape of her neck: a low, keening otherworldly sound of dreadful pain, primeval and all the more intense for being heard in the darkness.

Quickly Katie switched on the light, horror surging through her when she saw bloodstains on the floor, her appalled gaze tracking them from the open kitchen door to the sitting room.

Afterwards Katie couldn't remember exactly what she had thought standing there in the hallway – whether she had considered that the house might have been broken into, or that she herself might be in danger.

All she could remember was the feeling of anxiety that had cramped her stomach as she had hurried into the sitting room and switched on the light.

It was the smell that hit her first, vomit laced with alcohol, and blood, so pungent it made her own stomach heave.

Then she saw Zoë.

She was huddled into a corner of the room between the sofa and the window. Her bare arms, which were wrapped round her hunched-up knees, were covered in blood. There was blood and vomit on the carpet and Zoë's clothes. Instinctively Katie covered her nose with her cupped hand to block out the smell. There were marks on Zoë's face that looked as though someone had raked her skin with something sharp, just like that other time, only now the fingers of Zoe's right hand were curled round the hilt of a kitchen knife.

For a second Katie couldn't move. She felt as though the blood in her veins had turned to ice. Her brain's instinctive response was denial. Zoë couldn't surely have inflicted those dreadful cuts herself? But deep down inside, Katie knew that she must have done.

Katie ran to Zoë's side. The other girl was rocking to and fro, making the unearthly noise Katie had heard from the hallway. She was staring straight ahead of herself, her eyes open wide, her gaze fixed and unblinking, oblivious to Katie's presence.

Saying her name quietly, Katie slid the knife from Zoë's grip.

'Zoë, it's me, Katie.'

Was she imagining it or did something flicker in the staring blankness of Zoë's fixed gaze?

She couldn't deal with this on her own, Katie knew. She needed help. *Zoë* needed help.

There was only one person she could trust and rely on to know what to do and that was Tom. But Tom was in London, probably with his girlfriend, and it was now gone midnight.

'Zoë?' Katie tried again to rouse her friend from her trancelike state but this time not even a flicker of awareness disturbed Zoë's fixed stare.

She could always ring for an ambulance, of course, to take Zoë to A & E. What would Tom prefer her to do? Katie knew the answer to that.

The phone was in the hall. Although Katie knew the number for Zoë's parents' London house, she still had to punch in the numbers twice, her fingers were trembling so much. Ridiculously, she realised, as she curled the wire round her index finger whilst she listened to the phone ring out at the other end, as well as holding her breath, she was also crossing the fingers of her left hand behind her back.

The phone seemed to ring for ever. Katie pictured Tom waking up in bed, perhaps removing his arm from around his girlfriend. They would both be sleeping naked, of course. Despite the fact that Zoë teased Tom for being a dull boring banker, Tom's body was that of a sportsman, lean, with nicely honed muscles. He had rowed for Oxford and still played rugby at weekends.

'Tom.' The sound of his voice, so calm and clear, momentarily left Katie herself speechless.

'Tom, it's me, Katie,' she managed shakily.

'Yes, I recognise your voice.'

'It's Zoë, she isn't very well, and—'

'What kind of not well?'

'I think you need to be here, Tom.'

There was a small silence, and then she heard him say in a clipped voice, 'Right. I'm on my way.'

That was it – nothing more. No questions or demands for explanations, just that one simple, calm and oh-so-reassuring sentence that immediately lifted the weight of anxiety from her shoulders.

Replacing the receiver Katie, leaned back against the wall. The bloodstains on the floor caught her eye. Now that her primary duty to her friend was done, she had secondary obligations to their friendship to occupy her, Katie recognised. In the kitchen, filling a bucket with hot soapy water, she reflected that this wouldn't after all be the first time she had removed the evidence of Zoë's excesses in order to protect her friend. It would also give her something to do whilst she waited anxiously for Tom to arrive.

Thankfully the bloodstains soon lifted from the wooden floor. Cleaning up the carpet, though, and Zoë herself, was nowhere near as easy. Katie was reluctant to hurt her friend and provoke another of those hair-raising howls of pain, and she was also concerned that if Zoë was badly hurt she might make the injury worse by moving her.

In the end, although she managed to clean up the worst of the mess, it was impossible for her to disguise that Zoë had been sick, as no amount of disinfected hot water or fresh air could remove the smell of vomit.

She'd done her best to gently sponge as much of the dried blood as she could from Zoë's face but she'd been reluctant to touch the stomach-churning ripped flesh on her cheek.

It was with a mixture of relief and anxiety that she looked up to see car headlights illuminating the road, and realised that Tom had arrived.

Although he had his own key, she still went to let him in.

His face and arms were tanned, his hair covering the collar of the fine silky-knit polo shirt he was wearing with jeans. Immaculately clean jeans, of course, worn with brown loafers. His expression was sombre, a small crease in his forehead betraying his anxiety. Tom looked exactly what he was, Katie thought tenderly, a sensible, conservative young man who took his responsibilities seriously.

'I'm sorry I had to drag you all the way here,' Katie began, 'but I just didn't know what to do.' When he didn't respond she continued uncertainly, 'I expect your girlfriend is furious with me for waking you both?'

Again there was no response, other than an un-expectedly assessing look that made her face burn as Katie wished she had not been so obvious.

'What's happened?' Tom made towards the stairs, forcing Katie to dart in front of him. Her standing on the first stair still didn't bring her up to his height.

'She isn't in her bedroom, she's in the sitting room.'

When Tom turned towards the sitting room, though, Katie reached out to stop him again. She wanted to warn him – and to protect him? But she couldn't bring herself to put into words what she feared. Instead, all she could manage to say was, 'She's been very sick. I've tried to clean her up.'

Nodding, Tom turned back.

'Tom . . .,' Katie begged him urgently, '. . . there are some cuts on her arms and . . . and her face.'

'Cuts?' Tom was clearly alarmed now. 'What kind of cuts?'

Katie could only shake her head. Perhaps it was better, kinder, to let him see for himself and come to his own conclusions. Zoë was his sister, Katie reminded herself. He loved her. Katie's tender heart ached for him as she followed him into the sitting room, biting down hard on her bottom lip as she saw the shock on his face.

'What . . . what happened?' he demanded.

Katie's throat was so dry, she had to swallow before she could answer. 'I don't know. I found her like this when I came in. There was . . . there was a knife on the floor beside her.'

'You mean she's done this to herself?'

Katie hung her head as though somehow she herself was to blame – or was it because she just couldn't bear to see what she knew she would recognise in Tom's eyes?

'I'm sorry,' was all she could say. She knew how much Tom loved his sister and how protective of her he was. That was why she had telephoned him, after all.

Tom was now crouching on the floor beside Zoë, talking urgently to her, begging her to answer him. When she didn't he turned back to Katie.

'Why? Why would anyone do something like this to themselves?'

'I don't know,' Katie admitted. She wanted to tell him that she was as shocked as he was, but somehow she felt that there was a barrier between them, a unity of sibling blood and comprehension between Tom and his sister that she, as Zoë's friend, could not cross.

'Did she say anything to you, give you any idea?'

Again Katie shook her head.

'I don't understand. I don't understand how anyone could do this to themselves.'

To Katie Tom's words sounded almost like an accusation, but there was nothing she could say to him to defend either herself or Zoë. Some instinct urged her not to say anything to him about Axel.

'She's obviously taken something,' Tom continued.

Katie still didn't say anything. She couldn't.

'Oh, come on, Katie.' He was impatient now. 'She has to have taken something: she's completely out of it. Totally zeroed and zombied, and if you think that by refusing to say so you're helping her—'

'I'm not. I don't know what she's taken.' It was the truth. 'Shouldn't we call a doctor?' Tom gave her a grim look. 'Yes, but not here. I'm going to take her back to London with me. I think it best that she sees our family GP. Luckily the parents are away at the moment, so they won't need to know. I know I've no need to ask you not to discuss anything that's happened tonight with anyone else – for Zoë's own sake.'

Katie nodded, not trusting herself to speak.

'I'll need your help to get her into the car,' Tom told her.

Zoë wasn't making any sound now, her body slumped into the corner, her chin dropping down onto her chest.

It took them over ten minutes to get her into Tom's car. She was a dead weight in their hold, slumping against Tom as they half carried and half dragged her outside.

They put her on the back seat, wrapping the seat belts round her.

Tom had got into the driver's seat and was about to close the door when Katie begged him urgently, 'You will telephone, won't you, and let me know how she is?'

Giving her a brusque nod Tom pulled the car door closed, not looking at her as he started the engine.

When she went back inside the house, Katie was surprised to see that it was almost three o'clock in the morning.

The sitting room might be empty but Katie could still see Zoë's hunched body in the corner. She could still see her slashed and bloody arms. Why hadn't she guessed that Zoë was cutting herself, the first time she had seen her cut arms? Why hadn't she known? Zoë was her friend, after all. She should have known, instead of thinking that it had been Axel who had inflicted the wounds on her. If she had known, maybe now things would have been different. Guilt filled her. She could still smell the rank odour of vomit. That at least she could do something about.

Ten minutes later she was down on her hands and knees, scrubbing at the carpet, the windows wide open, but no matter how hard she scrubbed she could not erase the shocked revulsion that the evening had carved on her brain. How could Zoë have done such a thing? Zoë, of all people? Her behaviour went against everything Katie had believed she knew about her friend.

It was pointless going to bed. She wouldn't be able to sleep. She wouldn't, she knew, be able to do anything until Tom had telephoned her to let her know how Zoë was.

* * *

186

'The announcement of your engagement appeared in the Society columns only a few days ago and since then the telephone has hardly stopped ringing. I must have had five telephone calls from Emerald already today, the first one at half-past six this morning.'

'She must have forgotten about the time difference between London and New York,' Olivia tried to placate her mother, as she spooned the froth off the top of her cappuccino. They were sitting in a window table in one of their favourite delis. The smell of pastrami, coleslaw and coffee filled the air, along with the sound of the counter staff's Brooklyn accents as they called up the orders from the queue of customers waiting to brown bag their lunch sandwiches.

This was New York as Olivia loved it, but she knew that Robert did not share her affection for the city's traditional eateries, or the food. He was strictly a silver service, French menu and maître d' diner.

'She also seems to have forgotten that you are my daughter and that it is the prerogative of the bride's mother to organise the wedding, not the groom's.'

There was a hint of angry colour in her mother's face and an unusual sharpness to her tone. Her hands curled into small fists, which she rested on the table, her pastrami on rye sandwich forgotten as she gave vent to her feelings.

Olivia reached across the table, covering her mother's right hand with her left, the diamonds in her ring blazing fire in the light coming in through the window.

'Robert says that he doesn't think she's doing it deliberately to outmanoeuvre you and take over, Mom.'

Ella gave a small elegant snort of disapproval. She was

187

wearing a lemon silk Bill Blass dress teamed with a short, strawberry-pink silk, long-sleeved fitted jacket – an outfit that was wholly and completely New York. Some of her American friends teased her that sometimes she seemed more American than they. Ella loved New York, but right now she itched to be in London, making sure that Emerald knew just whose responsibility it was to organise the wedding to celebrate the marriage of their son and daughter.

'And because Robert says it, it must be true, is that it?' she teased Olivia wryly. She was glad that her daughter was so deeply in love with the man she was going to marry, but she didn't want Olivia to be so blinded by love that she forgot that she was an independent woman with a mind of her own.

'He says that he believes his mother wants to outdo his grandmother the Princess, rather than take over from you.'

Ella sighed faintly as she looked at her daughter. Livvy looked so pretty in the Chloé skirt and T-shirt she had bought in London. The warm peach colour suited her colouring, although no outfit, however pretty, could compete with the glow of happiness that positively shone from her. The glitter of Olivia's engagement ring caught her eye. To Ella's mind it was old-fashioned and ugly, and an elegant Tiffany solitaire would have suited Livvy's slender fingers far more, but as Olivia had told her, as Robert's wife-to-be she had an obligation to wear the Lauranto royal betrothal ring, no matter how ugly it was. Ella knew how much Olivia loved Robert but she did worry inwardly that Livvy might not fully realise how many sacrifices of her own ideas, her own taste, her own right to define and direct her own life, she was going to have to make in her role as the wife of the Crown Prince of Lauranto. After all, it was Robert she had fallen in love with, not a crown prince. She knew better than to voice such thoughts, though, knowing that Livvy would immediately defend both Robert and their love, just as she would have done herself in Livvy's shoes.

'Robert did say that it might be a good idea if you were to go over to London and work with Aunt Emerald organising the wedding.'

'I can't. I'd love to, but you know that being trustees of the foundation means that your father and I have a full diary here and on the Hamptons for virtually the whole of the summer . . .'

Of course she was happy for her daughter, Ella told herself later after she had returned home, but at the same time she knew that she was going to miss Olivia dreadfully. Somehow she had assumed that Olivia would marry an American and live in New York, not marry Robert and go and live on the other side of the Atlantic.

The telephone rang. Ella picked up the receiver and then closed her eyes and counted to ten when she heard Emerald's voice.

'Yes, I do realise that decisions need to be made, Emerald,' Ella agreed, 'but we do have stationers here in New York who are perfectly capable of printing wedding invitations, you know, and I really don't think it's necessary for you to send me samples from Smythson. I can organise them from this end . . .'

Ella distinctly heard Emerald give vent to an exasperated sigh.

'Ella, I appreciate that you have become more American than any American in believing that American is best, but I really cannot see the sense in you ordering the wedding invitations in New York when the wedding is being held here in London, and besides, Smythson know exactly what to do. After all, they've been printing family invitations for us for ever. What I really wanted to discuss with you is numbers. Drogo thinks we should try to keep it under five hundred because that's probably as many as the gardens here at Lenchester House will hold comfortably, once a marquee's been put up, but of course, I have no idea how many people you'll be wanting to invite . . .'

It was going to be a very long telephone call, Ella could see.

The sound of the telephone ringing woke Katie, who had fallen asleep downstairs on the sofa. Hastily, she got up, hurrying into the hallway to answer.

'Katie, it's Tom.'

Katie's fingers curled tightly round the receiver. 'How's Zoë?'

'She's fine. Dr Rawson came to see her first thing this morning. She was still very groggy, but she was able to confirm what he'd already suspected – that her sickness was probably caused by her eating some shellfish that must have been off.'

With every word Tom said, Katie could feel her disbelief growing. 'Last night you said –' she began.

But Tom interrupted her sharply, 'I'm not a doctor, Katie. I had no idea that Zoë had been eating shellfish. She's always been slightly allergic to them, even when

190

they're fresh.' His voice was clipped and hard, warning her off challenging him, but she couldn't let the matter drop.

'What about her arms?'

'Her arms?' What was happening? Tom must know what she meant. Why was he pretending that he didn't. 'You know what I mean, Tom,' she protested.

For several seconds he didn't speak and then he told her coldly, 'No, actually, Katie, I'm afraid I don't.'

Katie realised now why Tom was behaving this way. He wanted to protect Zoë – that was natural – but his manner towards her still hurt. Tom didn't need to protect Zoë from her. She was as concerned about her as Tom was. Surely he knew that? Katie was still appalled by what she had seen, appalled and desperately concerned. Surely Zoë's family needed to know why she had done such a thing, not pretend that she hadn't?

When she didn't say anything Tom continued curtly, 'Look, Katie, Zoë has insisted to Dr Rawson that the cuts were caused by her falling against a piece of broken glass. I've already told her that she should never have tried to walk home from the party on her own, when she was feeling so ill. And perhaps she wouldn't have done if you hadn't behaved in the way you did.'

'Me. I wasn't even with her,' Katie protested.

'There's no point in lying to me, Katie. Zoë's told me everything. I admit I was angry with her at first when she admitted that she'd been seeing Axel again, but when she broke down and told me that you'd betrayed her with him, and that she'd found you in bed with him, well, I have to say that I felt sorry for her and could understand how she must have felt.'

'It's not true!' Katie protested, too shocked not to blurt out her innocence.

'Look, Katie, I haven't got time to listen to your lies. Zoë, my sister, is my prime concern right now. I suppose I should have guessed there was someone else when you didn't return my phone calls. Zoë tried to protect you, of course, by saying that she must have forgotten to tell you that I'd phoned.'

Tom had telephoned her? Zoë had lied to her? Katie felt sick with shock and despair. She wanted to protest her innocence again and to beg Tom to listen to her but she could tell that he would refuse and that he wouldn't believe her. Because of Zoë. Because Zoë was his sister and his loyalty lay with her; because Zoë had lied to him about her, and lied again to her about Tom. How could she have been so cruel and so . . . so manipulative? That simply wasn't Zoë. Was it? Her friend had changed Katie knew, but now she felt she barely recognised the person she had become.

There was nothing Katie could say, nothing in truth that she wanted to say, as she struggled to overcome her own feelings of betrayal and to admire instead Tom's loyalty to his sister.

'I've already informed the College that she won't be well enough to attend any lectures for a while, but once she does return to Oxford I'd appreciate it if—'

'When will Zoë be coming back?' was all Katie could allow herself to say.

'I don't know. Not for a few weeks. I'm going to take her away for a bit of a break. She's had a rough time of things and needs cheering up. I'll give you a ring when we get back and tell you when to expect her. Katie, there is one other thing. I know it's not my business, but, well, everything I said to you about Axel with regard to Zoë must apply equally to you. I'd hate to see you ruin your life over someone like him.'

Katie's heart thumped. 'Axel means nothing to me,' she told him heatedly.

She thought she heard Tom sigh before he said coldly, 'For your sake I hope that's true, although it does make your behaviour and disloyalty to Zoë even more unforgivable.'

He'd ended the call before Katie could say anything in her defence.

The only explanation Katie could come up with for Zoë's behaviour was that the other girl wanted to keep something hidden from her brother, and Katie suspected that that something involved Axel. She wouldn't be able to confirm that, though, until Zoë came back to Oxford and she could question her in person, and she certainly intended to do that, Katie promised herself, as she replaced the telephone receiver.

Later, sitting in on her late morning lecture, she found her thoughts drifting back to what had happened. It was strange how suddenly seeing a person from an unfamiliar perspective could completely change how one felt about them. And even stranger that somehow it was easier for her to forgive Zoë her lies about her than it was to forgive Tom for believing them.

'I've brought the photographs to show you that I took at Easter when Harry and David were both at home,' Janey announced, adding proudly as she passed one of them over to Amber, 'This is my favourite.'

It was a good photograph, Amber acknowledged, before passing it on to Cassandra. In it John was looking happy and relaxed as well as proud, standing tall, flanked by his two sons.

The three of them were sitting in Denham's pretty sitting room, the early spring sunshine showing off the fresh spring green of the lawn beyond the window. The first dark-plum-streaked white petals of the magnolia Amber and Jay had planted the May after the twins had been born, to celebrate the end of the war, were opening, their colour echoed by the deep dark purple of the tulips planted beneath them.

'Mind you, John was a bit miffed when he had to admit that both boys are now taller than he is, and how like Daddy they look.'

Like Jay, their grandfather? Or were their de Vries looks so clearly discernible because they had a double measure of them from both their mother and their father?

Barrant de Vries had, after all, not only been Jay and Cassandra's grandfather, and thus Janey's great-grandfather, he had also secretly been her own cousin Greg's grandfather, and Greg might have been John's father. Might have been. There was no proof of that, Amber reminded herself firmly. Even so, she had to lift her hand toward her heart in an attempt to stifle its unsteady anxious beat, stopping when she saw that Cassandra was watching her with a knowing look in her eyes.

As calmly as she could she told Janey, 'Yes, I noticed over Christmas that the boys both have the de Vries looks.'

There, that should silence any comments Cassandra might feel like making.

Even so, Amber was relieved when Mrs Leggit's arrival with the tea trolley made it impossible for Cassandra to say anything about the resemblance.

'Shall I pour?' Janey asked after the housekeeper had gone.

'If you wouldn't mind, dear.' Amber gave her a grateful look. The rheumatism in her hands had been playing up a little, probably because she and Jay had been overindulgent during the sunny spring days in working in the garden, something they both loved.

'Goodness, Janey, with your weight problem I'm surprised you're eating a scone,' Cassandra commented when the tea was poured. 'I remember how John's dear father always admired slender women, but then as yourself acknowledged earlier when you remarked on your sons' resemblance to Jay, sons do not always take after their fathers. To be truthful, I sometimes find it hard to believe that John is my dear late husband's son, he is so unlike him.'

Amber felt as though all the air had been driven out of her lungs. She wished desperately that Jay was with them. He knew how to deal with Cassandra when she was in one of her spiteful moods, and how to diffuse situations that, to Amber, seemed too dangerous to risk enflaming.

Janey, of course, was totally unaware of the double meaning and the malice in Cassandra's statement. Janey, after all, had no idea that her husband might not have been fathered by the late Lord Fitton Legh, and that Amber's cousin Greg could have fathered him. No one knew, thankfully, other than Amber herself, Jay and, of course, Cassandra.

What was it about Cassandra that made her enjoy being so cruelly unkind to others, Amber wondered. She knew that Cassandra had been passionately in love with John's mother, but it had been a cruel, destructive love. Cassandra did not think or feel for the rest of humanity as Amber herself did. She was selfish; self-obsessed really.

It was a great pity that Cassandra knew about Greg's affair with John's mother. It gave her a power over John and Janey and their sons that they might not know she possessed, but that Amber knew about, and she was concerned that one day, out of petty spite and unkindness, Cassandra might use that power to hurt them very badly indeed.

Amber realised that she had let her thoughts drift, and now she saw that Cassandra's unkind comment about Janey's plumpness had extinguished the maternal pride from Janey's eyes and brought bright red coins of colour to her round cheeks.

Putting down her teacup Amber said protectively, 'John loves and values Janey for what she is – a wonderful wife and mother – and quite rightly as well. Her loving heart gives her more beauty than any stick-thin model could ever possess, and if you were to ask John he would be the first to say the same thing. Why, he was telling me only the other day how grateful he is to her for all that she's done to help him with Fitton and how he couldn't cope without her.'

Janey forced herself to smile. She knew that Amber meant well and that she was trying to protect her, but deep down inside, a much younger Janey cried with pain at the thought of being wanted only because of

196

what she 'did'. That Janey longed to be alluring and beautiful, in the way that she had noticed over Christmas all her female peers in the family were. That Janey wanted John to look at her with awe and admiration. That Janey wanted him to spoil her and cherish her and not say, as John had said this morning, that since David wasn't going to be available to help with the farm work this summer, it was just as well that Janey could drive a tractor since she would have to fill in for him.

She was overweight, she knew, but it didn't help that she felt obliged to spend most of her life wearing old work clothes. She had some lovely things, thanks to Ella. And thanks too to her own dressmaking skills she'd been able to alter them to make them fit, but she seldom had the chance to wear them, and anyway, John tended to get upset about the fact that she was wearing her sister's cast-offs.

When she'd first fallen in love with John it had been because he had seemed so safe and steady, so masterful and reliable. She had known, of course, how much Fitton meant to John but she had thought then of Fitton as the magical place of her childhood, a wonderful heritage that she and John would care for together. She'd also envisaged a marriage in which John would be a traditional husband, providing well for his wife and family. The reality was rather different. They had the kind of financial problems she'd never experienced growing up; John loved her, she knew that, but sharing him with Fitton was almost like sharing him with another woman, in the sense that Fitton was always at the forefront of his mind – Fitton and not her or the boys. He loved them all, of course, he was proud of his sons, but Fitton and his duty to it came first. There was never any money to spare for treats, never mind luxuries for the boys or her, never really any time to spare for them either.

It wasn't John's fault. They both might have lost their mothers young but she and Ella had grown up loved by Amber as their stepmother, whilst poor John had had only Cassandra, who was so mean and unkind. John's father, unlike her own, had been a cold, critical, distant man. John had grown up somehow believing that he wasn't really good enough for Fitton, and that was something Janey found hard to forgive both Cassandra and his father for.

Janey had been determined that things would be different for her own sons, that their lives would be happier, their spirits lighter, their laughter freer than John's She had tried discreetly and with maternal love to bring up Harry and David to understand that the girls they eventually loved and married should receive all the small considerations that John overlooked, and that they should not be shut out of their thoughts and conversation whilst her sons retreated within themselves.

Sometimes Janey almost wished that instead of their living at Fitton they had an ordinary house, somewhere in Alderley Edge or Prestbury, the kind of house and the kind of life that John despised, where he caught the train into Manchester every morning and she met up with other women in Wilmslow for coffee in Hoopers store.

The kind of life in which there was no Cassandra, with her sharp, malicious tongue.

*　*　*

'That dress you tried on in Droopy & Browns was out of this world,' Fran told Katie, as they sat together at a table in the Lamb and Flag, where they had paused in their search for suitably stunning ball gowns for the Commem Ball.

Katie managed what she hoped was an enthusiastic smile. The last thing she wanted to do was to spoil Fran's enjoyment of their shared shopping trip for ball gowns but the terrible situation surrounding Zoë was weighing very heavily on her heart, and on her conscience. She might not have any interest whatsoever in Axel but Katie still felt responsible for the fact that they had quarrelled and that she had let Zoë go back to that awful party without her. If she hadn't, if she had stayed with her . . .

'Hey, where have you gone?' Fran demanded.

Katie apologised for her lack of concentration, and told herself that she now owed it to Fran to put her guilt to one side and to focus instead on their shared shopping trip.

The Lamb and Flag was empty of Miles and the others, as the 'men' were either preparing for the Eights Week boat races or cheering on their friends in the teams.

'And so was the price,' Katie pointed out, although in reality she admitted that she had fallen in love with the oh-so-simple and oh-so-expensive Grecian-style pale lilac silk evening dress she had tried on in the most expensive and exclusive of Oxford's formal wear shops. 'Perhaps we shouldn't have started out with the most expensive shops,' she added. 'That icy-green number you tried in Annabelinda was breathtaking.'

'Trust me to pick one of the most expensive dresses

in the shop,' Fran groaned. 'And now that I've seen it, I just know that nothing else is going to come anywhere close to looking as good.'

'It would be wasteful to spend so much money on dresses we'll probably only wear once,' Katie said sensibly.

They looked at one another.

'But imagine how we're going to feel years from now if we don't get dresses that suit us so well. After all, a girl's first Commem Ball is something special, and since they hold one only every three years, we won't get a second chance to attend one.

'We can still look at Monsoon and some of the charity shops,' Katie felt bound to say.

'Yes,' Fran agreed, 'just as long as we leave enough time to get back to Annabelinda and Droopy & Browns before closing time. I'd hate to see two other girls turning up at the ball wearing our dresses.'

It was so easy being with Fran, Katie acknowledged, and just acknowledging that was enough to make her feel guilty all over again. Guilty and disloyal to Zoë.

Their lunch eaten, they hurried back out into the spring sunshine, heading for the Carfax, the centre of Oxford where the High Street, St Aldates, Queen Street and Cornmarket Street all met, window shopping as they walked. It being a Saturday, Oxford was busy with shoppers as well as students and tourists.

Doing their best to avoid tourists clutching street maps, and student cyclists on ancient boneshakers, the girls paused outside Monsoon, Fran digging Katie in the ribs and trying hard not to giggle as she nodded her head in the direction of a too dapperly dressed thirty-something man standing next to a parked Porsche Boxster car and shouting into a mobile telephone the size of a brick, his black attaché case open on the car seat.

'Talk about trying too hard,' Fran laughed as they hurried into Monsoon. 'My cousin's got one – he's a merchant banker – a "latent spiv", my father calls him, and we all take the piss out of him every time we see him with it. They weigh a ton and you can never get a good connection My aunt Jean, his mother, says that they remind her of trying to listen to Radio Luxembourg on the car radio when she and Uncle George were courting – every time a record she liked came on, the reception faded.

They weren't the only girls in Monsoon searching for ball dresses. The selection was really nice, they both agreed, but not to be compared with what they had already seen.

'I feel a bit awkward about my parents being prepared to buy me something so expensive when some of the girls who'll be going will really struggle to afford something,' Katie said.

'Well, don't,' Fran told her matter-of-factly, 'because if you do, then I'll have to as well, and I really did love that dress in Annabelinda. We'll be expected to put on a decent show, and look the part. I've got a cousin who attended the last one. She still talks about it now. They had everything – nonstop flowing champers, fairground rides, a hog roast, as well as the usual string quartets in the hall kind of thing.'

Katie tried to feel as excited as Fran but it was hard

when she was so anxious about Zoë. When would she come back to Oxford? What would happen when she did? Zoë hadn't made any attempt to get in touch with her, and neither, of course, had Tom.

Chapter Thirteen

'Ready to give in?' Fran demanded nearly two hours later.

'There's still The Ball Room. We haven't been there yet,' Katie pointed out. 'It's got a really good reputation.'

'Mmm . . . it's very Sloaney,' Fran agreed, 'but I've heard at least a dozen girls saying that they're going to be wearing something from there, either bought or borrowed.'

The exclusive shop by Magdalen Bridge was one of the best ball gown shops in the city, and both girls admitted when they left it later in the afternoon that they had been tempted.

'Tempted, but I have stayed true to my first love,' Fran laughed, assuming a mock dramatic pose. 'And now I can't wait to be reunited with it.' Then she paused, standing still in the middle of the street. 'I've just had the most terrible thought. What if we go back to the shops and we don't like our dresses after all?'

'Don't you dare even think that,' Katie protested, laughing. She had to admit she felt far more relaxed with Fran than she ever did these days with Zoë.

Pushing that thought aside, Katie fell into step with Fran as they set off again, heading first for Annabelinda.

'Have you thought any more about what I said about moving in with us when Jenny goes at the end of term?' Fran asked Katie.

Fran lived in a house with four other girls, one of whom was moving out to share with her boyfriend.

'It's really kind of you to suggest it but I've decided to stay with Zoë,' Katie thanked her, as they reached Gloucester Street and Annabelinda.

Inside her head she had an image of Zoë as she had been when Katie had found her, staring unseeingly into the dark place her life had become, and tormented by who knew what demons.

Katie gave a small shiver.

They'd done it: both dresses had been tried on again, to be admired and approved, and finally secured with deposits whilst the girls waited for parental funds with which to pay the full bill.

'Feel like calling in at the KA?' Fran asked. The King's Arms was a popular student pub at the south end of Parks Road.

Katie agreed, adding, 'Although after trying on our dresses I feel as though we should be drinking Pimm's not halves of lager.'

The cocktail party was being hosted by a banker from Goldman Sachs and his wife. Hugely wealthy, they were very much the leaders amongst the American banking community in London. Robert had been invited by virtue of the commission he had completed for Simon

Wineburgher's wife, Rebecca – the internal combining of the two Belgravia houses next door to one another, which she had bought with her husband's bonus.

The cocktail party, the purpose of which was officially to celebrate the month of June, was in reality being given so that Rebecca Wineburgher could show off her house, its furnishings and the antique diamond choker, which had supposedly once belonged to the ill-fated last Tsarina of Russia and had been bought at auction by Simon Wineburgher as a gift for his wife.

The stiff cream invitation had specified 'Black tie'. The million-dollar-bonus-earning bankers knew a dinner suit looked better on a man who had eaten rather too many business lunches than casual clothes might have done, and, of course, the formality gave their wives an opportunity to wear the rewards of their husband's success.

Normally Robert would have declined. He found such events brash, but given that he was going to have to raise money to fund the work he wanted to do on Lauranto's classical buildings, he knew that it made sense to cultivate rich people who might be prepared to help him in his endeavours. A charitable trust to raise money and then distribute it for work on Lauranto's crumbling architecture would be his best course of action, Robert had decided after seeking the advice of his future father-in-law and others. The charitable trust would, of course, have to benefit those who benefited it. It was the opportunity, perhaps, to set up and therefore control the banks Robert intended should provide a tax-free haven for the very rich in Lauranto. As Crown Prince he could ease through laws to accommodate that.

Rather than emptying the little that was left in Lauranto's royal coffers, it made sense to let the modernisation of the country pay for itself via the benefits he would offer to those willing to invest in it: the opportunity to become involved in financing the construction boom that would see marinas being built for the yachts of the millionaires who would place their money in Lauranto's new bank accounts, and villas for those who wanted summer homes there. At the same time, the the super rich could feel good that their money would bring the huge improvements to the principality's infrastructure, along with the building of new schools and homes for its people.

But first Robert needed a core of recognised 'money men' publicly ready to invest in him. Then others would follow. Simon Wineburgher was one of those he wanted to target.

Rebecca Wineburgher certainly knew how to spend her husband's money, Robert acknowledged half an hour into the cocktail party.

From the huge displays of cream and white roses and lilies that ornamented every room, through the 'room scent' that Rebecca had told him she had specially blended for the occasion by her own 'personal perfumier', to the Baccarat crystal in which the guests' 'Rose White' champagne cocktail was served, the whole event was pervaded by something far more powerful than Rebecca's 'room scent', and that was the combined smell of power, position and money. It was everywhere, breathed in and then exhaled, and multiplying with each breath rather like compound interest. It was heady and intoxicating, but probably poisonous if you didn't possess at least one part of the potent combination.

His, Robert suspected, was 'position', thanks to the news, now out in the gossip columns, that he was going to be stepping into his late father's shoes.

Robert had already lost count of the number of people who asked him about Lauranto and his 'title'.

'Robert, do let me introduce you to people.' Rebecca was at his elbow, and Robert guessed that it was no coincidence that her gold lamé cocktail frock went so well with the gilded frames of the profusion of mirrors ornamenting the walls of the large drawing room.

The diamond necklace glittered beneath the light from the Bavarian antique chandeliers as she moved. Lithe and tanned – all the American wives seemed to play tennis very competitively in the summer – her perfectly straight white teeth flashed in a photo opportunity perfect smile. 'Did I tell you that I hired the event organisers Lords of the Manor for tonight?'

Robert shook his head. Lords of the Manor, owned and run by an old Etonian, organised most of London's top events.

'I really wanted to have a word with Si,' he told Rebecca.

'Oh, Si.' Rebecca pulled a face. 'He's probably in the library with his cronies. He treats it as an extension of his New York Club. No, there he is.'

Si Wineburgher was standing with his back to them. Tell and burly, with iron-grey hair, he was flanked by several other dinner-suited men.

'Si, darling, do say hello to Robert, and congratulate him on his engagement.'

Robert had received a telephone call from Rebecca already to tell him that she had heard the news, and

Robert had little doubt that she had been angling for an invitation to the wedding. He must have a word with his mother and warn her that he would want to invite several of the big players in the banking world.

'What a pity your fiancée is in New York and couldn't be here.'

Simon Wineburgher turned to greet him, the movement of his body allowing Robert to see through the small phalanx of male bodies to the woman standing behind them and with whom they had obviously been engaged in conversation.

Charlotte Meredith.

His whole body tensed as though a hypodermic needle had been plunged into a vein.

She was wearing a red dress, high-necked, long-sleeved and extremely close fitting – the perfect visual conflict for any heterosexual male gaze fastening on her, Robert thought cynically. The fit of her dress and its colour screamed sexual availability, the high neckline and long sleeves instructed 'don't touch me'.

How clever she was not to have painted her nails or her lips the same sensual red as her dress, Robert acknowledged. Her nails were painted silver instead, her lips merely warmed with an almost natural flush of colour.

He couldn't take his gaze off her, as he heard Rebecca saying formally, 'Robert, may I introduce Charlotte, Lady Meredith, to you? Charlotte meet Robert Lenchester, soon to be Crown Prince Robert of Lauranto.'

Their fingertips touched, her handshake cool and unexpectedly firm. Robert felt as though he was drowning, going down for the third time, fighting for air.

'Hey, Bob,' Si was bellowing in his ear, using the diminutive form of his name that Robert most disliked, 'do we have to address you as "Your Highness" now?' whilst subjecting Robert's hand to a bone-crushing grip – to let him know who really was top dog between them, Robert knew.

'Not yet. I haven't been crowned yet,' Robert answered with a smile, joining in the laughter – at his expense, of course, but he had no intention of allowing Si to bait him for his own entertainment and that of his fellow bankers, especially not with Charlotte Meredith looking on.

'Poor Robert is separated from his fiancée by the Atlantic so we must try to cheer him up. Have you set a date for the wedding yet?'

'September, after Labor Day,' he answered Rebecca, referring to the national holiday that signalled the end of summer to Americans. 'The invitations will be going out around mid-July.' His smile for Rebecca was warm and meaningful, earning him a delighted smile in response that said she now knew she and Simon were on the guest list.

'Your fiancée is American then, is she?' Charlotte's voice was clear and cool, immediately taking her admirers' attention back to her.

'Olivia has dual nationality.'

Listening to the way Robert's voice and expression softened as he spoke his fiancée's name, Charlotte was filled with a surge of emotion she wouldn't let herself name. Sharp and painful, it held her in claws that dug deeper into her the more she tried to struggle free of it.

'Olivia's parents are British,' Robert was saying, 'but

Olivia herself was born in New York. Her father heads up an American charity foundation,' he added for Si Wineburgher's benefit.

'But you'll be getting married here in London?' Rebecca asked.

'Yes,' Robert confirmed. 'My mother would have liked us to marry in the chapel at Osterby, the family country home, but since I believe that that is a privilege that really belongs to my stepsisters and -brother, we've compromised and agreed on Westminster Abbey for the marriage service, with the wedding breakfast at the Savoy, followed by a reception at my parents' London home, Lenchester House.'

'Your mother, of course, is the daughter of the previous Duke of Lenchester, as well as the wife of the current duke.' Charlotte's voice was precise and cold.

'Yes.' Robert deliberately turned his back on her to tell Rebecca, as though in confidence, 'My wife and I will be hosting a reception in Lauranto once we take up residence there, although I should warn you that at the moment visitor accommodation is such that I would recommend renting a yacht, should you wish to attend.'

'A yacht.' Rebecca's eyes sparkled. 'You know, I've been telling Si we should be thinking about buying one. Now we shall have to.'

The waiters were circulating with fresh drinks; Robert reached for one at exactly the same time as Charlotte. Her fingers were slender and white, her hands those of a woman who was pampered and sensual. Even the way her fingers curled round the stem of the glass was deliberately erotic, Robert felt sure, each one closing separately and slowly, so that no man watching her could prevent himself from imagining her long white fingers closing just as purposefully and knowingly around his sex. Even the way she almost absent-mindedly stroked the pad of her thumb against the glass was designed to be sexual. Infuriatingly, Robert found his body was responding to the signals she was sending out. Once again, awareness of her had touched him, jolting through him with the same discomfort as a minor electric shock. But what really mattered was that she was a woman whose mere presence could affect him against his will. A woman who threatened his control over himself and his life. Robert picked up a glass from the tray and moved back from her, deliberately angling his body to relieve what he could of the pressure of his erection.

Determinedly Charlotte turned away from Robert. The effort it had taken her not to immediately release her glass when his flesh had touched her own, but instead to force her fingers to grip it, had shaken her – because of his attitude towards her, because he had deliberately humiliated her, and in public, by turning his back on her, as though she were nothing and no one, as though . . . As though what? She was still a child from the slums?

Charlotte glanced discreetly at her watch – a Cartier Tank, a present from herself to herself. It was just over an hour now since Rebecca had invited her 'closest girl-friends' amongst the guests to an escorted tour of the house, which had ended in the sitting room of what Rebecca called her 'private space': a suite of rooms comprising a bedroom she did not share with her husband, a bathroom, a dressing room, and the sitting room into which a couple of dozen or so of them were now all crammed, most of them exhibiting the after effects of the 'special treat' Rebecca had arranged for them – lines of cocaine spooned out of a silver box with a silver spoon, cut with a Gold American Express card and duly snorted by her guests via brand-new hundred-dollar bills – Rebecca's signature way of taking her cocaine, so she had told them.

Charlotte had managed both not to take part and to conceal the fact that she hadn't. She never touched drugs. You simply didn't when you had seen the reality of the slime of rotting humanity it led to, via a childhood where taking drugs was the final desperate act of women whose lives and bodies had already been wrecked by a succession of previous addictive habits. Taking drugs was the road to the hell that was lack of control over every single aspect of a person's life. She'd learned that from her father, who had laughed about the 'whores' he had got addicted during his younger days as a drug dealer.

Now Charlotte was ready to leave. More than ready. She stood up, smoothing down the skirt of her Alaïa dress, and started to make her way over to where Rebecca was leaning back into her off-white silk velvet-covered sofa, looking totally out of it.

Officially the male guests were supposed to be using the downstairs lavatory, leaving the lavishly appointed marble and gold 'guest bathroom' for the female guests, but the pressure was building on his bladder and the downstairs lavatory door remained locked. So, seeing no one either on the stairs or the landing above it, Robert took the stairs two at a time, pleased to discover that the upstairs lavatory was unoccupied.

It was a warm evening, but Charlotte had brought a fine pashmina to use as a wrap on her way home. She had almost reached the top of the stairs when she paused to remove it from her bag, just as Robert opened the lavatory door. For a second they glared at one another in mutual hostility. Robert was closer to the top of the stairs than she was, but something – the need not to be outdone by him, not to have to cede anything to him, simply not to let him go first – impelled Charlotte to move quickly to the head of the stairs.

Instinctively Robert responded to her challenge; good manners demanded that he allow Charlotte to precede him and he assured himself later that he would have done so, even though he had reached the top of the stairs first, if Charlotte had not deliberately challenged him by stepping forward so that they were standing almost body to body.

Charlotte could feel her heart pumping heavily, the effort to get enough air into her lungs almost punishingly hard. She wasn't going to give in and step back, though. No way. She was every bit as good as Robert. Better, since what she had achieved she had achieved for herself, whilst he had inherited everything that he had and was. She lifted her chin, angry contempt glittering in her eyes. When she breathed in her breasts lifted, straining against the fabric of her dress. Robert could see the outline of her nipples. Anger gripped him. He didn't want this awareness of her sexuality intruding into his thoughts. He had fought it off once, after all; conquered the unwanted ache she had made him feel.

He reached out for the banister, expecting her to step back but she didn't.

For a moment Robert didn't move, and then a fierce, mindless reaction to her contemptuous defiance surged through him, a need to remove her from his path, and from his thoughts. He reached out instead for her, and took hold of her, gripping her arms, their mutual fury crackling on the air between them.

And then it happened. How, Robert had no real idea. He only knew that one minute he was about to release her, the next she was in his arms and he was kissing her, if a savagely furious battle of lips and tongues, in which they both fought to demolish the other, could be called a kiss.

It ended as swiftly as it had begun, both of them breathing heavily as they stood and stared at one another in silence. A flush of colour lay along the tops of Charlotte's cheekbones, her breathing unsteady. Furious with himself, Robert wiped his hand across his mouth and then turned back to the stairs.

Charlotte watched him go, shuddering angrily at the way he slammed the front door behind him.

Outside on the street Robert had to resist the desire to wipe his hand across his mouth a second time. His heart was pounding, his stomach churning with nausea, revulsion for himself and what he had done gripping him like a fever. He had no idea why he had behaved as he had. No idea, no explanation, no excuse. Such behaviour, such emotion, was completely alien to him. He had no rationale, no pathway through his own understanding to tell him why he had done it. His head had started to ache, a dull pounding that mirrored his relentless demand to know what had happened.

Still inside, Charlotte was furious with herself for letting him kiss her and then wipe the taste of her from his mouth with such contempt. Well, he would pay for that. Somehow she would make him pay, she promised herself.

'Zoë!'

The unexpectedness of seeing her friend seated at the kitchen table, brought Katie to a standstill, despite the heavy weight of the books she was carrying.

'You might at least pretend to be pleased to see me, even if you aren't,' Zoë responded.

'Of course I'm pleased to see you,' Katie protested, putting down her bag. 'It's just that I wasn't expecting you back just yet.'

'I couldn't stand having Tom fussing round me any longer. It was more like living with a gaoler than a brother,' Zoë complained.

Her face looked thinner and paler, apart from the dark smudgy shadows beneath her eyes, the fine blue veins in her wrist standing out as she lit the joint she had been making when Katie walked in, her hands shaking as she inhaled deeply, then released the sweet smell into the air.

'What's that look for?' she snapped.

'I wasn't giving you a "look".' Katie protested truthfully.

'Yes you were,' Zoe argued, angry colour mottling her face as she sucked fiercely on her joint. 'For fuck's sake, don't *you* start going all prissy on me, Katie. It's a spiff, that's all.'

When Katie didn't say anything, she continued fiercely, 'It's not as though I'm mainlining heroin or . . . or . . . snorting up lines of crack cocaine, is it, much as both you and my dear brother would love to be able to accuse me of doing so?'

'Zoë, that's not true, and it's not fair either.'

'*Zoë, it's not true,*' Zoë mimicked cruelly exaggerating Katie's voice.

Katie could feel her face starting to burn. She was normally pretty even-tempered but Zoë's unkindness had touched a raw nerve.

'I'm not the one who doesn't tell the truth,' she told Zoë heatedly.

Zoë's lack of an immediate response, coupled with the way she was avoiding looking directly at her, told Katie all she needed to know.

'You lied to Tom about me, Zoë,' Katie pressed home her point.

'I couldn't help it. I didn't want to, but he kept going on and on at me, wanting to know . . . It's your own fault, anyway. If you hadn't overreacted and telephoned him, then he'd never have known anything, would he?'

'Overreacted?' Katie was almost incandescent with incredulity. 'If I hadn't phoned Tom I'd have had to call an ambulance, and you'd have ended up in hospital, so you tell me which option was the right one.'

'All right,' Zoë backed down, 'so I was in a bit of a state.'

'A bit of a state! Zoë, you were totally out of it. You'd been sick, and your . . . you were covered in blood.'

'I fell over on the way home and cut my arms on some broken glass.'

216

'No you didn't, you made those cuts yourself,' Katie insisted.

For a moment she thought that Zoë was going to deny it, but then tears filled her eyes and she admitted, 'Yes, I did.'

'Why? Why would you do something like that to yourself?'

'It makes me feel better.' When Katie looked at her shocked, distressed and utterly uncomprehending, Zoë went on, 'It's like . . . it's like what they used to do in the olden days, to get rid of people's evil humours, you know, blood-letting. I get so wound up, so filled with hatred for myself that I feel I'm going to burst. I want to punish myself for being so worthless, to hurt myself, and then when I do I feel better. It helps me, Katie. It makes me feel that it's something that I have to do to pay the price for what I am.'

'Oh, Zoë . . .' Compassion filled Katie's heart. She had intended to tell Zoë how angry she was about her lying to Tom about her, but now, after listening to her friend revealing her pitiful despair and distress, Katie knew that she couldn't.

'There must be something . . . some kind of help,' she began, but Zoë shook her head violently.

'No! That was what Tom wanted. He wanted me to say that I was mad so that I could be locked away somewhere and questioned by some psychiatrist, but I'm not mad. I just love the wrong person, that's all.'

'But—'

'I won't do it any more, Katie, I promise. I won't need to now that I've told you about it, because I can tell you when I'm feeling bad, can't I?'

Katie didn't know what to say.

'I did it only a couple of times. I mean, it wasn't like I was doing it all the time, you know. It was only after I'd seen a girl in Klosters doing it.'

Was that the truth? Katie hoped so. She certainly hadn't seen any signs of Zoë harming herself before she had met Axel, she acknowledged.

The smell of Zoë's joint was so strong that Katie suspected she'd get high on it herself. Already Zoë was calmer, her tension visibly easing.

'You shouldn't smoke so much of that stuff,' Katie felt obliged to warn her.

'Oh fuck, you've turned into a real boring old fart whilst I've been away. I'll soon change that. Let's do something really wild and exciting during the long vac, Katie; just pack our passports and loads of dosh and go.'

'I can't. I've promised Granny that I'll spend some time in Macclesfield helping her sort out her silk archives.'

Immediately Zoë's mood changed, a scowl replacing her earlier smile.

'Look, Katie, I can understand that you're pissed off with me for letting Tom think it was your fault that I ended up in such a mess, but there's no need to be like this about it, to punish me.'

'It isn't like that at all,' Katie protested. 'I promised Granny over Christmas.'

'And, of course, Miles will no doubt be in Macclesfield. I don't know what you see in him, I really don't.'

'We can't always like the same people.' Katie felt obliged to defend her friendship with Miles, but once again Zoë chose to misinterpret her words.

'If that's a dig at me because of Axel—'

'Of course it isn't.'

Zoë stubbed out her joint and stood up, pushing her chair back, the squeal of the legs against the floor making Katie grit her teeth.

'Did he ring at all whilst I was away?' Zoë asked gruffly, her back to Katie now.

Katie shook her head, then, realising that Zoë couldn't see her denial, she walked round to face her, saying quietly, 'No,' pity for her friend filling her when she saw the look in Zoë's eyes.

'I hate myself for the way I feel about him,' Zoë told her, 'but I can't help it, even though he's been so cruel to me. I don't want to feel like this, Katie, but I can't help that either. I keep trying not to think about him and . . . and not to want him, but then just when I think everything's all right and it won't happen again, it does.'

There was no mistaking the real anguish Zoë was feeling.

'Sometimes I feel that the only way I'll stop loving him is by cutting my heart out. It's like he's put a spell on me, Katie. Don't laugh – that *is* how I feel.'

'I wasn't laughing,' Katie assured her. What Zoë was saying was far too sad for her to laugh about it.

'He makes me want him. He makes me go back to him. I can feel him doing it, willing me to go back, dragging me back, even though I can't see him. People like you can't understand what it's like, loving someone the way I love Axel. It's like . . . like being bitten by a vampire; it changes you for ever, possesses you. You can never be the same again, and there's nothing you can do about it. Axel has made me his and sometimes I think that I'll always be his until the day I die, no matter how hard I try not to be. You'll help me, Katie, won't you?' Zoë begged her. 'You'll hold on to me when he tries to drag me back?'

'Oh, Zoë.' Wrapping her arms around her, Katie held Zoë tight. 'Of course I will.'

'I'm sorry that I let Tom think it was your fault.' Zoë's voice was muffled against Katie's shoulder. 'He was asking too many questions, pushing me, Katie. I had no choice. After all, I could hardly tell him that all I wanted to do after Axel chucked me was to die.'

Katie couldn't control the shock stiffening her body.

'You're shocked,' Zoë guessed. 'I was shocked myself, but like I've already told you, Axel has done something to me, changed me. He said that we were soulmates, and I believed him, no matter how dark both our souls are. In fact, that only made it seem more as though it were meant to be, as though we were both so wicked that we were destined to be together.'

'Zoë, you aren't wicked.'

'Yes I am. Deep down inside, I am, Katie. You have no idea how truly wicked part of me wants to be, or how much it relishes the idea of . . . of the darkest and deepest kind of depravity and . . . and everything that goes with it. Perhaps I'm going mad? Didn't Shakespeare say that being in love is a form of madness?'

Katie didn't know what to say. She felt desperately sorry for her friend, but everything she was saying felt so alien to her own emotional makeup.

'Tom wanted me to go into the Priory. I told him there was no chance and that I'd run away if he tried to take me. If Tom knew that I'd deliberately cut my arms because I hated my life so much without Axel in it, and I hated myself for being so weak and for going crawling to Axel when I knew he didn't want me any more, he would have me dragged there in a strait-jacket. And perhaps that's what I deserve.'

'Oh, Zoë, of course you don't.' Torn between love and despair, Katie hugged Zoë tightly again, whilst Zoë sobbed on her shoulder.

'Help me, please, Katie; you've got to help me.'

'You know I will,' Katie assured her.

'I know I've got to stop wanting him.'

'You will, just give yourself time. Look, there's a crowd of us going to the Commem Ball – why don't you come too?'

'There won't be any tickets left and they're doubles, anyway.'

'That doesn't matter. Miles is on the Committee; I'm sure he'll be able to get you a ticket and find you a partner. Oh, Zoë, say that you'll come. You'll enjoy it.'

Zoë looked so drained and vulnerable.

'OK.' Her voice was listless and unenthusiastic, but her agreement made Katie feel as though she had steered her friend away from the edge of a dangerous chasm. The truth was that the chasm was still there, Katie knew, just as she also knew that from now on it would be her job to keep Zoë safe from its danger.

Chapter Fourteen

It wasn't because of what had happened with Robert that she was feeling like this, Charlotte assured herself, as she rode the escalator down to the ground floor of Harvey Nichols, having stalked the designer room floor, flicking impatient dismissive glances over the clothes on offer, in a bid to vent the anger that was burning dangerously inside her.

She stepped off the escalator and turned towards the stands of designer sunglasses. Removing the Oliver Peoples Chelsea sunglasses, which, with their large round frames, were her signature style, she tried on a pair of turquoise-tinted Chanel's and then removed them. A man, forty-ish, expensively business suited, his dark hair cut short in the style favoured in the main by the higher echelons of the American bankers in London was watching her. Charlotte glowered at him. She did not welcome men trying to pick her up, even in Harvey Nichols – especially in Harvey Nichols, she decided, putting her sunglasses back on and heading for the exit. She'd already turned down an invitation from a girl-friend to have lunch with her at San Lorenzo, but the prospect of returning to her apartment didn't appeal to her. Right now nothing appealed to her other than making Robert pay for the way he had behaved towards her, treating her as though she was nothing, less than nothing, someone he could come on to and then walk away from when he'd had what he wanted, whilst his precious wonderful fiancée was protected from the kind of treatment he meted out to her.

Why had this happened to her? She had had everything that she wanted in her life until he'd come back into it, reminding her of things she did not want to remember, ripping the scabs off old sores to expose a vulnerability she had not known existed. Her six-year-old self had done the same thing, picking the scabs off her knees and realising too late that the pink flesh beneath them hurt. That had been self-inflicted pain but this pain was being inflicted on her now by someone else. Pain? Robert was causing her pain? He wasn't capable of causing her pain. No man was.

She was so engrossed in her angry thoughts that she didn't realise she had exited Harvey Nichols until she was standing outside on Sloane Street.

Kensington and Sloane Street, Knightsbridge, very much the territory of the wealthy and well bred, women like Robert's mother. She had an equal right to be here, Charlotte reminded herself. She now had money, and a title, and she was damn sure she had taught herself enough about what it meant to have 'good breeding' to pass for the genuine article, even here in its heartland. This was her territory now, and no one could take what she had achieved from her, least of all Robert. But he could withhold from her what he was giving so freely to his fiancée – all those things that could be wrapped up in a certain look, a certain softness in the voice, a certain determination, as Robert himself was wrapping up his fiancée in the protective public status their engagement gave her. When had that ever happened to her? When had any man, even the one who had married her, ever wanted to give her that? The men in her life might want her but they did not care enough about her to make their relationship with her public, to be proud of it and of her. A feeling she was unfamiliar with enveloped her, a slow aching sense of aloneness and exclusion.

A young woman walking past her, gripping the hand of a little girl, caught her attention. The child was beautifully dressed in what were obviously expensive clothes. She was chattering away confidently to the woman. That child belonged here; this was her place in society. Charlotte thought again of her six-year-old self. Some vulnerabilities could never ever be totally erased or forgotten. But they could be kept hidden; they must be kept hidden. In the life she now lived the people she knew would fall on her like vultures and destroy her if they knew she was vulnerable.

Her head had started to ache. She might as well walk on to Beauchamp Place. There was a coffee shop there she liked, where she was bound to bump into someone she knew, and right now anything was better than going home to shut herself away with her thoughts.

Rose was upstairs in her studio at the Walton Street shop when Emerald arrived. Going down to greet her, she told the pretty young shop assistant, a Courtauld Institute student who worked for them in her spare time, that she might as well go for her lunch, and that she would 'mind the shop'. Rose knew that Emerald wouldn't want anyone else to overhear their conversation.

The samples for the new silk for Amber's surprise eightieth birthday present had arrived from Angelli's the previous day. Rose had been thrilled with them, as she knew from the note that had accompanied them that Polly was as well, but she wanted Emerald to approve them before she sent them to Janey so that she in turn could arrange for the new designs to go into production at Denby Mill, ready to surprise Amber for her late November birthday.

Rose knew that Emerald was hostile to the whole idea of using *The Silk Merchant's Daughter* as inspiration for their new designs. She also knew that Emerald was unlikely to admit to or discuss that hostility without Rose using a great deal of tact and coaxing, which was why she had telephoned her this morning and asked her to come to the shop.

Why was it that she could never enter the Walton Street shop without believing she could smell her mother's favourite scent on the air, Emerald wondered, as she pretended merely to suffer Rose's warm hug. In reality, the warmth Rose always showed her inspired in Emerald a warm feeling in return that she hoarded and protected like a small perfect priceless jewel. Rose had shown her compassion and care at one of the worst periods of her life, when she had been so badly physically abused by Max Preston that she could have lost her life. That time was their shared secret, something they never discussed, but it had been the key that had turned the lock and opened the door of her life to the happiness she had gone on to find with Drogo. Emerald, though, was happiest dealing with practical matters, not emotional ones.

'Coffee?' Rose offered her. 'We could go up to my studio.'

Emerald shook her head. 'I can't stay long. In fact, I've arranged for Robert to meet me here at one o'clock. When I spoke to Olivia on the phone the other day she mentioned how appalling the palace décor is. Of course, that's only to be expected, given Alessandro's mother's meanness and lack of taste and style. I've told Robert that, as a wedding gift, Drogo and I will pay for the refurbishment of their apartment in the palace using Denby silk.'

Rose made a mental note to check whatever Emerald chose was what Olivia actually wanted. Emerald could be every bit as managing and determined to have her own way as the ex-mother-in-law she was now criticising.

'OK. As you haven't got much time I'll go upstairs and get the samples Polly has sent now.'

Whilst she waited for Rose to return, Emerald paced the shop, occasionally touching the bales of silk, feeling its texture between her thumb and forefinger as she had seen the other female members of her family do all their lives. Emerald did not share what she thought of as their mother's almost emotional relationship with the fabric. Emerald saw Denby Silk as a business venture. When she touched the silk she did not connect with it emotionally herself. She had a mental image of her mother touching it, the look on her face absorbed and almost reverential, and never more so than when she had first shown Emerald the piece of silk she had been given by her painter lover, Emerald's own father. Her mother had wanted her to feel for the fabric what she herself felt, but all Emerald had felt was anger and revulsion. To her the painter wasn't her father, but someone who had deprived her of the aristocratic father she had believed to be hers. The wounds inflicted by her anger then were long healed, but sometimes they still ached. Now she feared that what should be a happy celebration of her mother's eightieth birthday would be marred for her by that old wound aching, and that Amber would sense that and her celebration would be spoiled.

Although Rose knew nothing of Emerald's real father, out of all the female members of her extended family, Rose was the one to whom she now felt the closest.

'Here they are,' Rose announced as she came back downstairs, carrying several folded pieces of silk. 'When I drew up the designs for the patterns, I used several of the classical images Amber's father used, but I've also designed some that I think are quite fun.'

As she spoke Rose unfolded the lengths of silk and placed them on the long cutting tables side by side.

'This one I've overprinted with Greek vases in shadow outline so that the off-white and amber stripes still show through. The design will come in three different colour-ways: this one, off white and amber with pale grey and violet . . .'

'Great-grandmother Blanche's favourite colours,' Emerald acknowledged, unexpectedly touched that Rose should have thought of that particular colourway, knowing how unkind Blanche had been to Rose as a child.

'Then there's this one,' Rose smiled, 'emerald green and almost royal blue teamed with black, and finally, because I liked it myself, this one: off white, light and granite grey, and a touch of black. I've used the same colourways for each of the different designs. They comprise this one, the stripe with the Greek vase; this, where I've used the colours to produce an abstract sort of marbled effect; this one, which is spots and stripes; and this, which is my own personal favourite.'

As Rose unfolded and spread out the final design – silhouetted etched profiles in black on plain cream, pale or slate-grey backgrounds – Emerald frowned.

'These profiles, there's something about them . . .'

Rose laughed. 'Yes, they are ours, all of us: Blanche, Amber, you, Ella, Janey, me, Polly, Cathy and your girls.'

Emerald touched the fabric, and then suddenly, on an impulse she couldn't hold back, she found that she was smoothing the silk in a gesture she had seen her mother use countless times. A sense of peace and of healing warmed her heart like a good brandy warmed the stomach.

'It will cost a fortune to produce this lot, especially this one,' she informed Rose almost sharply, before relenting and telling her emotionally, 'You are a genius, Rose. I love it and I love you. Mummy will be over the moon.'

Then they were hugging one another, both of them close to tears, both laughing.

Walton Street. Charlotte hesitated as she saw the familiar sign and then glanced down the street. She could just about see Walton Street Silk, the interior design business owned by Robert's family, and whose name it was hard to avoid if, as Charlotte did, one studied the elegant room arrangements in magazines such as *Interiors*. Without making the decision to do so she discovered that she was walking towards the shop, pausing to study its elegant window display, and then turning the handle.

The sound of the shop bell pinging had Rose and Emerald releasing one another, Rose turning towards the door to greet the potential customer, whilst Emerald carefully folded up the lengths of silk.

Charlotte tensed. She shouldn't have come in here, but it was too late to step out of the shop now without looking either foolish or rude. The slender dark-haired woman smiling at her quite obviously had Chinese blood. Elegantly dressed in a black trouser suit that Charlotte suspected was Armani, she breathed the kind of quiet self-assurance and serenity that Charlotte herself longed to have.

'I've been thinking about redoing my guest bedroom,' Charlotte told Rose. It needn't, after all, be a lie.

'Have you anything specific in mind?' Rose asked.

The smart designer-clad blonde was very much the kind of client with whom she was familiar, too well-dressed to be blue-blooded and old money, but at the same time a long, long way from the kind of *nouveau riche* person whose idea of good taste was to smother everything in gold. And yet, despite her confident veneer, Rose gained the impression that the stunningly beautiful young woman was ill at ease, and that unexpected vulnerability made Rose warm to her as she calmly tried to tease out of her exactly what kind of décor changes she had in mind.

She should bring this to an end, Charlotte knew. She shouldn't really be here; she didn't feel comfortable being here, which was ridiculous when all she was doing was standing in a shop open to the public.

As Robert headed for Walton Street and his appointment with his mother, he wished that he had not agreed to meet up with her to discuss possible silks for the refurbishment of that part of the royal apartments that would be his and Olivia's marital home. In fact, right now he wished that he didn't have to think about anything whatsoever to do with his marriage to Olivia. Not because he didn't want to marry her. He did. Logically there was no one who would make him a better wife in his role as Lauranto's new Crown Prince. She was the ideal buffer between his mother and his grandmother, a choice of bride that neither of them could object to, and that neither could claim had been chosen by the other. Yes, Olivia was the logical choice for him as Crown Prince. But what about him as a man? What about the needs within him that were not logical; the desires and hungers that belonged to the buried secret places within him, and could not be satisfied by the sensible practical relationship he would have with Olivia?

Robert stopped in mid stride, forced to apologise to the pretty young woman behind him who bumped into him – a very pretty young woman, he acknowledged, an Olivia type of young woman, whose appreciative smile for him did nothing to raise his pulse or activate the gnawing hunger within him that a woman like Charlotte Meredith could arouse simply by his thinking her name.

Charlotte Meredith. What resentful destructive fate had elected to bring her into his life just at the very time when he was most unable to deal with her being there? Had he met her six months ago, by now he would be over the no doubt intense and passionate affair they would have enjoyed. And which he ached and burned still to enjoy, even though he had committed himself when he had decided to marry Olivia to remaining faithful to her? No! He fully intended to adhere to that commitment. His future life was going to be enough of a demanding balancing act, without him bringing into it the added complication of a mistress and an affair. Passionate affairs required dedication, a certain amount of personal freedom, and, for him, the knowledge that when he indulged in one he was not betraying or hurting anyone. It stung his pride that he had already betrayed his own principles in simply wanting Charlotte Meredith, never mind physically giving in to his desire for her. That went against everything he believed about himself, namely that he was a man of honour.

It irked and infuriated him that she had been able to get under his skin, to taunt him with her power to make him want her.

He had reached Walton Street.

Emerald saw Robert first, putting down the folded silk and going towards the door as he pushed it open, telling him, 'Robert, you have to see the wonderful designs Rose has produced for your grandmother's birthday surprise. They will be perfect for your and Olivia's apartment in the palace. Oh, and I want to talk to you about the menu for the wedding breakfast. Ella is being terribly American about everything.'

Charlotte, who was standing behind Rose, who had turned away from her when Robert had entered the shop,

232

froze. There was no way she could escape from the shop without Robert seeing her. Why had she come here? He was bound to think that she had done so because of him. He was that kind of person: self-satisfied and arrogant. If only his mother would take him upstairs and she could get away.

Robert bent to kiss his mother's cheek before turning to greet Rose.

And then he saw her, standing there staring at him with that haughty look she wore as provocatively as another woman might have paraded in front of him in a revealing dress, mocking him, daring him to tear it from her so that she stood before him naked and available.

Their gazes met and locked.

She had to get away. Another minute and he'd see in her eyes what she would die rather than let him see: how much it mattered to her still that she should be an outsider, not good enough to be admitted to the magical circle that enclosed people like Robert and the women they chose as their wives.

'I'm sorry, I've got a lunch appointment. I must go,' Charlotte apologised quickly to Rose, somehow managing to make her way to the door and out into the street, where she was fortunate enough to find a cruising taxi, almost collapsing into its hard leather seat in her blind panic to get away.

'Janey, how lovely to see you.'

Amber's greeting to her stepdaughter was as warm as the hug in which she enveloped her. 'I'll ring for Mrs Leggit to make us some coffee.'

'No.' Janey's voice was unfamiliarly sharp with tension, and as she looked more thoroughly at her Amber thought she could detect signs of recent tears. 'I mean, I'd love to stay, but I need to get back. Is Dad in?'

'No, I'm afraid he isn't. He's gone to Home Farm with one of the men from the Ministry, and I'm not expecting them back until later.'

In view of Janey's obvious tension Amber didn't want to say that she had assumed that John would also be attending the meeting until she'd found out what had upset her stepdaughter.

'He isn't here, but I am, Janey. Can't I help?'

Janey's mouth trembled. She pushed a hand into her hair and shook her head, her distress taking Amber back years to that time when Janey had been a little girl. Then she had come running to her with her little troubles, to be picked up and cuddled and things made better, but of course she wasn't a little girl any longer.

'Janey,' Amber put her hand on Janey's arm, 'come and sit down, and tell me what's wrong. No, don't shake your head. It's obvious that something has upset you and whilst it's only natural that the first person you should think of turning to is Jay, you are my stepdaughter, and I would be very hurt if I thought that you felt you couldn't confide in me. You and Ella and Rose are very dear to me for your own sakes, and for the sake of your father.'

As she talked, Amber was guiding Janey towards the sofa. It grieved her to see how shabby Janey's clothes were and how furrowed with anxiety her forehead. Of all the girls, Janey had the hardest life, Amber always thought, and not just financially. Although she would never have said so to anyone but Jay, Amber did think that John couldn't be an easy husband. It was not so much that he had changed since he and Janey had married as the fact that the less progressive and less outward-going side of his nature was now more evident. The money he had lost just before Jay had had his heart attack had been a huge blow to his self-respect, and Amber tended to believe that it was from that date that he had started to obsess about money and the spending of it on anything other than necessities. Janey was a wonderful wife and mother. Amber didn't think she had ever heard her speak one word of criticism about John, but it was obvious to both her and Jay that life wasn't easy for her. They did what they could, of course, giving John good annual rises in the payment they made him for managing their land alongside his own. Jay always insisted on buying whatever new or replacement farm machinery was needed, tactfully finding some reason why he, and not John should foot the bill. Jay knew very well what it was to be a 'poor relation' from his own childhood and early manhood, but Jay had always had that sweetness about his nature that made him so generous about not resenting the good fortune of others. That was one of the things Amber loved about him. It was always painful when a much-loved child did not as an adult seem to be properly valued and appreciated by his or her spouse, but of course one could never interfere.

'It isn't that I don't want to tell you, it's just that . . . well, John would be furious with me if he knew what I was doing, but I just don't know where to turn. I thought that Dad might be willing to have a word with the Bank on our behalf. I know they won't lend us any more money on our own account. Poor John's been working so hard this year, and when the letter came it was just the last straw. I've never seen him so . . . so defeated. He was even talking about us having to leave Fitton – perhaps let the house and rent somewhere smaller.'

Janey's muddled explanation increased Amber's concern. She knew how much Fitton meant to John – they all did – and privately she'd always thought that the only way John would ever leave Fitton would be when he was carried out in his coffin.

'I'm going to ring for Mrs Leggit. No, Janey, I insist. I need a cup of coffee, even if you don't, and then you can tell me properly about this letter.'

Twenty minutes later they were alone in the sitting room, Janey clutching the mug of coffee she preferred whilst Amber breathed in the delicious smell of a cup of dark espresso. Espresso with one of her favourite amaretto biscuits was her mid-morning treat. Janey, though, had refused the biscuits, her work-worn hands with their unvarnished nails trembling slightly as she held her mug.

'Right, now, tell me exactly what's happened. John got a letter this morning presumably asking for money?'

'Yes,' Janey agreed weakly. 'Well, not so much as actually asking for all of it, just a percentage, and we could always refuse, but with it being a local company and everything . . . You know how important reputation is to John. His pride—'

'Yes, of course,' Amber intervened, gently shepherding Janey back to the main issue. 'And John would like Jay to have a word at the bank with regard to payment of this bill?'

Janey looked horrified. 'No! John mustn't know that I've told you. Oh, how could Cassandra be so mean and do this to him when she knows—'

'Cassandra?'

'Yes. She's only had someone round from that hugely expensive new interior design shop in Alderley Edge and given them instructions to get in kitchen and bathroom designers, to redesign those rooms, as well as placing orders for new furniture and soft furnishings. The estimate she's accepted comes to over forty thousand pounds, and she's obviously told them that John will be paying. Of course, if he cancels everything she's going to tell them that it's because he can't afford to pay the bill, which is true.'

Janey was crying now and Amber wasn't surprised. She was appalled.

'I've never seen John so angry or so upset,' Janey continued.

'Where is he now?' Amber asked. She didn't want to alarm Janey but she couldn't help being concerned that John had evidently not met Jay as arranged, now that she knew what had happened earlier.

'He's gone to see Cassandra. Not that that will achieve anything. She must have known what she was doing and the effect it would have on him. Why is she so . . . so spiteful to poor John when he's done everything he can to meet her demands, even if that's meant us having to go without? Fitton hasn't been decorated since David was born, and as for a new kitchen and bathroom . . .' Janey's voice was bitter now, as well it might be, Amber thought sympathetically.

'We've no option now other than to try to borrow the money to cover what she's ordered or risk the whole of Alderley Edge knowing that we can't afford to pay for it.'

Amber took hold of one of Janey's hands and patted it reassuringly. 'We'll sort something out, don't worry.'

Fresh tears squeezed out from beneath Janey's tightly closed eyelids.

'I hate having to come here like this, like a beggar, always asking for help and for money, especially when . . .'

'When what?' Amber prompted. Janey's despair was rather like the head on a deep-rooted carbuncle, the poison needing to be fully removed before the wound it left could heal.

'When I know that Dad hasn't really got any money of his own and that you are the one who will end up helping us, and you aren't . . . I'm not . . . I don't have any right to your help.'

'You mean that I'm not your mother?'

'Cassandra can't resist pointing out to people that Dad made a good move when he married you, and that Ella and I have both benefited financially from that, especially me. The vicar came to see her the other day and she mentioned it then, and not . . . not in a kind way.'

Amber knew immediately what Janey meant, and she also knew how clever Cassandra had been in her spite-fulness. Normally the first thing Amber would have done would have been to tell Jay what had happened, so that they could discuss it together and decide what to do, but the unpleasant reality was that Jay himself was sensitive about the fact that what she would have preferred to be their shared wealth, was in reality hers. Not that they had ever let that come between them in any kind of way. Amber had insisted on giving Jay outright a large sum of money when they had married – his independence from her, she had called it. Jay had protested that he didn't want or need it, but Amber had stuck to her guns. All the children had had trust funds established for them, but there was no escaping from the fact that the source of the family's wealth was Amber's grandmother Blanche, and Amber's first husband, Robert.

Jay too had his pride, and Amber knew that had Jay been here when Janey had arrived and she had blurted out Cassandra's spitefulness to him, he would have refused to allow Amber to be the one to help his daughter.

Cassandra had manipulated them all so cleverly, first by using John's pride against him, knowing he wouldn't want to risk the humiliation of not being able to settle her bills, and secondly by making it impossible for Janey to turn to them by publicly underlining the fact that it was Amber who had the money.

'Why does she keep doing things like this to us?' Janey asked helplessly.

'Bitterness and resentment.' The words were out before Amber could stop them and now Janey was looking at her uncertainly.

'But why should she feel like that? John's been a wonderful stepson to her. She was close friends with his mother, and with mine.'

She had not been their close friend; she had been

their lover and their tormentor, implicated in both their deaths, if not physically then certainly mentally and emotionally, although of course Amber could not say that. Some secrets were best left unrevealed. But Janey was looking at her and waiting for an answer, so Amber said as convincingly as she could, 'I rather think that Cassandra regrets the fact that she did not have children – a son – of her own, with John's father.'

Janey's forehead crinkled. 'But even if she had, he could not have inherited, if that's what you mean. John would have been the eldest.'

John's father would have been bullied into calling John's paternity into account and disinheriting him in favour of Cassandra's own son, was more like it, Amber suspected, but she could hardly say so.

Still frowning, Janey added, 'John's always wanted to treat her properly as his stepmother, but she's never shown him or the boys the least little bit of affection.'

'I rather suspect that Cassandra isn't actually capable of feeling affection, and that it's that lack within her that makes her such an unhappy and therefore unkind person,' Amber answered her.

No, Cassandra couldn't feel affection. Intense, driving, demanding, dangerous passion, yes, but the gentle life-enhancing warmth of true, deep affection, no.

'I must get back. John will be wondering where I am. He'll be furious with me if he knows I've come here telling you our problems.'

'That's what parents are for, Janey. Just because you are grown up with children of your own that doesn't mean that to your father and I you are no longer our child. You were the prettiest, happiest baby. I can remember how proud Jay was of both you and Ella. I used to call and see your mother when she and Jay lived in the Gate House, just for the pleasure of cuddling you both. To me, you and Ella are my daughters just as much as Emerald, Polly and Cathy, and as Rose is loved by me just as much as all of you. To me, you are all my children.

'Now, tell me, what would you do if one of your boys had come to you with the tale you have just brought to me?'

The immediate indignation and maternal protective-ness Amber could see sparkling in Janey's eyes made her smile and say gently, 'Exactly. You go home to John, but before you leave I want you to promise me that you won't worry about this unfortunate matter any more.'

'What are you going to do?' Janey was both relieved and slightly alarmed. Amber always seemed so gentle, so sheltered by Janey's father from the harsh realities of life that Janey felt guilty for having confided in her, sure that her father would wish that she hadn't.

'Nothing that you need to worry about.'

Since Amber was standing up Janey felt obliged to do the same.

'What about John?' Janey felt rather like a child again, trusting in an adult to make things right.

'Everything will be all right,' Amber assured her.

It was already nearly midday and she was anxious for Janey to leave so that she could do everything she needed to before Jay came home.

The two women hugged and Amber walked out onto the gravelled forecourt to the house with Janey, to wave her off.

Chapter Fifteen

Fury versus longing, guilt versus need, the chance to prove himself a better crown prince than the father who had rejected him versus the chance simply to be himself. All those emotions and more were raging inside Robert when he left Walton Street. But he was determined that there could be only one outcome. He had invested too much of himself in too many different ways in becoming Lauranto's Crown Prince to risk that investment now. He had a duty not just to himself but to Olivia, to his paternal grandmother, to Lauranto and to his own pride. He could not and would not become Crown Prince as a man in thrall to a woman who was next to being an adventuress, no matter how discreetly she concealed that fact. He needed Olivia as his wife in order for him to be the kind of man he needed to be to attract the financing he had to if he were to make a success of Lauranto. He needed her because, whilst he liked her, she did not and could not get under his skin in a way that meant he could be in danger of putting his desire for her before his desire to prove himself. Some may have thought his reasoning cold-blooded and selfish, but they had not been rejected by their father and deprived of their right to their inheritance. If he was to succeed he needed to save all his energy and his willpower for the task ahead in Lauranto. What he did not need was Charlotte Meredith in his life. What the devil had she been doing at the Walton Street shop? He didn't trust her – he didn't trust her one little bit – and he intended to let her know that right now.

Oh, dear God, what was happening to her? She felt unclean, as dirty as she had done as a child loathing the sensation of dirt on her skin, knowing the other children looked down on her because of it. This time, though, the dirt was mental rather than actual. What on earth had she thought she was doing going into that shop? Was she really so pathetic that she needed almost to stalk Robert? She felt sick with fear. Then came the sound of someone banging loudly on her front door, increasing the pounding inside her head as she went to answer it.

Expecting to see a disgruntled delivery man, she was shocked out of her customary control at the sight of Robert. She simply stood there, holding the door open, allowing him to thrust his way into the hall, bringing with him the power of his raw anger.

'What's going on?' he demanded as soon as he had slammed the door closed. 'What the hell were you doing at Walton Street?'

The fact that he needed to ask and that he hadn't guessed what was happening to her, and how ridiculously and dangerously emotionally involved with him she had allowed herself to become, gave her the chance to gather up her defences and to attack him in return, taking cover behind a mask of cool mockery.

'Perhaps I wanted to ask your mother if she was sure it was wise to press ahead with wedding plans when the groom was already breaking his vows of fidelity before they had even been made.'

Her taunt confirmed Robert's worst fears.

'Damn you,' he swore. 'Damn you to hell and back.'

'You are the one who is damned, Robert, and you've damned yourself,' Charlotte told him coldly. 'You came on to me, not the other way around.'

'That meant nothing.'

His words were like a torch applied to dry tinder, setting fire to her pride.

'No? I'm sure your fiancée wouldn't think that. Face it, Robert, the reason you are here, the reason you can't keep away from me, is that you want me. You want me more than you want your well-bred, acceptable bride-to-be. You want me gut deep, and so badly that the heat of that wanting scalds and burns you, so much that you'll never be able to rid yourself of that wanting.'

Every word she said felt like a whip cutting into Robert's self-respect.

'No,' he denied, reaching for her, gripping her forearms and shaking her in his fury.

Charlotte leaned back and laughed mockingly up at him.

'Yes,' she told him. 'Every time you bed her you'll think about me. You'll ache for me and want me. Can you live with that, Robert?'

'Olivia is everything I want in a wife.' It was true. It had to be true. He was a man of honour.

'In a wife, maybe,' Charlotte continued to taunt him,

'but not in a woman. In a woman, a lover, you want me not her.'

'No!' Robert cried out, his voice full of anguish as he pulled Charlotte to him, and kissed her with all the pent-up emotions that were tearing him apart.

The light from the chandelier danced and twinkled in the mirrors either side of the hallway, positioned just as the mirrors in Olivia's much smaller hallway were.

Olivia. He tried to cling to her name and what she was to him like a drowning man clinging to a frail branch. He couldn't even conjure up her image, never mind the sound of her voice, or the touch of her hand. All were sent to oblivion by the power that Charlotte had over his senses. Like a man caught in a dream over which he had no control, powerless to resist what was happening to him, Robert kissed Charlotte's mouth and then her throat, tugging down the zip of her dress as he did so, driven by a need to satiate his senses' hunger for her. He wanted to smell the scent of her skin, to stroke it and taste it, to lick delicately at its firmness and to bite tenderly into its soft sweetness with a lover's hunger.

Charlotte allowed her unzipped dress to slip to the floor and pool at her feet before stepping out of it. She was wearing a delicate silk La Perla chemise with matching French knickers as her only underwear, silk holdups covering her legs. She felt the shudder that ran through Robert when he stepped back to look at her. Charlotte knew she had a stunningly sensual body, narrow-waisted, with a neat curve to her hips and firm breasts with large dark nipples, which right now were visible beneath the fine silk.

Robert felt the surge of his desire break over him. He couldn't help himself. This was what he had been born for; she was what he had been born for. One of the straps of her chemise had slipped free of her shoulder, so that the ring of dark flesh of her aureole was revealed. Like a man giving himself up to a dark force, Robert reached out and slowly pulled the chemise lower until her nipple was revealed in its entirety, whilst Charlotte stood in silence and watched him.

Charlotte heard the sound of despair and submission grating in Robert's throat as he bent his head to her breast, to draw her nipple into his mouth, his hand sliding into the open leg of her French knickers to caress her sex.

Now it was her turn to moan her protest at this invasion of her self-will by a force determined to destroy it. Her chemise and knickers joined her dress on the floor as Robert kissed and licked his way down her body.

In the mirror Robert could see their reflections, he on his knees in front of Charlotte, his hands clasping her naked body. A shudder tore at him, a memory, a knowledge and a shame that only he knew, but which had no power to halt what was happening now. Here, with Charlotte, he could feel and enjoy what he could not with Olivia. His tongue searched for and found the cleft of her sex and stroked it apart to allow him entrance. She was wet and soft, her flesh alive and pulsing with her arousal.

Charlotte too looked into the mirror. There was something almost pagan and very definitely erotic about their conjoined image, Robert's tongue might be probing her, and possessing her, but he was on his knees to her, whilst she stood over him, both of them in thrall to something that neither could control.

Charlotte arched her back to thrust her pelvis closer to his mouth so that she could move her sex against the stroke of his hard tongue. In the mirror they were dark and light, man and woman, need and the satisfaction of that need, raw and elemental, and surely destined to come to this point together. Her orgasm was close; she reached for Robert, urging him to his feet. Without any need for words he understood her. There wasn't time for him to undress, merely to unzip and thrust deeply and fully into her, her own muscles taking him as the fierce contractions of her orgasm brought him to his.

As soon as she was sure Janey had gone, Amber hurried inside at a rather brisker pace than usual, going in search of Mrs Leggit.

'I need to go into Alderley Edge; do you think Mr Leggit will be able to drive me? I know it's his day for tidying out the greenhouse.'

Amber wasn't just liked and respected by her employees, she was almost adored and worshipped. As Mrs Leggit quickly assured her, Mr Leggit would be ready to drive her the minute she was ready to be driven.

Upstairs in the bedroom she and Jay had shared since the night they had declared their love for one another, Amber's hands trembled a little as she hurried to change her clothes. The new Chanel might be rather over-dressed for Alderley Edge, but she wanted to make the right kind of impression. She wanted to look like a woman used to having her own way, she wanted to look very well-to-do, and rather imperious. She wanted, in effect, she admitted ruefully, to be like her grand-mother Blanche.

If Mr and Mrs Leggit thought it odd that their employer should want to be driven into Alderley Edge without warning, dressed in Chanel and wearing her grandmother's pearls, they were far too discreet to say so.

'I shouldn't be very long,' Amber told Mr Leggit once he had parked the Bentley in the car park next to the town's small supermarket.

Alderley Edge's shops lined both sides of the A34, the main road that passed through it. These shops were a mix of the old-established, which included a grocer's, a chemist's, and the post office, generally frequented by elderly ladies wearing good tweeds and carrying wicker shopping baskets, interspersed with modern 'designer boutiques' and the like, favoured in the main by the influx of rich men's wives from Alderley Edge itself and the neighbouring village of Prestbury – home to several top football players. The recently opened Interior Design Shop patronised by Cassandra fell into this latter category. The frame of its large window, divided into small panes, and its door were painted in a flat chic dark grey, the name of the shop written in gold italic script. Underneath, in smaller letters, was written 'Proprietor – Ruth Pepper'. It sat neatly in a row with a small boutique, a bank and Alderley Edge's famous No. 15 Wine Bar, and the notice in one corner of the window stated that it offered a 'bespoke service covering every aspect of interior renovation and design'. Amber had read in *Cheshire Life* that its target clientele were the rich wives who wanted perfect homes but who did not have the time or the inclination to set about achieving the requisite 'fashionable' look themselves.

The doorbell gave a pleasant ping when Amber opened it. A red-headed woman was standing behind the hand-painted and distressed desk, speaking into the telephone. Her quick, 'Look, I must go. I've got a customer,' accompanied a smile in Amber's direction as she ended her call.

'Ms Pepper?' Amber asked.

'Yes,' the other woman confirmed, inviting Amber welcomingly, 'Please do sit down. People always think they aren't allowed to sit on the chairs, but that's what they're there for.'

'They're very pretty,' Amber told her, returning her smile as she added truthfully, 'I do love to see our silk being used.'

Ruth Pepper's sherry-coloured eyes widened as she looked from Amber to the chair and then back again.

'You're connected with Denby Silk?' she guessed. 'How wonderful. I do love to use local fabrics when and where I can and I particularly love the combination of colour-ways on this stripe.'

'My father designed it,' Amber informed her, sitting down. It was just as well that Jay wasn't here. He would have been astonished to see her behaving in such a boastful and uncharacteristic way. 'My first husband and I used it in one of the state rooms when he inherited Osterby from his grandfather.' Amber paused to let the information sink in before continuing, 'And I'm afraid that I'm not exactly a customer.'

'Oh, well, that doesn't matter at all, er, Your Grace . . .'

Ruth Pepper was on the ball, Amber acknowledged, and obviously had enough local knowledge to place her correctly, and to know enough about her to use her title. Not that Amber herself ever used it. In the eyes of the world she might technically be able to call herself the Dowager Duchess of Lenchester, but she much preferred to be known simply as Mrs Fulshawe, the wife of the man she loved.

'No. Actually it's about my cousin by marriage Cassandra that I'm here.' Amber lowered her voice. 'Such a very sad situation and so unfortunate. I dare say it wouldn't have happened if her regular . . . companion hadn't been away on holiday.'

Ruth Pepper's expression was attentive but guarded now. 'I'm sorry?'

Amber congratulated herself that so far everything was going according to plan.

'This is all so very difficult. I must ask for your discretion. One hesitates to discuss a family member, especially when . . .'

'Of course. You may rely on me.'

'Well, the fact is that poor Cassandra isn't, what shall I say . . . quite *normal* mentally, if you know what I mean. These things happen when one grows old. My son-in-law Lord Fitton Legh does what he can, but it isn't easy. I know some people might think that it would be sensible to find somewhere for her to live where she'd be . . . well, that would suit her condition rather more than the Dower House, but she's so attached to it and to Fitton, and John is such a kind stepson that he won't hear of her being moved, despite the problems that tend to arise. What makes it all so much more difficult, of course, is that she can appear completely normal for weeks at a time, but then she has a relapse. We found her wandering on the main road once . . .'

'I'm so sorry.'

'Yes. Thank you, my dear. One hesitates to mention family difficulties outside the family, as I have said, but in this instance . . . John would have come to see you himself but he feels it so. Cassandra was his own mother's best friend, you know.'

'Yes.'

Was that a note of desperation entering the other woman's voice? Amber certainly hoped so. She didn't know how much longer she could go on creating the fiction that Cassandra was losing her marbles without getting something wrong.

'We're all so sorry that she's got you involved, giving you a commission that it's just impossible . . . Well, she has her pension, of course, but . . .'

'She assured me that her stepson, Lord Fitton Legh, was going to pay.' There was a definite note of anxiety in Ruth Pepper's voice now. 'I've already passed on the order to the kitchen supplier and—'

'Oh, please.' Amber was immediately contrite. 'Of course the last thing the family would wish is for you to be out of pocket. Naturally, we shall pay your bill. I shall do that today. No, my dear, I'm not here about the money,' Amber stressed, watching relief relax the other woman's face. 'No. The thing is . . . oh dear, this is such a delicate matter. Well, as I've already explained, Cassandra is not herself any more. She thinks that she is perfectly normal, and we tend to go along with that rather than upset her. Of course, with her condition it would be impossible for any kind of work to take place in the Dower House. Having strangers around always makes her worse. I have to confess that she can get quite violent. The thing is that I'm afraid that she will telephone you and demand to know when the work will commence and that sort of thing. She may even try to get away from her nurse to come in and see you.'

Ruth Pepper gave a small shudder, no doubt thinking of the havoc that an elderly madwoman could create in her elegant shop, and, even worse, the effect it could have on would-be customers.

'We would be eternally grateful to you if you would simply ignore her, if she should telephone or come in, and of course I do ask that you keep our conversation just between the two of us. People do know, of course – these things are impossible to hide completely – but I think you will be able to imagine how much it distresses my husband and my son-in-law to hear people gossiping about poor Cassandra. She's my husband's cousin, after all.'

'Yes, of course. You can rely on me.'

Ruth Pepper was beginning to look distinctly unsettled.

Amber gave her a beaming smile and then reached down for the Hermès bag Emerald had given her for her sixtieth birthday. Personally Amber thought it far too showy; she had never felt comfortable carrying a bag made from the skin of a wild creature even if that creature was a crocodile.

'I knew we could rely on you.' She opened her handbag and removed her cheque book – not the one from their local bank but the one from Coutts, where her grandmother had opened an account for her, and then uncapped her gold fountain pen. 'Now,' she said briskly, 'your bill was, I think, in the region of £40,000?'

'It's £41,125.18,' the redhead informed her faintly.

'Excellent,' Amber told her. 'Then I shall make out the cheque for £45,000 and we shall say no more about the whole business.' She wrote the cheque, signed it and handed it over, standing up to say with another smile, 'There, I knew I could rely on you, my dear. I sensed it the moment I saw our lovely fabric on this chair. One always knows.'

She certainly hoped that 'one' did, Amber thought wryly as she left the shop to cross the road and then make her way back to Mr Leggit and the car. Because what she was hoping was that Ms Pepper would totally ignore her request and lose no time at all in telling her closest friends about Cassandra's incipient dementia. 'Home?' Mr Leggit, a man of few words, asked her, as he opened the rear passenger door of the car for her.

'Yes, please.' Amber told him. Then, as he started the car: 'No, actually I think I might as well pay a call at the Dower House whilst I'm out. Janey did say this morning that Cassandra hasn't been too well. Yes, the Dower House, please, Mr Leggit.'

'Well, at least we've managed to sort out your dress for the ball,' Katie reminded Zoë as she tried to jolly the other girl out of the withdrawn and angry mood that Zoë had woken up with, and that had grown worse as the day had grown longer.

Immediately Zoë rounded on her, demanding wildly, 'For fuck's sake, will you stop talking about this shitty ball as though it's something I want to go to?'

Katie felt her heart sink. 'You said you did want to go,' she reminded her.

'That was before I knew I was going to have to dress up in some God-awful dress and be partnered by an even more God-awful rower with a brain the size of a pea and a prick to match,' Zoë responded.

Katie sighed, thankful they were at home and not in the pub, where Miles and the others could overhear Zoë's angry outburst, knowing as she did that nothing could stop Zoë from saying what she thought once she was in this kind of mood, certainly not any convention of 'good manners'.

'Ian's nice really,' she protested.

'He's a boring dullard.' Zoë jumped up from the chair on which she had been crouching and started pacing the kitchen floor before turning to face Katie and announcing, 'God, I need a smoke. I feel like I'm frigging dying, living the way I am at the moment.'

Katie's heart sank. This wasn't the first time Zoë had turned on her, or exhibited this kind of behaviour. Katie would have been tempted to get in touch with Tom again, for Zoë's sake, despite everything, if Zoë hadn't told her that he was working in New York.

Now, just as quickly as Zoë's anger had flared up, it died down again, and she flung her arms round Katie.

'I'm such a bitch. I'm sorry, but I can't help it. It's Axel. I know I've got to forget him, but it's so hard.'

Katie's heart ached for her.

'I don't know how you put up with me. I do want to

go to the ball really,' Zoë admitted, pleading, 'Say you forgive me?'

Katie nodded. What else could she do?

'Amber.'

Cassandra's too-light-blue-eyed gaze slid away from Amber's, her mouth pursing unwelcomingly.

'I was on my way home and I thought I'd call in and see you,' Amber smiled and waited.

'Well, I suppose you'd better come in then,' Cassandra offered ungraciously, 'but I warn you, you'll be freezing cold. *I* certainly haven't got the money to keep this place heated, and there's no Mrs Leggit here to wait on *me* hand and foot. It's no way to treat a woman of my age, to have to live denied the comforts that should be mine by other people's selfishness. You have no idea what I have to put up with, living here.'

'Well, you know you're always welcome to come and live with us at Denham,' Amber told her cheerfully, stepping determinedly forward so that Cassandra was forced to step back and allow her inside.

'Give up the Dower House?' Cassandra gave her a bitter look. 'Oh, yes, that would suit everyone, wouldn't it? Well, if you've come here to try to force me out of my home—'

'You were the one who told me that you aren't comfortable here,' Amber pointed out reasonably as she followed Cassandra into the drawing room, which seemed to Amber to be perfectly adequately heated.

Predictably Cassandra did not offer her any refreshment, but then she was glad that she hadn't, Amber admitted to herself, in view of what she was about to say.

It was hardly good manners to accept someone's hospitality and then say to her what Amber had to say.

'Janey came to see me this morning,' she announced without preamble.

Cassandra didn't say anything but the pale gaze flickered and the small smile replacing the earlier pursed lips had a definite twist of triumph about it.

'She and John are both very upset about the way you've gone behind their backs and commissioned someone to carry out some very expensive work to the Dower House.'

The triumphant smile deepened. 'My late husband made it clear in his will that my standard of living was not to suffer after his death.'

'Cassandra, it is less than five years since you last refurbished the Dower House, and you know John and Janey's financial situation. Heaven's, Janey has to cook for a family in a kitchen that hasn't been modernised since John's mother's day. John simply can't afford the work you commissioned and you know it.'

'That is their problem, not mine.'

'Actually, no, it isn't their problem, not any more,' Amber announced. 'You see, I've just been to Alderley Edge to see Ms Pepper, who you commissioned to take charge of the work. I explained to her that sadly you suffer from a mental condition that leads to you behaving in, shall we say, a rather irrational manner.'

Cassandra's hissed intake of breath, combined with the mottled blotches of angry colour on her face, exposed her reaction. Amber didn't take any pleasure in knowing she had outmanoeuvred Jay's cousin, leaving her marooned on the moral equivalent of a very small piece of stable land in the middle of a quagmire. It was simply something she had had to do, no matter how unappealing or unpleasant, to protect those who were vulnerable and undeserving of the misery Cassandra wanted them to suffer.

'I have asked Ms Pepper for her word that she will not breathe anything of your unfortunate mental condition to anyone,' Amber continued. 'She was most charming and understanding, and of course, the work you commissioned has now been cancelled.'

'You're making this up,' Cassandra accused Amber. 'You wouldn't dare do something like that. You don't fool me, Amber. I know you, remember. You always were a scared rabbit of a person. You couldn't even stand up to your own grandmother, never mind a stranger.'

'My grandmother has been dead for nearly forty-five years, and you'd be surprised just how hard and effectively rabbits can kick when they need to, Cassandra. You've hurt John enough.'

'Oh, so you're doing this for John, are you? Well, I might have guessed, mightn't I, seeing who his father was?'

'That's the desperately sad thing about elderly people when their mental powers fail and they become confused: they can't see for themselves that they are becoming mentally senile, even though those around them can. They say things that simply don't make sense,' Amber sighed, as though sympathising with Cassandra's supposed lack of mental stability. 'Everyone knows that John's father was your late husband, Cassandra,' she pointed out with a gentle smile. 'You know, Cassandra, the more I listen to you the more I wonder if it *is* actually safe for you to be living here on your own. I think I should have a word with Dr Phillips.'

'There's nothing wrong with me. You're the one who's crazy, telling people lies about me, trying to make out that I'm losing my mind.'

Cassandra was blustering, panicking, Amber could tell. She could see it in her eyes and hear it in her voice. She really ought to feel ashamed of herself, Amber knew. What she was doing was manipulative and even cruel. But Cassandra herself had been cruel, especially to poor John, bullying him and making his life a misery. It was a matter of fighting fire with fire.

'Well, you are perfectly free to say so if you wish, Cassandra,' Amber agreed in the kind of tone one used to humour a fractious child.

'And as for John and his real father—' Cassandra began heatedly.

Immediately Amber stopped her, pointing out, 'Cassandra, I am really surprised that you are willing to risk bringing up such a subject, in view of what it might ultimately bring to light.'

'What on earth are you talking about?'

'I'm talking about the role you played in John's mother's life,' Amber paused and then said very deliberately, 'and in her death.'

Cassandra's face lost its colour. 'That was nothing to do with me. She took her own life because of the shame she had brought on herself.'

'Did she?' Amber challenged her. 'Well, that is between you and your conscience, Cassandra, but if I were you I wouldn't start casting aspersions on John's legitimacy, in case rather more than you bargained for is *exhumed* for the sake of establishing the truth. Now,' Amber announced in a brisk tone, standing up, 'I'm going to go up to Fitton and tell Janey and John how guilty you feel about allowing Ms Pepper to persuade you into agreeing to have all that work done. That's the trouble when we get older, isn't it, Cassandra? Our brains don't work as quickly as they once did, and we end up getting confused. Such an appropriate name for her, don't you think, in view of the colour of her hair? I dare say she has a peppery temper too when people annoy her.'

The warning was firm and pointed. Cassandra need not think she would get any benefit from getting in touch with Ruth Pepper.

For a long time after Amber had left, Cassandra didn't move. She had always disliked and resented Amber. Born without her own advantages of breeding and aristocratic connections Amber had nevertheless had something that Cassandra, with her plain features and bony body, had ached for – her beauty. With such beauty how different her own life could have been. She could have won and held on to the love of John's mother, Caroline Fitton Legh, her first and only real love. But Caroline had made a fool of her, pretending that she loved her when all the time she had been allowing – no, not just allowing, but inviting – that worthless fool Greg Pickford into her life and her bed. The others who had come after her, including Jay's first wife, had never meant anything like as much to her. How could they have done? Cassandra truly believed that she had been destined to love only once.

She got up and started to pace the room, her gait

awkward, her movements fast, as though she were desperate to escape from something.

Caroline had even loved the brat Cassandra was sure that Greg Pickford had fathered on her, but which she had pretended was her husband's, more than she had done her. Well, she had made sure that he paid for that and she intended to make sure he would go on paying.

Someone had to pay for all that she had suffered, and that someone, she had decided, must be Caroline's son, John. And he *would* pay, she was determined on that. Amber might have saved him this time, but there would be other times, and she would be ready and waiting to make use of them.

Poor Mr Leggit, Amber thought a little guiltily as the Bentley came to a halt outside Fitton Hall. He must be parched and longing for a cup of tea and a slice of Mrs Leggit's homemade cake.

She could still remember the awe and wonder she had felt the first time she had visited Fitton Hall properly with her cousin Greg. She had loved its black and white exterior, and its beamed great hall, hung with the fabrics especially designed for it by her own father. Then she had been so naïve that she had been oblivious to the intimacy between John's mother and Greg. Oblivious to it and bewildered by Cassandra's furious jealousy of her cousin.

'How's John?' Amber asked Janey after her step-daughter had let her in, via the back door, which the family tended to use as it was closest to the kitchen, where Janey could most often be found.

Janey gave her a wan attempt at a smile. 'He's in the

estate office, writing to a couple of the local estate agents about finding a tenant for Fitton.'

Amber could hear the despair in her stepdaughter's voice, but she didn't say anything other than a calm, 'I'm glad he's in because there's something I've got to say and I want him to hear it.'

Fitton's kitchen was cavernous and dark. As Amber had pointed out to Cassandra, it hadn't been touched since John's mother had come to Fitton as a bride in the years between the wars. Heavy wooden cupboards and shelves lined the rear wall, and whilst a stone sink might have come back into fashion, it had not come back in the stained and chipped manner of Fitton's kitchen sink. At least she had the good fortune to have an Aga, Janey always said, and the solid scrubbed oak table was better than any plastic-topped unit.

'John isn't in the best of moods, I'm afraid,' Janey felt obliged to apologise in advance to Amber. 'He always hates being disturbed when he's doing any kind of paperwork, and of course the thought of having to leave Fitton is just so upsetting for him. He feels he's letting his father down.'

Amber patted Janey's arm. 'He will feel much happier once we have disturbed him and I've said what I need to say,' she assured her.

Fitton's estate office, like Denham's, was situated at the back of the house, and, also like Denham's, it smelled faintly of leather and damp Barbours, the June sunlight penetrating the dimness through the single small window, its beam gleaming on the metal hinges of the gun cupboard.

John was seated at his desk, writing furiously, sheets

of paper spread all around him, some of which had fallen on the floor. Uncharacteristically he made no attempt to acknowledge her or stand up, which showed the effect the whole situation had had on him, Amber acknowledged, because normally John was scrupulously polite.

Janey's too bright, 'Do say hello to Amber, John,' deflected his attention from the papers, causing him to look up not so much at her as through her, Amber recognised. Poor John. He had so much on his mind, and that was visible in the tension drawing his skin tightly across his checkbones.

'Actually I'm here on behalf of Cassandra,' Amber told them both, beginning the speech she had hurriedly prepared in the car.

'Cassandra?' John half started up from his chair, almost in panic, Amber thought compassionately. Poor man, and poor Janey too. Amber knew she was so lucky in Jay. He was such a wise, gentle and yet very strong person, his shoulders broad enough to carry whatever burdens life handed him. John, though, Amber suspected, whilst having been brought up in the same tradition, had a rigidity about his nature that made it difficult for him to cope with anything that was 'outside' his very narrow 'beliefs'. The sad truth was that John had been educated to take his father's place but never taught by example how to adapt to changing times, never allowed to develop the confidence to break with tradition when necessary.

'Cassandra telephoned me this morning in a bit of a state,' Amber continued. 'She's done the silliest thing, and she's feeling dreadfully guilty, but she's too embarrassed to come and apologise to you herself, so I'm here as her emissary.'

Amber paused to make sure she had John's full attention. It was so important that she struck exactly the right note now and did not say or imply anything that would alert him to the fact that she had intervened to protect him and Janey. His old-fashioned pride would not be able to tolerate that. No, instead she must make it seem as if this were a matter of silly, vulnerable, light-minded females, rather like fictitious Victorian heroines, getting themselves into a 'muddle' and then throwing themselves on the mercy of strong men. Right now, Amber guessed, John needed to believe that.

'It seems that some woman from Alderley Edge more or less browbeat her into agreeing to have some totally unnecessary work done on the Dower House, by getting her so flustered that she simply didn't know what she was doing. Of course, she knows she should have asked you for help, John, the minute this woman started pestering her, but you know Cassandra: she's her own worst enemy about asking for help. Now, of course, she's being hounded by this woman for money and it appears that she's even threatened to get in touch with you, John.'

'Oh, yes . . . we had an invoice for it this morning, didn't we, John?' Janey joined in Amber's charade. 'John was rather annoyed about it, weren't you, darling?'

Janey was looking strained, her voice reflecting her tension, and no wonder, Amber thought sympathetically.

'Well, I'm not surprised. Cassandra and I both went to see this woman at her shop, and it's been agreed that the whole thing will be forgotten. Cassandra has had to pay the woman some compensation, of course, but as Cassandra said herself, she felt she had a moral obligation to do so. The last thing she wanted was for John to feel that he should pay after all he's done for her already. Of course, Cassandra should really have come and apologised to John herself, but she just feels too ashamed to face him. I've promised her that nothing will be said about it, John. I hope you don't mind, but she was getting herself in such a state at the thought of you being cross with her.'

'As John has every right to be,' Janey put in loyally.

'Well, yes, of course, but what do you say, John? Are you willing to let the matter drop and accept Cassandra's apology via me?'

'Yes . . . yes, of course.' John's voice was unsteady. His face flushed. Poor man, Amber thought, and yet at the same time she couldn't help wishing that Janey had a different husband, someone stronger and less rigid in his ability to deal with difficult situations. Her own marriage to Jay was so filled with love and a genuine admiration for one another that it hurt her to think of any of 'her children' not having that wonderful blessing within their own relationships.

'Cassandra should have told you before, she knows that,' Amber repeated. 'I think she's learned her lesson, though. Now I must go. You are so generous and kind, John. Cassandra really is lucky to have such a good stepson.'

John was standing up now, so that Amber was able to kiss his cheek before turning to give Janey a swift hug.

'I'll see you out,' Janey offered.

As soon as they were out of earshot Amber told Janey quietly, 'Everything's all right now, and you are not to worry any more.'

'I don't know how on earth you managed to persuade Cassandra to do what she did,' Janey whispered emotionally. 'Thank you so much.'

'There's no need to thank me, Janey, and no need to say anything to your father either.'

They exchanged mutually understanding looks.

For a long time after Amber had gone Janey simply sat at her kitchen table trying to compose herself before she went in to John. The tension, the strain had been so bad that it was almost as though her brain could not accept that there was no need for it any longer. If she felt like that, then how must John be feeling? How must the relief be affecting him? Janey couldn't ask herself why she felt so reluctant to be with John, and she definitely couldn't ask herself why she felt so unable to discuss either his feelings or her own with him.

Chapter Sixteen

Olivia was smiling to herself as she stepped out into the street and flagged down a cab.

'Le Cirque, please,' she told the driver. She was having dinner there with her parents, but Robert had telephoned unexpectedly just as she was about to leave. 'Not for any reason,' he had told her, except to say how much he loved her and how much he was missing her.

He had been so reluctant to end their telephone call and let her go that she was now running late, not that her parents would mind, she knew.

She and her mother had spent the afternoon at Chanel's New York store, having a private viewing of the season's bridal gowns, specially flown over from Paris for them to see. They'd both fallen for the same dress, a fluid classic column of heavy white jersey sprinkled with diamanté and pearls, which started at the top just here and there, but which, by the time they reached the hem of the dress and its train, formed a deep shimmering band.

Olivia had loved the elegance of the cowl neckline and long sleeves, and they had both said how much they preferred the slender column to the bouffant meringue style of wedding dress made so popular by the Princess of Wales.

'Emerald is insisting that you wear the Lenchester tiara,' Ella had told her, 'more for Robert's grandmother's benefit than mine.'

Olivia had laughed.

They were all agreed that Emerald and Cathy's daughters should be invited to be bridesmaids.

'I rather suspect that Emerald is a bit disappointed that Sam and James are too old to be persuaded to be pageboys,' Ella had said ruefully, referring to her own and Emerald's youngest offspring.

'They can be groomsmen, though, along with Harry and David, and Aunt Polly's two boys,' Olivia had pointed out.

Aunt Emerald had faxed over sample menus, and was now pressing her mother for a decision on the Order of Service.

It was a warm clear night, and Olivia was glad that she'd chosen to wear a simple cream strappy Armani sheath-style dress, its bolero-style jacket with just a hint of detail in the small appliquéd leaves, studded with single diamantés, ornamenting one shoulder. With it she was wearing toning high-heeled sandals and carrying a matching clutch bag.

'Very regal,' her mother, who had obviously been waiting for her to arrive, teased her, adding, 'We'd better go and join your father. He's talking foundation business, and unless we stop him we'll never be able to drag him away.'

Tucking her arm through her mother's, Olivia let herself be led through the busy bar area, a smile curving her lips when she caught sight of her father, only to disappear when she realised who it was he was talking foundation business with.

Tait Cabot Forbes.

'What's wrong?' Ella asked when she felt Olivia freeze.

'How can Dad lower himself to talk to *him* after that article he wrote?' Olivia hissed angrily.

Ella gave Olivia a surprised look. 'Darling, that was a mistake, and it's all water under the bridge now, you know that.'

It wasn't water under the bridge for her, Olivia acknowledged with hostility, as both men stood up to greet them. Deliberately keeping her back to Tait, she returned her father's warm hug. She had to acknowledge him, of course, but she did so with as obvious reluctance as good manners allowed.

'That was a nice piece of reporting you filed the other month on the use of child labour abroad.'

After her cool response to his presence, a professional compliment was the last thing she had expected, and instinctively Olivia examined it for potential traps, rather in the manner that she might have lifted a stone and waited until all the creepy-crawlies had disappeared before touching the newly exposed ground beneath.

'Can we expect to read future articles filed from Lauranto? Or do you plan to give up journalism on your marriage?'

On the surface it might appear to be a reasonable enough question, but Olivia rather thought she had seen the booby trap waiting for her.

'There are plenty of social issues that my fiancé will need to address once he becomes Crown Prince – that's only to be expected in a country that hasn't as yet experienced the benefits of modernisation and democracy – but I doubt they would be interesting enough to American readers for me to write about them.'

'I'm sure New York's banking community will be interested since I hear that your fiancé plans to set up some pretty beneficial tax-free banking concessions in Lauranto.'

'Naturally Robert wants to attract money and investment into Lauranto for the benefit of his people,' Olivia responded sharply.

'By a democratic process or by using his powers as outright ruler?'

Olivia had had enough. She knew exactly what Tait was trying to infer.

'Are you asking off the record, or because you plan to write an article about Lauranto as ill informed as the one you wrote about my parents?'

Olivia could hear her mother's indrawn gasp and see her father's lifted eyebrow. She had broken one of the strictest rules of good manners and diplomacy, but she didn't care.

'Thanks for your offer to join you for dinner, Oliver,' Tait said. 'Maybe next time? Ella.' His smile for her mother was warm, drawing covert female glances, no doubt attracted by his air of raw masculine energy and, of course, his undeniable good looks.

'Olivia.' Disconcertingly she could see amusement gleaming in his eyes as he shook her hand although that amusement faded, she noticed, after he had looked deliberately at her engagement ring and then back at her. His words were for her ears alone.

'It looks rather heavy.'

'And that reminds me of what a privilege it is to be wearing it,' Olivia retorted.

He obviously wasn't finished with her, though, because he drawled, 'With privilege comes responsibility,' before releasing her hand and then striding away from them.

'What was all that about?' her mother asked her curiously.

Olivia's gaze was still on Tait's departing back. He'd stopped to talk to a pin-thin overexcited blonde who had flung herself into his arms.

'He doesn't like me and I don't like him back,' Olivia answered.

'You were rather rude to him, darling,' Ella remonstrated gently.

'He was sneering at me.' Olivia's face was flushed. She knew from the looks her parents exchanged that she was overreacting and, worse, behaving like a child caught out in bad behaviour and defiantly trying to blame someone else for it, but that only made her feel even more resentful and indignant. Her parents should be on her side, not Tait Cabot Forbes'. After all, she had only been protecting them and Robert. 'I could see it when he looked at my engagement ring.'

'He's a Boston Brahmin, descended in a direct line from the Founding Fathers. Remember, they left England because they prized democracy,' her father pointed out. 'Of course he's going to take a pop at anything and anyone he thinks is antidemocratic. It's in his genes.'

'I don't think he was actually sneering at you, darling,' her mother tried to soothe her. 'And I do think you are being a tad oversensitive to think that.'

'Yes he was.' Ridiculously, Olivia discovered that she was close to tears. 'And Robert isn't antidemocratic. One of the main reasons he's agreed to become Crown Prince is to help the people of Lauranto.'

Again 'that look' was exchanged between her parents. It made Olivia feel like stamping her foot and demanding that they treat her as a fully functioning adult instead of like a silly child.

'Yes, of course it is,' her mother agreed.

'But?' Olivia challenged, sensing her mother's unspoken thought.

It was her father who answered her, though, coming over to her and putting his arm round her shoulders.

'I guess it's just that the very words "Crown Prince" tend to stick in the American craw a bit.'

'You mean they stick in the craw of certain WASP males,' Olivia corrected him, adding unkindly, 'They certainly don't seem to stick in the craws of any of their female relatives, judging from the way so many of them just love boasting about it the minute one of their daughters marries a title.'

'Olivia,' Ella protested, 'that isn't very kind.'

'It's the truth. And it's also the truth that the reason men like Tait Cabot Forbes are so antagonistic to men like my Robert is because they know that no matter how many billions of dollars they have, when it comes to the wider world a title counts, and they can never have one.'

Olivia could see that she'd shocked her parents, who were both fiercely proud to be honorary Americans via their long-time residence in the United States, but like a child in the grip of a tantrum she was too wrought

272

up to want to take back the words even if she could have done.

'I don't think for one moment that Tait envies Robert his title, if that's what you're trying to suggest,' her mother said quietly. 'I'm really surprised that you should even think something like that, Livvy, never mind say it. I don't understand why you are so unpleasant about Tait. He's been a marvellous help to your father with the foundation, thanks to all his contacts, and aside from that he's also charming and intelligent.'

'Now you're taking his side against me, just because he's American and Robert isn't. Can't you see what he was trying to do, asking me those questions?'

'I dare say he felt it was a pity that someone with your talent would have to give up her career plans because of her marriage,' Oliver said.

Olivia looked at her father. 'No he wasn't. He was trying to make out that Robert is only taking on the role of Crown Prince for his own benefit, and that isn't true at all.'

Once again her parents exchanged looks.

'Why do you keep looking at one another like that, as though you don't believe me?' Olivia demanded, too upset to conceal her distress.

'Of course we believe you,' her mother assured her. 'But it's also the truth that the needs of his people are not Robert's only reason for agreeing to step in Alessandro's shoes. In fact, if you were to ask me, I would say that I think his decision is balanced seventy-thirty in favour of these buildings he keeps going on about raising money for.'

Olivia opened her mouth and then closed it again

before saying quietly, 'Of course Robert wants to protect and preserve such an irreplaceable heritage for future generations. The historical value of the buildings is incalculable. They're unique.'

'They're buildings, Livvy. Bricks and mortar. Important, yes, but so far as I am concerned people matter more.'

'Come along, you two, let's go and sit down,' Olivia's father suggested. 'The maître d's been hovering for the last ten minutes.'

'I don't think I want any dinner right now,' Olivia told them both.

'Don't be silly, darling. Arranging a wedding is very stressful. You need to eat properly.'

So it was her 'stress' over the wedding that was going to be blamed for the now miserable atmosphere between them, Olivia thought resentfully as she allowed herself to be guided towards their table, and not the real cause, Tait Cabot Forbes, who had succeeded in doing something she had never imagined could happen, and that was driving a wedge between her and her parents.

'Something's worrying you, what is it?' Jay's gentle question followed by his warm smile, as they walked round the garden together, pausing to admire and enjoy the old-fashioned scented roses, which had been a Golden Wedding Anniversary gift to them, filled Amber's heart with increased guilt. They never normally kept secrets from one another.

'I've done something you won't like,' she admitted.

Jay looked at her tenderly. 'I could never not like anything about you, Amber, you know that.'

'You have far too good an opinion of me,' Amber told him. 'Why not let me be the judge of that? It's self-indulgent and selfish of me to want to tell you. A sort of letting you carry the burdens of my conscience for me, when I know that what I've done was morally wrong, even if I do tell myself that it was necessary to do it.'

'Tell me,' Jay encouraged her.

Quietly and carefully Amber did just that.

'I'm not sure what I feel most guilty about,' she concluded, 'the dreadful lies and insinuations I've told about and to Cassandra, or the fact that, in creating such a fiction of lies to protect John, what I've really done is belittle him. He would be so hurt if he knew, Jay, but you know how proud he is. That was exactly why Cassandra did what she did, I'm sure, knowing his pride and wanting to humiliate him through it. I feel so guilty sometimes that we have so much whilst Janey and John . . .'

Jay squeezed her hand with his own. 'I feel it too, you know. It's only natural for parents to want their children to be happy. Poor Janey looks so tense and unhappy sometimes. Marriage to John, much as I like him, can't be easy for her.'

Amber gave Jay a grateful look. It was so typical of him that he had known immediately that her guilt was because of their own love and happiness and not because of her wealth.

'What makes it worse is having to listen to Janey saying that she can't understand why Cassandra is so unkind to them both, but especially to John, when of course I know exactly why but can't say. It's such a pity that Cassandra didn't do as you suggested years ago, Jay, and move to Brighton to live near that friend of hers.'

'I agree that it would have been better for Janey and John if she had moved to Brighton, and healthier for her too. She might even have found some measure of peace and happiness if she'd been able to put the past behind her and make a new life for herself.'

'I think she resents us all, especially you and me, Jay, for the happiness we have had together, when she has had none. I do feel sorry for her in that regard.'

'Her lack of happiness is her own responsibility,' Jay told Amber, the uncharacteristic note of criticism in his voice causing her to look questioningly up at him. 'I don't have your generous nature, Amber. Cassandra was indirectly responsible for the death of one of her lovers, and perhaps even directly responsible for the death of another and that other's unborn child.'

Now it was Amber's turn to squeeze Jay's hand in a gesture of comfort. She knew that the lover whose death Cassandra had been indirectly responsible for was Jay's first wife, whose mental instability Jay believed had been exacerbated by Cassandra's seduction of her.

'No one is more generous towards the vulnerabilities of others than you, Jay,' she insisted.

'You say that, but you didn't want to tell me what you'd done because you thought I would judge you harshly.' Now his voice was burdened with sadness.

'Never that,' Amber reassured him fiercely. 'I'm shallow enough to enjoy basking in your good opinion so much that I didn't want to risk forfeiting it.'

'That could never happen. Nothing you could ever do or say would change by a breath my love and admiration for you, Amber. You are the heart of my life, it is you and our love that sustains me.' It is because of you that I fought back from death's door and the sweet relief from all mortal pain, Jay knew he could have told her, but he knew too that Amber hated being reminded of his heart attacks and the fragility of human life.

They stood together in the rose garden, two elderly people, grey-haired and stooped, Jay's arm around Amber's shoulders, her cheek resting against the warmth of his chest.

'Sometimes I think that you and I aren't just blessed to have found and loved one another. Our love isn't just for us, it's for Barrant and Blanche and their sons, and for all the love that they never had.'

Jay kissed the top of her head and pulled her closer.

It was half-past eleven in the morning. Robert's eyes still felt gritty from being awake half the night tormented by anger over his lack of control. Anger, and guilt as well, at a need born out of something he couldn't explain or even comprehend himself, an ache within him for one specific woman who was not part of the plans he had made for his life. It should have been easy to subdue that need, to deny its existence, but instead he had given in to it and as a result of that it – and she – now had the power to destroy everything he had planned and worked for, everything he really wanted his life to be.

Had the power, if the person holding that power chose to use it.

Robert could remember quite plainly how much more comfortable he felt when his life and those things that touched most closely on it were under his own control. It had been when his mother had told him she was going to marry Drogo, and so give him the stepfather he had so much wanted. There had been no need then for him to be afraid any longer that the thug Max Preston, or someone like him, would come back into their lives. He had felt happy and safe. He had boundaries that he could control so that he had a safe area within them. What had happened last night had breached those boundaries.

He had been awake all night wondering what he should do. Telling Olivia about Charlotte was, of course, impossible. He knew women. She loved him, she would forgive him, but then there would be the questions, the accusations thrown up at him in times of discord between them. In short, telling Olivia would mean ceding control of their relationship to her, and he didn't want that.

That had left him with two remaining options: either to do nothing and hope that Charlotte Meredith would keep her distance from him, or to go to her, and ask her for the promise of her silence.

Given true freedom of choice, Robert would have opted for the first of these two, but he did not have freedom of choice.

Which meant going for the second option. Which was why right now he was standing outside Charlotte Meredith's door, and hoping that she would be in so that he could get the whole unpleasant business over and done with and then put it behind him, out of his life, the life he intended to live with Olivia.

Charlotte had only just returned from seeing her stockbroker to discuss the very pleasant increasing value of her shareholdings, when she heard the door knocker and looked down from her drawing-room window to see Robert standing on her front doorstep.

Her heart leaped. It was impossible for her to feel like this about him. About any man, but about him most of all. He disliked her, he despised her, he feared her. And he wanted her. And what did she feel for him? Nothing . . . or at least nothing that mattered. Nothing that could matter. She was accustomed, after all, to ignoring her own emotional pain.

One look at his face told her that whatever had brought him here, it wasn't a desire or a need to be with her as a woman.

The minute Robert stepped into the elegant hallway, the memory of what had happened the last time he had been here came flooding back, pressing in on him, filling him with a mixture of unwanted aching longing and an anger born of the fear of that longing. It would be typical of the kind of woman Charlotte was if she added to his discomfort by keeping him in the hallway with its unwanted memories, Robert thought.

But just as that thought formed, she confounded him and his judgement of her by saying, 'I don't know why you're here but I think that whatever you want to say can be said more comfortably in my drawing room.'

Robert followed her up the stairs. The first-floor drawing room was decorated with the same faultless good taste as the hallway, and had the same quirky, stylish individual touches. A man could feel at home in such a room, even though it had a certain female warmth to it. He was aware of the room's scent: earthy, warm, and yet at the same time crisp, with the promise of just enough sharpness to sting the senses. It reminded him of the pleasure of smelling and then biting into one of the apples that grew in the small orchard at Denham, a rare old English variety that he particularly loved. The drawing room smelled as it looked, understated and yet full of charm for those with the taste to recognise its true value. Its décor of cool white and grey tones soothed the senses, the decorative detailing of the grey-painted-framed mirrors over matching console tables was perfectly judged to draw the eye to notice it without it being overwhelming.

'Very nice,' he commented reluctantly, when he realised that she was watching him study the room. 'Who was the designer? I don't recognise the style.'

'Me,' Charlotte told him truthfully. 'I can never understand anyone employing an interior designer. I much prefer to put my own stamp on what is mine.'

Watching Robert almost visibly flinch, Charlotte warned herself that she must not feel sorry for him. She had not, after all, begged him to betray his fiancée with her.

'I expect you know why I'm here,' Robert began awkwardly, adding more desperately, when Charlotte made no response, 'This . . . this thing that's happened between us, that keeps happening between us, can't go on.'

'Because you are an engaged man, and your fiancée would never forgive you?' Charlotte taunted him, to hide the pain that was burning into her pride. Of course it would be her that he chose to reject and deny. Of course!

'I think perhaps she would,' Robert felt bound to say, 'but I would never be able to forgive myself for hurting her.'

Charlotte felt a savage stab of envy and resentment of the woman he wanted to protect. No man had ever wanted to protect her. What must it be like to be that kind of woman? To be a woman a man would sacrifice his pride to save from being hurt?

She had a fierce urge to tear down the protective wall Robert had put up to protect his fiancée, to make him surrender to her so completely that he would be forced to admit that there was no protection from the desire he felt for her, least of all that of an engagement ring. But instead she queried calmly, 'I see. And how do you propose to ensure that your fiancée is not hurt?'

Robert allowed himself to relax. She wasn't going to create a scene. Mixed with his relief was an unwilling respect for her and an awareness of her emotional strength. A man could easily grow to admire such a woman and look to her for confirmation of his own judgement in difficult situations. She would possess a fierce loyalty to those who mattered to her, and would fight to defend them. In that, she was very much like his own mother, Robert recognised.

'I've come to ask if you would agree to forget everything that has happened between us.'

It was no more than she had expected, and the sour sense of desolation growing inside her told her that there was no point in her continuing the 'game' by further tormenting him. Doing so might bring her a certain sense of revenge, but Charlotte was beginning to fear that her own emotions were too closely involved for her to emerge unscathed herself. Better to set him free and save herself than to continue to pursue him like some vengeful harpy and then discover that she was caught in her own trap, her emotions so entangled that she couldn't bear to let him go.

She had opened her mouth to give him the promise of silence, with it his freedom, when he added brusquely, 'After all, it isn't as though what happened actually meant anything to either of us. I mean, you could have been anyone.' It was a lie and Robert knew it, but he had to say the words as though speaking them somehow made them true.

On such small statements empires can fall and so can human beings.

There was more going on between them than just a man's blind, uncaring need for sexual satisfaction, and Charlotte knew that Robert knew that as well as she did herself. Had he been honest about that, had he admitted it, then she would have felt compelled to help him. But he had not. Instead he had rejected that truth and her with it.

The outraged fury of a woman scorned ripped through Charlotte, opening up all the old wounds of her childhood and filling her with a ferocious desire to hit out at Robert and hurt him as he had just hurt her. Instead of giving him his freedom, she took a step towards him, widening her eyes as she fixed her gaze on him, and deliberately softened her voice to a low hypnotically sensual semi-whisper.

'I admire you for wanting to protect your fiancée, Robert, but that isn't true and you know it. We can't ignore our need for one another.' When he flinched again, Charlotte smiled seductively at him. 'I was awake for most of last night, thinking about you. Smouldering embers can burn for a very long time. Some say the best way to extinguish them is to let them burn themselves out with their own ferocity. Perhaps we should do that, just to be sure that there is nothing left that either of us might want to . . . remember.'

He mustn't listen to her, Robert told himself, but she was already pressing her body against his, wrapping her arms around him, kissing him, the pointed tip of her tongue stroking its unbearably erotic message against his mouth. He made an attempt to stop her, reaching up to detach her arms from his neck, holding her narrow wrists in his grip as he forced her back from him.

Charlotte laughed softly. 'Why resist,' she taunted him, 'when you know you want me? You wanted me before and you want me now.' She placed her hand on his body, stroking her fingertips the length of his erection with open confidence, and then unfastened his trousers with her other hand, before going down on her knees in front of him and expertly taking the head of his cock into her mouth, cupping his balls with her free hand. His desire was immediate and explosive, as hot and hard as that of a boy jerking off, unable to control his own sexuality.

She could control his, though, nipping at his flesh to stop him from coming and then standing up to tell him with a smile, 'Let's do this properly.'

Before he could do or say anything she was removing her dress, revealing palely luminous flesh. A fine silk bra cupped her breasts without concealing the dark aureoles surrounding her nipples.

Unlike any woman Robert had known, she did not remove her bra first, but instead slid down her matching silk briefs, exposing the neat tightly curled triangle of natural blonde pubic hair, opening her legs as she reached for his hand and placed it on her mound.

'What's stopping you? You know you want to,' she told him.

Desire surged through him in a dark orgiastic flood that tore away his resistance, roaring out of control into every cell of his body.

He took hold of her, dragged her to him, cupping her face and then sliding his hands into her hair to tilt her head back as he kissed her, bruising her mouth and his own, tasting the soft scented flesh of her throat, tearing the silk barrier from her breasts so that he could hold and knead the receptive flesh of her breasts, and plucking and tugging at her nipples as he felt the warmth of her long exhaled breath against his forehead. When he reached for her nipple with his mouth, though, she stopped him.

'Not until you take your clothes off. You aren't the only one who's allowed to have fun, you know.'

She'd got him – Charlotte could see it in his eyes. He wanted her and he would have her, and then *she* would have *her* revenge.

Rose took a deep breath before raising her hand to lift the knocker on the front door of Nick and Sarah's house – or rather Sarah's house now, since Nick had moved out.

The surprise she felt when the door was opened, not by Sarah's au pair but by Sarah herself, was quickly superseded by the shock of recognising not just how much weight Sarah had lost, but how very distressed and unwell she looked, her eyes swollen from crying and her face blotchy. Sarah's reaction to seeing Rose was plain in her look of hostility.

Sensing that her daughter-in-law was about to close the door in her face, Rose stepped into the hall, telling her quickly, 'It's all right, I'm not here on Nick's behalf. I've just come to say how much Josh and I miss seeing the boys, and to ask if there is any chance of them spending a couple of days with us during the summer holidays.'

Whilst Rose was speaking, Sarah had lifted her hand to her temple, massaging it as though she was in pain.

'You'd better come through to the kitchen,' she told Rose, leading the way into the hand-painted kitchen Rose privately thought far too fussy. However, it wasn't the fussiness of the décor that wrinkled her forehead in concern so much as the room's chaotic untidiness – anathema to Rose, who loved orderliness.

'It's a mess, I know,' Sarah apologised tiredly, 'but Anya walked out this weekend. I'm afraid my father was rather sharp with her over the boys' behaviour.'

Sarah had her back to her as she filled the kettle, but Rose could hear the distress in her voice.

Putting her handbag down on the floor Rose went over to her. 'Sarah . . .'

'Please don't say anything. I really can't bear any more.'

She was crying, tears pouring down her face, her whole body shaking. She looked, Rose realised, like someone on the verge of a breakdown.

'Come and sit down,' Rose instructed her.

'Everything's going wrong,' Sarah wept, sinking into one of the kitchen chairs. 'Daddy keeps insisting that

I take the boys up to Scotland but then when we're there he gets cross with them and complains that they're unruly and need disciplining, and that I'm spoiling them. Then they get upset and start playing up. When Nick comes round he criticises Daddy in front of them and says nasty things about him to them. Sometimes I just wish that I could escape and that they'd both leave me alone.'

The kettle had boiled so Rose made them each a cup of tea.

'I suppose you think that I'm being unfair to Nick,' Sarah guessed, her hands wrapped round the mug Rose handed her, and her shoulders hunched.

'I think perhaps you're being unfair to yourself and to the boys,' Rose told her gently. 'Have you thought of taking a holiday, Sarah?'

'Daddy wants us to go up to Scotland as soon as the boys break up from school.'

Rose shook her head. 'No, I meant a proper holiday, just you and the boys perhaps. Somewhere where you could have some time to yourself.'

Fresh tears fell. 'I'd love that but it's just not on. I don't think I could cope. Daddy's right, I have let the boys get out of control.'

'I expect they're feeling confused and upset,' Rose said tactfully, instead of pointing out that Nick's sons might be missing him, their father. She was rewarded with a grateful smile.

'Daddy loves them, of course, but he doesn't always realise . . . that is, they're only young and he frightens them a little bit when he gets angry.'

'Have you told him that?' Rose asked her.

Sarah looked horrified. 'No, I couldn't. He'd be so cross with me. I mean, he wouldn't really understand.'

What she meant, Rose reflected, was that she was as intimidated by and afraid of her father as her sons were.

'It wouldn't be so bad if Nick would just stop making things worse by coming round here and raging about Daddy. The boys hear him and . . . I just wish they would both leave me alone.'

Her heartfelt cry touched Rose's heart and increased her concern. 'Sometimes I feel like taking the boys and running away, going somewhere where neither of them could reach us. I suppose you think me a fearful coward.'

Rose shook her head. An idea had just occurred to her. 'If you really would like to get away, I think I know exactly the right place for you.'

Sarah looked wary. 'If you're going to suggest we come and stay with you—'

'No. I was actually thinking of Denham.'

'Denham? With Amber and Jay, you mean?'

'You'd be very welcome, I know, and it would give you some breathing space. Time to think properly about what you want and what the boys need, Sarah, rather than trying to please your father and at the same time placate Nick.'

'Daddy only wants the best for us. He loves me and the boys.' Her tone was defensive.

'Of course he does,' Rose agreed, 'but as you've just said yourself, the boys are reacting to your and Nick's separation, and you feel torn between pleasing your father and not exacerbating the difficult situation that exists between you and Nick.'

'But wouldn't Amber and Jay take Nick's side?'

'You've met them – what do you think?'

'I liked them very much, and Denham, but if Nick knows we're there—'

'I shall tell Nick that you need time to yourself and that he must respect that.'

'My father is expecting us to go up to Scotland. He'll be angry – I mean upset – if we don't go.'

'He loves you, Sarah, as you've said yourself. I'm sure he'll understand.'

She was tempted, Rose could see, and right now Rose couldn't think of anywhere that she'd feel Sarah would be safer in her present fragile state than with her own aunt Amber at Denham, but she didn't want Sarah to feel coerced into agreeing.

'Why don't you think it over?' she began, but Sarah shook her head.

'No. I've made up my mind. I want to go.'

Three hours later it was all arranged and the kitchen had been restored to some sort of order.

Sarah and the boys were to travel down to Denham by train once the boys had broken up from school at the end of the week. Josh and Rose would drive them to Euston and then telephone Janey to confirm which train they were on, and then Janey would pick them up from Macclesfield station.

Amber had spoken to Sarah and assured her that she and Jay would be delighted to have her and the boys to stay, and Sarah had even found the courage to telephone her father and tell him that they would not be going up to Scotland.

Chapter Seventeen

'It's a pity you can't come round here to get ready for the ball with us. We're going to have champers and strawberries, and Sally has a friend whose sister is a hairdresser and she's going to come over and do our hair for us,' Fran had said the previous evening when they'd all met up to finalise arrangements for the ball.

The truth was that right now she wished that she was with them, Katie admitted, as she tried to ignore the horrible charged atmosphere between them that was the result of Zoë changing her mind yet again and announcing that she didn't want to go, and that she had only agreed in the first place to stop Katie going on and on at her.

'You can't not go now, Zoë,' Katie protested. 'Think how left out poor Ian will be if he hasn't got a partner.'

It was a lame effort at persuasion, Katie knew, without needing Zoë's contemptuous look to tell her that.

'Why aren't you thinking about me,' she challenged Katie, 'instead of thinking about "poor Ian"? After all, you are supposed to be my best friend – at least you were until you started going around with Francesca and her crowd.'

Katie eased out a shaky breath, relieved to discover that it was jealousy over her friendship with Fran that was responsible for Zoë's bad mood and not something more serious. Something like Zoë saying that all she wanted was to be with Axel. But, Katie reassured herself, she was worrying unnecessarily. Zoë had told her over and over again that she was 'cured' of the 'madness' that had gripped her over Axel, and that he meant nothing to her now. To doubt Zoë would be mean and wrong. She had to trust her friend, and have faith in her. She owed Zoë that after all she'd been through, surely?

The truth was, though, that secretly Katie felt guiltily relieved to be having a break from Zoë when they both left Oxford for their respective homes for the summer. Zoë was flying out to New York to see Tom, who was now working there to gain a wider experience of the banking world than his own family bank could give him, according to Zoë. Katie could still hardly bear to hear her talking about Tom, but after witnessing what the pain of unrequited love had done to Zoë, Katie was determined that the same thing would not happen to her. Tom had rejected her, and that hurt – very badly – but she wasn't going to let it ruin her life. She was going to accept it and work as hard as she could to put it and Tom behind her. Somehow she would learn to live with the ache of loss and regret for what might have been that she carried inside her.

From New York Zoë was flying to Paris and then travelling to Antibes to join her parents.

Katie's own summer plans were far less glamorous. She had willingly given up the chance to visit Venice with her parents and Jamie, to spend a week with the Angelli family and catch up with Emma, in favour of going to Denham. Ostensibly she was going there to gain some proper experience of working on the Denby Silk archives and help her grandmother to start cataloguing all her own personal silk-related archives, but in addition to that Katie had been entrusted by her mother and her aunt Rose with a secret mission. She was to liaise between the manager of Denby Mill and all those who were working hard to ensure that Amber received their special secret eightieth birthday gift in the form of the new silk designs. Katie felt sure that these responsibilities would keep her too busy to dwell on Tom and what she felt she had lost.

'Don't be silly,' she chided Zoë now. 'You will always be my best friend, you know that.'

'Spit on your finger and swear to God?' Zoë demanded, repeating a childhood mantra.

'Spit on my finger and swear to God,' Katie agreed. 'Come on, we'd better start getting ready, otherwise we're going to be late.'

'In a minute. I need a spliff first. It will stop me gagging at the thought of having to put up with boring Ian. Do you suppose he's ever had proper dirty sex? Mind you, I suppose he thinks that pushing it in and moving it about a bit is dirty.'

'Zoë . . .' Katie protested.

'I can take you to a party where we really can have fun. Why don't we, Katie?' Zoë's voice became urgent as she stopped in the middle of rolling her joint. 'I dare you not to go to the ball but to come with me instead to this party that I've heard about.'

Was that desperation and pleading she could hear in Zoë's voice? Katie's stomach churned with anxiety.

'No, Zoë, stop it.'

They looked at one another in silence.

'You promised me,' Katie reminded Zoë quietly.

'Oh fuck, fuck, fuck, all right then.' Zoë slammed her hand down hard on the table. 'I'll sodding well go, but don't blame me if I . . .'

'If what?' Katie demanded.

'If I end up dying of boredom.'

A sharp unwanted stab of misgiving caught at Katie's heart. Zoë wasn't still secretly yearning for Axel and all that he represented, was she? Surely she couldn't be after what he had put her through and her valiant battle to overcome the trauma he had inflicted on her? What should she do? If she started to question her then Zoë would naturally accuse her of not trusting her. But then she couldn't forget what Tom had said to her, and the sense of responsibility for Zoë his accusations had left her with. She couldn't imagine Emma, her own elder sister, balking at tackling such a duty.

She took a deep breath, and asked determinedly, 'Zoë, everything's all right, isn't it? I mean . . .'

'I know what you mean, and yes, of course I'm all right. Want to see for yourself, just to check, do you?' she asked angrily, starting to roll up her sleeves.

'No, of course not. I just wouldn't want you to think that you can't, well, talk to me if you need to.'

'Oh, Katie.' Suddenly Zoë was hugging her, half laughing and half crying as she told her fiercely, 'I don't deserve to have a friend like you, but I need you to be my friend, Katie, and I always will. You must never not be, no matter what I say or do. Promise me that.'

'I promise,' Katie assured her, hugging her back as tightly.

'Wow, the place is heaving, isn't it?' Fran said excitedly as the six of them, Fran and her partner, Rick, Katie and Miles, and Zoë and Ian, stood taking in the scene.

All the ticket holders had to pass through a rigorous checking process to get into the ball, admission to which was heavily protected by dozens of burly security guards, as well as the police.

Their tickets, which included a meal as well as admission to the free bar, had cost over £130 per couple. Although Zoë had poked fun at the boys in their dinner suits, secretly Katie thought they looked wonderful – really grown up and smart – and she had seen from the look that Miles had given her when they had arrived to collect them that he was equally pleased with her appearance.

It was a rule during the evening of a Commem Ball that those Fellows living in rooms at college but not attending the ball were not allowed to leave their rooms during the ball, just as it was a tradition that some undergrads would attempt to get into the ball without tickets, just for the fun of doing so. Stories of young men swimming across the river to reach the college gardens, carrying their evening clothes in plastic bags, were rife, as were more recent tales of luckless students ending up with telltale paint stains on their hands and clothes from trying to get in by climbing the walls, which had been painted especially to catch them out.

Grabbing the attention of a waiter circulating with a tray of champagne and Pimm's, Miles handed champagne to the three girls. Zoë drank hers in one go, reaching for a second glass before the waiter could move on, glowering defiantly at them all as she did so.

A string quartet had been engaged to play in the college's Hall, the music adding an air of glamour to the event, at least for Katie, who was loving the whole atmosphere of the event. Or at least she would have been if she hadn't been feeling so anxious about Zoë's behaviour. If privately she thought it was mean of Zoë to try to spoil things just because she herself had been reluctant to come, Katie knew better than to antagonise her further by saying so.

This year's ball might not, as some were saying, be able to rival that of three years ago, but to Katie it was everything a commem ball should be. There was dancing to a top group, fun to be had in the gardens, with fairground rides and a hog roast, and the predictable horseplay amongst some of the male undergrads of the type bound to occur wherever there is a combination of high-spirited young men, water and the potential of an audience of pretty girls. More than one dinner-suited young man could be seen emerging from the river as the night wore on.

'I think our dresses are the best here,' Fran whispered happily to Katie, and Katie was inclined to agree. Everyone was dressed up, but their dresses were just that little extra bit special, she thought. Zoë's insistence on wearing black, along with her offhand and even hostile attitude had drawn comments, just as Zoë had wanted it to do, Katie suspected. She had rather rudely, in Katie's opinion, been ignoring her partner for the last half an hour to stand watching the group instead, and now Katie could see her talking with one of their roadies, a muscular-looking man with a beard, wearing a leather waistcoat open over his bare chest and a pair of jeans, and the security guard who had been talking to him.

'Enjoying yourself?' Miles asked her ten minutes later as they danced together. He had to raise his voice so that she could hear him above the music.

Katie nodded enthusiastically, laughing as he grabbed hold of her and swung her round into an energetic jive. Being with Miles was rather like being with Harry and David, simple, uncomplicated by difficult emotions, safe and fun. She tried to imagine dancing with Tom like this and knew that it wouldn't be possible. She would be too aware of how she felt about him. Thinking about Tom made her heart ache. She didn't love him, she told herself. You couldn't love someone properly if you could only long for them from a distance, and if they didn't want you anyway. Thinking of Tom made her look round for Zoë her stomach muscles contracting when she couldn't see her.

'I can't see Zoë,' she told Miles.

He gave an impatient shrug, demanding, 'So what?' as he swung her round into a spin.

She couldn't explain to him how responsible she felt for Zoë; that would mean betraying Zoe's vulnerability to him.

'Have you seen Zoë?' she asked Fran the minute she and Miles had rejoined Fran and Rick.

'She was hanging around one of the roadies, the last time I saw her,' Fran responded.

Katie knew that Fran didn't much like Zoë, and in fact rather disapproved of her. It was there in her voice and her expression.

'Here's Ian,' Miles told Katie. 'Where's Zoë, Ian?'

Ian gave an awkward shrug. 'I don't know. She told me over half an hour ago that she needed another drink and I haven't seen her since.'

There was a small awkward silence, and Katie guessed that the others were thinking that Zoë was treating Ian badly in view of the cost of the double ticket. She couldn't tell them that Zoë had only agreed to attend the ball under pressure from her, and had complained all along that she didn't want to partner Ian. A little anxiously, Katie looked round, searching for Zoë, whilst acknowledging that it was going to be almost impossible to spot her amongst so many people. Unsure of what to do, Katie peered towards where the group were playing, hoping that she might after all see Zoë there, but there was no sign of either the roadie or her friend.

'Stop worrying about her,' Fran urged Katie, 'and don't say that you aren't because you are, I can tell. She's an adult, not a child, and you shouldn't have to take responsibility for her.'

'I know, and I don't, but—'

'But nothing,' Fran told her firmly. 'We've come here to enjoy ourselves, and if Zoë doesn't want to enjoy herself with us then that's up to her.'

Katie knew that Fran was right but she didn't know Zoë like Katie did. Fran couldn't be expected to understand how irrationally and self-destructively Zoë could behave if she felt so inclined. There, Katie admitted, she had said it, if only to herself: Zoë could be self-destructive.

'Come on, let's go and get something to eat,' Miles was urging, Rick and Ian agreeing enthusiastically. Reluctant to leave the dance without assuring herself that Zoë knew where they were going, Katie hesitated and looked round again.

'I'd better just check that she's not queuing for the loo,' she told the other four. 'I don't want her to come back and think that we've deserted her.'

The looks the others exchanged showed that they thought she was pandering to Zoë but what else could she do? She was responsible for Zoë being here, after all.

'We'll find a table to the right of the hog roast,' Miles offered practically, 'so you'll only have to look there for us.'

Katie gave him a grateful look. He was such a sensible, reliable, kind person. Zoë might mock him to her for not being exciting or sexy, but Katie admitted that she found his reliability comforting. He reminded her in many ways of her father, and she liked that.

The queue for the nearest ladies snaked for several yards and Katie made her way along its length, checking to see if Zoë was there, and even went and knocked on the doors of the cubicles themselves, calling out her name, before heading back to the stage where the group was still playing. There was still no sign of either Zoë or the roadie, but the heavyweight security guard was still there, watching the dancers with his arms folded, giving Katie a leering look that made her wish she didn't have to approach him. But she asked him if he knew where Zoë had gone, quickly describing her friend to him.

'Probably gone out for a quick shag with the roadie,' he informed Katie unpleasantly. 'She was certainly up for it.' His gaze narrowed speculatively. 'How about you and me nipping out for some of the same? You posh lot like a bit of rough.'

Quickly Katie stepped back from him, the angry look she gave him making it plain what she thought of his suggestion. Had Zoë gone off with the roadie? It was possible, Katie acknowledged. In fact it would be typical of Zoë to both amuse herself and punish Katie for bringing her to the ball by doing exactly that.

Katie felt a hand on her arm and spun round to find Fran looking at her wryly as she shouted above the noise, 'I thought I'd find you here.'

'I was looking for Zoë,' Katie told her unnecessarily.

'I don't know why you're wasting your time chasing round after her,' Fran said exasperatedly. 'She's an adult, not a child, even if she is behaving like one.'

'She didn't really want to come.' Katie felt obliged to defend her friend. 'I persuaded her to, and I sort of feel a bit guilty.'

'You feel guilty? She's the one who ought to be feeling that, but of course she won't be. I bet she's enjoying spoiling your night, but it isn't just your night she's spoiling, Katie. All three of the boys are pretty hacked off about her behaviour and the way she's got you running round after her, especially Miles.'

Fran's words brought Katie a fresh bout of guilt.

'Come on, let's go back and join the boys, and leave Zoë to come and find us if she wants to. It's not fair to spoil their night just because she's behaving the way she is. Do you think she's worrying about you and how you feel?' Fran pressed when Katie looked undecided. 'Well, I can tell you she won't be. Katie, this is the only time we'll be here. It's special, something we'll remember all our lives, and I'm not going to have it spoiled by Zoë, and if you've any sense neither will you. She's being selfish and mean.'

Katie sighed. There was a good deal of truth in what Fran was saying.

'Come on,' Fran urged her, grabbing hold of her hand and starting to physically drag her away.

Laughing ruefully, Katie gave in. 'All right.'

It was a special and wonderful occasion, Katie admitted over two hours later, as she and Miles walked hand in hand over the dew-damp grass, pausing to view the moon and stars reflected in the still waters of the Thames. Katie hadn't got used to referring to it as the Isis yet, in true Oxford tradition.

'Thank you for inviting me to be your partner tonight,' she told Miles.

The look he gave her was eloquent. Katie knew that he wanted to kiss her, but what she hadn't known until now was that she wanted to kiss him back. There was something so sweetly romantic and right about kissing a boy in a dinner jacket under a velvet-dark sky at one's first commem ball that was part and parcel of the ritual of the whole thing, she thought happily when Miles' arms closed round her and she lifted her face to his.

He was a good kisser, his mouth firm and warm, his tongue determined but not pushy or thrusting. She felt his hand move to her breast, the weight of it against

299

her flesh heavy and warm. Without breaking their kiss she moved it away, only to have Miles replace it. Beneath his kiss Katie smiled. She knew that Miles knew perfectly well that he wasn't going to get anywhere, just as she knew that the night called for him to make a determined try.

'I think I could very easily fall in love with you, do you know that?' he told her thickly.

Katie smiled. 'That's the champagne and Pimm's talking.'

And the champagne and Pimm's was telling her that it was very pleasurable indeed to be here with a boy who admired and desired her, and was prepared to tell her he could fall in love with her; so pleasurable, in fact, that she suspected she could easily tell him that she might let him. Why waste her time yearning for someone she could never have when there was someone here that she could have, and that wanted her in return.

Arm in arm they strolled back the way they had come. Dawn was starting to streak the sky, revealing the outlines of couples lying on the riverbank who had obviously decided to go a bit further than merely kissing. Katie smiled indulgently. On a magical night like this all manner of 'mischief' could surely be entered into, to be forgotten, if one chose, when tomorrow took the magic away.

It was all so perfect, so romantic, so gilded spires and golden youth and Oxford, and she was here, part of it.

'On a night like tonight it almost seems possible to believe we could be immortal,' she told Miles dreamily.

'I don't know about immortal,' Miles grunted in response. 'I do know, though, that I'm getting damnably hungry. What time are they supposed to be serving breakfast?'

Katie burst out laughing. She couldn't help it. She could feel the joy bubbling up inside her and as she laughed she recognised that, had Zoë been here with them she would not for one minute have understood why it gave her both amusement and pleasure to know that Miles had his feet planted so firmly on the ground.

Zoë . . .

'I'd better go and have another look for Zoë,' she told Miles.

'I don't know why you keep worrying about her.' Miles shook his head. 'You've gone off trying to find her at least a dozen times tonight. Hasn't it occurred to you that it should be her trying to find us, and apologising as well. You are not going to waste any more time on her, Katie,' he told her firmly, taking hold of her hand. 'You are going to come and have some breakfast and enjoy yourself. Zoë can take care of herself.'

In the sexually charged heat of the bedroom, the harsh groan of pleasure torn from Robert's throat met the ragged unsteadiness of their mingled breathing. His body slumped briefly against Charlotte's, his heart still slamming into his ribs in the release from his driving need to reach orgasm. He could see the gleam of Charlotte's eyes as he eased himself away from her, the night air cooling his sweat slick.

Every time he told himself that this would be the last time, that it wouldn't happen again, and every time the aching need he had for her brought him back. She was a sickness that possessed him, a fever that consumed him, and an ache that tormented him so that he hardly knew himself any more.

Take tonight, for instance. He had had dinner with his mother and stepfather. His mother had wanted to talk about the wedding, and Robert had wanted her to talk about it. He had wanted, needed, to hear her say Olivia's name so that he would focus on the reality of what his life was, instead of being sucked into this dangerous half-life that was no life at all.

After dinner he had gone home to work and to telephone Olivia. She had told him how much she was missing him and how much she was looking forward to his upcoming visit to America. They had talked about the wedding and their future together. Then he had gone to work on the alterations he was planning for the apartment his grandmother had promised him in Lauranto's royal palace.

He had worked until one in the morning, driving himself, wanting to exhaust himself so that when he went to bed he would sleep and not lie there thinking about wanting Charlotte. And then it had started; the gnawing, driving ache for her that was like a fever in his blood. If he could have ripped the need for her that possessed him out of his body he would have done, but he couldn't, and at two o'clock he had given in.

She had answered his telephone call at the sixth ring, laughing at him in that soft mocking way she had that only tightened the screws of his need.

Being with her, instead of satiating him, only seemed to increase his need, like a thirsty man drinking salt water.

Charlotte watched Robert through eyelash-veiled eyes.

He was a surprisingly good lover, aware and sensual, willing to spend time devoting himself to giving pleasure to her, but the pleasure Charlotte wanted the most was the one she would have when she drove him beyond his self-control, when he was totally possessed by his own need, when it overwhelmed him and controlled him and stripped him of everything that he was, when he had and was nothing. Then she would know all the pleasure she wanted.

Tonight he had come close to that; she had felt the battle going on inside him. That was something they shared; not just a desire, but a need to be in control. Losing his would make him feel humiliated and degraded. She was going to enjoy that.

'Somehow I don't think your little fiancée would approve of what you've just been doing,' she told him with a lazy smile, stretching her naked body with sensual ease.

Robert tensed. He didn't need reminding of his guilt. He had sworn he wouldn't do this again and yet he was here. This was something outside his real life, he assured himself. It could not and would not affect his relationship with Olivia or their marriage. Like a virus, it was simply something that needed to burn itself out, to destroy itself with its own energy. Other than that it meant nothing, to either of them.

Charlotte was not like the other women who had been his lovers. She asked no emotional intimacy of him, and seemed to find the fact that he was engaged to another woman amusing, rather than resenting it.

This time was the last time, he promised himself. An inner voice warned him that it was easy enough to tell himself that now, in the calm of release. He meant it, he assured himself. She was an aberration, a need within himself that was alien to everything he knew about himself, and that he simply hadn't given enough attention to controlling. It could be done. After all, he controlled every other aspect of his life, so of course he could control this one.

Chapter Eighteen

It was almost six o'clock in the morning, the sun coming up, burning the haze off the river, as Miles walked Katie back home.

A postman passed them without so much as a glance, as though the sight of people wearing evening dress, strolling through the city at six o'clock in the morning, was an everyday occurrence, which Katie recognised for him at this time of year it probably was.

She wasn't particularly looking forward to seeing Zoë, who would probably be in a sulk about the evening, having decided to leave them and go home.

Up above them, the milky early morning sky was turning pale blue.

'Isn't this perfect?' Katie told Miles happily. 'Just how early morning should be, with everything clean and fresh and full of promise for a beautiful day.'

Miles was still laughing at her when they turned the corner and saw the police car parked outside the house.

The immediate change from intense happiness to sharp fear sent Katie's heart plunging and then thudding into her chest wall. For a second she moved closer to Miles, seeking comfort and protection from her fear, but then she pulled free of him and started to walk faster.

'Katie,' Miles protested, but she shook her head as he lengthened his stride to keep up with her.

She was running now, half stumbling in her long dress as she saw the two policemen get out of the car and stand waiting for her.

She was out of breath when she reached them, her mouth dry with tension, 'Zoe?' she demanded breathlessly. 'Has—'

The policemen exchanged brief looks.

'Could we have your name and address, please, miss?' the older one, burly and almost fatherly-looking, asked her.

'It's Katie – Katherine Pearl Montpelier,' she amended, 'and I live here.' She gestured towards the house.

'What is it, Officer? What's happened?' That was Miles, standing at her side, reaching for her hand.

'And you, sir, do you live here as well?' the police officer asked.

Miles shook his head. No. I'm simply walking Katie home. We attended the Commemoration Ball last night and—'

'And Miss Zoë Mallory, she was with you?'

'Yes. At first, but then she left to come home,' Katie answered.

'She told you that, did she? That she was coming home?'

Katie looked at Miles. 'Not exactly.'

'Not exactly What does that mean?'

'It means . . . Oh, please, where is Zoë? What's happened?' Katie was pale and shaking with anxiety, tears not very far away.

'Would you happen to know the address and telephone number of Zoë's parents? She does live with her parents when she isn't at university, does she?'

'Yes. But they're in the South of France at the moment and Tom, that's her brother, he's in New York.'

'But you would be able to give us their telephone numbers?'

'I can give you Tom's, I'm not sure about her parents'. It's in our telephone book. But what about Zoë? Where is she . . . what's happened?'

Again that exchanged looks, followed by a firm, 'I think we'd better go inside.'

Katie's stomach was churning. But she walked obediently up to the front door, removing her key from her handbag, although her hand was trembling so much the police officer had to take it from her and open the door himself.

Inside, the hallway still smelled of the scent she and Zoë had sprayed on themselves last night before leaving for the ball, Jean Patou's Joy, which Zoe had 'borrowed' from her mother when they had first come to university in the days when wearing a scent like Joy was something she enjoyed, instead of something she now scorned, preferring, she told Katie mockingly, to 'smell of sex and men and joints'.

Remembering that, Katie's heart turned a double somersault. It was illegal to possess drugs. What if they were here to search the house for them because of something Zoë had said or done? Katie realised as her apprehension knotted her stomach that she had no idea whether or not Zoë had stashed 'something' somewhere in the house.

'If Zoë's done something and she's in trouble,' she said shakily, 'I'm sure she wouldn't have meant to do it.'

Behind her the younger policeman muttered something under his breath that Katie couldn't catch.

'Now if you could give us those telephone numbers, please, miss, and then tell us what happened last night. When Zoë left you. What happened before that. I expect you'd like a cup of tea or coffee first, though. Constable Peters here will make us all one.'

The younger policeman had just brought in the coffee cups on a tray when the telephone rang. Quickly Katie went to answer it, pressing the receiver to her ear when she heard Fran demanding anxiously, 'Katie, is that you? Have you heard the news about Zoë, about her throwing herself out of the top-floor window of Axel's house?'

'What! No!'

A large hand was covering her own, taking the receiver from her, a dark blue serge-uniformed arm guiding her back to the living room and helping her to sit down.

'I'm sorry, Katie.' The policeman's voice was kind and calm.

'It's not true, is it?' Katie begged him, white-faced, her teeth chattering. 'What Fran said about Zoë – it's not true?' Her voice had started to rise in panic.

She could hear Miles demanding to know what was going on. She could hear the younger policeman answering him, odd words imprinting themselves on her brain like darts thrown haphazardly into a darts board, words like, 'party', 'drugs', 'argument' . . .

Katie stood up. 'She's all right, isn't she? She's not . . . she's not dead?' She protested wildly when the three men looked at her, 'She's not. She can't be. Not Zoë.

She didn't really want to die. I know she said she did sometimes, because of loving Axel and him not wanting her, but she didn't mean it.'

The older policeman must have somehow pushed her back onto the sofa because she was sitting there again and Miles was sitting next to her, holding her hand.

'I'm sorry, Katie,' the policeman was saying. 'I know this must be difficult for you, but it's important that we know as much as possible about Zoë's plans and how she was feeling before . . . before she had her accident.

'Now. Last night the two of you attended the Commem Ball together . . .'

It was Miles who telephoned his own parents, who telephoned his grandparents, who telephoned Katie's father. Miles who held her hand as the police went through the events of the previous evening with her and Miles, who insisted on staying with her until her father arrived. But grateful as she was to him, nothing could take away the coldness inside her, the knowledge that from now until the last breath of her life, the word Joy and the scent of the perfume would forever remind her of this day and Zoë's death. Her suicide, because that was what she knew the police were trying desperately hard not to say, with all their talk about it not being possible yet to establish just what had happened, and that the fact that Zoë had smoked so much hash, and drunk so much, prior to her death, there was no way of knowing if she had intended to take her own life or if it had been a dreadfully tragic accident.

As for the argument that was supposed to have taken

place between Zoë and Axel and his new girlfriend, the police would say nothing to Katie, of course.

It was her father who went with them to identify Zoë's body, not Miles, who had volunteered to go. Katie had wanted to go, protesting that it was her duty and that Zoë had been her best friend, but a brief shake of the older policeman's head had had her father saying firmly that he believed that Zoë would want Katie to remember her alive and happy as they set off together in their dresses for the ball.

Now she was at home in her own bedroom in Lenchester House in London, and their family doctor had been round to give her some pills that he had said would help her to sleep.

Katie, though, didn't want to sleep. Zoë was sleeping, though Zoë was sleeping now for ever. Zoë was dead. And it was all her fault. She was to blame. She didn't deserve to sleep. She deserved to suffer. At least she was alive to suffer. Zoë wasn't. Zoë wouldn't ever feel anything ever again. And that was her fault. She had let Zoë leave the ball because she had been enjoying herself too much to care what had happened to her friend. It was because of her that Zoë was dead. And that guilt would be with her for the rest of her life, Katie knew.

'It's so kind and generous of you to have us here.'

Amber smiled at Sarah. 'We're enjoying your company, Sarah, and that of the boys.'

They looked out of the window to where Jay and Harry were teaching Alex and Neil to ride their bicycles.

It was less than a week since they had arrived at

Denham but already Sarah was feeling much better. She'd been too worn down and exhausted by the constant battle between her father and Nick to think properly about what being at Denham would be like when she'd first agreed to come. Then, when she'd got here, she had been on edge, worrying about the boys getting into trouble for being too noisy and undisciplined, and worrying that Amber and Jay might try to talk her into patching up her marriage, but gradually their calm acceptance of both the boys and her had helped her to relax.

'It's really kind of Jay to take so much trouble with the boys. He's so patient with them. My father gets very cross when they don't do as they're told. That's why he wants them to go to boarding school. He says I can't control them.'

'Control them?' Amber queried gently.

Sarah flushed. 'Daddy's a bit of a disciplinarian.'

'Well, it's true that children, especially young children, do need boundaries, but personally I think they're rather too young for boarding school yet. Sending them to boarding school young is very much an upper-class thing, I know. I remember the arguments I had with my first husband over our son. What does Nick think?'

The question was slipped in gently, Amber's wise gaze somehow conveying to Sarah that here, in her presence, it was safe for her to say what could not be said anywhere else.

'He doesn't agree with Daddy. In fact, he doesn't want them to go to boarding school at all. He thinks the school he went to is perfectly good enough.'

'But you don't think it will be?'

311

'Well, it is a good school, of course, but . . . as Daddy says, it isn't Eton, and Daddy says the right education is so important these days. I mean the boys won't have trust funds or anything, and of course I want the best for them.'

'Of course you do,' Amber agreed, 'and a good education *is* important.'

Sarah gave her a grateful look, relieved that Amber hadn't questioned or rejected what she'd said. She was so used to both her father and Nick telling her that she didn't know what she was talking about that it was something of a novelty for her to have someone agree with her.

'More than anything else I want them to be happy,' she admitted, emboldened by Amber's acceptance.

'Well, they look very happy at the moment,' Amber laughed.

'Oh, yes. They are really enjoying themselves. Jay is so patient with them, and Harry so kind. My father would never—' Sarah bit her lip. She didn't want to criticise her father, but she couldn't help contrasting the way Jay listened to and spent time with Alex and Neil with the way her father was always criticising them and punishing them. They'd 'played' chess with him in complete attentive silence the night before last, and then last night he and Harry had given them a billiards lesson. During the daytime there'd been cycling practice, and 'helping' with the farm work, as well as 'helping' Mrs Leggit in the kitchen, and Mr Leggit to wash the car. There'd been no tears and tantrums over bedtimes, no refusing to eat their meals, no angry male voice telling her and them that they were at fault for something or other.

'But surely Nick plays with them? They are his sons, after all.'

Amber's tone was so mild that Sarah didn't feel for one minute that Amber was deliberately bringing Nick into the conversation as a reminder that he was the boys' father, and her own father merely their grandfather.

'Yes. He does. Well, he did, but Daddy said that it was because Nick wasn't disciplining them properly that they were so naughty. He said that it couldn't be expected that Nick would know how to bring them up properly because of his own background.'

'And is that what you thought as well, Sarah? That Nick's background is a barrier to him being a good father?'

Put like that, it sounded terrible.

'No, of course not,' she denied immediately. 'I loved Nick so much when we first got married. He was so different from anyone else I knew. Being with him was exciting . . .'

'Because you knew your father wouldn't approve of him?' Amber guessed.

Sarah's eyes widened. 'No! Well, maybe a little . . .'

'But now you'd rather that Nick wasn't different, is that it?'

'No . . . I don't know. It just makes everything so difficult, him and Daddy not getting on and always arguing about everything the other one says. Daddy never wanted me to marry Nick. He says he doesn't know how to behave properly.'

Amber laughed. 'Oh dear. Poor Nick. You mean he slurps his soup and eats with his fingers.'

Sarah was horrified. 'No, certainly not, nothing like that. It's just that Daddy is . . .'

'A terrible snob.' Amber's smile took the sting out of her words. 'My grandmother was the same.'

Sarah looked at her. 'Was she?'

'Oh, yes, very much so. Only my grandmother possessed the kind of snobbery that comes from not being born into the upper class rather than from being born into it. She was determined that I would do what she had not been able to do, and marry a title. In my day we had no choice, we had to obey our parents. Your generation is much more fortunate and yet, at the same time, less fortunate.'

'What do you mean?'

'I mean that my generation had no choices, no freedom, so we could always blame those who chose for us if things went wrong. Your generation is free to make its own choices but that means you also have to shoulder the burden of the responsibility for those choices. You chose to marry Nick but now I think you rather wish that you hadn't because Nick's hopes and expectations for your sons are very different from you own.'

'Nick's the one who wishes he hadn't married me.' Sarah couldn't bring herself to look at Amber. 'Sometimes I just feel so worthless. I can't discipline my children and make them behave themselves. I can't stop my father criticising me.'

'You are not worthless, Sarah. You must never think that.'

Privately Amber was thinking that whilst both Nick and Sarah's father had a lot to answer for, for the way they had behaved, it was Sarah's father who could take most of the blame. From what Sarah had said about him, Amber judged him to be a snob and a bully.

'Have you talked to Nick the way you have to me, told him how difficult you find it to deal with your father, asked him for his support?'

Sarah looked warily at Amber. 'I can't talk to Nick about Daddy. He'd immediately think that he'd won and start being even more nasty about him. Anyway, he doesn't care how I feel. All he cares about is making life as difficult for me as he can.'

'Rose telephoned me this morning. Nick would like to come and see the children whilst they're here.'

'I knew something like this would happen,' Sarah claimed immediately, feeling betrayed. 'I suppose Rose only arranged for us to come here for Nick's benefit. She was just pretending to want to help me. She is his stepmother, after all.'

'No, Sarah, that isn't the case at all. Rose has told Nick that he mustn't come unless you've agreed that he can. He is her stepson, yes, and of course his feelings and his happiness are important to her, but Rose isn't someone who would deliberately interfere in someone else's life with the kind of ulterior motive you are implying.' There was just a hint of reproach in Amber's voice. 'If you don't want to see Nick, there is no need for you to do so. No one is going to bully you into doing or agreeing to anything you don't want to do here, Sarah, you have my word on that. You are free to make up your own mind.

'If Nick were to come down he could stay with Janey at Fitton – there would be no need for you to be involved. Jay could take the boys over to see him there, or if you prefer, he could visit them here and Jay would stay with them. Separation and divorce is never easy. You love your sons, I know that.'

Sarah thought about what Amber had said to her earlier about her generation having the responsibility that came with the freedom to make their own decisions. Her father had never really allowed her that freedom, which was why she had rebelled and married Nick, a childish action, not the action of an adult. Nick had always accused her of not being able to stand up to her father and of giving in to him, of not having a mind of her own.

She owed it to her sons to protect them as well as love them. She owed it to them to think of their needs above her own. She knew they missed Nick; they were always asking where he was. She and Nick might be estranged but did she really want her sons, *their* sons, growing up not knowing their father, cowed into obedience by their grandfather? She took a deep breath.

'How long . . . how long would he want to stay?'

'Only a weekend.'

Sarah sighed and then nodded her head reluctantly. 'Very well. But I don't want to see him.'

'I shall make sure that Rose knows that and passes that information on to him.'

Chapter Nineteen

Katie had the house to herself, apart from the staff; she was in the 'small' sitting room, reading the letter Fran had sent her, when Ingham, the butler – her mother insisted on having a butler – knocked on the door and told her that she had a visitor.

Tom! Katie had known – hoped – that he would come. No one would talk to her about Zoë, no one understood that she wanted to talk about her, that she needed to talk about her.

He looked taller and broader, and yet at the same time his face was thinner – tanned, but thinner – a man's face now, not a boy's.

'Oh, Tom . . .'

'I hope you're pleased with yourself. But of course you are. You're still alive, after all, aren't you. It's Zoë who's dead, Zoë who's lying in a coffin with her broken body, and her broken face mended so that she looks like a plastic doll, not you. No, you're fine.'

White-faced with shock, Katie stepped back, desperately holding on to one of the chairs to support herself, shivering beneath the onslaught of Tom's savage denunciation.

Sticks and stones may break my bones but words can

never hurt me. The old playground chant whirled shrilly through her head. How untrue it was. Words could and did hurt. They could pierce the flesh and bury themselves in the mind and the heart, poisoning both. Oh, yes, words hurt, could torment and torture, but not as much as her own guilt. That was far more painful than Tom's verbal assault on her.

Guilty – yes, she was guilty: guilty of false friendship, guilty of vanity, guilty of not caring enough, of not doing enough, guilty of not being there for Zoë when Zoë had needed her, guilty of not putting Zoë first. Guilty as charged, and she would have the weight of that guilt hanging over her for the rest of her life, waking with it in the morning and sleeping with it at night, a constant presence.

'You knew how vulnerable she was and yet you let her go. You danced with your friends whilst Zoë died.'

'Stop it!' Katie clapped her hands over her ears, but whilst she might be able to blot out the sound of Tom's fury she could not blot out the sound of her own grief and despair.

'You could have saved her. You could have been with her. You must have known what was going on, and the way she was living – the drugs, the fact that she had gone back to that . . . to Von Thruber.'

'No I didn't,' Katie protested emotionally.

'You must have done.'

The sitting-room door opened abruptly.

'What's going on?'

Katie looked numbly at her father, whilst Tom turned and stormed out. She could see her father half turn as though to go after him, and then turn back to her when she made a small keening sound of anguish.

'Katie . . .'

'Drogo, what on earth is happening?' Emerald demanded. 'Tom Mallory has just rushed past me in such a hurry that he nearly knocked me over, and not a word of apology, Katie . . . *Katie* . . .'

'Come on, Katie, it's all right. We're here now.' Her father was holding her as though she were still a little girl, rocking her in his arms as she struggled with the sobs of despair that racked her body.

'It's my fault that Zoë is dead. It's my fault . . .'

'No, Katie, it isn't your fault,' her mother was insisting with maternal determination to protect her.

'Yes it is. I knew . . . I knew about . . . about everything. I made her go to the ball when she didn't want to, and Tom was right. I was enjoying myself too much to care about Zoë. And now she's dead, and it's my fault.'

'Katie, listen to me.' Her father's voice was calm but firm. 'Of course you're upset about Zoë – she was your best friend – but the Zoë, I remember, was someone who always made up her own mind about what she wanted to do, not someone who took advice from or listened to others. Do you really think you could have made her go to the ball if she hadn't wanted to go, or stopped her from leaving if she hadn't wanted to leave? You are not to blame for Zoë's death, Katie, and I want you to promise me that you'll stop thinking that.'

Heathrow was busy, and Olivia had to queue for a taxi. She couldn't wait to see Robert. She hadn't even telephoned him to say she was coming, wanting it to be a surprise. She was longing to see him.

There was still a sore unhealed place inside her from the argument she had had with her parents the night they had gone out to dinner and run into Tait, and it hurt. She had never ever felt that she and her parents were on differing sides of an argument before, and it made her feel so alone and miserable, as though somehow her own judgement was lacking. Was it? Was that secretly why she had come here, because the upset with her parents had underlined for her all those small and, she had believed, unimportant issues about which her own feelings did not match with Robert's? She wasn't actually having doubts about the long-term viability of marrying Robert, was she, of their providing together the right environment for their children to grow to maturity, and for their own happiness, just as she had done in her parents' love?

She loved Robert, she protested to herself. Having any kind of second thoughts was disloyal to him. And love surely was more important than sharing the same point of view everything. About everything, yes, but when it came to certain important non-negotiable attitudes of mind it was important that they were shared. Defending Robert to her parents and Tait, she had unwillingly recognised in reality she felt more as they did than Robert did. That had scared her. The last thing she wanted now, with their marriage only weeks away, was to open the door to serious doubts about how well suited politically, in their attitudes to world affairs, and to the inequality amongst humankind, which her heated discussion with her parents and Tait had brought up.

It was Tait's fault that that door had been opened. If he hadn't been there, interfering, forcing her to see . . . Forcing her to see nothing. She loved Robert and that was all that mattered. Wasn't it?

Of course, on the surface everything was normal. She and her mother were still having lunch together to talk about the wedding, but deep down, Olivia felt that her parents had all but abandoned her by taking Tait's side against her. She was afraid that from now on they would be on separate sides of a deep chasm, and that marriage to Robert would divide them by far more than the Atlantic. That upset her. They were a very close family. She loved her parents and her younger brother. How was she going to feel, knowing that once she was Robert's wife she would have to put her duty to Lauranto before her love for her parents? A new shiver of doubt touched Olivia's spine. She desperately needed the reassurance that being with Robert would give her.

It had been a sudden decision to come to London, a need to be with Robert, who loved her. After all, it was Robert she would be spending the rest of her life with, not her parents.

It was gone midnight before the taxi dropped her outside Robert's apartment.

Going up in the lift, Olivia imagined how pleased he would be to see her. How he would take her in his arms and hold her safe and wanted.

She used her key to let herself into the apartment – she wanted it to be a proper surprise, after all – and her mouth curved into a tender smile as she remembered the way Robert had surprised her by creeping into her bedroom. This time she would be the one doing the surprising.

She pushed open the bedroom door, a shaft of moon-light from the uncurtained windows outlining the shapes of the two people on the bed quite obviously engaged in the act of sex. Two people: Robert and the woman lying beneath him as he arched over her, her blonde hair spread over the pillow, both of them naked.

Charlotte saw her first, her mouth curving into a mocking smile.

'You've got a visitor and I do believe it is your fiancée,' she told Robert coolly.

Robert whirled round, demanding, 'Livvy, what the hell are you doing here?'

He was getting off the bed, reaching for his clothes. The whole thing was surreal, a dark madness of nightmare proportions. But it wasn't a nightmare, Olivia told herself. It was real.

'I wanted to surprise you,' she told him.

She tugged off her ring and put it down, turning towards the door, barely able to see for the hot burning tears of shock and shame and anger – and yes, perhaps something that might almost be guilty relief – clouding her gaze.

Stumbling and fumbling, somehow she made it back out onto the street, where she was violently sick. She wanted to lie down and die, to crawl away into some dark place where she would never have to face the world again. She was shocked, all her dreams and hopes in ruins, and yet some part of her somehow was relieved, and that only made her feel worse.

Because Tait had been right? To hell with Tait. Why on earth was she allowing him into her thoughts now?

A cruising taxi caught her eye. She flagged it down.

'Where to, love?' asked the driver.

Where to? Not to hell – she was already there, or at least a version of it. Where was there for her to go? All she wanted was some deep dark place where she could hide away to escape from the public gossip and fallout from the ending of their engagement and plans to marry. There was no escape for her, though. She was a woman, not a girl; there were things to be done, the wedding and all its attendant arrangements to be cancelled.

'Heathrow, please,' she told the driver.

By the time Robert had pulled on his jeans and followed Olivia outside, the street was empty. Anger and guilt assaulted his mind and body. All his life Robert had done the right thing, stayed on the side of the good and the just, never been tempted or wanted to be tempted to cross the line between that life and experience what lay on the other side of it, knowing what the consequences of doing so might be. All his life he had needed to be in control, and sworn he would never allow that control to pass from him. But now he had done both. Like the child he had once been he tried to take refuge in the comfort of anger and blaming others.

What the hell had possessed Olivia to just turn up like that without warning him that she was coming? Why hadn't she stopped to think that he could easily not have been there, that he could easily have been away in Lauranto or . . . or staying with friends? Or in Charlotte's bed, as he had been virtually every night since he had first been there?

Why had he suggested that tonight of all nights they went back to his flat? He knew the answer to that. It was because he had felt that in his flat, on his territory, he would have more control.

He'd even been intending to tell her that it had to stop, that it was over between them, to remind her that he was soon to be married, Robert told himself with defensive virtue.

But for Olivia's uninvited visit, it could all have been over and she would never have needed to know anything about it. Lots of men had a final fling before marriage, a final grab for what they knew they were about to lose.

There was no point in him standing out here in his bare feet, wearing only a pair of jeans, Robert admitted, making his way back indoors. With luck – and he certainly deserved some – he'd be able to persuade Olivia that what she'd seen meant nothing, once she'd calmed down and got in touch with him.

In Robert's bedroom, all starkly utilitarian and mono-chrome – although thankfully he did have the good taste and the good sense to have top-quality Egyptian cotton bed linen – Charlotte looked at the ring she was balancing in the palm of her hand. It was, she acknow-ledged, incredibly ugly, a regal statement of power and wealth and status, with no modern pretensions to beauty about it whatsoever.

She was still looking at it and smiling when Robert strode back into the bedroom.

'Poor Robert,' she mocked him. 'How unfortunate. Now you've lost your fiancée, but fortunately not your crown jewels, which I assure you, you would have done had you been my fiancé.'

Her taunting *double entendre* increased Robert's furious resentment.

'I can assure you that there would be no chance of that, since I'd never have been engaged to you in the first place.'

'Meaning what? That I am nowhere near "good" enough to marry a man like you?'

Robert could feel his face starting to burn as he heard the cynical mockery in her voice.

'Do you know something?' she continued lazily. 'I rather believe that your little fiancée – I'm sorry, I mean your ex-fiancée – will come to thank me ultimately.'

'Olivia will still marry me. She loves me,' Robert insisted when Charlotte looked askance at him.

'I feel very sorry for her if that's true,' she told him, stretching her still naked body luxuriously against the rumpled sheets.

'I want you to leave,' Robert told her abruptly.

'Do you?' Charlotte teased him, sitting up and smiling provocatively at him. 'Are you sure?'

'Yes. Damn you,' Robert replied.

Charlotte started to laugh. 'Oh, poor Robert.'

'You wanted this to happen, didn't you?' Robert accused her angrily. He looked at the ring she had placed on the matt black cubed bedside table. 'Well, if you're hoping that you will get to wear this and become my wife—'

'Me marry you?' There was no laughter in Charlotte's expression now, only iron-hard cold cruelty. 'I don't intend to marry anyone – ever – but if I did you would be the last man on earth I'd want to be married to, Robert. Oh, yes, you can look at me as though you don't believe me. After all, you were born with a silver spoon in your mouth, and soon you'll be wearing a golden crown, so what you see is a perfect man, a marital prize any woman would be a fool not to throw herself gratefully at your feet for. That's what you think, isn't it? Admit it. Well, I've got a bit of a shock for you, Robert. You know, the way you see yourself as a man isn't the way I see you at all. What I see is an image without substance, a hollow straw creature wearing his bestowed finery with ignorance and vanity. You have done nothing to earn what you have, nothing to merit it or to take pride in achieving it. Even your work as an architect is a vanity you've created to allow you to "play" with the buildings of the really great architects so that some of their glory can be yours. You are nothing, Robert. Everything you have, everything you are, has all been given to you by others. You are empty of everything it would take for a man to persuade me to break my vow never to marry.'

'You hate me.' Robert understood. 'You wanted this to happen. You want to destroy me. Why?'

'Do you really want to know? Very well, come with me then.' Charlotte reached for her clothes.

In a daze Robert watched her dress, her movements calm and smooth, fluid and elegant, unlike his own as he pulled on his own clothes in the now tense hostility of his bedroom.

Half an hour later they were standing opposite one another in the square ground-floor room Charlotte used as her 'social office'.

She unlocked one of the drawers in the pretty antique mahogany writing desk and removed a folder.

'This is why I hate you, Robert, or rather why I did hate you. You're such a pitiful pathetic creature that I don't even think you are worthy of my hatred any longer.'

Robert looked at the folder.

'Open it,' Charlotte instructed him.

Robert's hands shook slightly as he did as she commanded. Inside the folder, in a clear Perspex wallet, was a magazine. Old and crumpled, it had a photograph of his mother on its front cover.

'Remember this?' Charlotte asked.

Robert nodded. 'Yes. The magazine did a feature on my mother. I had to be photographed with her. I remember how much I hated it. It seemed to take for ever. Why have you got a copy? Where did you get it? It must be well over twenty years old.'

'Yes, it is. And as to where I got it, I stole it from my mother. She wanted this magazine so badly that she spent her booze money on it. My mother was an alcoholic,' she explained without emotion. 'An alcoholic, a drug user, sometimes a hooker, occasionally a mother, but most of all my mother was a punch bag. That's how my father treated her, you see, as a punch bag. He would dope her up with drink and drugs until she was slobbering all over him and then he'd knock her around, as opposed to knocking her up. He saved that for his other women.'

Robert was watching her.

Charlotte paused and spaced out the words very deliberately. 'His rich, spoiled, titled women. Women just like your mother, Robert. In fact, your mother was one of his women, and whenever she rubbed him up the wrong way instead of the right way, he'd come round and beat hell out of my mother.'

Max Preston. Robert didn't know how he knew, he just did. His heart was jerking slowly and painfully as though reluctant to beat, just as his mind was reluctant to accept what he was hearing.

'Max Preston was your father.'

Charlotte smiled mirthlessly. 'He was responsible for my conception, yes, but he was never what you might call a father. And unlike your mother, Robert, mine didn't survive her relationship with him. She didn't come out the other side of an exciting affair with him to go on to marry someone titled and provide me with a rich stepfather. But then, of course, my mother wasn't a lady, a socialite enjoying the amusement of taking a rough East End criminal as her lover because it was the fashionable thing to do.

'Shall I tell you what my life was like when I saw this article and you for the first time, Robert? It was all about keeping out of my father's way whenever he came round, and keeping my mother from falling down the stairs and breaking her neck because she was too drunk to stand upright when he wasn't. It was about stealing food because I never got enough to eat, wearing rags, having stones thrown at me by the other kids, because I was always dirty – an outcast who no one wanted. But that life was heaven to the life I had once my mother died and I was sent to a children's home. Can you imagine what it's like living somewhere where the people caring for you regularly sexually abuse you, where you have to learn to turn tricks to get treats – and by treats I mean a basic meal. No, of course you don't. You are to be the Crown Prince of Lauranto, your experience of growing up is a world away from mine, but you and I are linked,

328

Robert. Our parents were lovers. My father shagged your mother. Just think, we could have shared a stepbrother or -sister. Imagine that.'

Charlotte laughed when Robert gagged.

He was shocked, appalled, angry and resentful, and, at some unwanted deeper level, he had a sense of knowing, of sharing her emotions, a sense of knowing that the two of them were somehow bound together by fate.

Angrily he pushed that awareness away. He didn't want to be reminded of Max Preston and the role he had once played in his mother's life, but most of all Robert didn't want to have to acknowledge that there was a bond between Charlotte and himself that went far deeper than Charlotte could know. He could hear in her voice, when she talked about her parents, every single emotion he himself knew so well and he knew that the cause of those emotions was the same for both of them: that it came from the destructive twisting of a child's understanding of the adult sexual world caused by exposure to too much too soon. He might only have witnessed the violence of the sexuality his mother and Max Preston had shared once, but its effect on him was burned into him for life. He did not need to ask himself how what she had experienced might have affected Charlotte. He knew.

'Nothing to say?' she mocked him.

Robert looked at her. 'I know why you've said and done what you have tonight, but it won't make any difference, you know.' He turned away from her and walked towards the door, pausing with his hand on the door knob to add, 'It won't put right for you what's wrong here.' He touched his chest, and then his forehead. 'Or here.'

They looked at one another in silence and then Robert opened the door and walked through it.

Perhaps it was because it is said that revenge is a dish best eaten cold that hers had lost its flavour, Charlotte reflected after Robert had gone. Consuming hers in the fierce heat of raw passion had certainly not brought her the satisfaction she had expected. Where there should have been satiation and delight, there was emptiness and pain. She picked up the magazine and put it back in the folder, which she returned to the drawer.

It was over, and time for her to move on.

If she could.

If she could . . . She had to. She must.

Chapter Twenty

'You've broken off your engagement to Robert?'

Olivia watched as her mother sank down into the chair, staring at her.

The flight back from London to New York had been more than long enough for her to prepare and rehearse until she was not just word-perfect, but expression-, emotion- and inward belief-perfect in her speech of renunciation of her engagement to Robert and her reasons for it. It had been easier, after all, to focus on that instead of constantly relaying inside her head what she had seen when she had opened the door to Robert's bedroom.

'Yes,' she confirmed to her mother. 'I flew to London to tell him personally and . . . and he understands and accepts my feelings.' Olivia produced the small wry smile she had practised.

'To be honest, I don't think he was entirely surprised when I told him that, much as I love him, I know that I'd never really be comfortable being the wife of a crown prince. You and Dad have succeeded far too well at bringing me up as an American.' Another smile. Wider and more genuine and truthful this time. 'I shouldn't

331

have let things go as far as they have, I know, but I wanted it to work so much, Mom. I wanted the whole fairy-tale thing, not of marrying a prince but of marrying my first love. But Robert is a man, not a cardboard cut-out. He has dreams and ambitions for Lauranto and a need to fulfil them that I can't share.' And a need for a woman who wasn't her, but she couldn't tell her mother that. Some things were best kept secret, for everyone's sake.

'I know that Aunt Emerald will be furious with me, but Robert and I are both agreed that it's better for us to part as friends now. I suppose that part of me got caught up in the whole fairy-tale princess thing, but when it came down to it, when I had to really think about what I'd have to give up in order to be the kind of wife Robert, as Crown Prince, will need I knew that I couldn't do it. It was what Tait said about wasting my education that did it, I think.'

What a pleasure it was to blame Tait Cabot Forbes, a small piece of much-needed sweetness in the bitterness of what she was having to stomach.

'I hadn't really thought about it before. I was too caught up in the whole being-in-love thing, but once he had said it, it got me thinking and added to what you and Dad said about the Atlantic being between us, and then the little hints Robert's grandmother has been dropping about court protocol and that kind of thing. I began to question if I could really adapt to that life. I do love Robert and I always will, but the weight of that engagement ring was beginning to feel like a ball and chain tying me to a life that I knew would never be comfortable for me.'

'Why didn't you say something to us . . . to me . . . talk about how you felt?'

'Come on, Mom, you know I couldn't have done that. It wouldn't have been fair to Robert.'

How easily the lies slipped from her tongue, every bit as easily as Robert had betrayed her.

'Mom . . .' Olivia reached for her mother's hand. This was it, the clincher, the all-important emotional nail through the heart to pin her argument firmly in place, 'if I had loved Robert enough, I would have been willing to give up my freedom. And if he had loved me enough he would have been willing to give up the throne. We've both agreed on that. When we held our love up to the stark sharp light of reality, it simply wasn't as strong as we both know it needed to be. There's no need for you to worry. There's no animosity or regret between us, other than the regret we both feel at all the fuss that cancelling the wedding is going to cause.'

'Does Emerald know yet?'

'I don't know. I assume that Robert will tell her, although we didn't discuss him doing so.'

'She won't be pleased.'

Olivia pulled a small face. 'I think that's something of an understatement,' she laughed. 'I'm rather glad that I'm on the other side of the Atlantic.'

'Oh, darling, I shouldn't say this, I know, but the truth is that I'm rather glad that you won't be marrying Robert.'

'Yes, I thought you would be.'

'It wasn't because of us, your father and me, and what we said?'

'No, of course not,' Olivia assured her mother instantly

and truthfully. 'I made the decision because I know it's the right thing for me to do.'

How true that was. There was no point in marrying a man you caught out having sex with someone else. Better to be hurt and suffer the humiliation and misery she was suffering now than to spend a whole lifetime humiliated by an unfaithful husband. Robert had never loved her. He couldn't have done. She'd had plenty of leisure on the return flight to remember some of the things he'd said to her. Phrases such as, 'You are perfect for me and for Lauranto', 'I know you are the right wife for me', and others of a similar nature had surfaced from her memory, not as the sweet tender words of a man deeply in love with her, but as the practical disclosures of a man looking for a wife whose suitability would allow him to get on with the more important things in his life.

If she had been deceived, then it was because in part she had wanted to be deceived, Olivia felt now. She had done the work of loving Robert for him; all he had needed to do was to say the words.

Perhaps she was a coward for not telling her parents the truth, but what was the point? Nothing they could say or do would remove or ease the humiliation and hurt scorching her pride and her heart. Knowing the truth, they would be bound to defend her and that would lead to repercussions within the family, with Aunt Emerald no doubt equally determined to defend Robert. The last thing she wanted was to be the cause of a family fallout with attention focused on her humiliation and the fact that Robert hadn't really loved her at all.

No, the fiction she had created wouldn't just save her

own pride, it would save family harmony as well. And as for Robert – perhaps a good ruler needed to be pragmatic and to put the needs of his country above human emotions. Perhaps he needed to be prepared to sacrifice truth and honesty and love when they involved only one person, in order to benefit the lives of so many others. Perhaps treasuring beautiful buildings was more important than treasuring the love that two people could share together. There was no 'perhaps', though, about whether she was more American than European, or how important the American values with which her parents had brought her up were to her. She had had a lucky escape, and from now on it was her career on which she would be concentrating, and the way she could benefit others through her writing. She had posted a letter to Robert before she had left Heathrow, and in it she had told him that she intended to tell her parents that she had come to England to break off their engagement because she felt that she could not adapt to the role of the wife of a crown prince, and that their parting had been amicable. Somehow she suspected that Robert would much prefer to go along with that than to admit to the truth.

'We're going to the Hamptons this weekend, Livvy – why don't you come with us? The break will do you good. We can let it be known before we leave that you've changed your mind about marrying Robert, and by the time we come back to the city in September, people will be talking about something else.'

Olivia nodded. The longest journey begins with the first step and right now she felt that she had a very long journey indeed to make.

* * *

Sarah couldn't settle. This was the morning that Nick would be arriving to collect Alex and Neil.

Nick . . . Her heart jumped inside her chest, her body aching for him in that way she simply seemed unable to get over. She had loved him so much. *Had* loved him? Wasn't it true that she still loved him? Yes, but she didn't feel secure with him. She didn't feel that he loved her. His work seemed to matter so much more to him than she and the boys did. That, and getting the better of her father. She had the boys to think of. The quarrels between her and Nick weren't good for them. Jay had offered to take the boys to Fitton so that Sarah didn't have to see Nick but, with the conversation she had had with Amber still very much to the forefront of her mind, Sarah had decided that it would be better for the boys if they saw that she was 'happy' for them to go off with their father. After all, Nick was hardly likely to start a row about either the boys or their marriage in front of his own family.

Both boys were excited at the thought of seeing their father. Nick had telephoned and spoken to them earlier in the week, and it had increased Sarah's guilt to recognise their eager anticipation.

Only last night, when she had bent to kiss them good night after reading them their bedtime story, Alex had told her happily, 'I like it much better here, Mummy, than going to Scotland. Can we come again?'

Nick had been ready to leave for Denham by eight o'clock. John and Janey were both early risers, especially in the summer, Janey had told him with a rueful smile, so that John and the men could make the most of the daylight and the good weather.

It had shocked Nick at first when Rose had told him that Sarah had taken the boys to Denham, but it had shocked him even more when Rose had added that she felt that Sarah had been pushed close to the edge of a breakdown by the antagonism between him and her father, and his neglect of her by putting his work first.

'The reason I work so hard is because I want her and the boys to have everything they need. She married me, but she lets her father rule our lives,' had been Nick's defence.

'She's afraid of him, Nick, and I rather think that she's afraid of you as well, albeit in a different way. And as for providing them with what they need, I believe that what Sarah really needs and wants for the boys and for herself is your support, and your love.'

'No,' Nick had denied. 'If she did . . . She wanted me to leave.' He had paused and then asked Rose grimly, 'You say she's afraid of me? If she's told you that—'

'No, she hasn't. And I don't mean to imply that she's afraid of you in any physical sense. It's your dislike of her father and your willingness to show it she fears, I suspect. She's been conditioned since childhood to obey her father or risk the consequences of his temper. He's a bully, that much is obvious, and Sarah has learned to do everything she can not to provoke him. When you antagonise him, it's Sarah and the boys he takes it out on, not you, and then you make things worse by criticising her for letting herself be bullied. What she needs is your support, not your criticism.'

'How the hell can I not criticise when she lets her father treat my sons the way he does, and when she says that everything I try to do for them is "common" and not good enough?'

Rose took hold of his arm and looked up at him in that way she had that said she meant he was to listen to what she had to say.

'Nick, Sarah has never known what it is to have the confidence a child gets from good loving parenting. Imagine how that must feel. Imagine what it must be like to go in fear, not of blows but of words. Sarah's grown up believing that if she avoids provoking those words then everything will be all right, but of course it isn't and it can't be. She needs your help and your support to overcome her fear of her father.'

'We're separated,' Nick had reminded his stepmother. 'Her choice, not mine.'

'Yes, but you are still both your sons' parents. You can't want to see them growing up taking on their mother's fear, and that's what will happen.'

'I've tried,' Nick had insisted. 'I've told Sarah over and over again that I won't have her father telling Alex and Neil what to do. I've told her that I don't want her taking them up to Scotland, but all she does is go on about where her father thinks they should go to boarding school and how he thinks they should learn to ride. What I say doesn't matter, but then it wouldn't, would it, since marrying me is the biggest mistake she's ever made and I'm not good enough for her?'

'You are the boys' father,' Rose had repeated. 'They need you, Nick. They need you to show them what good parenting is. They need to know that you are there for them.' She had paused, then added, 'Remember how you felt when you first came to us? Remember how it feels not to know if you're wanted and if you are safe? If the adults who should care for you love you enough to protect you?'

It was as a result of that conversation with his step-mother that he was here now, feeling wary, suspicious of being judged by Amber and Jay, who had no doubt heard all about his failings from Sarah, not even knowing if he was capable of spending a full day with his sons without getting bored and irritated.

'I don't know what I'm going to do to keep them occupied. And stop them wanting to be taken back to their mother,' he had admitted to Janey the previous evening after a couple of glasses of the Scotch he had brought down for John, and which John had insisted on opening.

'I could make up a picnic for you,' Janey had offered.

'And you could teach them to fish,' Harry suggested. 'Remember when you taught me and David, Dad?'

'I remember you coming back with Wellingtons full of pond water,' Janey laughed.

Teach them to fish! His only experience of fishing had been dangling a bit of line into the Thames with a worm on it, something Sarah's father would turn his aristocratic nose up at, no doubt.

Half-past eight. If he drove over to Denham slowly, and took his time, he shouldn't be there too much before nine.

'Will Daddy be here soon?' Neil asked impatiently.

Sarah forced herself to smile. 'I expect so, yes.

'I don't know how Nick will cope with having them for a full day. He isn't used to spending that kind of time with them,' she fretted to Amber.

'I'm sure the boys will find something to keep themselves and him occupied. I think they want to show him how well they can ride their bikes, and Alex was saying something about taking Nick to watch Jeff Lloyd training his dogs.'

One of Denham's tenant farmers was a very successful trainer of dogs for sheepdog trials and he taught them in a small paddock at Home Farm. Jay had been taking the boys with him when he went there, knowing they would enjoy watching the dogs.

Sarah tried to imagine Nick – urbane, elegant, a city dweller, so restless that he never even sat down to drink a cup of coffee – leaning on a fence, watching dogs round up sheep.

'Daddy's here.'

Neil's voice, sharp excited, broke through Sarah's thoughts. She could feel the colour coming and going in her face.

'I don't want to see him,' she told Amber. 'You said that I didn't have to.'

'Of course you don't,' Amber agreed.

'I'll need to remind him that Neil doesn't always remember to say he needs the lavatory when he gets excited. And not to give them chewing gum.'

Amber smiled and forbore to say that Jay could easily pass on those messages for her, instead waving to Nick through the window as Jay went out to greet him.

Nick had never thought of Amber and Jay as his grandparents – after all, they weren't – but Jay's welcome for him made it clear that in his eyes Nick was very much part of his family, the warmth of his unexpected hug catching Nick off guard.

'Thanks for everything you and Amber are doing for Sarah and the boys.'

'There's no need to thank us,' Jay assured him.

They were inside the hall now, his sons coming racing towards him, flinging themselves bodily against him, clutching at his jeans-clad legs. *His sons.* His flesh, pushing into him, demanding his attention, looking up at him. A surge of love rose up inside him, crashing through him like a wall of water too powerful to be denied. He wanted to gather them up in his arms and hold them to him.

A small movement caught his eye and he looked beyond them to see Sarah standing in the doorway, Amber at her side.

'They've grown,' was all he could think of to say.

'Yes.'

Awkwardly they looked at one another, and then looked away.

'We can ride our bikes properly now, Daddy,' Alex announced importantly.

'Yes, and Granddad Jay lets me keep the stabilisers on mine, even though I don't really need them any more, now that I'm five.'

Neil's voice was slightly anxious. Hearing it, Sarah flinched, remembering how her father had insisted on removing the stabilisers from his bike even though the little boy had kept falling off, telling him that he was a coward.

Nick kneeled down so that his face was on the same level as his son's. 'I had stabilisers on my bike until I was seven,' he fibbed.

Neil's eyes rounded. 'Did you?'

He turned round and looked at Sarah. 'Daddy had stabilisers on his bike until he was seven, and he isn't a coward,' he told her excitedly.

None of the adults spoke, Nick finally breaking the silence to ruffle Neil's hair and say softly, 'Wanting to be safe doesn't make anyone a coward. It's just good common sense. Now,' he announced, standing up, 'what would you like to do?'

Both boys started to speak at the same time, telling him happily about all the exciting things they'd been doing and wanted to show him.

A mixture of remorse, regret and the longing for what might have been flowered painfully in Sarah's heart as she watched the three of them. Nick looked up and caught her eye. Quickly she looked away, reminding herself of the misery the endless arguments between them had caused, the differences between them of upbringing and outlook, and the schism they had caused in their marriage, which could not be healed. What she was seeing now when she looked at Nick and their sons was a fantasy of a perfect family that did not and could not exist – for them.

'Olivia's broken off your engagement, but why?'

'I've already explained to you, Mother, she feels that she'd have problems adjusting to my role as Crown Prince.'

Publicly allowing Olivia to be the one to break their engagement, especially when she had come up with the reason she had for doing so, and suggested that for the sake of family harmony they remained 'friends', at least in public, was a small price to pay for the truth to remain hidden, Robert knew, even if having to listen to his mother's complaints was beginning to be tiresome.

'But she knew you planned to become Crown Prince. She seemed perfectly comfortable with the idea. Are you sure this isn't just some kind of last-minute bridal nerves, Robert? I mean, cancelling the wedding at this stage is bound to cause gossip. Surely you can talk to her, persuade her . . .'

'I have far too much respect for Olivia to want to try to put pressure on her, Mother.'

The faint rustle of the newspaper he was reading was his stepfather's only reaction to his comment, but his mother was far more vocal.

'Respect! For goodness' sake, Robert, you're talking about the girl you love and who loves you, and Olivia does love you.'

'And I love her. Too much to want to tie her into a way of life that she doesn't want. I'm afraid that it looks as though you are going to have to content yourself with a possible Habsburg daughter-in-law after all.'

His weak attempt at a joke didn't please his mother in the least, but it was his stepfather's comment that really stunned him.

Drogo put down his newspaper and said quietly, 'It isn't too late for you to withdraw from stepping into your late father's shoes, you know, Robert. I appreciate that you feel you have a duty to his people, but you also have a duty to yourself.'

'Drogo's right, Robert,' his mother agreed. 'You don't have to give in to your grandmother and become Crown Prince of Lauranto.'

His mother had never wanted him to leave England,

Robert knew, but he couldn't give up the pull of his dreams for the restoration of Lauranto's buildings.

'I could give up the throne,' he agreed, 'but I think that both Olivia and I know that if our love was strong enough that would not be necessary. The last thing I want is for her to feel that she has to marry me because I've made a sacrifice that she doesn't really want me to make. We probably rushed into things. We've both agreed that we'll remain friends – we are, after all, family. I'm leaving for Lauranto tomorrow. Obviously my grandmother will have to be told of the changes to my plans, and there are certain meetings I need to hold there with regard to the changes that need to be made in the law to enable us to set up a new tax-free banking system for overseas investors. Don't worry,' he told his mother, 'everything will work out fine, you'll see.'

Once Robert had gone Emerald turned to her husband angrily. 'What on earth have I done to be given children who cause us so many problems? First we've got Katie getting herself involved in Zoë's death, and all the fuss that's caused, Katie crying all over the place and Zoë's parents banning her from the funeral! And now Robert, of all people, has let Olivia break off her engagement to him when I'm right in the middle of planning their wedding.'

'Very inconsiderate of them both,' Drogo agreed mildly.

Emerald gave him a suspicious look. 'It isn't funny, Drogo.'

Drogo folded up his *Times* and stood up. 'There I do agree with you. None of it is remotely funny. Two of our children are currently suffering from varying degrees

344

of misery and despair – no loving parent can ever be anything less than concerned about something like that, or not try to guide them out of their misery into a happier situation. Sometimes though, we have to allow our children the opportunity to fight their own battles, make their own mistakes, and direct their own lives.'

Emerald opened her mouth to point out that she was far better equipped to do all of those things for them than any one of her offspring, given the current mess they were making of their lives, and then closed it again as she saw the look in Drogo's eyes. Only rarely did her husband look at her in such a way, and when he did . . .

'I only want the best for them,' she told him.

Drogo walked over and put his arms round her. 'I know you do,' he acknowledged, 'but they need to find out for themselves what that "best" might be, and when they do we need to be able to offer them all the support they might ask for in achieving that best.'

'You mean I shouldn't interfere.' Emerald put it to him succinctly.

Drogo smiled at her, the same sweet tender smile he had used all those years ago to undermine her opposition to him.

'Something like that,' he agreed.

'Katie.'

'Mmm.'

In what had once been the 'nursery' of Lenchester House, but was now the younger members of the family's 'sitting room,' Emma, who had just returned home for a short break, looked impatiently at her younger sister, who was curled up on one of the room's two comfortable sofas, staring into space, the book she had claimed to be reading lying open on her lap, '*Katie*,' Emma repeated, forcing Katie to focus on her. 'I was talking to you, telling you about Venice and working at Angelli's and the special dyes and design they're working on there for Grandmother's eightieth birthday, but you haven't heard a word I've said.'

'I was thinking about Zoë. If only I'd tried harder to find her.'

'Oh, for goodness' sake, will you stop brooding about Zoë. What happened wasn't your fault. If you ask me it was always obvious that something like that would happen. She was always such a drama queen and so . . . so wild and reckless.'

Katie shook her head. 'Stop it. Stop saying things like that about her. Don't you understand, she's dead. She's DEAD, Emma.'

Emma put her hands on her hips and glared at her sibling in disgust. Then Katie got up and ran from the room, slamming her door behind her.

In her bedroom Katie flung herself down on the bed and pressed her face into her pillow. She wanted to cry but she couldn't. There was a hard, hurting pain in her chest and her eyes were dry. Nothing seemed real any more, nothing seemed to matter. She could hear Zoë's voice inside her head so clearly that sometimes she thought she was really there and that all she had to do was to turn round and she'd see her.

If only she'd gone to look for her instead of enjoying herself; if only she'd found her then Zoë would be alive now. Tom was right to blame her. It was her fault.

'Katie, I'm sorry for what I said about Zoë.' Emma

346

was standing in the doorway to her bedroom, looking and sounding contrite. 'I didn't mean it; it's just that it makes me so cross to see you like this, blaming yourself when it isn't your fault.'

Emma sat down beside her on the bed and Katie felt the mattress depressing beneath her weight.

'I know she was your friend, but she wasn't your responsibility, Katie.'

'I could have gone and found her when she went missing during the ball.'

'But you wouldn't have found her, would you, because you didn't know where she'd gone. She lied to you, Katie. She told you it was all over between her and Axel.'

'I could have looked. I could have tried.'

'Oh, Katie . . .' Emma put her arms round her sister, hugging her tightly.

'Tell me about the silk then, for Grandma.'

Still hugging her, Emma told her quietly, 'It's beautiful, the colours are just right, just like those in the fabric from *The Silk Merchant's Daughter*, but somehow modern as well.' Emma laughed. 'I think that Uncle Rocco is a tiny bit jealous because Angelli's aren't going to be weaving it. Aunt Rose really is so clever. I wasn't sure I wanted to work at the Walton Street shop until I saw this new silk.' She pulled a small face. 'I mean, I love our silks but I'm not like you – you love the past and the archives. I like something more modern, and I've decided now that I'm going to ask Aunt Rose if she'll let me work with her on her own private work. Her commercial designs are so trendy.'

Katie listened and nodded. Talking about silk and the

business was much safer than thinking about Zoë and Tom and everything that she'd lost.

Olivia retreated deeper into the shade of the immaculately trimmed hedge of the Lawrences' Southampton Village garden. Neatly trimmed hedges were as much of a 'must' amongst certain sectors of the WASP Hamptons' summer visitors as homes whose décor favoured the Sister Parish interior design look, and the owners, Lilly Pulitzer dresses, and the men wearing their old Harvard and Yale crew shirts.

It was a world with which Olivia was very familiar, but not wholly a part of. Her parents were members of a more recent influx into the Hamptons not the 'old' élite.

Scott Fitzgerald would have felt perfectly at home at today's cocktail party, Olivia suspected. Southampton Village was one *the* most prestigious parts of the Hamptons in which to summer; the families who came had often holidayed here for generation after generation. The house and the garden had that uncopiable patina of status, tradition and money that spoke volumes about those who lived here and the way in which they lived. It was simply not 'WASP' to dress up for the Hamptons, and the more Bostonian WASP a family was, the more they gloried in their family traditions. Here on the sunshine-splashed lawn, society women put aside their designer clothes to dress themselves and their young daughters in their 'Lilly's' – skirts, dresses and shorts in the bright pinks and green that were the hallmark of Lilly Pulitzer's clothes, the colours a perfect foil for their summer-blonde tresses and honey-tanned limbs – and socialised with one another, their accents pure Boston and New York WASP. Men wearing linen trousers and blazers talked earnestly to one another, teenagers in madras cut-offs fooled around and flirted. Olivia could see her own parents in the middle of a group of fellow 'new' summer visitors to the Hamptons, wealthy New York socialites who, like the WASPS before them, had discovered the delights of the string of islands so convenient for New York and offering such a different summer lifestyle from the city.

Out of the corner of her eye Olivia caught a glimpse of a pair of Nantucket Reds, the shorts and trousers worn mainly by the sailing fraternity, which had originated from Murray's Toggery Shop on Nantucket Island. The shorts, like the muscular tanned legs they were on belonged to Tait and instinctively Olivia stepped deeper into the shadows, exhaling in relief when she could no longer see the shorts.

'So the engagement's off then.'

Olivia nearly dropped her barely touched glass of Pimm's. Tait must have gone round the hedge and sneaked up on her from the other side.

'Yes,' she agreed tersely.

'Fancy coming out sailing tomorrow?'

Olivia was just about to open her mouth to refuse when he added insouciantly, 'We need someone to man the bilge, and your father happened to mention that you're a pretty good sailor.'

As invitations went it was hardly a glamorous one, being invited to man the bilge pump on an open sailing boat, but . . . as little as she personally liked Tait, Olivia knew how anxious her parents were about her and how carefully other people were avoiding mentioning the cancellation of the wedding. The last thing she wanted was to be treated as an object of pity; she had her pride, after all. Being seen to be 'enjoying' herself might mean creating the kind of fiction that part of her despised, but another part of her demanded that she grit her teeth and put on the show of her life.

'I used to be,' Olivia agreed.

'Fine. I'll drive by and pick you up in the morning. Seven OK?'

She should tell him that she didn't want to go sailing, but their hostess had seen them and was coming over, and whilst Lulu might look like the sweetest old lady you could imagine, and all sugar and spice, the reality was that she was as sharp and shrewd as any one of her four lawyer sons, and Olivia certainly didn't want her to catch her in the middle of an argument with Tait.

'Yes,' she agreed helplessly, returning Lulu's smile and then making her escape when she saw that it was Tait who was their hostess's real quarry.

'There you are.'

Olivia returned her mother's smile as she joined them.

They'd come over to Lulu's for drinks after watching the polo, and this evening they were having dinner at Fresno Restaurant in East Hampton, supposedly one of the best eating places in the area. Unlike most of the other women Olivia wasn't wearing a 'Lilly'. She didn't think the pretty-pretty patterns or the colours suited her, and instead she was wearing a simple acid-yellow shift dress, bought originally with Robert's appreciation and their honeymoon in mind.

Robert. Olivia looked down at her bare left hand. She mustn't let it hurt. She wouldn't let it hurt.

'Did Tait find you?' her mother asked. 'Only he was asking where you were earlier.'

'Mmm. He's asked me to go out sailing tomorrow – they're short of someone to man the bilge pumps. He's picking me up around seven. I don't know who else will be there.'

'Jay, I don't think Cassandra is very well.'

Jay looked up from his copy of *Farmers Weekly*. Amber's forehead was pleated in a genuinely anxious frown.

'And this time I don't think she's putting it on. In fact she hasn't mentioned not feeling well at all but she's gone dreadfully thin and I don't think she's eating properly. I noticed when I was at the Dower House this morning that whilst she pretended to eat a biscuit, all she really did was crumble it up. I'd thought of having a word with Janey. She sees Cassandra more than I do. I don't want to fuss, of course.'

'I would have thought that if Cassandra isn't well, she'd have made sure that John and Janey knew about it.'

'Well, yes, if it was some minor ailment she could use to make more demands on their time, I dare say she might, but I can't help thinking that if it was something more serious, if she was really worried, then she might not.'

When Jay made no response, Amber got up and went over to him, putting her hand on his arm. 'I couldn't help thinking how awful it must be to be Cassandra,

Jay. She has no real friends, no close family, other than us, no one to turn to who loves her if she is really ill.'

'And whose fault is that? If no one loves Cassandra then I would suggest that it's because Cassandra has never offered anyone love herself.'

'Yes, I know, but I can't help thinking that if she is really ill, she must feel so frightened and alone, unable to tell anyone, fearful and unwell.'

Jay eyed his wife ruefully. 'What is it you want me to do?'

'She is your cousin. You grew up together. I thought if you visited her, just you, she might confide in you.'

'Cassandra confide in me? I doubt it.'

'Jay, I think she may be seriously ill.' Amber's voice was quiet and grave. 'She has gone shockingly thin in such a short time. Her mother died from stomach cancer, remember. Cassandra must be so frightened. Anyone would be.'

'You have the most tender heart of anyone I know, you know that, don't you?' Jay answered her.

'I'll have a word with Janey. You could speak to Dr Phillips. Perhaps he could visit Cassandra, just casually, you know, so as not to frighten her,' Amber suggested.

Jay gave a sharp bark of laughter. 'You're worried about Cassandra being frightened?'

'This is different. She's so alone, Jay. We have each other and I know I can face anything because I have you and your love, but without that . . . Besides, she is family.'

'Very well, I'll have a word with Dr Phillips.'

'And I'll speak to Janey,' Amber told him, kissing the top of his head, before changing the subject.

'The house seems dreadfully quiet now that Sarah and the boys have gone, doesn't it?'

'Yes. They were good little chaps.'

'Sarah seemed so much better when she left us. I do hope her visit to her parents won't set her back. Her father sounds like a dreadful bully, and an even worse snob.'

Jay patted Amber's hand. 'It's typical of you that you want to make everyone's life happy for them, but things don't always work out as we would wish.'

'I know,' Amber agreed. 'I was dreadfully worried at first that the fact that Robert and Olivia have decided they don't want to get married would cause a rift between Ella and Emerald, but according to Ella, when she telephoned the other day, their decision was mutual and amicable. I must say that I don't blame Livvy for feeling she couldn't cope with the protocol and formality that would go with being married to a crown prince. It wouldn't have been the easiest of lives. And since Robert has said that he wants to dedicate himself and his future to Lauranto it's better for them to part now than to create future unhappiness for themselves by marrying and then discovering it won't work. I'll go and ring Janey now and tell her that you're going to speak to Dr Phillips about Cassandra.'

Chapter Twenty-One

From where he was standing on the ramparts of the old fortified part of the castle, Robert could see out across the painting-perfect blue of the Mediterranean. Last night he'd hosted a banquet for the financiers and the financial journalists who'd come to Lauranto to talk about his now public plans to turn the principality into a tax haven – or a money box for the Crown, as one cynical American journalist had suggested – plans that had been received very well indeed by his audience. He already had several private pledges of support and money for the charity he was setting up – The Society for the Protection of Lauranto's Public Buildings – and his grandmother was delighted by the future prospect of getting the opportunity to find him a royal bride she deemed worthy of him, once he had had time to recover from his broken engagement, and having agreed that Robert would need time to establish himself and put his plans for the country into practice before he married.

Everything in his life was as near perfect as it was possible for it to be. The gleaming yachts down in the harbour below him weren't just carrying their wealthy owners, they were carrying his successful plans for the future.

One of those yachts had been chartered by the Wineburghers. Rebecca Wineburgher had made a special effort to seek him out in private to tell him how sorry she had been to hear about the broken engagement and to offer him some sexual solace. He'd been tempted to accept – until she'd happened to mention that Charlotte had been invited to join them as one of their guests on the yacht but that she had refused at the last minute.

'It must be because of a man,' Rebecca had told Robert confidingly, 'although she refused to tell me who he is.'

Those words, the mention of Charlotte's name, had immediately chilled and then withered his desire; that same desire that burned so hotly and unwontedly in him at night when he woke up aching for Charlotte, his body ignoring the commands of his mind to stop wanting her. One day he would stop wanting her. One day.

Far better to feast his gaze on the architectural treasure he had inherited, and the future that lay ahead of him, than to allow himself to admit that what he felt for Charlotte went beyond mere sexual desire. How it had happened he had no idea, but it had. She had engaged his emotions and possessed his thoughts and his feelings as no woman ever had, or, he suspected, ever would. To put it simply, she had his heart in her hands and he could not reclaim it, so he must therefore learn to live without it. His grandmother would never accept Charlotte as his consort, and Charlotte herself would never accept being forced to play the role of his hidden mistress while another woman played the public role of his wife. Nor would he want her to. For them it must be all or nothing, and he had chosen nothing. He had waited so long for this chance to prove himself worthy of being acknowledged as his father's rightful heir. There was so much he could do here in Lauranto, not just to confirm that worthiness but to turn the country round, to make it a shining jewel of historic beauty and financial success. He could achieve those goals, he knew it. At a deeper level he felt it was his destiny to achieve them. But he could not fulfil that destiny and accept that other destiny that called to him: to be with Charlotte, to heal her wounds whilst she healed him, to complete the circle he suspected they had been born to complete. He had to choose. He had chosen, taking a choice he had made long before he had met Charlotte or even known she existed. Had he met her first, would it have made a difference? He didn't know.

Tait's friends Ogden and Natalie Adams had a house at Sag Harbor. Ogden had been at school and then college with Tait, and the wife, Natalie, was the kind of young woman Olivia easily felt at home with, especially when it turned out they were sorority sisters, having been at Vassar three years apart but in the same sorority.

They sailed most of the day in the old sailboat that Natalie's grandfather had raced in his youth, eating the picnic lunch Natalie had prepared, in an atmosphere of relaxed good humour that Olivia could almost feel smoothing down the raised prickles of her defensiveness, and now they were back on dry land, Tait's hand steadying Olivia as she jumped from the boat onto the jetty, and then brushing down the back of her sunbleached denim cut-offs, her momentary tension and questioning glance drawing a grin from him.

'Looks like you sat in one of the sandwiches,' he informed her.

'Livvy, don't pay any attention to him,' Natalie told her. 'He's been eyeing up your behind all day, I swear it, and now he's finally got to do what he's been wanting to do. Men! There's nothing they like more than a peachy derrière in well-fitting denim.'

Even Livvy laughed, although she doubted that Tait's action had anything whatsoever to do with any male desire to touch her.

'Great day, guys,' was Ogden's verdict as they all tramped along the boardwalk, the men carrying the now empty picnic basket between them. The breeze coming in off the sea smelled of salt and the cooling of the day, the sun starting to dip towards the horizon.

'We're planning a clam bake for Saturday,' Natalie told Livvy. 'You'd be welcome to join us.'

Acceptance and the offer of friendship. She'd be silly to refuse either of them, Livvy acknowledged.

'I'd like that,' she accepted, and was rewarded by Natalie slipping her arm through Livvy's own and telling her confidingly, 'The last girl Tait introduced us to was dreadful. A real city type, you know.' She wrinkled up her nose. 'Wearing a white linen dress and heels for a day's sailing, and she was seasick. Ogden said he reckoned that Tait brought her along deliberately as a way of shaking her off.'

By the time Tait had dropped Ogden and Natalie off at their home, it was almost dusk, the sky pearling through palest blue to lemon and then deep rose, a sea mist rolling in off the ocean. Neither of them spoke until Tait brought his Jeep to a halt outside her parents' property, and then it was only to exchange 'good nights' and for Olivia to thank Tait for her day out.

Later that night, lying awake in bed and thinking about the day, she reached into the drawer of her bedside cabinet and withdrew the Tiffany box containing the diamond on its chain that had been Robert's Valentine gift to her. Suspending the chain from her fingertips she watched as the diamond shone in the moonlight coming in through the window. Tears filled her eyes, but not the bitter, lonely, cheated tears of the Olivia who had seen another woman naked in the arms of the man she loved. No, these were cleansing tears, which stung, yes, but that also healed.

She returned the diamond to its box and put it back in the drawer, telling herself that she must send it back to Robert and wish him well in his future. When Labor Day came in September to mark the end of summer, she would return to New York ready to begin the next stage of her life, ready to concentrate on her career. And ready to abandon her antipathy towards Tait?

Today she had enjoyed herself, but that enjoyment had come from proving to Tait that she wasn't broken-hearted over Robert, nothing more. *Nothing* more.

Cassandra had cancer and was dying. It had been officially confirmed by the doctors and now she was 'resting' at home in the Dower House, after undergoing various tests in hospital.

The disease was advanced and unstoppable. Cassandra herself had not been told, and a fiction was being maintained of a stomach disorder that meant that she must rest, which was why a nurse had been hired by the family – to make sure she did, and to make sure that she took the 'medicine' prescribed for her by the Hospital. Dr Phillips had assured them that with private nursing it would be possible for Cassandra to die at home in her own bed.

Cassandra had said nothing, nor given any indication that she knew that her life was drawing to its close. The vicar had become a regular visitor, but Janey had told Amber that Cassandra turned her head away and ignored him whenever he sat with her.

'Do you think Cassandra does know?' Amber asked Jay as they sat together in the garden, enjoying the warmth of the late August sunshine. 'I think she must really,' she answered her own question, 'what with us visiting her nearly every day, and the doctor calling round almost as often. She never says anything, though, Jay. In fact, she barely speaks at all. Nurse Jenkins says the same. She told Janey she'd never nursed anyone who was so determined not to communicate with her. She hates me, I know,' Amber told him. 'I can see it in her eyes when she looks at me. Poor Cassandra, it must be so uncomfortable having all that hatred and anger locked up inside her.

'Did you read Sarah's letter?' They'd received a letter from Sarah that morning.

Jay nodded. 'It seems that she's taking your advice and standing up to her father, at least where the boys are concerned.'

'Yes,' Amber agreed. 'And that can't be easy for her. She did tell me that she was reluctant to take them up to Scotland but that she would feel guilty if she didn't because her parents had made so many plans to entertain people whilst they were there. Rose told me that Nick is convinced her father is trying to arrange a match for Sarah with someone he approves of, before Nick and Sarah have even started divorce proceedings, and I rather think that Nick might be right. It's such a pity that the two of them couldn't make a go of things. I hate to think of those two little boys torn between their parents.'

'There's no reason why they shouldn't have an amicable divorce,' Jay pointed out. 'It can happen.'

'Yes. I know. But with Sarah saying to me that she felt that she and Nick have such different values and aspirations for the boys, my fear is that they will learn to be one person with their mother and a different person with their father,' Amber said sadly.

Janey stood in the morning cool of her kitchen, nursing her first precious early morning cup of tea and looking out of the window. The sun was coming up, dispersing the mist that hung over Fitton's pools. Her thoughts were on Cassandra, whose life was ebbing away, her body becoming a dry husk as the cancer ate into her.

The nurse had told Janey yesterday that she was going to have to ask the doctor to increase Cassandra's morphine and that the end could not be very far away.

Janey hoped it wasn't. There was something destructive to the human decency for both the dying and the waiting about a long-drawn-out process. Or was it because secretly, she was already thinking about the future, and how it would feel to be free of Cassandra's difficult presence? Such thought made her uncomfortable. She felt that she was like a vulture hovering over the dying, waiting to pick clean the carcass for her own benefit.

John came into the kitchen. He looked so careworn. Like her, he must secretly be thinking ahead, looking forward to his escape from Cassandra's constant financial demands, although she knew he would not say so, because he would deem it 'wrong' to speak in such a way.

The reality was, though, that once they didn't have to pay Cassandra's large jointure every month they would be so much better off. Backwards and forwards Janey's thoughts darted and scuttled, whilst she went through the motions of making fresh tea for John and putting toast in the toaster, whilst he poured some cereal into a bowl, and she thought about the day ahead.

How much longer would it be? The doctor had said just weeks, possibly a month or so. The nurse might be able to tell her more later this morning when she went over to the Dower House.

The nurse, Mrs Jenkins, was waiting for Janey when she reached the Dower House, having walked there, instead of driving, to enjoy the late summer warmth of the morning – and to delay having to sit with Cassandra, knowing that her feelings towards John's stepmother were not the kind of feelings a person should have towards someone who was dying.

The Dower House now had that clinical unpleasant hospital ward smell, through which something else was woven, which gripped the stomach muscles with its primeval message of impending death.

'She's asking to see your husband,' Mrs Jenkins told Janey without preamble.

John, in common with a lot of men, wasn't comfortable around the sick. He hated hospitals and the last thing he would want to do, Janey knew, was sit with his dying stepmother.

'He's out harvesting,' Janey told her. 'I can tell him when he comes in this evening.'

The nurse shook her head. 'That could be too late,' she said meaningfully.

Janey didn't know what to do. John wouldn't thank her for sending for him so that he could watch Cassandra taking her last breath, but Mrs Jenkins seemed determined that he must be sent for.

'It's her dying wish that she speaks to him,' she insisted, confirming Janey's thoughts. 'He ought to be with her and, take it from me, she'll fight to hang on until he is. I've seen it before.'

'Very well,' Janey agreed reluctantly. 'I'll have to drive out to Home Farm to tell him. It could be an hour before we're back.'

John received the nurse's news just as Janey had known he would, standing stiffly, his body tensed, torn between duty and his own personal feelings, whilst the men continued to work on.

It was Harry, on holiday from his work in Norfolk to help his father, who broke the difficult silence, announcing calmly, 'I'll come back with you and Mum as well, Dad,' as he hauled himself into the back of the Range Rover. Watching John move slowly and heavily, Janey couldn't help contrasting his stiff tired movements with those of their son. Farming was hard on the human body, and when you added to that the mental strain

John had been under for so many years because of their financial situation it was no wonder his shoulders were rounded and his head bowed. She wanted to reach for his hand and hold it, but she was afraid of her gesture being unwanted. They seemed to be growing so far apart, so unable to talk to one another, and that hurt her. She had loved John so much – she still did love him – but sometimes she needed him to show her that she was important to him.

It was wrong of her to look forward to the outcome of Cassandra's death, she knew, and she certainly couldn't voice her private thoughts to John, who would be shocked, but the reality was that life would be easier for them when Cassandra was no longer there. Sometimes Janey felt that Cassandra, with her constant reinforcement of how much Fitton meant to John, came between them as much as Fitton itself, forcing her to take an ever more backward place in her husband's life.

Back at the Dower House, Mrs Jenkins greeted them with a professional inclination of her head, falling into step alongside John in a way that excluded Janey. To prevent her from going into the room with him, or to ensure that he couldn't change his mind and refuse to enter it himself, Janey wondered, automatically falling back to wait with Harry.

'We'll have to let Granny and Gramps know,' he reminded her.

'Yes, of course.'

Her father was Cassandra's cousin, after all, and closer to her in blood than John.

The nurse was coming back to them – alone.

'How long do you think she has?' Janey asked uncomfortably. 'Only my father will want to be here. He's her cousin, and she and my stepmother were girls together.'

'Probably tonight, although it's hard to tell. I've phoned the doctor and he's going to call when he does his afternoon round.'

Janey looked up the stairs. Poor John. He would hate sitting in the hospital-smelling room, Cassandra lying in the bed with its immaculate hospital cornered sheets, her body so thin now that it barely lifted them, her face sunken and yellowing.

Chapter Twenty-Two

The light was fading from the August sky. They were still all at the Dower House, Janey and John, and Harry, along with Amber and Jay now, as well as the vicar and the nurse. It was several hours now since John had walked quietly out of Cassandra's room, closing the door behind him, his face grey and set.

He hadn't spoken about whatever might have passed between him and Cassandra, and Janey had sensed that he didn't want her to ask. She could only hope that his stepmother had, in her final hours, realised and recognised John's kindness to her and had thanked him for it. She longed to be able to go to him, to be held by him and to hold him in return, but still she felt that Cassandra and the adverse effect she had had on their marriage lay between them, constraining her. She felt, too, that she did not have the right to ask him what Cassandra had said to him. John had always been a very private man but how had it happened that that need for privacy had begun to exclude her? Was Cassandra right when she had intimated that the weight Janey had put on made her undesirable? Was that why John no longer turned to her in the shared intimacy of their bed?

These were questions she felt she could not ask him, and private shames she felt she could not discuss with anyone else either.

The grandfather clock ticked steadily in the hallway. Janey looked at it every time she passed it on her way up and down the stairs to relieve whoever was sitting with Cassandra, and then to be relieved in turn herself.

The stepmother who had tormented John so badly had slipped into a coma now, and though still alive, had gone beyond any awareness of them, her breath rasping in and out of her lungs as her strong heart fought against the morphine she had been given to ease her pain and her journey.

'Two o'clock in the morning, or thereabouts, it will be,' Mrs Jenkins said. 'You wait and see. The death hour, they used to call it.'

Amber glanced at the clock on the mantel. It was barely ten in the evening. Another four hours of sitting waiting. That sounded terrible and she certainly didn't want to hasten Cassandra's end, but it was so pitiful and sad, this gathering here of those she should have loved and been loved by in return, but who instead were here out of duty.

She and Jay had driven over the moment they'd been informed, and then later Mrs Leggit had sent over a basket of cold food, which so far only Harry, the nurse and the vicar had eaten.

Amber looked at Jay. Cassandra was his cousin, after all. As though he sensed her concern for him he gave her a reassuring smile.

Janey, who had just gone up to take Amber's place at Cassandra's bedside, was looking pale and tense, John withdrawn, poor man. Amber hoped that Cassandra had made her peace with him, for both their sakes. A sudden thought struck Amber as she looked out of the window at the darkening sky. Quickly she stood up.

'What is it?' Jay asked her.

'The window.' She told him urgently. 'We must open it so that her spirit can go free.'

The nurse was pursing her lips and frowning. She exchanged a look with the vicar that said she did not approve of such pagan country habits, but Harry had got to his feet as well.

'I'll go up and open it.'

Amber gave the vicar and Mrs Jenkins an apologetic look. 'I know it must seem superstitious, but I can't bear to think . . . well, you just never know, do you?'

'There is a good deal of kindness in the thought of speeding the soul home,' the vicar responded gently.

'Well, I don't think that having cold air blowing over a person in their last hours is a good thing at all,' the nurse told them, getting up herself, and then stiffening when they heard Janey calling from upstairs.

Mrs Jenkins, Vicar, I think you'd better come.'

Amber looked at Jay. 'I think we should be there,' she told him, the two of them taking the stairs together in the wake of the others.

There had been so many deathbeds over the years, Amber thought quietly to herself: Robert, her first husband, and Luc, her precious son; Greg, her cousin; Jay's first wife; her grandmother, Blanche, and others, but none that filled her with the same kind of sadness she felt now; the sadness of a life never lived as it could have been, the sadness of a heart that had never loved as it might have done, a human being whose death would not be truly mourned.

Janey had stepped back from the bed when the nurse had come in. The shock of seeing Cassandra try to raise her head from the pillow and then claw at her throat before falling back against it, her breathing ragged and noisy, had left her trembling slightly and glad of the fresh breeze coming in through the sash window that Harry had opened.

The room was silent apart from Cassandra's agonised breathing. Was she struggling to live or struggling to die, Amber wondered as the vicar took hold of Cassandra's fleshless hands and began to recite the Lord's Prayer. Gradually they all joined in, and Amber saw Jay flinch when the vicar raised his voice just as Cassandra's last breath rattled angrily in her throat.

'Oh, no!' Olivia's protest made to herself under her breath was caused by the fact that she had just seen Tait emerging from the foyer to her parents' apartment block as she crossed Fifth Avenue to go into it. She and her parents had returned to New York from the Hamptons earlier than planned after learning of Cassandra's death, and were due to fly to Manchester in the morning to attend her funeral, which was why Olivia was going to spend the night at home with them rather than in her own apartment.

It was too late to try to hide. Tait had seen her and was striding purposefully towards her.

'I've just seen your parents,' he announced. 'I was sorry to hear about your family loss.'

Olivia sighed, tempted to tell him that very few

members of the family would actually feel that Cassandra's death was a 'loss'.

'I'm glad to have bumped into you.' He had stepped to the back of the sidewalk, somehow or other taking possession of her arm as he did so, drawing her with him so that they were standing in the shadow of the building.

'This probably isn't the time, but there's something I want to discuss with you.'

'Like what?' Olivia demanded warily.

'I want an assistant to help me with the investigative work I need to do on an article I'm planning, and I'd like you to be that assistant.'

Confused thoughts filled Olivia's head. For a young, still-not-established reporter to be offered a chance of working with someone with Tait's reputation was like being handed the keys to a gold mine, and if she'd got any sense she'd be jumping to accept it, but . . .

Why should Tait offer her such a prestigious job? Why should he and why would he?

Olivia looked up towards the windows of her parents' apartment. She knew how much they loved her, how relieved they were that she wasn't marrying Robert, and how eager they were to encourage her to focus on her career. And they were certainly all three of those things enough to use their influence to, as they would see it, 'help' her.

'I get it,' she told him angrily. 'My parents have asked you to do this, haven't they? They've asked you to make up a job as your assistant and offer it to me, and you've agreed because you feel you owe my folks one for that article you wrote about them. You don't want me as your assistant, you want to buy off your guilt. Well, I don't need your charity. I don't need you or anyone else feeling sorry for me just because I found my fiancé in bed with someone else.' Olivia's eyes widened as she realised what she'd said.

For a minute they looked at one another in silence, and then Tait said, 'I'm sorry.'

'Well, I'm not,' Olivia told him angrily, surprised to discover as she said the words that it was true. 'I'm not sorry at all. In fact I'm glad. What I thought I was in love with was a silly dream leftover from my teens. I don't want you to be sorry for me, Tait, I don't want you to offer me a made-up job, and most of all I don't want to have to listen to you lying to me when I know damn well that you've got an ulterior motive for what you're doing.'

As she hurled the words at him, Olivia pulled her arm free and headed blindly towards the edge of the sidewalk, intending to cross the road, oblivious to the taxi bearing down on her until she heard the squeal of its tyres as Tait yanked her out of its path.

'Yes, I do have an ulterior motive for offering you a job,' he agreed.

He was breathing heavily and so was she, her heart pounding with the realisation of how close she had come to stepping under the wheels of the yellow cab.

'But it isn't because I want to please your father, it's because of this.'

'This' was his fingers biting into the soft flesh of her upper arms through the fabric of her silk blazer, and his mouth coming down hard on her own, in a kiss that was angry and hungry and a world away from the deliberate detached skill of Robert's kiss. This was the kiss of a man with real feelings, real anger, real need, real desire for her, and something inside her exulted in knowing that, as she started to push him away and then relented.

It was nothing like the kiss Robert had given her in his car on the drive to Denham but it did have one thing in common with that kiss, Olivia knew, and that was that this too signalled a new beginning. Her hostility that had masked her awareness of Tait had now been given a name and that name was 'maybe'.

'We can take things slowly,' Tait was saying to her, giving her that smile that she had previously labelled too confident, too WASP, and too male. 'I mean, my mom might phone me every week to ask if I've met the girl yet who'll be the mother of her grandchildren, but I promise I won't tell her about you. Well, I won't say too much, and you don't have to accept any invitations she'll send you.' He smiled at her again. 'So how about it, do you want the job?'

'The job?' she asked him. 'Or you?'

'You can have either, or both,' Tait offered hopefully. 'You can come home with me right now, if you like, and trial the goods on offer.'

Olivia started to laugh, to really laugh in a way that she couldn't remember doing in what felt like for ever. Something unfettered and free was unfurling inside her, a happiness that she didn't have to be anything or anyone other than herself.

'I'm flying to Manchester tomorrow, for Aunt Cassandra's funeral,' she told him.

'You know where to find me when you come back – if you want to,' Tait responded.

Olivia smiled.

Oh, she would want to, and she knew that her smile was telling him exactly that.

'Katie.'

Tom! What was he doing here in her father's library at Lenchester House? Katie backed towards the door. When her father had said there was someone waiting to see her in here she had never for a moment imagined it would be Tom. How could Dad have done this to her after the cruel things Tom had already said to her?

'Katie, no, please don't go. There's something I want to say to you.'

She had reached the door and now she leaned back against it, her hands behind her and clasping the handle so that she could make her escape if she needed to.

Tom's face was tanned, his hair slightly longer. He had what she thought of as a New York look about him, slicker, smarter, somehow, than his London equivalent. Katie noticed these things but noticing them was simply a way of holding at bay what she was really feeling and the fear gripping her that he had come here to hurt her again.

'I'm sorry, Katie, for what I said before about you and Zoë.' His voice was so low that she had to lean forward to hear it properly. 'Turning on you like that was wrong of me, cruel and cowardly, and totally unforgivable.'

'Then why did you do it?'

'Guilt, anger, fear, all of those and probably more. Guilt because I couldn't seem to help Zoë. Guilt, too, because I'd pretended not to see that. Just as I pretended to believe her when she blamed you for the cuts on her

374

arms. We were both very good at that – blaming you for our own flaws and weaknesses.'

She watched as his chest rose and then fell as he paused to take in air, before continuing bleakly, 'Anger against myself for failing Zoë, which I turned against you rather than accepting that it should have been directed at myself. But most of all fear, Katie. Fear of what it would mean to me as a brother if I were to admit to myself that Zoë had emotional problems that were rooted so deep inside her that it may have been impossible to cure them. Fear of having to live the rest of my life blaming myself because I wasn't there for her when I should have been. Fear of the yawning chasm of what her suicide said about her fear and loneliness, and my failure to see them and help her. Instead of accepting and confronting those things, I turned on you, blaming you for my faults and failings. I knew perfectly well that there was no power on earth that could stop Zoë when she had her mind set on something. You were her friend, not her gaoler. You weren't to blame for what happened, Katie. I was.'

There was a moment of silence, in which Katie tried to assimilate what he had said, before he continued, 'I don't have the right to ask you to forgive me but I can at least make sure that I free you from the guilt that is rightfully mine. I should never have allowed her to return to Oxford.' His voice was heavy with pain and remorse.

'It wouldn't have made any difference,' Katie felt bound to tell him. Tom was looking at her. She took a deep, unsteady breath and continued, 'We talked about how she felt. She said she wouldn't see Axel again. She didn't want to, but there was something inside her, something she couldn't control, which, when it took hold of her, she couldn't fight. It changed her, took possession of her, she said that herself. She told me that Axel was her soulmate and I think she truly believed that. She said she'd rather die than live without him.'

They looked at one another.

'I'm sorry I refused to believe you when you told me that Zoë had lied to me about you. In reality I think I knew all along that you were the one telling the truth.'

'Zoë told me that she'd lied to me about you,' Katie said. 'She told me that you hadn't telephoned when you had.' She paused. Then: 'She told me that you'd given her a message for me saying that you hoped I hadn't misinterpreted what you'd said to me when we had lunch together.'

He was still looking at her and although neither of them had moved, surely somehow there was less distance between them.

'I never gave her any message for you.'

'I never encouraged Axel – or wanted to.'

'Why would she do such a thing?'

'She was frightened, I think,' Katie told him simply. 'She thought that I'd tell you about her still seeing Axel.'

'Or maybe she was afraid that she might lose you to me. You were her rock, Katie. You were what secured her to reality. You were the best thing that ever happened to her, a true friend. I'm so sorry I misjudged you. Jealousy can be so destructive. I couldn't bear the thought of you not wanting my love that—'

'You loved me?'

They were closer. Close enough for her to see the dark length of his eyelashes and to feel the warmth of his breath on her skin.

Tom was shaking his head, his lips forming the word, 'No,' his denial filling the heart she had thought healed with fresh searing pain.

She started to turn away from him, but he caught hold of her hand, twining his fingers with hers, his voice filled with emotion as he told her, 'No, not *loved*, in the past, Katie, but *love*, as in the present, and for the future. I've never stopped thinking that we could have something very special.'

'Neither have I.' Her voice was shaking and so was her body, but it was a very different kind of tremor that gripped it when Tom took her in his arms and kissed her.

It only took a heartbeat for her to know what she wanted. Wrapping her arms tightly round him, she kissed him back.

'Zoë will always be part of us,' he told her when they had finally managed to stop kissing, 'but we'll make sure that hers is a loved and cherished presence in our memories, and that our memories of her are good ones that bond us together. I think she'd like that.'

'Yes she would,' Katie agreed.

'I'd better go. Your father said I could have fifteen minutes. He wasn't going to let me see you at all at first, until I told him what I wanted to say,' Tom admitted.

Smiling at her, he opened the door. Katie could see her father waiting in the hall, protective, caring, understanding; she was so lucky to have such a father, she knew.

Tom started to walk towards her father. Katie exhaled quickly and ran after him. Tom stopped and waited for her, holding out his hand to her. Katie took it, Tom's fingers curling round hers, his flesh warm and alive against her own.

Everything was going to be all right. Everything was going to be better than all right.

Chapter Twenty-Three

Cassandra's funeral took place at the small church where members of the Fitton Legh, and de Vries families had worshipped for generations, her body interred in the Fitton Legh family vault, the bars of September sunshine warming the ancient worn stone of the graves.

The family had turned out in force to pay their 'last respects' and, sitting in the drawing room at Denham House on their return from the service, watching those she loved, Amber thought of how many of their lives had been affected by Cassandra.

Like ripples from a stone thrown into a still pond one small personal action could have far-reaching consequences.

'I know I shouldn't say this, but it's a relief that she's gone,' Janey admitted to Ella, as the two sisters sat together. 'I know she was our mother's friend – what is it?' she asked when Ella recoiled so sharply that she almost spilled her tea into the delicate china saucer.

'Nothing,' Ella lied. Cassandra and their mother were both dead now, and there was no point in telling Janey after all these years that their mother and Cassandra had been lovers. At least now that Cassandra was gone she could learn to forget that awful image of the two of them in bed together, which had haunted her every time there had been a big family get-together. She had never been able to look at Cassandra without seeing it and them.

Rose smiled at Amber as she stood with Josh.

Smiling back, Amber reflected on how it had been Cassandra's malice in informing Lord Fitton Legh of Greg's affair with his wife that had led to her cousin being banished to Hong Kong, and there he had met Rose's mother.

Even she and Jay might not have shared their lives in the way that they had – as man and wife – if Cassandra had not tormented Jay's poor first wife so dreadfully that in her already vulnerable mental state she had been involved in the accident that had ended her life.

Poor Cassandra, always so bitter and so manipulative. Amber hoped that at last she was at peace.

Olivia smiled warmly at Robert. He hadn't been avoiding her exactly, but of course there had been a certain air of restraint between her own mother and his, and now in the spirit of generosity her own happiness had brought, she went over to him and told him quietly, 'It's all right, Robert. I think we both know that it wouldn't have worked for us. I'm more American than I realised, and sooner or later the restraints of the protocol of being "royal" would have irked me, and I wouldn't have been the suitable wife you wanted at all.'

'Thanks for being so decent about everything,' Robert responded. 'I didn't want it to happen, what you saw. I don't want you to think I'm the kind of bastard who thinks it's acceptable to make a public commitment to one woman and sleep with another. I just couldn't help myself.' It was an admission he'd never imagined he would make.

'She obviously means a great deal to you,' Olivia responded.

'No!' Robert's denial was immediate and defensive.

'Well, whatever the case,' Olivia said quietly, 'the reality is that we both created idealised versions of our perfect partners and then imposed them on one another.'

Now that she could see Robert clearly she realised that what she saw was a man with whom she had childhood ties and of whom she was fond, but not a man with whom she would want to spend her life. Robert now seemed so stiff and formal, so hidebound by the expectations of the role he had chosen for himself, so British compared with Tait, who was so American and whose outlook on life was so much closer to her own.

'Friends?' she asked Robert.

'Friends,' he agreed, smiling.

On opposite sides of the room two mothers, carefully pretending not to be watching them, gave two equally grateful sighs of relief, each naturally believing that it was her child who was the one to be applauded for generosity of spirit.

Most of the family were spending the night at Denham, but Robert had elected to return to London. He had several meetings to attend regarding his plans for Lauranto, prior to his return to that country.

The city had an end-of-summer air about it, a dustiness and weariness to the fading heat of summer. He parked his car and then went up to his apartment, stripping off his clothes to take a shower. He hadn't been looking forward to seeing Olivia, half expecting tears and recriminations, and he was relieved that that hadn't happened. It had surprised him how very American she had seemed, something he hadn't really noticed before. An American-minded wife. He grimaced to himself. That wouldn't have suited him at all. Out of nowhere a mental image of Charlotte formed inside his head along with an echo of Olivia's comment about her meaning a great deal to him. Charlotte wasn't American in any kind of way. Charlotte, if he had to classify her, he would class as European, sophisticated, sensual, and subtle.

Charlotte. He'd been thinking about her all day, or rather he'd been trying not to. And not just all day. She was in his head all the time. In his head and in his heart. He ached for her and missed her body and soul.

He threw down the towel with which he'd been drying himself, his heart thumping heavily and fast, the feeling inside his chest and his head similar to the one he'd felt the first time he'd stood poised at the top of a black ski run, one part of him wanting to meet its challenge and another more cautious part of him fearful of its danger and the risk he was taking. Then he had held his breath and taken that leap into the unknown, and the exhilaration, the excitement, the supreme aware-ness that he was living life to the full and challenging all his own vulnerabilities had transported him to a sense of such intense fulfilment and joy that he had never forgotten it.

He thought of Lauranto's buildings and his plans for them, the opportunity to own them and restore them to their original glory without interference from anyone else. Stone and brick – these were substances that could be touched and held; you knew where you were with them, unlike emotions. Emotions were dangerous, treacherous. They had the power to control you and, through you, to damage others. Charlotte would understand that. Their parents' affair had damaged them both in different ways. Charlotte . . .

He couldn't live in Lauranto as its Crown Prince with her. And he couldn't live as himself without her. Once admitted, the truth was impossible to call back, as was telling himself that it was pointless his risking everything for a woman who probably didn't even want him. Some ski jumps had to be made. Some risks had to be taken.

Charlotte had only just returned home when Robert knocked on her front door. She was expecting Nat to call round so she opened the door without looking to see who was outside, more affected than she wanted to admit by the discovery that it was Robert, and frowning when he stepped into her hallway without asking permission. He was casually dressed – for Robert – wearing jeans and an open-necked shirt, his hair ruffled and damp. He was also wearing an unRobertlike air of mixed intensity and determination.

'There's something I want to say to you,' he announced.

Charlotte allowed her eyebrows to lift in mocking query. 'Yes?'

'I love you. I love you,' Robert repeated, 'and I want us to be together, as a couple.' He paused and then said huskily, 'As husband and wife.'

'You want to marry me?'

A long time ago a little girl in shabby clothes had sat on the pavement with her feet in the gutter, wishing with all her heart that she could grow up to be a beautiful princess with a charming prince to marry her, just like the woman in the magazine her mother had bought, and that same little girl had wept tears of bitter anger and frustration because even then she had known that for girls like her there were no handsome princes waiting to whisk them away to a land of happy-ever-afters. She had sworn then that she would never fall in love, especially not with anyone who looked like the boy staring back at her from the magazine.

'Why?'

Robert shook his head.

'I don't honestly know. I just know that without you I can't be whole. You complete me, Charlotte. You know me, you know what I am, and what has made me. You know my past; with you I can be myself. I need you to be myself.'

She wasn't going to let him think it was going to be easy. She did know him and she knew that Robert needed to believe he had had to strive for what he wanted.

'I like my freedom to do as I please, Robert. What if I don't want to live by the rules that come with being the wife of a crown prince?'

'That won't matter. It won't be a crown prince you will be marrying, it will be me. My grandmother is already looking for a suitable bride for me, a bride who will make me good enough, in her eyes, to step into my father's shoes. I've wanted that so much. To be accepted by her as my father's son and rightful heir.' Robert paused. 'But I want you more. I love you more.'

Charlotte's heart missed as beat. 'You'd give Lauranto up for me?'

'Yes.'

One small word, but it meant and contained so much. It held more value, more weight than a hundred royal engagement rings.

Knowing him as she did, Charlotte understood what a difficult decision that would have been for him. An unfamiliar tenderness filled her.

'You do realise how much everyone will disapprove of what you're doing – your parents, your grandmother – and how much opposition there will be to our marriage, don't you?' she challenged him.

'I don't care,' Robert told her simply, and Charlotte could see that it was true and that he meant that.

Love, sweet and tender and whole, filled her. 'I think,' she told him very carefully, 'that this matter needs further discussion, and that the best place for that would be upstairs, in my bedroom.' She paused. 'Ruling Lauranto matters a great deal to you, doesn't it?'

'Yes,' Robert admitted. 'But you mean more.'

'Your grandmother will come round to our marriage.'

Robert shook his head. 'No she won't. You don't know her.'

'I don't need to know her,' Charlotte told him briskly. 'I know myself, and I know that if being Crown Prince of Lauranto is what you want then I'll find a way of making sure you are. There's always a way, Robert, always, and your grandmother needs you and the sons you and I will have much more than we need her.'

She was so like his mother, Robert recognised. They

would challenge one another constantly, and he suspected form a bond that nothing could break.

'I don't care about Lauranto,' he told her. 'I can live without being its Crown Prince, but I can't live without you, and I don't intend to.'

Charlotte smiled the secret smile of a woman in love and loved in return, a powerful, a strong woman, who would break every taboo there was for her man and her children. Robert would rule Lauranto, and she, of course, would rule him.

'John, there you are, I've—' Janey broke off as her eyes adjusted to the dim shuttered gloom of the estate office, and she realised that, far from listening to her, John was sitting holding his shotgun and staring into space.

Her heart was hammering against her ribs, her gaze drawn to the gun.

'John,' she begged, relief easing the tension from her when he finally turned towards her. But it was a relief that was short-lived.

'I have to do it,' he told her. 'You see, I'm not really a Fitton Legh after all. Cassandra told me everything. Her deathbed confession.' A muscle twitched in his face.

'Of course you're a Fitton Legh, don't be silly,' Janey protested. Harry was in the kitchen, but she dare not call out to him to come. John's finger was crooked round the trigger of the shotgun, both barrels now pointing at his chest.

'This was his gun, you know. Made for him.'

'Your father's gun – yes, I know.'

'No, not my father. Greg Pickford was my father.'

Janey could hear Harry coming down the stone-flagged passage towards them. John looked at the window.

'I was never a Fitton Legh.'

Janey looked into the passage and gestured silently to Harry. She could see the shock seize and change his expression as he came into the room.

'That can't be true, John. Cassandra was just being spiteful, or . . . or confused.'

'No. She said that it was true. She said that Mother confessed the truth to my . . . to Lord Fitton Legh after I was born, when he had already publicly accepted me as his heir.'

Harry had been edging closer to the desk whilst his father talked and stared out of the window.

'I have no right to the Fitton Legh name or the Fitton Legh land. None of us has.' His finger tightened on the trigger just as Harry leaped forward to wrestle it from him.

The sound of the barrels discharging made Janey's ears ring. The shattered glass from the window lay everywhere. There was blood on Harry's hands from where small shards of it had cut him.

'You shouldn't have stopped me. Can't you see that it's the only honourable thing left for me to do? I can't live without Fitton,' he told them both, 'and I can't live with the shame of what I am.'

Harry had taken the precaution of locking both the gun cabinet and the estate office door, and keeping the keys himself. John was upstairs in bed, sleeping, thankfully, after Janey had persuaded him to drink a cup of tea in to which she put two of the sleeping tablets that had been prescribed for Cassandra earlier in the year, and which she'd put to one side to return to the pharmacy when she had time.

'Is it true, do you think?' Harry asked her. 'Is Dad really not a Fitton Legh?'

Janey thought of all the comforting things she could say in answer to his question, and then admitted, 'I don't know. But I do know that Lord Fitton Legh brought your father up to be his heir. We all grew up together and it was always clear that your father would inherit Fitton. There was never any question about that.'

'So why did Cassandra say what she did? She must have believed it to be true. I mean, you wouldn't say something like that, would you, if it wasn't true? Not when you were dying.'

'No, Harry. I don't think you would,' Janey agreed.

'What's going to happen?'

Janey looked at her son. 'I don't know. But I'm going to telephone your grandfather. He'll know what to do.'

'Do you think Dad really would have turned the gun on himself if we hadn't stopped him?'

'Yes. Knowing how he feels about Fitton, Harry, I think he probably would. It means so much to him, you see, being a Fitton Legh of Fitton. It means everything to him. Fitton has been his life.'

Chapter Twenty-Four

Jay and Amber sat looking at one another. It was less than hour since Janey had telephoned, almost too distraught to tell Jay properly at first what had happened. Jay had done his best to reassure her but they both knew there was one reassurance they could not truthfully give.

'How could Cassandra do that to him?' Amber asked Jay. 'John, of all people, who has never really had the strength to stand up to her. She must have known how much Fitton means to him – and not just Fitton but his father, I mean Lord Fitton Legh. Even as a child John was always desperate to gain his father's approval. I never thought Lord Fitton Legh a good father, but he never gave any indication that he didn't consider John to be his, or that he wanted to disinherit him.'

'I don't think for a minute that he did. Whatever he might privately have suspected about John's paternity, John was his heir and he brought him up as such. The devil of it is, though, that I suspect that no matter how strenuously any of us say that to John, he will refuse to accept it without proof that he is a Fitton Legh. It's a damnable thing that Cassandra has done.'

'A cruel, cruel thing,' Amber agreed.

There was a small silence and then she said, 'I think we are both agreed that Lord Fitton Legh planned for and wanted John to succeed him, no matter what Cassandra may have said to John on that score.'

'Yes.'

'No one really knows the truth,' she pressed on, 'nothing has ever been proved, nothing can ever be proved. Oh, I know there is that new DNA test that has been mentioned in the papers, but for that they would need surely to have samples from both Greg and Lord Fitton Legh, and they are both dead.'

'I'm not sure how the process works,' Jay replied, 'but I do know it takes a very long time. Given John's current mental state, and since, as you have said, both the men who might have been his father are dead, I don't think that is an avenue it would be possible to pursue. No, I'm afraid that if John has convinced himself that he is not Lord Fitton Legh's son—'

'You mean if Cassandra has convinced him that he is not Lord Fitton Legh's son,' Amber interrupted him. 'And since she did that, it must be possible for someone else to convince him that she was wrong.'

Jay looked at her. 'We have no proof that Lord Fitton Legh was his father.'

'And neither do we have any proof that he wasn't,' Amber told him, reaching for his hand and holding it tightly. 'I know what Greg said, Jay, but he was only making an assumption. Maybe Caroline did tell him that John was his son but did she herself actually know which of them had fathered him – her husband or Greg, her lover? It could have been that she was deliberately tormenting Greg. Poor woman, she was so desperately tormented herself. It isn't just John who will suffer through Cassandra's malice – we both know that. There is Janey, as well, and the boys. There have been so many secrets in this family that would have created scandals had they become public; maybe it's time that one of those secrets was made public to prevent a scandal. I must tell John what Greg told me.'

'What Greg told you, or what you want John to believe he told you?'

'It has to be done, Jay. We have no choice. It is what my grandmother would have done, and your grandfather too.'

'That is no recommendation.'

'Maybe not, but we cannot – *I* cannot – let poor John suffer as we both know he will be suffering, and through him, Janey and the boys, and to what purpose? It would be different if there was another heir but there isn't. And yes, I know we could perhaps buy Fitton Hall and give it to Janey and John, but we both know that all that would do would be to humiliate John further, at least in his own eyes. He had such pride in being a Fitton Legh. As a young man he spoke so often of being worthy of stepping into his father's shoes when the time came. I know you think he has taken far better care of his inheritance than Lord Fitton Legh ever did, but that is not the point. John put his father on a pedestal, Cassandra knew that. She could not know who fathered John any more than anyone else could, not even Caroline herself. I shall go over to Fitton in the morning and speak with John. Will you telephone Janey and tell her?'

Her words were shorthand for asking him to support her in her decision, Jay knew.

'Some secrets once shared are better forgotten for ever,' Amber told him. 'Throughout history there must be many a son who has succeeded a father, who is not really his father at all, and who despite that has proved to be a good and loyal son to his dynasty and his inheritance. John has given his heart and soul to Fitton. Fitton needs John every bit as much as he needs it.'

'Very well,' Jay agreed. 'I'll go and telephone Janey and warn her to expect you in the morning.'

'It's kind of you to offer to speak to John, but I must warn you that he isn't himself,' Janey told Amber as she ushered her towards the library. Amber could tell that her stepdaughter didn't think that Amber could say anything to John that would improve the situation.

'Daddy said not to ring the solicitor until you've seen John, but I know you won't be able to change his mind. He is adamant that we don't have any right to be here at Fitton and that we must leave. I think he wishes that Harry and I hadn't taken the gun off him.'

Amber patted Janey's arm sympathetically, and then knocked briefly on the library door before pushing it open without waiting for a response.

John was sitting in the worn leather chair in which Lord Fitton Legh had sat before him. Several papers lay on the desk, amongst them what looked like birth and marriage certificates.

He stood up when he saw Amber, and then subsided back into the chair when she begged him to do so. He looked dreadfully careworn and defeated, a man who had lost everything he held dear, Amber thought sadly. It was not her place to suggest to him that his wife and sons should matter more to him than Fitton. She knew there was no point. John had been raised from birth by a proud and often harsh parent who had instilled into him the importance of their bloodline and the estate. Nothing mattered more to a Fitton Legh than Fitton itself.

'I remember the first time I visited Fitton,' Amber began conversationally. 'My cousin Greg brought me here.'

She could see John flinch but ignored his reaction, and continued, 'I was only seventeen. I remember how beautiful your mother was. Your father was so proud of her, and of you.'

John was tense now but Amber ignored his tension, just as she had ignored his flinch.

'Poor Greg was desperately in love with your mother – we could all see that – but of course she was a married woman, far above him in status, and the wife of a man he greatly admired.'

Amber paused. Then she said quietly, 'I know what Cassandra told you, John, but she was wrong.'

'You can say that but I know it isn't true. She said my own mother had told her.' In his voice was the painful cry of a lost child.

Amber took a deep breath, and then reached out and placed her hand on his shoulder as she stood beside him, as a mother might a small child.

'John, I'm going to be very honest with you and tell you something I wish I did not have to tell you, something that I've always sworn I would never tell anyone or discuss with anyone other than Jay. It concerns Cassandra and, unfortunately, your mother.'

John looked at her.

Amber prayed for the strength to say what had to be said.

'In her youth Cassandra was a woman who, to put it bluntly, desired her own sex, rather than the male sex, despite the fact that she later married your father. Just like Greg, she fell in love with your mother.'

She could see his shock as he struggled to speak.

'It's all right,' she said gently. 'Of course it goes without saying that Cassandra's feelings were unwanted and unreciprocated. Your mother, as I have already said, was a young wife and mother who had befriended Cassandra as a member of her husband's family, and taken her under her wing. However, I'm afraid instead of accepting Caroline's gentle rejection of her, Cassandra turned against her, letting her bitterness provoke her into a desire to hurt your mother because she herself had been hurt. Unfortunately, as a young woman Cassandra was subject to intense emotions and passions that she couldn't always control. It is my belief that her assertion that you are Greg's son came from that same bitterness, and those passions.'

John's gaze was fixed on her now.

'I can't tell you what cruel and vengeful thoughts might have filled Cassandra's head in the last hours of her life. I do know that she resented your birth because she could see that Caroline's love was given to you, her child, and to her husband. Your mother and Lord Fitton Legh were so proud of you, a first-born son, an heir for Fitton. Your mother's death was a terrible tragedy, depriving you of a loving mother and your father of a wife and second child.'

'Cassandra told me that Greg was sent away because of his affair with my mother, and that Lord Fitton Legh was preparing to send her away in disgrace when she drowned.' John's voice was clipped and harsh.

'That is true, yes,' Amber agreed, 'but it is also true that it was Cassandra who put it into Lord Fitton Legh's head that your mother had been unfaithful to him. In public she played the part of friend to your mother but in private she was determined to have her revenge on her for rejecting her. My grandmother knew that. She told me as much, just as Cassandra admitted to Jay that she had persecuted poor Caroline out of malice and jealousy.

'No one has ever disputed that my cousin admired and revered your mother, John, but Cassandra's talk of anything more between them than worshipful admiration on Greg's part and a happily married woman's kindness to a young man on your mother's part was purely that – talk. There was and is no evidence of any wrongdoing between them.'

'According to Cassandra I am that evidence.'

'There is no proof of that.'

John looked away from her.

'It is my belief that Cassandra said what she did to you in a deliberate attempt to hurt you because of your mother. Cassandra was so embittered and so resentful, her whole personality warped because her pride had been stung by your mother's rejection of her. She was driven by a need to destroy what your mother had created, and that included you.'

'Your belief? How am I to believe you? How am I ever to know whether I am a Fitton Legh or not? And if I can't know that, I cannot remain here.'

This now was the crossroads Amber had known she would reach. Did she have the courage to take the darker path? She could almost sense her grandmother's presence at her elbow and hear the snort of derision she would have given. When the pattern in the silk becomes distorted then the weaver must correct that distortion to hold the pattern true, just as the painter must sacrifice the reality of feature and expression to create the image he can see inside his head, in order to complete the greater plan. These things must be done for the greater good.

'I can't make you believe me, John,' she agreed, 'but what I can do is tell you that on his deathbed, when he begged for forgiveness for the errors of his life, my cousin made me promise to refute any lies Cassandra might seek to spread about your mother and his relationship with her. This is the first time I have been called upon to make good that promise.'

'Think, John,' she urged him. 'Do you really believe for one minute that Lord Fitton Legh would have brought you up as he did, as his son and heir, if he had thought that there was any doubt about the matter? He was a very proud man, a man of honour, to whom Fitton was everything, just as it is for you. Do you really think he would have handed Fitton into the hands of anyone other than another Fitton Legh?'

Now at last she could see something in John's expression, a struggling, a recognition of the truth of what she had said.

'Would you really destroy everything that Lord Fitton Legh worked for, and not just for yourself but for your sons and their sons after them, on the malicious words of an embittered woman? I dare say Cassandra might have hoped to have a son of her own with your father, and I think also that the fact that she did not added to her bitterness and jealousy, but you were always the only son and heir your father wanted, John. Look at how he prepared you for your role, how determined he was that you would be worthy of it, how proud he was of you when he knew that you were.'

John's head was bowed. 'I never felt that I truly pleased him.'

Amber's heart ached for him. 'That was just his way. Jay's grandfather Barrant was very much in the same mould. You did please your father, John; he handed Fitton on into your care, didn't he? Do you really believe he would have done that if he had not had faith in you and if it had not been his wish?' she repeated. 'Do you not think if he had had any doubts of any kind he could have and would have used the excuse Cassandra was all too ready to give him to doubt you and your right to succeed him?

'You knew your father, John. Do you not think that he was perfectly capable of telling you you were not his son had he thought that? Do you think he would want you to throw away everything he gave you because of the spite of one woman? Is that what he would have expected of you, John, or would he have expected you to stand tall and remember the promises you made him when you took onto your shoulders the responsibility he handed on to you, in trust for the generations to come. Lord Fitton Legh would not have allowed you to inherit from him if he had not believed you to be his son and it is that that you must allow to guide you, not Cassandra's troublemaking.'

Amber held her breath. She knew how hard Lord Fitton Legh had been on John and she prayed as she had never prayed before that now, as he stood at his crossroads, John would take the upward broader path into the light and not the fork that led downwards.

'You are right. He . . .' his voice weakened and then gathered strength as he continued, '. . . my father would never have allowed me to inherit if he had had any doubts about me.'

Then he put his head in his hands, huge sobs racking his body.

Amber stroked his down-bent head as though he were a small child. 'You must do as your father would do now, John, and put all this behind you. You must not think of it again. There is no need. Instead you must do what your father would expect of you. You have a wife and two sons who need your strength, as does Fitton. You must not fail them.'

Her words might sound hard but Amber knew that to John they would echo the teachings of Lord Fitton Legh, and that he would respond to them because of that.

'I shan't.' John raised his head. There was a new zeal in his eyes. 'You are right to remind me of my duty to Fitton, and to my family.' He was sitting upright now, straightening his shoulders, looking resolute and determined.

Amber allowed herself to begin to relax. It was extraordinary how weak and shaky she felt. Her grandmother would not have approved, or sympathised.

'You are right, I am sure, when you say that my step-mother harboured bitterness against my mother and that this was the cause of her lies. My father must never have known how she felt.'

'No, I don't think he did,' Amber agreed, relieved to be able to say something she felt was the truth.

'If he had he would never have married her,' John continued firmly. 'Cassandra deceived him, just as she tried to persuade him that my mother had deceived him.' John's voice rang with conviction. He suddenly looked at least ten years younger, his entire manner brisk and purposeful. He would be all right now. Everything would be all right now.

Amber walked to the door. She was stiff from standing, her chest tight from holding her breath, her conscience pricking her for what she had done. As she opened the library door she thought she caught a hint of a once familiar scent – Blanche's scent – and heard her grandmother's familiar exasperated sigh.

You're right, she agreed inwardly, a guilty conscience is an unnecessary self-indulgence.

Tiredly she walked towards the kitchen where she knew that Janey and Jay would be waiting.

The moment she saw John, Janey knew that everything was going to be fine. Automatically she went to him, and then stopped so that it was John who crossed the divide between them, taking her in his arms to hold her and hug her tightly in an unaccustomed display of emotion. Tenderly, and filled with gratitude, Janey hugged him back. This would be a new start for them, she promised herself, a new start filled with love and shared gratitude for all that they had together.

A parent who loved their child would sacrifice anything for that child's happiness and peace of mind, including the right to call that child their own. Her grandmother had taught Amber that and if she had made that decision on behalf of her cousin, then she had done so knowing that Greg too would have made that sacrifice for John, if he were his father.

The past was best left to lie. It could not be changed, and the business of the living lay with the present and the future, not the secrets or the scandals of the dead.

Chapter Twenty-Five

Sarah smiled dutifully as Charles brought his car to a halt outside her parents' home. She would have much preferred it if her father had not so obviously thrown her together with Charles McKenzie, the nephew of a neighbour, but it would be rude to refuse Charles's invitation to dinner, even though she knew that, pleasant though he was, he was certainly not someone she could ever be interested in romantically.

She had come to Scotland in part to please her father and in part to prove to herself that she was capable of standing up to him when it came to the boys, but their visit had not gone as well as she had hoped. She was glad that they would be returning to London in a few days. And glad too that Nick would be meeting them off the train?

Sarah frowned to herself as Charles got out of the driver's seat of the car and went round to the passenger door to open it for her.

Of course, it was a good thing that she and Nick were now on speaking terms, for the boys' sake, if nothing else. It had been her stay at Denham that was responsible for that. Watching Nick with their sons had showed her how much they genuinely meant to him and how much they loved him, and that had made her determined to keep things as amicable as possible between them.

The hall to Broderick Castle, her parents' home, always felt cold and slightly damp. Its walls were decorated with the antlers of various stags shot by her father and his father before him, and her father himself was on hand to greet them, offering Charles a nightcap.

Forced to join the men with their generous tumblers of whisky whilst her father poured her a small too-sweet sherry, Sarah acknowledged that whilst she might not know what she really wanted her future to be, she knew that she didn't want it to be a life like her mother's – the life her father was pushing her towards via Charles. She might have got it wrong with Nick, but marrying someone like Charles would be equally wrong for her. The trouble was that there was no neat pigeonhole for her to fit into. She had rebelled against her upbringing by marrying Nick, and then discovered that she could not fit into his world, but at the same time she had come too far and changed too much to go back and fit into her parents' world.

She stifled a yawn – of boredom, not tiredness. She wanted to go up and check on the boys and then go to bed, but her father would consider any attempt to leave the room before Charles said good night an act of such bad manners that he'd be going on about it for days.

Thankfully, though, Charles finally drained his glass and stood up. Dutifully Sarah accompanied him and her father to the door.

At last Charles had gone and she could go up to bed.

After saying a brief good night to her father, Sarah ran up the stairs, hurrying along the corridor that led to the bedroom the boys were sharing, opening the door quietly and then stepping inside, her mouth already curling in a tender smile of maternal love as she looked towards the two beds.

The two empty beds, as she could see from the night-light Neil always insisted on having left on.

It took her several seconds to accept that the boys really weren't there, and several more to check the bathroom, whilst her mind whirled and her heart pounded and the sick fear inside her grew and grew until it possessed and shook her in its hold. She even looked beneath the beds and then pulled back the bedclothes in case the boys were playing some kind of joke on her, even though she already knew they were not. That was when she saw the carefully printed note in childish uneven handwriting, left beneath Alex's pillow, like a tooth left for the tooth fairy. Her hands trembling, Sarah smoothed it out and read it.

'Der mummy, grandfather doesn't like us and tonite he made me cry because I wouldn't eat my supper, so we are going to Denham on the train cos we like it better there. Lots of love, Alex and Neil xxx.'

No! No. No. She had to clap her hand over her mouth to stop herself from screaming hysterically, her mind racing in top gear. Her sons, her precious little boys, had been so frightened and upset that they had run away, and she hadn't been here to protect and reassure them. She hadn't been here for them to turn to, because she had been out with a man she hadn't wanted to go out with just to placate her father, because, like her sons, she was afraid of him. Oh dear God, what had she done?

There was only one telephone in the castle and it was in the hall. Frantically she ran back down the corridor, almost bumping into her father, who was on his way upstairs.

'What the devil . . . ?' he began, but she ignored him, her fear for her sons so great that it overwhelmed her normal anxiety about confronting her father.

'I need to speak to the police, and then I am going to telephone Nick. The boys are missing.'

She could hear her father objecting that she was over-reacting and that the boys were playing her up and were probably hiding somewhere, enjoying all the fuss they'd caused, but Sarah ignored him, her fingers trembling as she punched in 999.

The police were wonderful, assuring her that they would come immediately, their reassurance leaving her free to dial Nick's number.

She was too angry to be afraid. That would come later, when she had done what she had to do, what her father should have done, what it would not have been neces-sary to do if she had not gone out and left them. Oh dear God, if anything should happen to them . . . had happened to them. Sarah thought of the winding unlit road that led from the castle to the small town and its station. She mustn't cry. Not now. She must be strong.

And she was, until she heard Nick's voice, warmed with sleep so that she could picture him lying in bed – he always slept naked; she hoped he was alone. And then she was sobbing frantically as she told him what had happened, and what she had done.

'They've left a note saying that they're going to Jay and Amber. The police are on their way. They'll check the trains, of course, but, Nick, it's five miles to the station and then they'd have to change at Glasgow, and then again at Manchester.'

She could hear him cursing and then he was saying, 'I'm coming up there. I'll ring Denham and Fitton and let them know what's happening, and Dad and Rose as well, just in case.'

By the time she'd replaced the telephone receiver the local police had arrived.

Immediately Sarah made it clear that they were to deal with her and not her father, stepping up to them, stifling her tears, taking charge, because after all, the boys were her sons, hers and Nick's, and until Nick got here it was up to her to do whatever had to be done, and not her father, who had already proved that he could not be trusted.

The police were kind but firm, telling her that the boys could not have got very far. They naturally asked for the details of what had happened before the boys had run away and Sarah could see the local police inspector's mouth hardening as he looked at her father after she had explained the events of the evening.

Sarah wanted to go with them but they had told her that it would be better if she remained where she was. After they had gone to begin their search, Sarah ignored her father, who was now trying to bully and bluster her into apologising for her 'hysteria' and giving the police completely the wrong impression, too concerned for the boys to feel anything when he actually fell silent and then said he was going to bed, meekly accompanied by her mother. Poor Mummy, Sarah thought, what a miserable life she had.

The house was silent apart from its familiar creaks and groans, the sound of an old house, rheumaticky and grumpy with age.

Sarah opened the heavy front door. A new moon gleamed from the clear sky. The night had such a different quality up here in the North from the night sky over London. The stars seemed so much closer. And brighter, as though there was less distance between sky and earth. An owl flew silently, its swoop followed by a shrill scream from its victim, the sound making Sarah shudder. Beyond the boundaries of the castle grounds lay her father's precious moors with their heather and their grouse, and surely, please God, her children. If they had reached the station then someone would have seen them. At least it was September and the nights still relatively warm. But what if they were not lying safely asleep in the heather? What if the unthinkable, the unbearable, happened and someone had seen them, someone had stopped, someone had taken them? The need to start looking for them now, this minute, immediately, ignoring the dark, ignoring everything but her need to find her sons and keep them safe, burst through her. Sarah set off at a run and then stopped. She must not panic. She must not – for the boys' sake.

She made her way back inside and then up to the bedroom the boys shared where she lay down on one of the small single beds. Not because she was tired and certainly not because she thought she might sleep – that was impossible – but because she could smell them still on the pillows and the bedding and she wanted to hold that scent, their scent to her, for as long as she could. The terrible thought that this might be all she would now have of them lay beneath the surface of her self-control like a jagged reef lying just beneath the waves. She must not accept that thought. She must push it away from her and concentrate instead on willing fate to keep her sons safe. She might deserve to be punished for not being a good mother, but they did not deserve any punishment.

Dawn was just beginning to streak the sky when Nick arrived, the wheels of his car crunching over the gravel, its headlights arcing light through the thin curtains of the boys' room, sending Sarah to her feet and then running down the stairs to pull open the heavy door for him.

Somehow it seemed the most natural thing in the world to run to him and be held in his arms as they tightened round her.

'I'm sorry, I'm sorry, it's my fault. It's all my fault.' Her voice was muffled against the fabric of his shirt as he rocked her against his chest.

'No, it's mine,' he told her. You are my wife, they are my sons. It's my job to protect you, but I had too much of a chip on my shoulder to see that. I was enjoying revelling in my own stupid self-pity too much to put the three of you first.'

Their confessions were spoken swiftly in the time-honoured shorthand of two people who formed a unit, each knowing automatically what the other meant, both of them united in their fear and their love for the children they had created together.

'I thought I could stand up to Daddy. I thought I was strong enough.'

'You are strong, but your father has no respect for your sex.'

'I shouldn't have brought the boys here. I knew they didn't want to come. They had such a wonderful time at Denham. It was so lovely to see the way they interacted with Jay and Amber, but especially with Jay, and seeing them with you . . . You are their father, Nick, and they love you and . . . oh, Nick.' She was in tears now, clinging to him, telling him how very afraid she was as well as how dreadfully guilty she felt.

It was the first time she had actually turned to him for comfort, the first time she had let down her defences and spoken to him about her father without immediately leaping to the other man's defence – the first time he had felt that they were united as a couple against her father – and Nick felt his own emotions respond to her need.

'Come on, let's go inside. It's going to be all right,' Nick told her with a confidence he was far from feeling, but that he knew she needed to see in him.

Within minutes of Nick's arrival the police returned, shaking their heads when Sarah asked if the boys had been found. Her hopes crumbled into fresh fear when they asked her for items of clothing recently worn by the boys.

'We're going to bring in the dogs to work with the scent,' the inspector in charge explained to her. 'They can't have got far, and it will be much easier looking for them in daylight than it was in the dark.'

'Not walking,' Sarah agreed. 'But what if—'

'Don't say it,' Nick told her fiercely, 'and don't think it either.'

* * *

The police dog handlers had arrived, along with two sniffer dogs, half a dozen members of a mountain search and rescue team, and just as soon as the sun had burned off the low-lying mist from the moor, a search and rescue helicopter team from RAF Kinross would be 'going up to take a look round,' according to the police inspector in charge of the 'operation'.

More to keep herself busy than anything else, Sarah had gone down to the almost medieval kitchen to grill bacon for sandwiches for the men, an action that reminded her in a way of her days as a chalet girl whilst she had been at university.

Out of the corner of her eye, as she sliced and buttered bread, she watched Nick, who was listening to the police inspector explaining to him how they intended to conduct their search. Nick had very much taken on the role of the family's alpha male, Sarah knew, whilst her own father sat at the table, growling about potential damage to the moor and being virtually ignored by everyone.

Nick's concerned but courteous readiness to listen to what the authorities had to say had won them over to his side, Sarah could see, and she was not surprised to hear him announce that he intended to go with the men who would be searching either side of the road.

'No need for that,' her father criticised Nick. 'You don't know anything about the countryside. Bound to get in people's way. Far better to stay here.'

'Actually, sir,' the police inspector told Nick, having listened to her father and then turned away from him, 'your presence could be beneficial. Bairns who think they're in trouble tend to fear that the fact that the police are looking for them means they are in even more trouble, d'you ken? If the bairns see their own father and hear him calling to them, then chances are that if they are hiding out, as we hope, they'll show themselves.'

'Sentimental claptrap,' Sarah heard her father snort. 'Look at you, man, you can't go out on the moor dressed like that.'

Everyone turned to look at Nick, who was wearing a T-shirt, a pair of jeans and had trainers on his feet.

Sarah took a deep breath. It was the safety of her sons that was at stake, after all, and that mattered far more to her right now than her father's pride and need to be right.

'Don't be silly, Daddy,' she told her father firmly. 'Nick is dressed perfectly sensibly.'

She turned to her husband and added clearly, 'Please go with them, Nick. I'll feel so much better knowing that you're there. I know if the boys are hiding if they see you they'll know that it's all right to show themselves.'

Her father's face was puce, a sure sign that he was furious, and normally that would have been enough to have her feeling positively sick with dread of what was to come, but right now the smile Nick was giving her meant far more than her father's anger; that and the need to do everything she could to ensure that her sons were found safe and speedily.

The men had eaten their bacon sandwiches and drunk the strong tea her mother had made. Outside the mist was lifting, the clear blue sky bringing the promise of a fine day.

The search party was starting to move out of the

kitchen, the dogs waiting outside. Sarah's heart shook when she saw their handlers removing the boys' T-shirts from the plastic bags and offering them to the dogs so that they could pick up her sons' scent.

Engrossed in the battle going on inside her between hope and fear, she was taken off guard when Nick came to her and put his hand on her shoulder – in a gesture of comfort or a gesture of possession aimed at her father? Sarah didn't care. The warmth of his touch was comforting, and so was the promise he made her as he told her, 'I'm not coming back until we find them,' before bending his head to kiss her briefly, a husbandly semi-preoccupied mundane kiss of the kind exchanged between couples in established relationships every day, and yet right now it meant so much because it said that she was not alone and that they were united in their desire for the safety of their sons.

It was over two hours since the men had left, heavy walking boots crunching over the gravel, Nick walking ahead with the police inspector.

Sarah could hear her father still complaining, blaming first the boys for their disobedience, then her for spoiling them and instigating that disobedience, and then finally Nick.

All the time he was complaining Sarah had been helping her mother, who was insisting on preparing lunch, even though Sarah knew that the last thing she felt like doing was eating anything. However, the moment her father started on Nick, Sarah put the cutlery she had been holding down onto the table with careful deliberation and faced her father.

'I appreciate that things have changed since you were

a boy, Daddy, and of course you didn't have sons your-self so you haven't had the experience of bringing up boys, as Nick and I have. Nick is an excellent father. The boys love him and he loves them, and it's been very wrong of you to criticise Nick in front of them. It upset the boys and it upset me. I'm sure you didn't mean to do that, but you did. As for me not disciplining the boys – boys are different from girls, it's in their nature. What you think of as disobedience is simply boys pushing against the boundaries. Remember, Daddy, one day they will be men. It is my fault that the boys are missing, not because I don't discipline them, as you said, but because I brought them up here in the first place, when I know how unkind you can be to them. Nick has been a saint not to throw that in my face. I doubt I could have been as generous in his shoes. *That* is being gentle-manly, Daddy, showing kindness and consideration for others, not bullying them and frightening little children into running away.'

Sarah heard a gasp from her mother behind her. Her father was still puce-faced, but although he opened his mouth, obviously intending to say something, he closed it again to glare at her.

Eventually he said bitterly, 'So he's finally done it, has he? He's finally turned you against your own blood, and your own kind. Well, more fool you. And you needn't come crawling back here to me and your mother when he leaves you for someone of his own class. There'll be no place for you here. I always warned you he wasn't good enough for you.'

The air stirred behind her, her mother moving, Sarah guessed.

'Far from being not good enough for me, I am the one who has not been good enough for him – not good enough or wise enough to recognise just how lucky I was to meet him and be loved by him. And as for me coming back here, the only place I want to be is with Nick and our sons, and if that means never seeing you again, if that is the choice you intend to force me to make, then I may as well tell you now that my choice is already made, and it is Nick I choose.' A heady, dizzy, unfamiliar feeling had taken hold of her, and that was because her emotions had scented freedom, Sarah recognised – freedom and the opportunity to finally be herself on her own terms.

'There never has been a place for me here, Daddy, not really. Not a place for me, only a place for the person you wanted me to be.'

'He's divorcing you.'

'Yes,' Sarah was obliged to agree. 'But my loyalty and my love are still his.' It was the truth, even if it had taken her until now to recognise it.

'Sarah.'

She spun round at the sound of Nick's voice. How long had he been there? How much of what she'd said had he heard? But then when she looked into his eyes her feelings about her father and about Nick became nothing.

'The boys?' she whispered.

'The dogs picked up their scent and followed it down to the river. They haven't been able to pick it up again. The river's still in full spate after the heavy rain last week, so Inspector McIntyre is sending for some police divers.'

'No! No!' Nick caught her as she collapsed, hugging her grief tightly to herself, the keening noise of mourning she was making rising up like a lone piper's lament to pierce the bitter silence of the kitchen.

It was one of the sniffer dogs that found the boys. It had been wandering around sniffing at the shale bank of the river when suddenly it was off, nose down, heading for the rocky outcrop where the land rose and from which the river fell into the deep pool that the divers were going to search. None of them paid any attention until the dog started whining and pawing at one of the slabs of rock, its handler calling it to heel. Then some instinct, or maybe it was desperation, Nick said later, made him follow the dog, clambering up the shale to find the narrow entrance between the slabs of rock at which the dog was pawing. It was too narrow surely for any child to climb into, but the dog was trying to do just that, and had to be hauled back, and then they could all hear a thin sound that might be a child crying or might be an animal frightened by the dog.

'Boys, it's Daddy,' Nick called out, putting his mouth to the gap. 'Are you there?'

No sound. Nothing.

And then blessedly a small voice said unsteadily, 'Daddy, it's dark in here and we can't get out.'

It took four hours to free them, Nick and Sarah, who had been called in, talking to them all the time whilst the rescue team worked to widen the gap, and Sarah promised herself she would not think about what would happen if the small space they had crawled into collapsed and filled with earth and stone.

The boys told them that they'd been frightened and

tired walking along the road, and thirsty as well, so they'd come down to the river to get a drink. They'd been climbing up the rocks when they'd found the 'cave', as they called it. Climbing into it had been an adventure – somewhere to sleep and hide for the night. But when they'd woken up in the morning they'd discovered that the earth walls of their cave crumbled when they tried to climb up to reach the opening and get out.

Sarah wept listening to their story, hearing how frightened they'd been when 'Grandfather' was cross and said they were going to be punished, and how they'd decided to go to Denham, to Jay and Amber. Nick put his arm round her and told her it wasn't her fault even though she knew it was, and she'd seen the sheen of emotion in his eyes as well when the boys said how much they wished their parents were still living together.

'Maybe that's one wish we can make come true?' Nick whispered to her, and Sarah nodded, weeping a few more tears when Nick's hold on her hand tightened.

They were nothing, though, to the emotion that overwhelmed her when Alex was finally lifted out of their prison and handed to her. It was almost like giving birth all over again and feeling the wonder of holding the new life she and Nick had created together in her arms, a warm, living, wriggling child, who was demanding to be put down and who seemed more interested in the sniffer dogs than he was in his parents. When Neil was lifted free and about to be handed to her, Sarah shook her head and looked at Nick, who took hold of him instead. She knew from the look he gave her that he understood the symbolism of her gesture and that it was her way of telling him of her trust in him as a man and a father.

Epilogue

'And now, Mummy, we've got a very special birthday surprise for you.'

Amber looked from Emerald's uncharacteristically excited expression to Jay, but she could read nothing in his face to tell her what her surprise might be.

It had been a wonderful day – a wonderful week, in fact – with family arriving to celebrate her eightieth birthday and no special gift could be more valued or cherished to her than the gift of themselves, the gift that they all of them were to her.

Just looking round Denham's drawing room now filled her with joy, her love for them overflowing her heart.

Emerald looked positively girlish in her excitement, Drogo watching her as ever with tenderness and understanding and love. Very much the same emotions she could see in Robert's gaze when it rested on Charlotte. What a surprise to them Robert's announcement of his intention to give up the throne of Lauranto to marry her had been. Somehow, though, Amber rather thought that between them Charlotte and Emerald would find a way of making sure that Robert had the woman he so obviously loved – and Lauranto.

And then there was Olivia, who Robert had been going to marry, standing so proudly within the arm of her charming and oh-so-good-looking American fiancé. Amber could understand why Ella and Oliver were so happy about the match. It was obvious how much in love Olivia and Tait were.

At John's side Janey was exchanging smiles with her husband. It was a true joy to see them both so happy and contented. The weight Janey had lost during those dreadful months when Cassandra had been dying made her look years younger, her whole appearance revitalised, and the sparkle she had lost back in place. The way she looked now reminded Amber, as she felt it must do John, of the Janey he had fallen in love with.

Amber had a special smile for Nick and Sarah and a special place in her heart for them as well. She was so pleased that they were giving their marriage a second chance.

'Are you ready, Mummy?' Emerald was demanding.

Amber nodded, looking towards the doors to the drawing room as Emerald clapped her hands and Jay and Drogo opened a door each to admit a line that comprised Cathy, Polly, Rose, Emma and finally Katie, all of them wearing plain black dresses, and each carrying what looked like small bales of silk.

Amber felt her heartbeat increase.

'This is our gift to you, Mummy,' Emerald told her, going to the opened-out afternoon tea table, which Amber had thought must have been brought in ready for a celebration tea, but which was still clear. Emerald opened one of its drawers and removed from it . . . Amber's eyes widened as she recognised the piece of silk her eldest daughter was spreading on the table. It was the silk upon which Jean-Philippe had painted her as *The Silk Merchant's Daughter*, the silk that Emerald had always abhorred and refused to touch, because of what it represented.

Uncertain what to expect, Amber looked to Jay. His smile for her was loving and reassuring, telling her that there was nothing for her to fear.

Her younger daughters, her niece and granddaughters were standing in line in front of Emerald.

Taking the bale from Cathy, the first in the line, she threw it down with an expert and dramatic twist that unravelled the silk to spill in rich waves of brilliant sea colours onto the original silk it represented, causing her audience to gasp in awe, as she declared, 'This, Mummy, is "Emerald".'

The next in line, Polly, stepped forward and offered her bale to Emerald, who repeated her previous gesture. This time the silk that spilled across the table was a combination of rose pinks, and Amber wasn't surprised when Emerald announced, 'This is "Rose".'

Everyone was beginning to grasp the idea now, and share in the excitement, all the family pressing closer when Rose stepped forward with the third bale.

This time it was shades of grey and lilac that mingled on the table, and Amber was already saying her grandmother's name before Emerald stated, 'This is "Blanche".'

How perfectly the colours represented her grandmother, Amber thought emotionally. How much love had gone into the creating of this very special gift to her, woven together for her by her family, as her love for them wove them together and bound them to her.

Now it was Emma's turn, and Amber saw the look that Rose and Emerald exchanged before Emerald took the fabric from her elder daughter.

For a moment, as the rich shades of gold and amber fell across the table, there was silence, and then Emerald was saying, 'This, of course, is "Amber"'.

The rest of the family were starting to clap, but Emerald shook her head to stop them.

It was Katie, her most beloved granddaughter to whom the final honour fell, and Amber didn't miss the silent plea for reassurance she sent to her boyfriend, Tom, with a brief look that was returned with love and pride before she stepped up to her mother.

'This one, Mummy,' Emerald told her, almost hugging the silk to herself this time instead of revealing it, 'we have decided to call "Life"'.

With that, Emerald very gently revealed the final silk and Amber's heart turned over when she saw the profiles of herself, her grandmother, her own mother and the female descendants who had come after them etched across the elegantly striped silk.

'Rose did the designs,' Emerald was telling her, 'and Angelli made up the dyes and the samples for us. We all did something to make this gift of love for you, Mummy.'

Yes, they had all done something, but it was Emerald who had given her something so precious that it was hard for her not to cry, because Emerald had accepted the silk that had come to Amber from the lover – Emerald's father – whom her daughter had previously rejected and loathed.

Champagne corks were popping and the men of the family were doing what men were so very good at, filling glasses, handing them out, whilst Mrs Leggit wheeled in a trolley with a huge cake on it.

'Amber . . . Mummy . . . Grandmother.' So many voices filled with love and raised to toast her birthday, all of them precious and much loved by her in return, but none more than the one that chimed the sweetest in her heart, that of her husband, Jay.

The silk lay in billows on the table still, and later she would touch it and hold it and feel again a renewal of the awe and delight silk always gave her. When she did she would think of her own parents, and of her grandmother, of her cousin Greg, of her lover, Emerald's father, and of Robert her first husband, and Luc, the lost child who was always in her thoughts. She was so very fortunate to have had the life she had, and to have had and shared the love she had.

She raised her own glass and toasted softly, 'To silk.'

Scandals Reading Group Questions

1. How is adultery portrayed throughout the novel?

2. *Scandals*, as the title suggests, examines past and present scandals. Consider the ways in which these scandals have impacted the characters' lives.

3. Originally, Robert cannot decide whether or not to accept his birthright. Does he make the right decision in becoming Crown Prince? Do you consider him to be a good ruler?

4. Does Kate make the right decision in choosing her step-children over her lover?

5. Kate grows up believing that she is not as good as Emerald or Emerald's children. How does this outlook impact her life?

6. Olivia has an exciting and demanding career as a photo journalist. In what ways does her career define her?

7. Sarah ends up with Josh's illegitimate son Nick. Are they a good match in the long run, or is she just looking for someone to lean on? Do you think that their background influenced their decision to be together?

8. Did you wish that the novel had ended differently?

9. Compare and contrast the different parental figures within *Scandals*. How are motherhood and fatherhood valued throughout the novel?